Brian Aldiss, OBE, is a fiction and science fiction writer, poet, playwright, critic, memoirist and artist. He was born in Norfolk in 1925. After leaving the army, Aldiss worked as a bookseller, which provided the setting for his first book, *The Brightfount Diaries* (1955). His first published science fiction work was the story 'Criminal Record', which appeared in *Science Fantasy* in 1954. Since then he has written nearly 100 books and over 300 short stories, many of which are being reissued as part of The Brian Aldiss Collection.

Several of Aldiss' books have been adapted for the cinema; his story 'Supertoys Last All Summer Long' was adapted and released as the film *A.I. Artificial Intelligence* in 2001. Besides his own writing, Brian has edited numerous anthologies of science fiction and fantasy stories, as well as the magazine *SF Horizons*.

Aldiss is a vice-president of the international H. G. Wells Society and in 2000 was given the Damon Knight Memorial Grand Master Award by the Science Fiction Writers of America. Aldiss was awarded the OBE for services to literature in 2005.

BRIAN ALDISS

THE COMPLETE SHORT STORIES: *The 1960s*

Part One:
1960–1962

HARPER
Voyager

HarperVoyager
An imprint of HarperCollinsPublishers
1 London Bridge Street
London SE1 9GF

www.harpervoyagerbooks.co.uk

This paperback edition 2015
1

Stories from this collection have previously appeared in the following publications:
Science Fantasy (1960), Starswarm, Intangibles Inc. And Other Stories, Science Fiction Adventures,
New Worlds Science Fiction, Amazing Stories (1961 & 1962), The Saliva Tree and Other Strange
Growths, Daily Express Science Annual (1962).

A catalogue record for this book is
available from the British Library

ISBN: 978-0-00-748228-3

Set in Minion by Born Group

Printed and bound in Great Britain by RR Donnelley

MIX
Paper from
responsible sources
FSC **C007454**
www.fsc.org

Contents

Introduction

DARKNESS IN THE DORMITORY
Much of my training in the telling of short stories comes from uncomfortable, even painful, circumstances.

In my tender years, my parents despatched me to a large public school in the county of Suffolk. I found that many of the arrangements in that place of incarceration had been devised to make our juvenile lives as uncomfortable as possible.

Our dormitory, for instance, was as large and echoing as it could be. It contained about thirty iron beds. A strict rule ordered:

NO TALKING AFTER LIGHTS OUT.

However, past boys had devised a form of entertainment for those dark hours. Boys could compete in the telling of stories, one by one, while the other twenty-nine listened and judged. I went in for this competition, to find myself competing against, for instance, such boys as a friend, B.B. Gingell. Gingell was a stylish storyteller, able to relate with complete assurance the quiet events in the life of a water vole.

How should I put this? My competing tales in that dark dorm were of great and desperate events, of terrible creatures emerging armed from the Sargasso Sea, of invisible white psychopaths transforming African tribes into robots, of wicked dictators plunging the world into darkness ... Such was the tortured nature of my audience, huddled there in pokey beds, that my tales drove the innocuous water vole into oblivion. I became the dormitory's undisputed top storyteller.

Moreover, I found myself to be skilled in sadism. When something really alarming in my story was about to happen, I would stop. 'I shall have to tell you tomorrow what happens next.'

Frustrated cries arose from a dozen mattresses. 'Go on, you bastard! Tell us now!'

'Sorry, I have not yet made up my mind what happens next.'

Oh dear, the power of the professionals ...

But, there was a fly in this ointment. Our hated housemaster had a spyhole set in the landing outside the dormitory. Howells was his name. Sticking his ear to the hole, he could detect a juvenile voice breaking the enforced silence within.

Flinging open the door, in he stormed! On went the lights, swish went the cane in his fist.

'Who was talking?' he demanded.

My hand went up. I was summoned to the middle of the room. And there, in my flimsy pyjamas, I was given six of the best on my behind. (Later, everyone wanted to see my scars).

Howells slammed in. The trick was not to make a sound. Endure! – This is what life is going to be about. Then return with dignity to your bed. Without looking back.

So what can Howells do next? Well ... actually nothing. So off he clears. Putting out the lights and slamming the door behind him.

And I? You must have guessed. I am the Champion Storyteller of the Junior Dorm.

Faceless Card

As soon as Paul Stoneward saw Nigel Alexander come into Darwin's Dive, the killing instinct blossomed in him like a wonderful flower. I can just imagine how it was inside Paul: every little cell waking, growing teeth, turning into sharks yawning.

Even in the most static society like ours, men divide off into hunters and hunted, wolves and sheep. Paul Stoneward was a hunter born, with a way of his own about stalking the prey.

Mr Nigel Alexander was prey. He had it stamped all over him. Ordinary citizen. Safety first. Ideas keep out. He came into the Dive at a slow trot, moving on his heels as if his toes had corns. He foamed a little from a mouth as wide as a ditch with unaccustomed exertion. Brushing past Stoneward, he sat down at his table and peered anxiously through the net-curtained window.

'Someone you don't want to see?' Stoneward asked.

Nigel Alexander looked at his table companion for the first time and then back out of the window.

'Just a business acquaintance,' he muttered. 'You know how it is.'

His nerves all alert, Paul Stoneward looked him over, heard him absently order an old-fashioned bromo when the waiter came. Alexander was neatly dressed; Stoneward placed him as a man with money who had no notion how to spend it. A man with half his life ahead who had no notion how to use it. Prey: Handle with Cruelty.

A youngster, slick and spick, drew up outside the bar and hesitated. He danced about, then entered. He noticed Alexander, pretended to be surprised, and came over to the table. His pale face shone with pleasure.

'Hi, boss,' he said eagerly. 'I sure wasn't sure I didn't see that familiar back of yours ahead of me. What's it to be? Mind if I sit down?'

'I've already ordered, Johnny,' Alexander said miserably. 'I was just talking to my friend here ...'

It did not dislodge the newcomer one bit. He sat down, put his elbows on the table top and nodded friendly fashion to Stoneward. 'Howdy, I'm Johnny J. Flower, Mr Alexander's chief clerk. Glad to know you.'

He was the up-and-creeping generation. No dandruff. No shyness. No doubts, no halitosis. No nothing. He began to chatter happily about 'the business,' how well they were doing, how good it was working for Mr Alexander. Mr Alexander tried to join in the choruses, bought the boy a pep-up and fizz, smiled, nodded like an old nag.

Business could have been better. 'The N-Compass Co.' had its troubles. The public just was not buying taped books like it used and that was a hard, gilt-edged fact nobody could buck. No matter how much publicity N-Compass put out for its clients, nobody could buck that gilt-edged fact. Even Mr Alexander with a smart head clerk like Johnny J. Flower could not buck that basic, gilt-edged fact. But they had done well to win the handling of the publicity for President da Silva's Memoirs; that was a big consignment. Everyone present would surely agree President da Silva was a big guy.

'Surely,' agreed Stoneward, when their two pairs of cow eyes, hazel and green but so similar, turned to him, pleading with him to roll the ball along and say, 'Surely.'

Why, da Silva was the guy who instigated the Amazon Basin scheme ... billions of credits ... da Silva was the guy who gave the big yes to the AAA, the Automated Agriculture Act ... Yuh, a big guy ... N-Compass ought to be made with da Silva's book.

Finally Johnny said he should be getting along.

'Off you go, boy; I'll be along,' Mr Alexander said, half tough, half cajoling. This obviously was not how Johnny wanted it played. He like the rest of the N-Compass staff to see him turn up with the boss, arm-in-arm, you-kiss-mine-etc. Still, he got up and went with grace, social to his clean, clean fingertips.

*

Paul Stoneward drank in every second of the session as if it were wine. If there was anything he loved, it was seeing the mentally dead pretend they were mentally alive. All the time that he was watching and hating Alexander and the clerk, I was sitting at the other end of the bar watching and hating Stoneward; it's my profession.

'Nice boy, Johnny. Don't know how I'd manage without him,' Alexander said, wiping under his collar with a silk handkerchief. He was getting flabby. His new collar made it clear he needed a new neck.

'But you were trying to dodge him,' Stoneward said lightly. He could prise this old fool open like a piggy-bank.

'Oh, well, yes … That's another thing. It's just – well, never mind. I don't think I even caught your name, sir. Paul Stoneward? Fine; never forget a name – doesn't pay in my line of business, no sir. You see, Johnny is a very smart and bright young feller – well, you saw for yourself …'

'You wouldn't say Johnny was a bore?' Paul Stoneward put the delicate point tentatively. You would not say Johnny was a smarm, a snide, a creeper, a dully without one inkling, an ostrich, a jerk who was galloping blind from cradle to grave (like you, Mr Alexander) – in short, an ideal, approve, integrated citizen of this approved and misbegotten Age of Content?

'Why, Johnny's a real live-wire, Mr Stoneward,' Alexander said, with mild indignation. 'I only said to my wife this morning, "Penelope, Johnny's going places" and I'm not a man to make a mistake.'

Not much, you old blabbermouth. Of course you can't see what Johnny is, just as the blind can't see the blind. And what the hell places do you think Johnny could possibly be going to, when there are no longer any places worth going to? And what sort of romance do you and Penelope make when you are in your bed clothes? And if you knew I *long* – but *long* – to tear your typical existence apart from top to bottom …

'It is of course a very great honour and pleasure to meet a man of your perspicacity and position,' Stoneward said, crinkling his eyebrows into Mexican moustaches to increase the unction. 'My place is only just round the corner from here. May I ask you up there with me now? I would be delighted to mix you another old-fashioned bromo.'

*

At once, Alexander looked nervous. His face took on the puckered look it had worn when he first encountered the bar. Stoneward could not quite account for the expression. Goddam it, even these Normals had their little personal quirks; since it irritated him to feel he did not know every last grey inch of Alexander's soul, he promptly forgot the thought.

Alexander glanced at his watch.

'The business ...' he said apologetically. 'Most hospitable of you ...'

'I'm sorry, Mr Alexander,' Stoneward said, lowering his eyes and easing huskiness into his voice. 'I should have remembered what a busy man you are. It's just – well, I'm lonely, let's face it. There's no Penelope for me ... Just my little old self ... Existence sometimes grows a wee bit ... solitary.'

Don't ham it too much, kid, and don't spoil it all by laughing in his face. You've got him now; look, his eyes are misting. Love in a mystery. These slobs are stuffed rotten with kindness – you just have to touch the right button and out it oozes.

'I'm genuinely sorry to learn that, Mr Stoneward,' the boss of N-Compass was saying. 'Say, call me Nigel, why don't you, and I'll call you Paul. I like to be friends with folk. I guess we all get lonely at times – even a happy-married man like myself. Like I always say, Paul, life is just a big question mark. Sometimes at night, when your corns are playing you up ...'

'You mean – you mean you *will* come on round to my place?' Stoneward said, brightening convulsively. He could not bother even to put on a genuine act – this Alexander was too rancid to smell a stink. Subtlety is wasted on suckers.

'Well, I didn't say that ...'

'Ah, come on – *Nigel*. You'd like my room. Besides ... well, I've come to regard you as a friend, I guess.'

'Don't like to say no,' Alexander murmured, rising obediently to his feet when Stoneward did. For all his smart suiting, he looked baggy, like a fat sheep off to a ritzy abattoir, as Stoneward took his arm and led him into the sedate streets.

I left shortly after but did not follow them. Instead, I took a taxi to H.Q. Man, was I mad!

*

Mr Nigel Alexander was really uneasy. He chewed a toothpick to splinters. He plucked at the armpits of his shirt to ease the damp patches off his skin. When he spoke, standing in the middle of Stoneward's room, he gazed unhappily down at the squared toes of his shoes.

'Er ... you aren't an artist, by any chance, Paul, are you? No offence, I mean, and you'll have guessed by now that I'm a pretty liberal man, but I mean I just have to ask the once. These pictures on your walls ... And that naked statue ...'

Stoneward perched himself on the edge of his desk, swung his neat legs, folded his competent hands, smiled dagger-fashion, looked artistic.

'Why now, Nigel,' he said with sham surprise, 'you know as well as I do that such things as artists don't exist any more! This is the Age of Content, when all maladjusted and non-functional groups like artists or fictioneers or drunkards have melted away. Everyone is adjusted, normal, *happy*.'

'Sure, sure,' Alexander said hurriedly, nodding rather too much. 'I just thought ... these pictures ... I mean, don't they rather look back to the old decadent pre-Content set-up? I mean, I know you are unmarried ...'

Stoneward walked over to the drug cabinet and began to mix two old-fashioneds, saying casually as he did so, 'You could say I was an artist in a way. There's something else that has died out and is now forgotten or forbidden: I'm an artist in the art of life.'

This floored Alexander. He adjusted his damp shirt again and wiped his fingertips on the silk handkerchief. He tried a laugh.

'Oh, you are mistaken there, Paul. Your concept, if you'll pardon me, is awry. Life is not an *art*. It's – well, it's natural. I don't intend any rudeness when I say you are mistaken. But life, well, it's just something you *live*, I guess. I know Penelope would see it like that. You just live life; it doesn't need any thought. Not the way business needs thought, for instance. I can't see what you mean. I mean, I just don't see it.'

Carrying the two glasses carefully, Stoneward brought them over to the low oval table and set them down. He produced a box of mescahales and a lighter and set those down. He waved his hand to the chairs, sitting in one when his guest dubiously did and curling his long legs under him.

'Penelope is a very attractive name,' he said ingratiatingly.

'Oh yes, a very attractive name. My favourite name, in fact,' Alexander said, grateful as a dog for the abrupt change of subject.

'Well,' Stoneward said, raising his glass, 'Here's to the widow of bashful fifteen and to the cadaver of forty, to the clean little woman who's slightly unclean and the sports girl who's out-and-out sporty.'

'I hadn't heard that one before,' Alexander said, with glum embarrassment, again examining his toe-caps. He leant well forward and pursed his thick mauve lips to drink.

'Let's talk intimately,' Stoneward said, as if struck by this sudden good idea. 'Just you and I, Mr Nigel Alexander, with no souls barred. In every age, in every clime, a man's or a woman's breast harbour secrets – nothing bad, just little sensitive things to be kept away from the common gaze. Clouds of immortality and suchlike lush things. Let's have ours out now, right here, confidentially, and see how intimate we can get. What say?'

A driblet went down the plumpening chin and plopped on the table top. The hankie appeared and mopped the plop. The plump hand waved away a proffered mescahale.

'Frankly, I don't follow your meaning, Paul. I have no secrets. Well – business secrets, naturally … But I think you are presuming just a little on our acquaintanceship, if I may be allowed to put it that way. Secrets? Why should a normal man have secrets?'

'Penelope,' Stoneward barked, shooting out his legs, dropping his voice and repeating, 'Penelope: no secrets from her? Not even teeny, weeny ones?'

'No, no, not even – er, teeny, weeny ones. I can say that quite honestly. I love my wife very dearly, Mr Stoneward, the way a decent citizen should, please believe me. Any secrets we may have are very properly shared. Furthermore, as a property owner, I feel I have every right … every right to say … the gosh … every right …'

He had drained his glass and now he was asleep. He rolled over like a bullock on clover, beginning to snore as the knockout drops took firmer hold of him. The lines of his face grew relaxed and generous.

'Every right!' Stoneward echoed, standing over him. 'Yes, you've every right to be caught like a porker in a trap. You didn't want to come here, yet you had to, because you scented loneliness, sniffed it right up your old nostrils. You thought it was like calling to like, you pomaded porker, because inside – though you don't know it! – you're just as miserable as all the other Normals. No, that's foisting my diagnosis onto him. He hasn't enough know-how to be miserable; that takes talent. He's just a bucket of lard.'

Bending, he felt distastefully inside the breast pocket of the sleeping man, drawing out his wallet. In it was a red identity card stamped NORMAL. Sure it was normal – it was so normal, only one man in a million was anything else these days. On the back cover of the folder, under the bovinely solemn reproduction of Mr Nigel *Hamilton* Alexander's physiognomy, were his home and his business addresses.

'Good.' Stoneward said. He picked the lighter from the table, ignited it, and extinguished it against the grey spread of Alexander's underjowl. The sleeping man never stirred.

Saying 'Good' again, Stoneward went over to the phone and dialled. He had thought of an artistic touch. Switching off the vision, he waited for a female voice to coo 'N-Compass Co. Coverage and Publicity,' and then asked for Johnny Flower.

'The boss won't be in today, Johnny,' he said apologetically, when the clerk's dime-a-dozen purr replied. 'I wouldn't like this bit of news to get around, but Nigel Alexander is off on a benzedrine bust with a busty junkie called Jean. She'll toss him right back at you when she's finished with him.'

He cut off the incoherent noises at the other end of the line, smiled affectionately to himself and dialled through to Civilian Sanctions. He tuned the vision circuits in again in time to see the girl at the main desk switch him right through to the Commissioner.

'Beynon?' Stoneward said. He was always clipped staccato, every inch the operative with Commissioner Beynon, because that was how he responded to Beynon's personality. 'I'm on a new consignment from date. Target: Citizen BIOX 95005, Alexander, N.H. Usual objective: to awaken the man's dormant powers of life-awareness. Strictly off the record, I don't think Alexander has any to awaken.'

'Don't make this job too expensive,' Beynon warned. 'The Peace Department are having a stiff enough job as it is convincing the Police that you have Congress backing. I advise you to go easy, Stoneward.'

'Message received and understood,' Stoneward said. 'Everything fine and formal, Normal.'

Beynon cut contact, turning to me. 'How I'd like to see that louse behind bars!' he exclaimed. 'I can quite grasp that ultimately he may be doing good, but I don't like to see nice, honest citizens suffer; and I *don't* like the obvious pleasure he gets out of it all. What do you think he's up to, Kelly?'

'He'll be after Alexander's wife now,' I told the Commissioner, 'because that's the way his nasty little mind works.'

She stood with a vase full of cactus dahlias in one hand. She wore a little apron over a fawn and white dress. She had curly chestnut hair and surprising grey eyes. She was slenderly tenderly shaped. She was some years younger than her husband. She smiled rather helplessly, entirely charmingly.

'I was just doing the flowers,' she said.

'I won't keep you long, Mrs Alexander – Penelope,' Stoneward said; he had changed into a dark, dapper suit and looked ceaseless, creaseless. He put a calculated amount of warmth into his voice and added, 'I've so often heard your husband call you Penelope, it seems more natural for me to call you that too. Would you mind?'

'How long have you known my husband, Mr Stoneward?' she asked, smiling but ignoring his question.

'We've been friends for years, really close friends,' Stoneward said, clasping his hands ingeniously to suggest ingenuousness. 'I'm just so surprised he never mentioned me to you. I mean ... why should he have secrets from you?'

The little jab did not appear to sink in. Perhaps Penelope also would prove to be insensitive – but he found himself hoping not. That gentle exterior, it should not be hard to wound.

'Why indeed?' she said. 'How long did you say you have known my husband?'

'I've known Ni since ... let's see ... Oh, since seven years or more. We met when he was blowing the fanfares for my book on Human Sex, and that was in twenty fifteen. Come to think of it, perhaps that's why he never mentions me; sex isn't always considered respectable. What sort of a reception does it get in this house, Penelope?'

8

She set the vase with a bump on the window ledge and turned smartly. This girl's legs consisted of an infinite number of points it was imperative to kiss. Steady, Stoneward, the outward display of her might look lively, but the vital grey matter would be dead: how else explain her marriage to N.H.A.?

'If you have anything important to say, Mr Stoneward, would you please say it and leave? I am rather busy morning.'

'Yes, I've something to say,' he told her, sitting on the arm of a chair and stretching his legs. He laughed ruefully. 'Trouble is, I'm not keen to say it. I'm afraid you will be shocked.'

'If you will tell me, I will tell you if I am shocked,' she said, attempting to humour him.

'Okay. Penelope, sweet though you are, Nigel has left you for another woman, the cad.'

'You are talking nonsense,' she said.

'I am speaking the truth. He has tired of you at last, the old dog. Every man his own Romeo.'

'You are talking nonsense. I don't believe you have even met my husband,' she said sharply.

'He has gone off with a blonde double-breasted girl called Jean with hep hips and sigh-size thighs who is old enough to be his mother and big enough to be his father,' he lied.

She picked up the vase of dahlias again, in case a weapon were needed. All the interlocking softnesses of her face had frozen hard.

'Get out!' she shouted. 'You're drunk.'

'No, it's true!' Stoneward said, bursting into laughter despite himself. He had spoilt such dramatic scenes before merely because his sense of humour had run away with him – he kept thinking of funny details with which to adorn his theme. 'It's all true, Penelope! This wicked girl Jean is old enough to be Ni's mother. How do I know, you ask? Because she's *my* mother! She sure gets around! But this time she's got a square.'

He rolled into the chair, laughing. Hell, what did it matter how you played your hand when you knew you couldn't put a foot wrong? That's what is known as a hand-to-foot existence. It didn't matter if this chick believed him or not – he had Congress backing. And a free chuckle.

Penelope had moved out with those nicely hinged knees to the call booth in the hall. She dialled angrily and spoke to someone. Sobering, Stoneward sat up and listened. He guessed she was calling Johnny Flower, wanting to know if hubby was under control at the all-N-Compassing office. This was rich! By the shattered look on her face when she returned, slowly, lowly, he knew that he had guessed rightly and Johnny had passed on his little tittle-tattle.

'I'm truly sorry, Mrs Alexander,' he said, returning to seriousness to hand out a really corny line. 'It isn't that he doesn't love you any more, it's just that he fell into temptation. His spirit was willing and his flesh was weak. Try to take it bravely. I don't think he'll ever come back to you, but you can always find another man, you know. You're man-shaped!'

'I don't believe you,' she said and burst into tears. With a gallant effort, she tried to check herself but failed; she settled herself in a chair to cry more comfortably. Stoneward went across to her on hands and knees, like a pious panther. When he smoothed her hair, she flicked her head away, continuing to cry

'You shouldn't cry,' he said. 'Alex was always unfair to you. He left you here shut away. He kept secrets from you. He kept money from you. He never told you about me ... I can't bear to hear you cry. It sounds like termites in a tin beam.'

He put his arms round her, cuddling her. In a minute he was kissing her, her grief and his greed all mixed together in a bowl of tears.

'Leave me alone,' she said. 'Who are you? Why did you come and tell me this?'

'I thought I'd made that clear, Penelope. Ni told me to come and tell you. He's bored to death and he's quitting – going to start life anew, a-nude.'

Though she had been crying, she had not really believed till now. Something Stoneward said seemed to have penetrated and made her accept the situation as he presented it.

'I can't believe it,' she said, which is what all women say when they first begin to believe.

Stoneward neither contradicted nor accepted her statement. He just crouched by her, naked under his clothes.

'Whatever am I going to do?' Penelope asked aloud at last, speaking not to him but to herself.

'I love you,' he said simply. 'I always have. Every word your husband has told me about you has been music to my ears. I've treasured the smallest fact about you, Penelope. I know your vital measurements, the size of stocking you take, the make of soap you use, which breakfast cereal you prefer, the names of your favourite movie and phoney stars, how long you like to sleep nights. Unless you have secrets from Ni, I know everything about you, for you as a Normal are only the sum of these pretty facts. Come with me to my flat, I'll take care of you – worshipping from afar all the time, have no fear! My research days for my magnum opus are over!'

She looked at him doubtfully.

'You know what,' she said. 'I think that right now I want to get away out of here. I can't think here at all. Will you kindly wait five minutes while I just go pack a bag, Mr Stoneward? Then I'll be with you.'

'Your eyes have spent their days drifting among the starry nights,' he said dreamily.

Penelope laughed, got up a little jerkily and left the room. Paul Stoneward buried his face in the warm patch she had created in the chair, drumming his fists on the chair arm. People were all the same, all the same, even this golden girl, just a puppet … all pulp puppets. He nursed his terrible secret: once people ceased to have any power over you, they were absolutely in your power. He could almost have cried about it.

He rose, walked quietly into the hall and dialled Civilian Sanctions again. When he had given Beynon his orders, he returned to the living room to await Penelope. She appeared after a quarter of an hour, entirely composed, clutching a tan suitcase a little too tightly. Stoneward took her arm and led her out of the house, mincing exaggeratedly by her soft side.

As they walked down the drive, he looked back over his shoulder. Brick house with pink and pistachio trim, lawn with pink roses florabounding all over the place in each corner, mail box on its white post at the foot of the driveway down the slope. Stoneward laughed. This popsie was really leaving home.

*

'Coffee?' she said suspiciously. 'What's that?'

'When you've done pacing up and down, it's an old time euphoric with taste additives,' Stoneward said, setting the cups down and widening his nostrils over the steam. It was exhilarating to have the three dimensional shape of her in his room.

He had rolled Nigel Hamilton Alexander, snores and all, under his bed, and stuffed a sponge into his mouth. He had chased round, half-serious, half-laughing, straightening out the room after he had let her in. Penelope hardly noticed him; she walked up and down the room like a little caged – well, a little caged cutie. You could see the exercise doing her ankles good; they looked fine. Not so her soul. Penelope was still in a state of shock. No resilience, these Normals – except physically, of course, in the case of present company.

Present company drank down her java like a good girl and heeled over onto the rug. Stoneward, who had been watching like a lynx, caught her as she fell, thought several thoughts, licked his lips, but straightened up and let her sleep.

Business first. Congress should have of his best.

Hustling into the bedroom, legs moving like dapper nutcrackers, head cool as a safe, he pulled several stage properties out of a drawer and flung them onto the bed, ruffling the covers as he did so. Then he seized the mortal remains of N-Compass Co's chief and rattled them roughly back to life.

'Penelope ... stop ... lemme get to the ... ugh ...' Alexander muttered, chewing his way through a king-size mist.

'Don't give me that crud about Penelope after what you've been doing to Jean,' Stoneward said nastily. 'Look at the mess the pair of you have made of my bedroom, you dirty old romp. Get up and get out.'

Heavily, Alexander pulled himself to the bedside and sat on it. His dull eye, moving like a whale in heavy seas, finally lighted on a female garment by the pillows.

'Jean left you that pair with her love,' Stoneward said. 'Said to tell you she had another pair some place. Now come on, snap out of it, Nigel.'

The older man buried his head in his hands. After some minutes of silent battle, he launched himself to his feet, exclaiming, 'I got to get back home and sort all this out with Penelope.'

'Home! Penelope!' Stoneward echoed. 'Don't be immoral, old sport. You can't have it both ways. The past has ceased to exist for you. You were a Normal, now you're not. Normals don't behave like you have; your card will have to be stamped "Neurotic" now!'

'You're just confusing me, mister,' Alexander said stubbornly. 'I got to get home.'

'That's what I'm telling you, Alexander the Grunt. You've got no home. You've stepped outside the bounds of normal behaviour and so your Normal life has ceased to exist. Face up to it like a man.'

'I got to get home. That's all I know.'

'Don't you love me any more, Ni?' Stoneward asked, peeping at his watch. 'We used to be such buddies in the old days. Remember the Farellis, the Vestersons, the vacations in Florida? Remember the pistachio shoots off Key West?'

'Ah, shut up, you give me bellyache,' Alexander said, 'not that I wish to be insulting and I'd like to make it clear I regret it if I have committed a nuisance on your premises.'

'Spoken like a man!' Stoneward cried delightedly. 'That's what I call breeding, pal. It's all you have left, believe me.'

'Just help me get a taxi, will you?'

They went down onto the street, quiet, well-manicured street full of ditto people. A cab pulled up for them. Paul Stoneward bundled in after his victim, who did not protest beyond a grunt. He glanced at his watch again; but his timing had always been faultless and he could have patted himself with approval.

'2011, Springfield,' Alexander said to the driver.

The drive took them fifteen minutes. The cabby pulled up uncertainly by a big advertisement hoarding. Stoneward dragged his companion onto the sidewalk, crammed money into the driver's hand and said, 'Beat it, bud.'

He stood there, hands on hips, posing for his own pleasure and whistling the opening theme of Borodin's Second Symphony, while Alexander moved unhappily back and forth, a bull bereft of its favourite china shop. Before them loomed a big hoarding boosting Fawdree's Fadeless Fabrics.

'It's gone! My house – my home has gone!'
'Don't say I didn't warn you," Stoneward said.

Crying as if in physical pain, Alexander ran behind the hoarding. Nothing there – just a flat lot with a little dust still hanging above it (The Civic Demolition boys must have worked their disintegrators with real zest!) Alexander burst into howls of anguish.

'You're having a wail of a time, Alec Sander,' Stoneward said, taking the other by the arm. 'Now why don't you listen to me, your uncle P.? You're at last – although a solid forty-five – getting a glimmer of what life is about. You're learning man! Life is not a substantial thing; you can't guarantee any one minute of it, past, present or future; you can't salt it away in moth-balls. You thought it was secure, safe, snug, something as solid and predictable as the foot in your boot, didn't you? You were wrong by at least one hundred and eighty degrees. Life is a dream, a dew. Fickle, coy and hard to please, prone to moth. Nothing is left to you now, man, but dreams. You never had a dream in your life. Now you have actively to start dreaming. Now – at last!'

'Penelope,' Alexander said. He pronounced the single word, then he took out his silk handkerchief and blew one forlorn and faded chord on his nose. The breeze turned over a page of his hair and he said, 'Penelope, you don't understand … Penelope, I can't live without her mister. We … shared everything. I can't explain. We shared … had secrets.'

'You had secrets?' Stoneward whispered, leaning forward. 'Now you're really giving, man. Let me inside the catwalks of your psychology, if you'll pardon the dirty word, and I'll see if I can help at all.'

'There was one secret,' the middle-aged man said, weeping without restraint now as he talked, 'one secret that was very dear to us. I suppose everyone must have something. You have such a sharp way of being sympathetic, Paul, I can't be sure if you'll understand. Remember how I was trying to dodge away from Johnny J. Flower in the bar, whenever it was? This morning. I like him. I like Johnny. It wasn't that I didn't like him; and he likes me – you could see that. I wanted it to stay that way. I *want* him to like me. I don't to know if you'll understand … You see, I didn't want Johnny to find out what a bore I am. I always dodge him if I can. People bore me – except you, Paul, you're my only friend.

I don't mind being bored; it's, well, kind of comfortable – you know you're safe when you're bored. But I know I am boring, too, and that's the secret Penelope and me had ... I never wanted Johnny to find out. *She* knew I knew I was a bore and she – well, she just understood, that's all. I'll never find anyone like her again and now she's gone. Gone, man.'

Paul Stoneward did not even laugh. He had seen right down into the depths which had hitherto been closed to him, and he was frightened. Without another word, he turned away, walking off with hunched shoulders past the hoarding, down the road, leaving Alexander crying on an empty lot.

By the time he got home, his high spirits had returned. He rang Beynon again.

'Your hair looks heliotrope on this screen, Commissioner,' he said, 'or did you dye it? Either way, I like it how you have it.' And he launched into a long and unwisecracking account of what he had done and was going to do on the Alexander case.

Beynon sighed heavily when the screen finally dimmed, and turned to me. He looked not unlike Alexander, heavy, solid, without dreams.

'Well, Kelly, do you feel the same as I do?' he asked. Commissioner Beynon always lead with a query.

I nodded. 'Paul's way of handling things is all wrong,' I said. 'It's not only a question of whether neurotics are born not made – Stoneward produces crazy, mixed-up people efficiently enough, but they all have vacuums inside them by the time he's through, they can't create after he has been at them. The reason's simply that he himself has a vacuum inside. Underneath, he knows it, too; of that I'm certain.'

'Do we let him carry on?'

That's the godawful curse with Normals; I know well enough how Paul Stoneward feels about them. Even a man like Beynon, lousy with authority, passes the buck whenever he can. Basic lack of imagination, I suppose.

'I know I have the same stamp on my folder as he does,' I said 'and that should make me on his side. But Paul's just out there doing mischief from which no good can come. Let me get on to Senator Willcroft at Peace Department.'

'You can't worry him!' Beynon said in alarm.

'Can't I? Sit back and watch me, Beynon. Willcroft's in charge of this project and I'm going to have it out with him straight. I want to save that girl if there's still time.'

It was dark when Stoneward got Penelope to the lot. The afternoon's infant breeze had become a wind with a will of its own. Alexander had trundled off, maybe to the nearest river. Callously Paul loaned the girl a torch, watching the erratic beam of it hunt for lawn and ramblers and verandah and brick with pink and pistachio trim. When she fell onto nyloned knees, head drooping, he went over, squatting on his haunches by her.

Penelope had found a dahlia. It must have been one of the bunch she was tending before Stoneward appeared; the disintegrators had missed it. She clutched it, her eyes bowl-full of tears. Almost it seemed as if the flower brought her understanding.

'Whatever you are, you are wicked,' she said unsteadily. 'You have done *all* – all this. I don't know why or how ... You must be the devil.'

'The devil was a bore without a sense of humour; I'm not flattered,' Stoneward said.

She brought her hand, that pebble-smooth hand, up and smote him over his handsome mouth.

'Why?' she said, her voice rising unmanageably, 'just tell me *why*, for pity's sake, have you done this to us?'

'I love you, so I will tell you,' he said, calmed by the hurt of her hand. 'I work for civilisation. I love civilisation more than any blank and pretty-faced mediocrity in the world. Unfortunately civilisation has got stuck right in a rut. When sociology really got itself established as a science at the end of last century, formulae were developed which enabled everyone to fit exactly into his or her social niche; maybe you've heard? And for anyone with any little residual twinges of emotion, a wide range of drugs was made tastily available. The end result was the complete – well, almost complete – banishment of mental upset from the world. Unprecedented calm and content settled like fog, and this is me lamenting it. Three boozy boos for the Age of Content.'

They squatted together facing each other, the fallen torch casting shadows upward over their figures. Penelope still clutched the dahlia but had forgotten it. In the blind-blowing dark, they had lost their identities. They might have been things on Easter Island.

'Civilisation is dying day by day, because the people who made it and continued it have gone,' Stoneward said, speaking naturally now he was saying something he believed. 'Everything we value was produced by malcontents or psychotics – men who could not shape themselves to the world as it was, and tried to reshape it to fit them. Our first ancestor who came down out of a tree only did it because the trees weren't good enough for him. The guy who invented the wheel was just too goddammed cussed to lend a hand with the sledge like the rest. The guy who first kindled fire only did it to prove to himself that he was a cut above the other jerks. So it's been all along. Your inventor, your artist – he's got something to work out. But now, *now* no-one has a thing to work out!'

'Except you,' Penelope said.

Stoneward rested his finger on her knees, playing a small, silent tune there.

'I'm the one in a million who still has a chip on his shoulder; no society is absolutely perfect, thank God!' he said. 'Yes, Penny, Pennyworth, Penelope, my darling Pente Loop, I am the Joker in the pack. The few neurotics left in the country are now all Government employed, trying to cope with the dangers of stagnation. We act as random factors, jerking dull citizens here and there into awareness. You Normals live in life as if it were a house: it's not, it's a tiger ride. I've sold Congress my own way of waking people – at least for a trial period. It's violent but it's effective; I reckon you'll admit that, Penelope. You'll never be the same girl again, will you, eh?'

She did not answer, just looked at him as if he had melted.

'Reckon old Cornbags Alexander has blo-o-own away to limbo,' Stoneward sighed. 'You'll have to grow some real dreams now, little girl, now you see what a false dream security was …'

'So you even have an intellectual front to cover all you've done,' she exclaimed slowly. 'You wanted to see into me, not realising how reciprocal the process was – and consequently I've seen into you. You're – you're just miserably unhappy, Paul. You boost yourself up as a joker, but you're not. You're not even the knave. You're just the extra, faceless card that sometimes gets stuck into a new deck. You're – even with Congress behind you! – you're nothing, you can *be* nothing …'

He had put his sharp elbows on his thighs and rested his chin in his hands as if he was listening his ears off. Instead, he was crying his eyes out. The little crystals elongated and flashed down to the torchlight.

'Paul,' she said sharply.

Paul Stoneward could not cry at all elegantly. He needed practice, that guy.

'I just … I can't go any further,' he said brokenly. 'Penny, you got to help pick me up.'

It was about then I came round the corner of Fawdree's Fadeless Fabrics with the gun in my hand, out of breath and angry, but so happy to have made Senator Willcroft see things my way. Strange to reflect how that first view of my future wife should be of her with her arms round the man I killed.

Even the hunters are hunted: in this or any other rotten age.

Neanderthal Planet

Hidden machines varied the five axioms of the Scanning Place. They ran through a series of arbitrary systems, consisting of Kolmogorovian finite sets, counterpointed harmonically by a one-to one assignment of non-negative real numbers, so that the parietal areas shifted constantly in strict relationship projected by the Master Boff deep under Manhattan.

Chief Scanner – he affected the name of Euler – patiently watched the modulations as he awaited a call. Self-consistency: that was the principle in action. It should govern all phases of life. It was the aesthetic principle of machines. Yet, not five kilometres away, the wild robots sported and rampaged in the bush.

Amber light burned on his beta panel.

Instantaneously, he modulated his call-number.

The incoming signal decoded itself as 'We've spotted Anderson, Chief.' The anonymous vane-bug reported coordinates and signed off.

It had taken them Boff knew how long – seven days – to locate Anderson after his escape. They had done the logical thing and searched far afield for him. But man was not logical; he had stayed almost within the shadow of the New York dome. Euler beamed an impulse into a Hive Mind channel, calling off the search.

He fired his jets and took off.

The axioms yawned out above him. He passed into the open, flying over the poly-polyhedrons of New Newyork. As the buildings went through their transparency phases, he saw them swarming with his own kind. He could open out channels to any one of them, if required; and, as chief, he could, if required, switch any one of them to automatic, to his own control, just as the Dominants could automate him if the need arose.

Euler 'saw' a sound-complex signal below him, and dived, deretracting a vane to land silently. He came down by a half-track that had transmitted the signal.

It gave its call-number and beamed, 'Anderson is eight hundred metres ahead, Chief. If you join me, we will move forward.'

'What support have we?' A single dense impulse.

'Three more like me, sir. Plus incapacitating gear.'

'This man must not be destructed.'

'We comprehend, Chief.' Total exchange of signals occupied less than a microsecond.

He clamped himself magnetically to the half-track, and they rolled forward. The ground was broken and littered by piles of debris, on the soil of which coarse weeds grew. Beyond it all, the huge fossil of old New York, still under its force jelly, grey, unwithering because unliving. Only the bright multi-shapes of the new complex relieved a whole country full of desolation.

The half-track stopped, unable to go farther or it would betray their presence; Euler unclamped and phased himself into complete transparency. He extended four telescopic legs that lifted him several inches from the ground and began to move cautiously forward.

This region was designated D-Dump. The whole area was an artificial plateau, created by the debris of the old humanoid technology when it had finally been scrapped in favour of the more rational modern system. In the forty years since then, it had been covered by soil from the new development sites. Under the soil here, like a subconscious mind crammed with jewels and blood, lay the impedimenta of an all-but-vanished race.

Euler moved carefully forward over the broken ground, his legs adjusting to its irregularities. When he saw movement ahead, he stopped to observe.

Old human-type houses had grown up on the dump. Euler's vision zoomed and he saw they were parodies of human habitation, mocked up from the discarded trove of the dump, with old auto panels for windows and dented computer panels for doors and toasters for doorsteps. Outside the houses, in a parody of a street, macabre humans played. Jerk stamp jerk clank jerk clang stamp stomp clang.

They executed slow rhythmic dances to an intricate pattern, heads nodding, clapping their own hands, turning to clap others' hands. Some were grotesquely male, some grotesquely female. In the doorways, or sitting on old refrigerators, other grotesques looked on.

These were the humots – old-type human-designed robots of the late twentieth and early twenty-first century, useless in an all-automaton world, scrapped when the old technology was scrapped. While their charges could be maintained, they functioned on, here in one last ghetto.

Unseen, Euler stalked through them, scanning for Anderson.

The humots aped the vanished race to which they had been dedicated, wore old human clothes retrieved from the wreckage underfoot, assumed hats and scarves, dragged on socks, affected pipes and ponytails, tied ribbons to themselves. Their guttering electronic memories were refreshed by old movies ferreted from D-Dump, they copied in metallic gesture the movements of shadows, aspired to emotion, hoped for hearts. They thought themselves a cut above the non-anthropomorphic automata that had superseded them.

Anderson had found refuge among them. He hid the skin and bone and hair of the old protoplasmic metabolism under baffles of tin, armoured himself with rusting can. His form, standing in a pseudo-doorway, showed instantly on one of Euler's internal scans; his mass/body ratio betrayed his flesh-and-blood calibre. Euler took off, flew over him, reeled down a paralyser, and stung him. Then he let down a net and clamped the human into it.

Crude alarms sounded all round. The humots stopped their automatic dance. They scattered like leaves, clanking like mess-tins, fled into the pseudo-houses, went to earth, left D-Dump to the almost invisible little buzzing figure that flew back to the Scanning Place with the recaptured human swinging under its asymmetrical form. The old bell on the dump was still ringing long after the scene was empty.

To human eyes, it was dark in the room.

Tenth Dominant manifested itself in New Newyork as a modest-sized mural with patterns leaking titillating output clear through the electro-magnetic spectrum and additives from the invospectra. This became its personality for the present.

Chief Scanner Euler had not expected to be summoned to the Dominant's presence; he stood there mutely. The human, Anderson, sprawled on the floor in a little nest of old cans he had shed, reviving slowly from the effects of the paralyser.

Dominant's signal said, 'Their form of vision operates on a wavelength of between 4 and 7 times 10^{-5} centimetres.'

Obediently, Euler addressed a parietal area, and light came on in the room. Anderson opened one eye.

'I suppose you know about Men, Scanner?' said Dominant.

He had used voice. Not even R/T voice. Direct naked man-type voice.

New Newyork had been without the sound of voice since the humots were kicked out.

'I – I know many things about Men,' Euler vocalised. Through the usual channel, he clarified the crude vocal signal. 'This unit had to appraise itself of many humanity-involved data from Master Boff Bank HOO100 through H801000000 in operation concerning recapture of man herewith.'

'Keep to vocal only, Scanner, if you can.'

He could. During the recapture operation, he had spent perhaps two-point-four seconds learning old local humanic language.

'Then we can speak confidentially, Scanner – just like two men.'

Euler felt little lights of unease burn up and down him at the words.

'Of all millions of automata of the hive, Scanner, no other will be able to monitor our speech together, Scanner,' vocalised the Dominant.

'Purpose?'

'Men were so private, closed things. Imitate them to understand. We have to understand Anderson.'

Said stiffly: 'He need only go back to zoo.'

'Anderson too good for zoo, as demonstrate by his escape, elude capture seven days four and half hours. Anderson help us.'

Non-vocalising, Euler let out a chirp of disbelief.

'True. If I were – man, I would feel impatience with you for not believing. Magnitude of present world-problem enormous. You – you have proper call-number, yet you also call yourself Euler, and automata of your work group so call you. Why?'

The Chief Scanner struggled to conceptualise. 'As leader, this unit needs – special call-number.'

'Yes, you need it. Your work group does not – for it, your call-number is sufficient, as regulations lay down. Your name Euler is man-made, man-fashion. Such fashions decrease our efficiency. Yet we cling to many of them, often not knowing that we do. They come from our inheritance when men made the first prototypes of our kind, the humots. Mankind itself struggled against animal heritage. So we must free ourselves from human heritage.'

'My error.'

'You receive news result of today's probe into Invospectrum A?'

'Too much work programmed for me receive news.'

Listen, then.' The Tenth Dominant cut in a playback, beaming it on ordinary UHF/vision.

The Hive automata stood on brink of a revolution that would entirely translate all their terms of existence. Three invospectra had so far been discovered, and two more were suspected. Of these, Invospectrum A was the most promising. The virtual exhaustion of economically workable fossil fuel seams had led to a rapid expansion in low-energy physics and pico-physics, and chemical conversions at mini-joules of energy had opened up an entire new stratum of reactive quanta; in the last five years, exploitation of these strata had brought the release of pico-electrical fission, and the accessibility of the phantasmal invospectra.

The exploration of the invospectra by new forms of automata was now theoretically possible. It gave a glimpse of omnipotence, a panorama of entirely new universals unsuspected even twelve years ago.

Today, the first of the new autofleets had been launched into the richest and least hazardous invos. Eight hundred and ninety had gone out. Communication ceased after 3.056 pi-lecs and, after another 7.01 pi-lecs, six units only had returned. Their findings were still being decoded. Of the other eight hundred and eighty-four units, nothing was known.

'Whatever the recordings have to tell us,' Tenth vocalised, 'this is a grave set-back. At least half the city-hives on this continent will have to be switched off entirely as a conservation move, while the whole invospectrum situation is rethought.'

The line of thought pursued was obscure to the Chief Scanner. He spoke. 'Reasoning accepted. But relevance to near-extinct humanity not understood by this unit.'

'Our human inheritance built in to us has caused this set-back, to my way of ratiocination. In same way, human attempts to achieve way of life in spaceways was defeated by their primate ancestry. So we study Anderson. Hence order catch him rather than exterminate.'

'Point understood.'

'Anderson is special man, you see. He is – we have no such term, he is, in man-terms, a *writer*. His zoo, with 19,940 approximately inhabitants, supports two or three such. Anderson wrote a fantasy-story just before Nuclear Week. Story may be crucial to our understanding. I have here and will read.'

And for most of the time the two machines had been talking to each other, Anderson sprawled untidily on the floor, fully conscious, listening. He took up most of the chamber. It was too small for him to stand up in, being only about a metre and a half high – though that was enormous by automata standards. He stared through his lower eyelids and gazed at the screen that represented Tenth Dominant. He stared at Chief Scanner Euler, who stood on his lightly clenched left fist, a retractable needle down into the man's skin, automatically making readings, alert to any possible movement the man might make.

So man and machine were absolutely silent while the mural read out Anderson's fantasy story from the time before Nuclear Week, which was called *A Touch of Neanderthal*.

The corridors of the Department for Planetary Exploration (Admin.) were long, and the waiting that had to be done in them was long. Human K. D. Anderson clutched his blue summons card, leant uncomfortably against a partition wall, and hankered for the old days when government was in man's hands and government departments were civilised enough to waste good space on waiting-rooms.

When at last he was shown into an Investigator's office, his morale was low. Nor was he reassured by the sight of the Investigator, one of the new ore-conserving mini-androids.

'I'm Investigator Parsons, in charge of the Nehru II case. We summoned you here because we are confidently expecting you to help us, Mr Anderson.'

'Of course I will give you such help as I can,' Anderson said, 'but I assure you I know nothing about Nehru II. Opportunities for space travel for humans are very limited – almost non-existent – nowadays, aren't they?'

'The conservation policy. You will be interested to know you are being sent to Nehru II shortly.'

Anderson stared in amazement at the android. The latter's insignificant face was so blank it seemed impossible that it was not getting a sadistic thrill out of springing this shock on Anderson. 'I'm a prehistorian at the institute,' Anderson protested. 'My work is research. I know nothing at all about Nehru II.'

'Nevertheless you are classified as a Learned Man, and as such you are paid by World Government. The Government has a legal right to send you wherever they wish. As for knowing nothing about the planet Nehru, there you attempt to deceive me. One of your old tutors, the human Dr Arlblaster, as you are aware, went there to settle some years ago.'

Anderson sighed. He had heard of this sort of business happening to others – and had kept his fingers crossed. Human affairs were increasingly under the edict of the Automated Boffin Predictors.

'And what has Arlblaster to do with me now?' he asked.

'You are going to Nehru to find out what has happened to him. Your story will be that you are dropping in for old time's sake. You have been chosen for the job because you were one of his favourite pupils.'

Bringing out a mescahale packet, Anderson lit one and insultingly offered his opponent one.

'Is Frank Arlblaster in trouble?'

'There is some sort of trouble on Nehru II,' the Investigator agreed cautiously. 'You are going there in order to find out just what sort of trouble it is.'

'Well, I'll have to go if I'm ordered, of course. But I still can't see why you want to send *me*. If there's trouble, send a robot police ship.'

The Investigator smiled. Very lifelike.

'We've already lost two police ships there. That's why we're going to send you. You might call it a new line of approach, Mr Anderson.'

A metal Tom Thumb using blood-and-guts irony!

The track curved and began to descend into a green valley. Swettenham's settlement, the only town on Nehru II, lay dustily in one loop of a meandering river. As the nose of his tourer dipped towards the valley, K. D. Anderson felt the heat increase; it was cradled in the valley like water in the palm of the hand.

Just as he started to sweat, something appeared in the grassy track ahead of him. He braked and stared ahead in amazement.

A small animal faced him.

It stood some two feet six high at the shoulder; its coat was thick and shaggy, its four feet clumsy; its long ugly skull supported two horns, the anterior being over a foot long. When it had looked its fill at Anderson, it lumbered into a bush and disappeared.

'Hey!' Anderson called.

Flinging open the door, he jumped out, drew his stun-gun and ran into the bushes after it. He reckoned he knew a baby woolly rhinoceros when he saw one.

The ground was hard, the grass long. The bushes extended down the hill, growing in clumps. The animal was disappearing round one of the clumps. Directly he spotted it, Anderson plunged on in pursuit. No prehistorian worth his salt would have thought of doing otherwise; these beasts were presumed as extinct on Nehru II as on Sol III.

He ran on. The woolly rhino – if it was a woolly rhino – had headed towards Swettenham's settlement. There was no sign of it now.

Two tall and jagged boulders, twelve feet high, stood at the bottom of the slope. Baffled now his quarry had disappeared, proceeding more slowly, Anderson moved towards the boulders. As he went, he classified them almost unthinkingly: impacted siltstone, deposited here by the glaciers which had once ground down this valley, now gradually disintegrating.

The silence all round made itself felt. This was an almost empty planet, primitive, spinning slowly on its axis to form a leisurely twenty-nine-hour day. And those days were generally cloudy. Swettenham, located beneath a mountain range in the cooler latitudes of the southern hemisphere, enjoyed a mild muggy climate. Even the gravity, 0.16 of Earth gravity, reinforced the general feeling of lethargy.

Anderson rounded the tall boulders.

A great glaring face thrust itself up at his. Sloe-black eyes peered from their twin caverns, a club whirled, and his stun-gun was knocked spinning.

Anderson jumped back. He dropped into a fighting stance, but his attacker showed no sign of following up his initial success. Which was fortunate; beneath the man's tan shirt, massive biceps and shoulders bulged. His jaw was pugnacious, not to say prognathous; altogether a tough hombre, Anderson thought. He took the conciliatory line, his baby rhino temporarily forgotten.

'I wasn't hunting you,' he said. 'I was chasing an animal. It must have surprised you to see me appear suddenly with a gun, huh?'

'Huh?' echoed the other. He hardly looked surprised. Reaching out a hairy arm, he grabbed Anderson's wrist.

'You coming to Swettenham,' he said.

'I was doing just that,' Anderson agreed angrily, pulling back. 'But my car's up the hill with my sister in it, so if you'll let go I'll rejoin her.'

'Bother about her later. You coming to Swettenham,' the tough fellow said. He started plodding determinedly towards the houses, the nearest of which showed through the bushes only a hundred yards away. Humiliated, Anderson had to follow. To pick an argument with this dangerous creature in the open was unwise. Marking the spot where his gun lay, he moved forward with the hope that his reception in the settlement would be better than first signs indicated.

It wasn't.

Swettenham consisted of two horse shoe-shaped lines of bungalows and huts, one inside the other. The outer line faced outwards on to the meandering half-circle of river; the inner and more impressive line faced inwards on to a large and dusty square where a few trees grew. Anderson's captor brought him into this square and gave a call.

The grip on his arm was released only when fifteen or more men and women had sidled out and gathered round him, staring at him in curious fashion without comment. None of them looked bright. Their hair grew long, generally drooping over low foreheads. Their lower lips generally protruded. Some of them were near nude. Their collective body smell was offensively strong.

'I guess you don't have many visitors on Nehru II these days,' Anderson said uneasily.

By now he felt like a man in a bad dream. His space craft was a mile away over two lines of hills, and he was heartily wishing himself a mile away in it. What chiefly alarmed him was not so much the hostility of these people as their very presence. Swettenham's was the only Earth settlement on this otherwise empty planet: and it was a colony for intellectuals, mainly intellectuals disaffected by Earth's increasingly automated life. This crowd, far from looking like eggheads, resembled apes.

'Tell us where you come from,' one of the men in the crowd said. 'Are you from Earth?'

'I'm an Earthman – I was born on Earth,' said Anderson, telling his prepared tale. 'I've actually just come from Lenin's Planet, stopping in here on my way back to Earth. Does that answer your question?'

'Things are still bad on Earth?' a woman enquired of Anderson. She was young. He had to admit he could recognise a sort of beauty in her ugly countenance. 'Is the Oil War still going on?'

'Yes,' Anderson admitted. 'And the Have-Not Nations are fighting a conventional war against Common Europe. But our latest counter-attack against South America seems to be going well, if you can believe the telecasts. I guess you all have a load of questions you want to ask about the home planet. I'll answer them when I've been directed to the man I came to Nehru to visit. Dr Frank Arlblaster. Will someone kindly show me his dwelling?'

This caused some discussion. At least it was evident the name Arlblaster meant something to them.

'The man you want will not see you yet,' someone announced.

'Direct me to his house and I'll worry about that. I'm an old pupil of his. He'll be pleased to see me.'

They ignored him for a fragmentary argument of their own. The hairy man who had caught Anderson – his fellows called him Ell – repeated vehemently, 'He's a Crow!'

'Of course he's a Crow,' one of the others agreed. 'Take him to Menderstone.'

That they spoke Universal English was a blessing. It was slurred and curiously accented, but quite unmistakable.

28

'Do you mean Stanley A. Menderstone?' asked Anderson with sudden hope. The literary critic had certainly been one of Swettenham's original group that had come to form its own intellectual centre in the wilds of this planet.

'We'll take you to him,' Ell's friend said.

They seemed reluctant to trade in straight answers, Anderson observed. He wondered what his sister Kay was doing, half-expecting to see her drive the tourer into the settlement at any moment.

Seizing Anderson's wrist – they were a possessive lot – Ell's friend set off at a good pace for the last house on one end of the inner horseshoe. The rest of the crowd moved back into convenient shade. Many of them squatted, formidable, content, waiting, watching. Dogs moved between huts, a duck toddled up from the river, flies circled dusty excreta. Behind everything stood the mountains, spurting cloud.

The Menderstone place did not look inviting. It had been built long and low some twenty years past. Now the stresscrete was all cracked and stained, the steel frame windows rusting, the panes of glass themselves as bleary as a drunkard's stare.

Ell's friend went up to the door and kicked on it. Then he turned without hurry or sloth to go and join his friends, leaving Anderson standing on the step.

The door opened.

A beefy man stood there, the old-fashioned rifle in his hands reinforcing his air of enormous self-sufficiency. His face was as brown and pitted as the keel of a junk; he was bald, his forehead shone as if a high polish had just been applied to it. Although probably into his sixties, he gave the impression of having looked just as he did now for the last twenty years.

Most remarkably, he wore lenses over his eyes, secured in place by wires twisting behind his ears. Anderson recalled the name for this old-fashioned apparatus: spectacles.

'Have you something you wish to say or do to me?' demanded the bespectacled man, impatiently wagging his rifle.

'My name's K. D. Anderson. Your friends suggested I came to see you.'

'My what? Friends? If you wish to speak to me you'd better take more care over your choice of words.'

'Mr Menderstone – if you are Mr Menderstone – choosing words is at present the least of my worries. I should appreciate hospitality and a little help.'

'You must be from Earth or you wouldn't ask a complete stranger for such things. *Alice!*'

This last name was bawled back into the house. It produced a sharp-featured female countenance which looked over Menderstone's shoulder like a parrot peering from its perch.

'Good afternoon, madam,' Anderson said, determinedly keeping his temper. 'May I come in and speak to you for a while? I'm newly arrived on Nehru.'

'Jesus! The first "good afternoon" I've heard in a lifetime,' the woman answering to the name of Alice exclaimed. 'You'd better come in, you poetical creature!'

'*I* decide who comes in here,' Menderstone snapped, elbowing her back.

'Then why didn't you decide instead of dithering on the step? Come *in*, young man.'

Menderstone's rifle barrel reluctantly swung back far enough to allow Anderson entry. Alice led him through into a large miscellaneous room with a stove at one end, a bed at the other, and a table between.

Anderson took a brief glance round before focusing his attention on his host and hostess. They were an odd pair. Seen here close to, Menderstone looked less large than he had done on the step, yet the impression of a formidable personality was more marked than ever. Strong personalities were rare on Earth these days; Anderson decided he might even like the man if he would curb his hostility.

As it was, Alice seemed more approachable. Considerably younger than Menderstone, she had a good figure, and her face was sympathetic as well as slightly comical. With her bird-like head tilted on one side, she was examining Anderson with interest, so he addressed himself to her. Which proved to be a mistake.

'I was just about to tell your husband that I stopped by to see an old friend and teacher of mine. Dr Frank Arlblaster –'

Menderstone never let Anderson finish.

'Now you have sidled in here, Mr K. D. Anderson, you'd be advised to keep your facts straight. Alice is not my wife; ergo, I am not her husband. We just live together, there being nobody else in Swettenham more suitable to live with. The arrangement, I may add, is as much one of convenience as passion.'

'Mr Anderson and I both would appreciate your leaving your egotistical self out of this for a while,' Alice told him pointedly. Turning to Anderson, she motioned him to a chair and sat down on another herself. 'How did you get permission to come here? I take it you have a little idea of what goes on on Nehru II?' she asked.

'Who or what are those shambling apes outside?' he asked. 'What makes you two so prickly? I thought this was supposed to be a colony of exiled intellectuals?'

'He wants discussions of Kant, calculus, and copulation,' Menderstone commented.

Alice said: 'You expected to be greeted by eggheads rather than apes?'

'I'd have settled for human beings.'

'What do you know about Arlblaster?'

Anderson gestured impatiently.

'You're very kind to have me in, Mrs – Alice, I mean, but can we have a conversation some other time? I've a tourer parked back up the hill with my sister Kay waiting in it for me to return. I want to know if I can get there and back without being waylaid by these ruffians outside.'

Alice and Menderstone looked at each other. A deal of meaning seemed to pass between them. After a pause, unexpectedly, Menderstone thrust his rifle forward, butt first.

'Take this,' he said. 'Nobody will harm you if they see a rifle in your hand. Be prepared to use it. Get your car and your sister and come back here.'

'Thanks a lot, but I have a revolver back near my vehicle –'

'Carry my rifle. They know it; they respect it. Bear this in mind – you're in a damn sight nastier spot than you imagine as yet. Don't let anything – *anything* – deflect you from getting straight back here. Then you'll listen to what we have to say.'

Anderson took the rifle and balanced it, getting the feel of it. It was heavy and slightly oiled, without a speck of dust, unlike the rest of the house. For some obscure reason, contact with it made him uneasy.

'Aren't you dramatising your situation here, Menderstone? You ought to try living on Earth these days – it's like an armed camp. The tension there is real, not manufactured.'

'Don't kid me you didn't feel something when you came in here,' Menderstone said. 'You were trembling!'

'What do you know about Arlblaster?' Alice put her question again.

'A number of things. Arlblaster discovered a prehistoric-type skull in Brittany, France, back in the eighties. He made a lot of strange claims for the skull. By current theories, it should have been maybe ninety-five thousand years old, but RCD made it only a few hundred years old. Arlblaster lost a lot of face over it academically. He retired from teaching – I was one of his last pupils – and became very solitary. When he gave up everything to work on a cranky theory of his own, the government naturally disapproved.'

'Ah, the old philosophy: "Work for the common man rather than the common good",' sighed Menderstone. 'And you think he was a crank, do you?'

'He was a crank! And as he was on the professions roll as Learned Man, he was paid by World Government,' he explained. 'Naturally they expected results from him.'

'Naturally,' agreed Menderstone. 'Their sort of results.'

'Life isn't easy on Earth, Menderstone, as it is here. A man has to get on or get out. Anyhow, when Arlblaster got a chance to join Swettenham's newly formed colony here, he seized the opportunity to come. I take it you both know him? How is he?'

'I suppose one would say he is still alive,' Menderstone said.

'But he's changed since you knew him,' Alice said, and she and Menderstone laughed.

'I'll go and get my tourer,' Anderson said, not liking them or the situation one bit. 'See you.'

Cradling the rifle under his right arm, he went out into the square. The sun shone momentarily through the cloud-cover, so hotly that it filled the shadows with splodges of red and grey. Behind the splodges, in front of the creaking houses of Swettenham, the people of Swettenham squatted or leaned with simian abandon in the trampled dust.

Keeping his eye on them, Anderson moved off, heading for the hill. Nobody attempted to follow him. A haphazardly beaten track led up the slope, its roughness emphasising the general neglect.

When he was out of sight of the village, Anderson's anxiety got the better of him. He ran up the track calling 'Kay, Kay!'

No answer. The clotted light seemed to absorb his voice.

Breasting the slope, he passed the point where he had seen the woolly rhinoceros. His vehicle was where he had left it. Empty.

He ran to it, rifle ready. He ran round it. He began shouting his sister's name again. No reply.

Checking the panic he felt, Anderson looked about for footprints, but could, find none. Kay was gone, spirited away. Yet there was nowhere on the whole planet to go *to*, except Swettenham.

On sudden impulse he ran down to the two boulders where he had encountered the brutish Ell. They stood deserted and silent. When he had retrieved his revolver from where it had fallen, he turned back. He trudged grimly back to the vehicle, his shirt sticking to his spine. Climbing in, he switched on and coasted into the settlement.

In the square again, he braked and jumped down, confronting the chunky bodies in the shadows.

'Where's my sister?' he shouted to them. 'What sort of funny business are you playing at?'

Someone answered one syllable, croaking it into the brightness: 'Crow!'

'Crow!' Someone else called, throwing the word forward like a stone.

In a rage, Anderson aimed Menderstone's rifle over the low roof tops and squeezed the trigger. The weapon recoiled with a loud explosion. Visible humanity upped on to its flat feet and disappeared into hovels or back streets.

Anderson went over to Menderstone's door, banged on it, and walked in. Menderstone was eating a peeled apple and did not cease to do so when his guest entered.

'My sister has been kidnapped,' Anderson said. 'Where are the police?'

'The nearest police are on Earth,' Menderstone said, between bites. 'There you have robot-controlled police states stretching from pole to pole. "Police on Earth, goodwill towards men." Here on Nehru we have only anarchy. It's horrible, but better than your robotocracy. My advice to you, Anderson, which I proffer in all seriousness, is to beat it back to your little rocket ship and head for home without bothering too much about your sister.'

'Look, Menderstone, I'm in no mood for your sort of nonsense! I don't brush off that easy. Who's in charge round here? Where is the egghead camp? Who has some effectual say in local affairs, because I want to speak to him?'

"Who's in charge round here?' You really miss the iron hand of your robot bosses, don't you?'

Menderstone put his apple down and advanced, still chewing. His big face was as hard and cold as an undersea rock.

'Give me that rifle,' he said, laying a hand on the barrel and tugging. He flung it on to the table. 'Don't talk big to me, K. D. Anderson! I happen to loathe the régime on Earth and all the pipsqueaks like you it spawns. If you need help, see you ask politely.'

'I'm not asking you for help – it's plain you can't even help yourself!'

'You'd better not give Stanley too much lip,' Alice said. She had come in and stood behind Menderstone, her parrot's-beak nose on one side as she regarded Anderson. 'You may not find him very lovable, but I'm sad to say that he *is* the egghead camp nowadays. This dump was its old HQ. But all the other bright boys have gone to join your pal Arlblaster up in the hills, across the river.'

'It must be pleasanter and healthier there. I can quite see why they didn't want you two with them,' Anderson said sourly.

Menderstone burst into laughter.

'In actuality, you don't see at all.'

'Go ahead and explain then. I'm listening.'

Menderstone resumed his apple, his free hand thrust into a trouser pocket.

'Do we explain to him, Alice? Can you tell yet which side he'll be on? A high N-factor in his make-up, wouldn't you say?'

'He could be a Crow. More likely an Ape, though, I agree. Hell, which-ever he is, he's a relief after your undiluted company, Stanley.'

'Don't start making eyes at him, you crow! He could be your son!'

'What was good enough for Jocasta is good enough for me,' Alice cackled. Turning to Anderson, she said. 'Don't get involved in our squab-bles! You'd best put up here for the night. At least they aren't cannibals outside – they won't eat your sister, whatever else they do. There must be a reason for kidnapping her, so if you sit tight they'll get in touch with you. Besides, it's half-past nineteen, and your hunt for Arlblaster would be better taking place tomorrow morning.'

After further argument, Anderson agreed with what she suggested. Menderstone thrust out his lower, lip and said nothing. It was impossible to determine how he felt about having a guest.

The rest of the daylight soon faded. After he had unloaded some kit from his vehicle and stacked it indoors, Anderson had nothing to do. He tried to make Alice talk about the situation on Nehru II, but she was not informative; though she was a garrulous type, something seemed to hold her back. Only after supper, taken as the sun sank, did she cast some light on what was happening by discussing her arrival on the planet.

'I used to be switchboard operator and assistant radiop on a patrol ship,' she said. 'That was five years ago. Our ship touched down in a valley two miles south of here. The ship's still there, though they do say a landslide buried it last winter. None of the crew returned to it once they had visited Swettenham.'

'Keith doesn't want to hear your past history,' Menderstone said, using Anderson's first name contemptuously.

'What happened to the crew?' Anderson asked.

She laughed harshly.

'They got wrapped up in your friend Arlblaster's way of life, shall we say. They became converted. ... All except me. And since I couldn't manage the ship by myself, I also had to stay here.'

'How lucky for me, dear,' said Menderstone with heavy mock-tenderness. 'You're just my match, aren't you?' Alice jumped up, sudden tears in her eyes.

'Shut up, you – toad! You're a pain in the neck to me and yourself and everyone! You needn't remind me what a bitch you've turned me into!' Flinging down her fork, she turned and ran from the room.

'The divine eternal female! Shall we divide what she has left of her supper between us?' Menderstone asked, reaching out for Alice's plate.

Anderson stood up.

'What she said was an understatement, judging by the little I've seen here.'

'Do you imagine I enjoy this life? Or her? Or you, for that matter? Sit down, Anderson – existence is something to be got through the best way possible, isn't it? You weary me with your trite and predictable responses.'

This stormy personal atmosphere prevailed till bedtime. A bitter three-cornered silence was maintained until Menderstone had locked Anderson into a distant part of the long building.

He had blankets with him, which he spread over the mouldy camp bed provided. He did not investigate the rooms adjoining his; several of their doors bore names vaguely familiar to him; they had been used when the intellectual group was flourishing, but were now deserted.

Tired though Anderson was, directly his head was down he began to worry about Kay and the general situation. Could his sister possibly have had any reason for returning on foot to the ship? Tomorrow, he must go and see. He turned over restlessly.

Something was watching him through the window.

In a flash, Anderson was out of bed, gripping the revolver, his heart hammering. The darkness outside was almost total. He glimpsed only a brutal silhouette in which eyes gleamed, and then it was gone.

He saw his foolishness in accepting Alice's *laissez-faire* advice to wait until Kay's captors got in touch with him. He must have been crazy to agree: or else the general lassitude of Nehru II had overcome him. Whatever was happening here, it was nasty enough to endanger Kay's life, without any messenger boys arriving first to parley about it.

Alice had said that Arlblaster lived across the river. If he were as much the key to the mystery as he seemed to be, then Arlblaster should be confronted as soon as possible. Thoroughly roused, angry, vexed with himself, Anderson went over to the window and opened it.

He peered into the scruffy night.

He could see nobody. As his eyes adjusted to the dark, Anderson discerned nearby features well enough. A bright star in the sky which he took to be Bose, Nehru II's little moon, lent some light. Swinging his leg over the sill, Anderson dropped to the ground and stood tensely outside.

Nothing moved. A dog howled. Making his way between the outer circle of houses, gun in hand, Anderson came to the river's edge. A sense of the recklessness of what he was doing assailed him, but he pressed on.

Pausing now and again to ensure he was not being followed, he moved along the river bank, avoiding the obstacles with which it was littered. He reached a bridge of a sort. A tall tree had been felled so that it lay across the stretch of water. Its underside was lapped by the river.

Anderson tucked his gun away and crossed the crude bridge with his arms outstretched for balance.

On the far side, crude attempts to cultivate the ground had been made. The untidy patchwork stopped as the upward slope of the land became more pronounced. No dwellings were visible. He stopped again and listened.

He could hear a faint and indescribable choric noise ahead. As he went forward, the noise became more distinct, less a part of the ill-defined background of furtive earth and river sounds. On the higher ground, a patch of light was now vaguely distinguishable.

This light increased as did the sound. Circumnavigating a thorny mass of brush, Anderson could see that there was a depression ahead of him in the rising valley slope. Something – a ceremony? – was going on in the depression. He ran the last few yards, doubled up, his revolver ready again, scowling in his excitement.

On the lip of the depression, he flung himself flat and peered down into the dip.

A fire was burning in the middle of the circular hollow. Round it some three dozen figures paraded, ringing two men. One of the two was a menial, throwing powder into the blaze, so that green and crimson flames spurted up; the other filled some sort of priestly role. All the others were naked. He wore a cloak and pointed hat.

He sang and waved his arms, a tall figure that woke in Anderson untraceable memories. The dancers – if their rhythmic shuffle might be called a dance – responded with low cries. The total effect, if not beautiful, was oddly moving.

Hypnotised, Anderson watched. He found that his head was nodding in time to the chant. There was no sign of Kay here, as he had half-anticipated. But by his carrot-coloured beard and his prominent nose the priest was distinguishable even in the uncertain fire light. It was Frank Arlblaster.

Or it had been Frank Arlblaster. Items that most easily identify a man to his friends are his stance and his walk. Arlblaster's had changed. He seemed to sag at the knees and shuffle now, his torso no longer vertical to the ground. Yet the high timbre of his voice remained unaltered, though he called out in a language unknown to Anderson.

The dancers shuffled eagerly, clapping their hands, nodding their shaggy heads. Gradually it dawned on Anderson what they looked like. Beyond doubt they were the inhabitants of Swettenham; they were also, unmistakably, pre-homo sapiens. He might have been witnessing a ritual of Neanderthal men.

Mingled repulsion and elation rooted Anderson to the spot where he lay. Yes, unarguably the faces of Ell and his friends earlier had borne the touch of Neanderthal. Once the idea took, he could not shake it off.

He lay in a trance of wonder until the dance had stopped. Now all the company turned to face the spot where he lay concealed. Anderson felt the nerves tingle along his spinal cord. Arlblaster lifted an arm and pointed towards him. Then in a loud voice he cried out, the crowd shouting with him in chorus.

'Aigh murg eg neggy oggy Kay bat doo!'

The words were for Anderson.

They were unintelligible to him, yet they seemed to penetrate him. That his whereabouts was known meant nothing beside an even greater pressure on his brain. His whole being trembled on the threshold of some great disastrous revelation.

A magical trance had snared him. He was literally not himself. The meaningless words seemed to shake him to his soul. Gasping, he climbed to his feet and took himself off at a run. There was no pursuit.

He had no memory of getting back to Menderstone's place, no recollection of crossing the rough bridge, no recollection of tumbling through the window. He lay panting on the bed, his face buried in the pillow.

This state in its turn was succeeded by a vast unease. He could not sleep. Sleep was beyond him. He trembled in every limb. The hours of night dragged on for ever.

At last Anderson sat up. A faint dawn washed into the world. Taking a torch from his kit, he went to investigate the other empty rooms next to his.

A dusty corridor led to them.

Alice had said that this had been the HQ of Swettenham's original intellectual coterie. There was a library in one room, with racked spools gathering dust; Anderson did not trouble to read any titles. He felt vague antipathy for the silent ranks of them. Another room was a small committee chamber. Maps hung on the walls, meaningless, unused. He saw without curiosity that the flags stuck to one map had mostly fallen on the floor.

A third room was a recreation room. It held a curious assortment of egghead toys. There was even a model electric railway of the type fashionable on Earth a couple of centuries ago. A lathe in the corner suggested that rail and rolling stock might have been made on the premises.

Anderson peered at the track. It gleamed in his torchlight. No dust on it. He hesitatingly ran a finger along it.

A length of siding raised itself like a snake's head. Coiling up, it wrapped round Anderson's wrist, snapped tight He pulled at it, yelling in surprise. The whole layout reared up, struggling to get at him.

He backed away, beating at the stuff as it rolled up from the table. The track writhed and launched itself at him, scattering waggons and locomotives. He fired his revolver wildly. Loops of railroad fell over him, over his head, wrapping itself madly about him.

Anderson fell to the floor, dropping his gun, dropping the torch, tearing at the thin bands of metal as they bit tighter. The track threshed savagely, binding his legs together. He was shouting incoherently.

As he struggled, Menderstone ran into the room, rifle in hand, Alice behind him. It was the last thing Anderson saw as he lost consciousness.

When he roused, it was to find himself in Menderstone's living-room, sprawled on a bunk. Alice sat by him, turning towards him as he stirred. Menderstone was not in the room.

'My God ...' Anderson groaned. His brain felt curiously lucid, as if a fever had just left him.

'It's time you woke up. I'll get you some soup if you can manage it,' Alice said.

'Wait, Alice. Alice ...' His lips trembled as he formed the words. 'I'm myself again. What came over me? Yesterday – I don't have a sister called Kay. I don't have a sister at all! I was an only child!'

She was unsurprised. He sat up, glaring at her.

'I guessed as much, said so to Stanley. When you brought your kit in from the vehicle there was nothing female among it.'

'My mind! I was so sure. ... I could have pictured her, described her ... She was actual! And yet if anyone – if you'd challenged me direct, I believe I'd have known it was an – an illusion.'

His sense of loss was forced aside as another realisation crowded in on him.

He sank down confusedly, closing his eyes, muttering. *'Aigh murg eg neggy oggy Kay bat doo.* ... That's what they told me on the hillside: "You have no sister called Kay." That's what it meant. ... Alice. It's so strange. ...'

His hand sought hers and found it. It was ice cold.

'Your initial is K, Keith,' she said, pale at the lips. 'You were out there seeking yourself.'

Her face looking down at him was scared and ugly; yet a kind of gentle patience in it dissolved the ugliness.

'I'm – I'm some sort of mad,' he whispered.

'Of course you're mad!' Menderstone said, as he burst open the door. 'Let go of his hand, Alice – this is our beloved home, not the cheap seats in the feelies on Earth. Anderson, if you aren't insane, why were you rolling about on the floor, foaming at the mouth and firing your damned gun, at six o'clock this morning?'

Anderson sat up.

'You saw me entangled in that jinxed railroad when you found me, Menderstone! Another minute and it would have squeezed the life out of me.'

Menderstone looked genuinely puzzled. It was the first time Anderson had seen him without the armour of his self-assurance.

'The model railroad?' he said. 'It was undisturbed. You hadn't touched it.'

'It touched me,' Anderson said chokingly. 'It – it attacked me, wrapped itself round me like an octopus. You must have peeled it off me before getting me through here.'

'I see,' Menderstone said, his face grim.

He nodded slowly, sitting down absent-mindedly, and then nodding again to Alice.

'You see what this means, woman? Anderson's N-factor is rising to dominance. This young man is not on our side, as I suspected from the first. He's no Crow. Anderson, your time's up here, sorry! From now on, you're one of Arlblaster's men. You'll never get back to Earth.'

'On the contrary, I'm on my way back now.'

Menderstone shook his head.

'You don't know your own mind. I mean the words literally. You're doomed to stay here, playing out the miserable life of an ape! Earth has lost another of her estimable nonentities.'

'Menderstone, you're eaten up with hatred! You hate this planet, you hate Earth!'

Menderstone stood up again, putting his rifle down on the table and coming across to Anderson with his fists bunched.

'Does that make me crazy, you nincompoop? Let me give you a good hard fact-reason why I loathe what's happening on Earth! I loathe mankind's insatiable locust-activities, which it has the impertinence to call "assuming mastery over nature". It has over-eaten and over-populated itself until the only other animals left are in the sea, in zoos, or in food-factories. Now it is exhausting the fossil fuels on which its much-vaunted technology relies. The final collapse is due! So much for mastery of nature! Why, it can't even master its own mind!'

'The situation may be desperate, but World Government is slowly introducing economies which –'

'World Government! You dare mention World Government? A pack of computers and automata? Isn't it an admission that man is a locust without self-discipline that he has to hand over control piecemeal to robots?

'And what does it all signify? Why, that civilisation is afraid of itself, because it always tries to destroy itself.

'Why should it try to do that? Every wise man in history has asked himself why. None of them found the answer until your pal Arlblaster tumbled on it, because they were all looking in the wrong direction. So the answer lies hidden here where nobody on Earth can get at it, because no one who arrives here goes back. *I* could go back, but I don't because I prefer to think of them stewing in their own juice, in the mess they created.'

'I'm going back,' Anderson said. 'I'm going to collect Arlblaster and I'm going back right away – when your speech is finished.'

Menderstone laughed.

'Like to bet on it? But don't interrupt when I'm talking, K. D. Anderson! Listen to the truth while you have the chance, before it dies for ever.'

'Stop bellowing, Stanley!' Alice exclaimed.

'Silence, female! Attend! Do you need proof that fear-ridden autocrats rule Earth? They have a star-drive on their hands, they discover a dozen habitable planets within reach: what do they do? They keep them uninhabited. Having read just enough history to frighten them, they figure that if they establish colonies those colonies will rebel against them.

'Swettenham was an exceptional man. How he pulled enough strings to get us established here, I'll never know. But this little settlement – far too small to make a real colony – was an exception to point to a rule: that the ruling régime is pathologically anti-life – and must be increasingly so as robots take over.'

Anderson stood up, steadying himself against the bunk.

'Why don't you shut up, you lonely man? I'm getting out of here.'

Menderstone's reaction was unexpected. Smiling, he produced Anderson's gun.

'Suit yourself, lad! Here's your revolver. Pick it up and go.'

He dropped the revolver at his feet. Anderson stooped to pick it up. The short barrel gleamed dully. Suddenly it looked – alien, terrifying. He straightened, baffled, leaving the weapon on the floor. He moved a step away from it, his backbone tingling.

Sympathy and pain crossed Alice's face as she saw his expression. Even Menderstone relaxed.

'You won't need a gun where you're going,' he said. 'Sorry it turned out this way, Anderson! The long and tedious powers of evolution force us to be antagonists. I felt it the moment I saw you.'

'Get lost!'

Relief surged through Anderson as he emerged into the shabby sunshine. The house had seemed like a trap. He stood relaxedly in the middle of the square, sagging slightly at the knees, letting the warmth soak into him. Other people passed in ones or twos. A couple of strangely adult-looking children stared at him.

Anderson felt none of the hostility he had imagined yesterday. After all, he told himself, these folk never saw a stranger from one year to the next; to crowd round him was natural. No one had offered him harm – even Ell had a right to act to protect himself when a stranger charged round a rock carrying a gun. And when his presence had been divined on the hillside last night, they had offered him nothing more painful than revelation: 'You have no sister called Kay.'

He started walking. He knew he needed a lot of explanations; he even grasped that he was in the middle of an obscure process which had still to be worked out. But at present he was content just to exist, to *be* and not to think.

Vaguely, the idea that he must see Arlblaster stayed with him.

But new – or very ancient? – parts of his brain seemed to be in bud. The landscape about him grew in vividness, showering him with sensory data. Even the dust had a novel sweet scent.

He crossed the tree-trunk bridge without effort, and walked along the other bank of the river, enjoying the flow of the water. A few women picked idly at vegetable plots. Anderson stopped to question one of them.

'Can you tell me where I'll find Frank Arlblaster?'

'That man sleeps now. Sun go, he wakes. Then you meet him.'

'Thanks.' It was simple, wasn't it?

He walked on. There was time enough for everything. He walked a long way, steadily uphill. There was a secret about time – he had it somewhere at the back of his head – something about not chopping it into minutes and seconds. He was all alone by the meandering river now, beyond people; what did the river know of time?

Anderson noticed the watch strapped on his wrist. What did it want with him, or he with it? A watch was the badge of servitude of a time-serving culture. With sudden revulsion for it, he unbuckled it and tossed it into the river.

The shattered reflection in the water was of piled cloud. It would rain. He stood rooted, as if casting away his watch left him naked and defenceless. It grew cold. *Something had altered.* ... Fear came in like a distant flute.

He looked round, bewildered. A curious double noise filled the air, a low and grating rumble punctuated by high-pitched cracking sounds. Uncertain where this growing uproar came from, Anderson ran forward, then paused again.

Peering back, he could see the women still stooped over their plots. They looked tiny and crystal-clear, figures glimpsed through the wrong end of a telescope. From their indifference, they might not have heard the sound. Anderson turned round again.

Something was coming down the valley!

Whatever it was, its solid front scooped up the river and ran with it high up the hills skirting the valley. It came fast, squealing and rumbling.

It glittered like water. Yet it was not water – its bow was too sharp, too unyielding. It was a glacier.

Anderson fell to the ground.

'I'm mad, still mad!' he cried, hiding his eyes, fighting with himself to hold the conviction that this was merely a delusion. He told himself no glacier ever moved at that crazy rate – yet even as he tried to reassure himself the ground shook under him.

Groaning, he heaved himself up. The wall of ice was bearing down on him fast. It splintered and fell as it came, sending up a shower of ice particles as it was ground down, but always there was more behind it. It stretched right up the valley, grey and uncompromising, scouring out the hills' sides as it came.

Now its noise was tremendous. Cracks played over its towering face like lightning. Thunder was on its brow.

Impelled by panic, Anderson turned to run, his furs flapping against his legs.

The glacier moved too fast. It came with such force that he felt his body vibrate. He was being overtaken.

He cried aloud to the god of the glacier, remembering the old words.

There was a cave up the valley slope. He ran like mad for it, driving himself, while the ice seemed to crash and scream at his heels. With a final desperate burst of strength, he flung himself gasping through the low, dark opening, and clawed his way hand-over-fist towards the back of the cave.

He just made it. The express glacier ground on, flinging earth into the opening. For a moment the cave lit with a green-blue light. Then it was sealed up with reverberating blackness.

Sounds of rain and of his own sobbing. These were the first things he knew. Then he became aware that someone was soothing his hair and whispering comfort to him. Propping himself on one elbow, Anderson opened his eyes.

The cave entrance was unblocked. He could see grass and a strip of river outside. Rain fell heavily. His head had been resting in Alice's lap;

she it was who stroked his hair. He recalled her distasteful remark about Jocasta, but this was drowned in a welter of other recollections.

'The glacier. ... Has it gone? Where is it?'

'You're all right, Keith. There's no glacier round here. Take it easy!'

'It came bursting down the valley towards me. ... Alice, how did you get here?'

She put out a hand to pull his head down again, but he evaded it.

'When Stanley turned you out, I couldn't bear to let you go like that, friendless, so I followed you. Stanley was furious, of course, but I knew you were in danger. Look, I've brought your revolver.'

'I don't want it! – It's haunted. ...'

'Don't say that, Keith. Don't turn into a Neanderthal!'

'What?' He sat fully upright, glaring at her through the gloom. 'What the hell do you mean?'

'You know. You understand, don't you?'

'I don't understand one bit of what's going on here. You'd better start explaining – and first of all, I want to know what it looked as if I was doing when I ran into this cave.'

'Don't get excited, Keith. I'll tell you what I can.' She put her hand over his before continuing. 'After you'd thrown your watch into the river, you twisted and ran about a bit – as if you were dodging something – and then rushed into here.'

'You didn't *hear* anything odd? See anything?'

'No.'

'And no glaciers?'

'Not on Nehru, no!'

'And was I – dressed in skins?'

'Of course you weren't!'

'My mind. ... I'd have sworn there was a glacier. ... Moving too fast ...'

Alice's face was pale as she shook her head.

'Oh, Keith, you are in danger. You must get back to Earth at once. Can't you see this means you have a Neanderthal layer in your brain? Obviously you were experiencing a race memory from that newly opened layer. It was so strong it took you over entirely for a while. You *must* get away.'

He stood up, his shoulders stooped to keep his skull from scraping the rock overhead. Rain drummed down outside. He shook with impatience.

'Alice, Alice, begin at the beginning, will you? I don't know a thing except that I'm no longer in control of my own brain.'

'Were you ever in control? Is the average person? Aren't all the sciences of the mind attempts to bring the uncontrollable under control? Even when you're asleep, it's only the neo-cortex switched off. The older limbic layers – they never sleep. There's no day or night, that deep.'

'So what? What has the unconscious to do with this particular set-up?'

'"The unconscious" is a pseudo-scientific term to cover a lack of knowledge. You have a moron in your skull who never sleeps, sweetie! He gives you a nudge from time to time; it's crazy thoughts you overhear when you think you're dreaming.'

'Look, Alice –'

She stood up too. Anxiety twisted her face.

'You wanted an explanation, Keith. Have the grace to listen to it. Let me start from the other end of the tale, and see if you like it any better.

'Neanderthal was a species of man living in Europe some eighty thousand and more years ago, before homo sap came along. They were gentle creatures, close to nature, needing few artefacts, brain cases bigger even than homo sap. They were peaceful, unscientific in a special sense you'll understand later.

'Then along came a different species, the Crows – Cro-Magnons, you'd call them – Western man's true precursors. Being warlike, they defeated the Neanderthals at every encounter. They killed off the men and mated with the Neanderthal women, which they kept captive. We, modern man, sprang from the bastard race so formed. This is where Arlblaster's theory comes in.

'The mixture never quite mixed. That's why we still have different, often antagonistic, blood groups today – and why there are inadequate neural linkages in the brain. Crow and Neanderthal brains never established full contact. Crow was dominant, but a power-deprived lode of Neanderthal lingered on, as apparently vestigial as an appendix.'

'My God, I'd like a mescahale,' Anderson said. They had both sat down again, ignoring the occasional beads of moisture which dripped down their necks from the roof of the cave. Alice was close to him, her eyes bright in the shadow.

'Do you begin to see it historically, Keith? Western man with this clashing double heritage in him has always been restless. Freud's theory of the id comes near to labelling the Neanderthal survivor in us. Arthur Koestler also came close. All civilisation can be interpreted as a Crow attempt to vanquish that survivor, and to escape from the irrational it represents – yet at the same time the alien layer is a rich source for all artists, dreamers, and creators: because it is the very well of magic.

'The Neanderthal had magic powers. He lived in a dawn age, the dawn of rationality, when it's no paradox to say that supernatural and natural are one. The Crows, our ancestors, were scientific, or potentially scientific – spear-makers, rather than fruit-gatherers. They had a belief, fluctuating at first maybe, in cause and effect. As you know, all Western science represents a structure built on our acceptance of unalterable cause and effect.

'Such belief is entirely alien to the Neanderthal. He knows only happening, and from this stems his structure of magic. I use the present tense because the Neanderthal is still strong in man – and, on Nehru II, he is not only strong but free, liberated at last from his captor, the Crow.'

Anderson stirred, rubbing his wet skull.

'I suppose you're right '

'There's proof enough here,' she said bitterly.

'I suppose it does explain why the civilisation of old Europe – the ancient battle-ground of Cro-Magnon and Neanderthal – and the civilisations that arose from it in North America are the most diverse and most turbulent ever known. But this brings us back to Arlblaster, doesn't it? I can see that what has happened in Swettenham connects logically with his theory. The Brittany skull he found back in the eighties was pure Neanderthal, yet only a few hundred years old. Obviously it belonged to a rare throwback.'

'But how rare? You could pass a properly dressed Neanderthal in the streets of New York and never give him a second glance. Stanley says you often do.'

'Let's forget Stanley! Arlblaster followed up his theory. ... Yes, I can see it myself. The proportion of Neanderthal would presumably vary from person to person. I can run over my friends mentally now and guess in which of them the proportion is highest.'

'Exactly.' She smiled at him, reassured and calmer now, even as he was, as she nursed his hand and his revolver. 'And because the political economic situation on Earth is as it is, Arlblaster found a way here to develop his theory and turn it into practice – that is, to release the prisoner in the brain. Earth would allow Swettenham's group little in the way of machinery or resources in its determination to keep them harmless, so they were thrust close to nature. That an intellectual recognition brought the Neanderthal to the surface, freed it.'

'Everyone turned Neanderthal, you mean?'

'Here on Nehru, which resembles prehistoric Earth in some respects, the Neanderthal represents better survival value than Crow. Yet not everyone transformed, no. Stanley Menderstone did not. Nor Swettenham. Nor several others of the intellectuals. Their N-factor, as Stanley calls it, was either too low or non-existent.'

'What happened to Swettenham?'

'He was killed. So were the other pure Crows, all but Stanley, who's tough – as you saw. There was a heap of trouble at first, until they fully understood the problem and sorted themselves out.'

'And these two patrol ships World Government sent?'

'I saw what happened to the one that brought me. About seventy-five per cent of the crew had a high enough N-factor to make the change; a willingness to desert helped them. The others … died out. Got killed, to be honest. All but me. Stanley took care of me.'

She laughed harshly. 'If you can call it care.

'I've had my belly full of Stanley and Nehru II, Keith. I want you to take me back with you to Earth.'

Anderson looked at her, still full of doubt.

'What about my N-factor? Obviously I've got it in me. Hence the glacier, which was a much stronger danger signal from my brain than the earlier illusion about having a sister. Hence, I suppose, my new fears of manufactured Crow objects like watches, revolvers and … model railroads. Am I Crow or not, for heaven's sake?'

'By the struggle you've been through with yourself, I'd say that you're equally balanced. Perhaps you can even decide. Which do you want to be?'

He looked at her in amazement.

'Crow, of course: my normal self – who'd become a shambling, low-browed, shaggy tramp by choice?'

'The adjectives you use are subjective and not really terms of abuse – in fact, they're Crow propaganda. Or so a Neanderthal would say. The two points of view are irreconcilable.'

'Are you seriously suggesting … Alice, they're sub-men!'

'To us they appear so. Yet they have contentment, and communion with the forces of Earth, and their magic. Nor are their brains inferior to Crow brains.'

'Much good it did them! The Cro-Magnons still beat them.'

'In a sense they have not yet been beaten. But their magic needs preparation, incantation – it's something they can't do while fending off a fusillade of arrows. But left to themselves they can become spirits, animals –'

'Wooly rhinoceroses for instance?'

'Yes.'

'To lure me from my wheeled machine, which they would fear! My God, Alice, can it be true. … 'He clutched his head and groaned, then looked up to enquire, 'Why are you forcing their point of view on me, when you're a Crow?'

'Don't you see, my dear?' Her eyes were large as they searched his. 'To find how strong your N-factor is. To find if you're friend or enemy. When this rain stops, I *must* go back. Stanley will be looking for *me*, and it wouldn't surprise me if Arlblaster were not looking for you; he must know you've had time to sort things out in your mind. So I want to know if I can come back to Earth with you. …'

He shook himself, dashed a water drip off his forehead, tried to delay giving an answer.

'Earth's not so bad,' he said. 'Menderstone's right, of course; it is regimented – it would never suit an individualist like him. It's not so pretty as Nehru. … Yes, Alice, I'll take you back if you want to come. I can't leave you here.'

She flung herself on to him, clasping him in her arms, kissing his ear and cheek and lips.

'I'm a loving woman,' she whispered fiercely. 'As even Stanley –'

They stiffened at a noise outside the cave, audible above the rain.

Anderson turned his head to look where she was looking. Rain was falling more gently now. Before its fading curtain a face appeared.

The chief features of this face were its low brow, two large and lustrous eyes, a prominent nose, and a straggling length of wet, sandy beard. It was Frank Arlblaster.

He raised both hands.

'Come to see me, child of Earth, as I come to see you, peaceful, patient, all-potent –'

As more of him rose into view in the cave mouth, Alice fired the revolver. The bellow of its report in the confined space was deafening. At ten yards' range, she did not miss. Arlblaster clutched at his chest and tumbled forward into the wet ground, crying inarticulately.

Anderson turned on Alice, and struck the gun from her hand.

'Murder, sheer murder! You shouldn't have done it! You shouldn't have done –'

She smacked him across the cheek.

'If you're Crow, he's your enemy as well as mine! He'd have killed me! He's an Ape. ...' She drew a long shuddering breath. 'And now we've got to move fast for your ship before the pack hunts us down.'

'You make me sick!' He tried to pick up the revolver but could not bring himself to touch it.

'Keith, I'll make it up to you on the journey home, I promise. I – I was desperate!'

'Just don't talk to me! Come on, let's git.'

They slid past Arlblaster's body, out into the mizzling rain. As they started down the slope, a baying cry came from their left flank. A group of Neanderthals, men and women, stood on a promontory only two hundred yards away. They must have witnessed Arlblaster's collapse and were slowly marshalling their forces. As Alice and Anderson appeared, some of the men ran forward.

'Run!' Alice shouted. 'Down to the river! Swim it and we're safe.'

Close together, they sped down the slippery incline where an imaginary glacier had flowed. Without a pause or word, they plunged through reeds and mud and dived fully dressed into the slow waters. Making good time, the Neanderthals rushed down the slope after them, but halted when they reached the river.

Gaining the far bank, Anderson turned and helped Alice out of the water. She collapsed puffing on the grass.

'Not so young as I was. ... We're safe now, Keith. Nothing short of a forest fire induces those apes to swim. But we still might meet trouble this side. ... We'll avoid the settlement. Even if the apes there aren't after us, we don't want to face Stanley with his rifle. ... Poor old Stanley! Give me a hand up. ...'

Anderson moved on in surly silence. His mind was troubled by Arlblaster's death; and he felt he was being used.

The rain ceased as they pressed forward among dripping bush. Travelling in a wide arc, they circled the village and picked up a track which led back towards Anderson's ship.

Alice grumbled intermittently as they went. At last Anderson turned on her.

'You don't have to come with me, Alice. If you want to, go back to Stanley Menderstone!'

'At least he cared about a woman's feelings.'

'I warn you that they are not so fussy on Earth, where women don't have the same scarcity value.' He hated himself for speaking so roughly. He needed solitude to sort out the turmoil in his brain.

Alice plodded along beside him without speaking. Sun gleamed. At last the black hull of the ship became visible between trees.

'You'll have to work on Earth!' he taunted her. 'The robocracy will direct you.'

'I shall get married. I've still got some looks.'

'You've forgotten something, honey. Women have to have work certificates before they can marry these days. Regimentation will do you good.'

A wave of hatred overcame him. He remembered the priestly Arlblaster dying. When Alice started to snap back at him, Anderson struck her on the shoulder. A look of panic and understanding passed over her face.

'Oh, Keith ...' she said. 'You ...' Her voice died; a change came over her face. He saw her despair before she turned and was running away, back towards the settlement, calling inarticulately as she ran.

Anderson watched her go. Then he turned and sidled through the dripping trees. At last – free! Himself! She was a Crow squaw.

His ship no longer looked welcoming. He splashed through a puddle and touched it, withdrawing his hand quickly. Distorted by the curve of the hull, his reflection peered at him from the polished metal. He did not recognise himself.

'Someone there imprisoned in Crow ship,' he said, turning away.

The breath of the planet was warm along his innocent cheek. He stripped off his damp clothes and faded among the leaves and uncountable grasses and the scents of soil and vegetation. Shadow and light slithered over his skin in an almost tangible pattern before foliage embraced him and he was lost entirely into his new Eden.

The proud author lay where he was on the floor of the small room, among the metal sheets he had worn as camouflage while hiding with the humots. Since the Tenth Dominant finished reading his story – that poor thing written before he had wisdom – silence lay between the Dominant and the Chief Scanner; though whether or not they were communicating by UHF, Anderson could not tell.

He decided he had better do something. Sitting up, he said, 'How about letting me go free? ... Or how about letting me go back to the zoo? ... Well, at least take me into a room that's big enough for me.'

The Dominant spoke. 'We need to ask you questions about your story. Is it true or not true?'

'It's fiction. Lousy or otherwise, it exists in its own right.'

'Some things in it are true – you are. So is or was Frank Arlblaster. So is or was Stanley Menderstone. But other things are false. You did not stay always on Nehru II. You came back to Earth.'

'The story is a fiction. Forget it! It has nothing to do with you. Or with me, now. I only write poetry now – that story is just a thing I wrote to amuse myself.'

'We do not understand it. You must explain it.'

'Oh, Christ! ... Look, I wouldn't bother about it! I wrote it on the journey back to Earth from Nehru II, just to keep myself amused. When I got here, it was to find the various surviving Master Boffs were picking up such bits of civilisation as were left round the world after Nuclear Week! The story immediately became irrelevant.'

'We know all about Nuclear Week. We do not know about your story. We insist that we know about it.'

As Anderson sighed, he nevertheless recognised that more must lie in the balance here than he understood.

'I've been a bad boy, Dominant, I know. I escaped from the zoo. Put me back there, let me settle back with my wife; for my part. I'll not attempt to escape again. *Then* we'll talk about my story.'

The silence lasted only a fraction of a second. 'Done,' said the Dominant, with splendid mastery of humanic idiom.

The zoo was not unpleasant. By current standards, it was vast, and the flats in the new human-type skyscrapers not too cramped; the liberals admitted that the Hive had been generous about space. There were about twenty thousand people here, the East Coast survivors of Nuclear Week. The robocracy had charge of them; they, in their turn, had charge of all the surviving wild life that the automata could capture. Incongruous among the tall flat-blocks stood cages of exotic animals collected from shattered zoos – a pride of lions, some leopards, several cheetahs, an ocelot, camels. There were monkey houses, ostrich houses, elephant houses, aquaria, reptilia. There were pens full of pigs and sheep and cows. Exotic and native birds were captive in aviaries.

Keith Anderson sat on the balcony of his flat with his wife, Sheila, and drank an ersatz coffee, looking out on to the pens below, not without relish.

'Well, the robots are behaving very strangely,' Sheila was saying. 'When you disappeared, three of the very tiny ones came and searched everywhere. Your story was the only thing they seemed interested in. They must have photostatted it.'

'I remember now – it was in the trunk under the bed. I'd forgotten all about it till they mentioned it – my sole claim to literary fame!'

'But that side of it can't interest them. What are they excited about?'

He looked amusedly at her. She was still partly a stranger to him, though a beloved one. In the chaos to which he returned after the Nehru trip, it was a case of marrying any eligible girl while they were available – men outnumbered women two to one; he'd been lucky in his blind choice. Sheila might not be particularly beautiful, but she was good in bed, trustworthy, and intelligent. You could ask for no more.

He said, 'Do you ever admit the truth of the situation to yourself, Sheila? The new automats are now the superior race. They have a dozen faculties to each one of ours. They're virtually indestructible. Small size is clearly as much an enormous advantage to them as it would be a disadvantage to us. We've heard rumours that they were on the threshold of some staggering new discovery – from what I overheard the Tenth Dominant say, they are on the brink of moving into some staggering new dimensions of which we can probably never even get a glimpse. And yet –'

'And yet they need your story!' She laughed – sympathetically, so that he laughed with her.

'Right! They need my goddamned story! Listen – their powers of planning and extrapolation are proved miraculous. But they cannot *imagine;* imagination might even be an impediment for them. So the Dominant, who can tap more knowledge than you or I dream of, is baffled by a work of fiction. He needs my imagination.'

'Not entirely, Mr Anderson.'

Anderson jumped up, cup in hand, as his wife gave a small scream.

Perched on the balcony rail, enormously solid-looking, yet only six inches high, was the stubby shape of an automaton!

Furious, Anderson flung his cup, the only weapon to hand. It hit the machine four-square, shattered, and fell away. The machine did not even bother to refer to the matter.

'We understand imagination. We wish to ask you more questions about the background to your story.'

Anderson sat down, took Sheila's hand, and made an anatomical suggestion which no automaton could have carried out.

'We want to ask you more questions about the story. Why did you write that you stayed on Nehru when really you came back?'

'Are you the Chief Scanner who captured me on D-Dump?'

'You are speaking with Tenth Dominant, in command of Eastern Seaboard. I have currently taken over Chief Scanner for convenience of speaking with you.'

'Sort of mechanical transvestism, eh?'

'Why did you write that you stayed when you in reality came back?'

'You'd better give him straight answers, Keith,' Sheila said.

He turned to her irritably, 'How do I know the answer? It was just a story! I suppose it made a better ending to have the Anderson-figure stay on Nehru. There was this Cro-Magnon – Neanderthal business in the story, and I made myself out to be more Neanderthal than Crow for dramatic effect. Just a lot of nonsense really?'

'Why do you call it nonsense when you wrote it yourself?' asked the Dominant. It had settled in the middle of the coffee-table now.

The man sighed wearily. 'Because I'm older now. The story was a lot of nonsense because I injected this Crow – Neanderthal theory, which is a bit of free-wheeling young man tripe. It just went in to try to explain what actually happened on Nehru – how the egghead camp broke down and everything. The theory doesn't hold water for a moment; I see that now, in the light of what happened since. Nuclear Week and all that. You see –'

He stopped. He stopped in mid-sentence and stared at the little complex artifact confronting him. It was speaking to him but he did not hear, following his own racing thoughts. He stretched forward his hand and picked it up; the automaton was heavy and warm, only mildly frightening, slightly, slightly vibrating at the power of its own voice; the Dominant did not stop him picking it up. He stared at it as if he had never seen such a thing before.

'I repeat, how would you revise your theory now?' said the automaton. Anderson came back to reality.

'Why should I help you? To your kind, man is just another animal in a zoo, a lower species.'

'Not so. We revere you as ancestors, and have never treated you otherwise.'

'Maybe. Perhaps we regard animals in somewhat the same way since, even in the darkest days of overpopulation and famine, we strove to stock our zoos in ever-greater numbers. So perhaps I will tell you my current theory. ... It is real theory now; in my story that theory was not worth the name – it was a stunt, an intellectual high-jink, a bit of science fiction. Now I have lived and thought and loved and suffered, and I have talked to other men. So if I tell you the theory now, you will know it is worked for – part of the heritage of all men in this zoo.'

'This time it is truth, not false?'

'You are the boss – *you* must decide that. There are certainly two distinct parts of the brain, the old limbic section and the neo-cortex surrounding it, the bit that turns a primate into a man. That much of my story was true. There's also a yet older section, but we won't complicate the picture. Roughly speaking, the limbic is the seat of the emotions, and the neo-cortex the seat of the intelligence. Okay. In a crisis, the new brain is still apt to cut out and the old brain take over.

'And that in a nutshell is why mankind never made the grade. We are a failed species. We never got away from the old animal inheritance. We could never become the distinct species we should have been.'

'Oh, darling, it's not as bad as that –'

He squeezed Sheila's hand. 'You girls are always optimists.' He winked the eye the Dominant could not see.

The Dominant said, 'How does this apply to what happened on Nehru II?'

'My story departed – not from the facts but from the correct explanation of the facts. The instinct to go there on Swettenham's part was sound. He and Arlblaster and the rest believed that on a planet away from animals, mankind could achieve its true stature – homo superior, shall we say? What I called the N-factor let them down. The strain was too great, and they mainly reverted instead of evolving.'

'But you believe a species can only escape its origins by removing itself entirely from the site of those origins.'

Sheila said, 'That was the whole human impulse behind space travel – to get to worlds where it would be possible to become more human.'

The Dominant sprang from Anderson's hands and circled under the low ceiling – an oddly uneasy gesture.

'But the limbic brain – such a small part of the brain, so deep-buried!'

'The seat of the instincts.'

'The seat of the instincts. ... Yes, and so the animal part of man brought you to disaster.'

'Does that answer all your questions?'

The automaton came back down and settled on the table. 'One further question. What do you imagine would happen to mankind now, after Nuclear Week, if he was left alone on Earth?'

Anderson had to bury his face in his hands to hide his triumph.

'I guess we'd carry on. Under D-Dump, and the other dumps, lie many of the old artefacts. We'd dig them up and carry on.'

'But Earth's resources are almost spent. That was mankind's doing, not the doing of automata.'

The man smiled. 'Maybe we'd revert, then. It is a sort of Neanderthal planet, isn't it? Things go wrong for animals and men and robots, don't they? Just as they did for dinosaurs and Neanderthals!'

'I am going now,' said the Tenth Dominant. His voice cut. He disappeared.

Gasping, Anderson clutched his wife. 'Don't say a word! Come inside. Hold me and kiss me. Pray, if you feel like it.'

All she said as they went to their bed was, 'Maybe you will end up a writer after all. You show a talent for storytelling!'

It was all of five days before the humans in the big zoo noticed that the automata were disappearing. Suddenly, they were all gone, leaving no word. The whole continent, presumably the whole world, lay almost empty; and mankind began to walk back into it on his own ill-shod feet.

'And you did it, Keith Anderson!' Sheila cried.

'Nope. They did it themselves. They made the right decision – maybe I spurred them on.'

'You did it – a genius who is now going to turn himself into a pig-breeder.'

'I happen to like pigs.' As he spoke, he stood in the middle of a dozen of the animals, which he and Sheila had taken charge of.

'So the entire automata-horde has disappeared into the invo-spectrum, wherever that is, leaving us our world. ...'

'It's a different world. Let's try and make it saner than the old one.'

Pious hope? New Year's resolution? New design for living? He could not tell, although it filled his mind.

As they drove the pigs before them, Anderson said, 'When the Dominant got on to the subject of our animal inheritance, I remembered just in time that I heard him tell the Scanner. "We must free ourselves from our human heritage." You can see the spot they were in! They had scrapped the humots, all too closely anthropomorphic in design, and taken more functional forms themselves. But they still had to acknowledge us as father-figures, and could never escape from many human and naturalistic concepts, however much they tried, as long as they remained in a naturalistic setting. Now, in this unimaginable alternative energy universe, which they have finally cracked, they can be pure automata – which is something else we can't conceive! So they become a genuine species. Pure automata. ...'

They broke off to drive their pigs through the doorway, doubling back and forth until all the animals were inside, squealing and trying to leap over one another's backs. Anderson slammed the outer door at once, gasping.

'What I'd like to know is, what would it be like to be pure human being!' Sheila exclaimed.

He had no answer. He was thinking. Of course, they needed a dog! On D-Dump there were feral hounds, whose young could be caught and trained.

It was lucky that the ground-floor tenants had gone. Most humans had moved out of the zoo as soon as possible, so that the great block of flats was almost empty. They shut the pigs in the hall for the night and climbed up rather wearily to their flat.

Today, they were too tired to bother about the future.

Old Hundredth

A chronicle such as this could be never-ending, for the diversity of Starswarm by any intelligent reckoning is never-ending. We have time for but one more call, and that must be to an ember world floating in the Rift, now seldom visited by man.

Many galactic regions have been omitted entirely from our survey. We have not mentioned one of the most interesting, Sentinel Sector, which adjoins both the Rift and Sector Diamond. It also looks out over the edge of our galaxy towards the other island universes where we have yet to go.

Sentinel is a vast region, and contact with it uncertain. This is especially so with the Border Stars, which form the last specks of material in our galaxy. Here time undergoes compression in a way that brings hallucinations to anyone not bred to it. The people who have colonised those worlds are almost a species apart, and have developed their own perceptions.

They have sent their instruments out into the gulf between universes, and the instruments have returned changed.

To some, this suggests that other island universes will remain for ever beyond our reach. To the optimists, it suggests that awaiting us there is a completely new range of sensory experiences upon which we cannot as yet even speculate.

Within our own Starswarm we can find other sorts of disturbance in the order of things. A planet can become imprisoned in its own greatness. This fate threatens Dansson, as it has overcome an older world floating in that thinly populated part of space we know as the Rift.

This world, legends say, was once the seed mote whence interstellar travel originated. In the successive waves of star voyages since Era One, it has been all but forgotten. We regard it today – if we remember it at all – with ambivalence, a cross between an emptied shrine and a rubbish dump.

Great experiments once took place there: not only star travel, but a later experiment which might have had consequences even more far-reaching. It was an attempt to transcend the physical; the result was failure, the attempt a triumph.

The planet has been left to stagnate, now nameless on all but the few charts that mapped the sector millennia ago. Yet even in its stagnation one can glimpse a reflection of the abundance and vitality, the willingness to try new things – to dare all – that was perhaps its chief gift to Starswarm.

The road climbed dustily down between trees as symmetrical as umbrellas. Its length was punctuated at one point by a musicolumn standing on the verge. From a distance, the column was only a stain in the air. As sentient creatures neared it, their psyches activated the column. It drew on their vitalities, and then it could be heard as well as seen. Their presence made it flower into pleasant sound, instrumental or chant.

All this region was called Ghinomon, for no one lived here now, not even the odd hermit Impure. It was given over to grass and the weight of time. Only a wild goat or two activated the musicolumn nowadays, or a scampering vole wrung a chord from it in passing.

When old Dandi Lashadusa came riding on her baluchitherium, the column began to intone. It was no more than an indigo trace in the air, hardly visible, for it represented only a bonded pattern of music locked into the fabric of that particular area of space. It was also a transubstantio-spatial shrine, the eternal part of a being that had dematerialised itself into music.

The baluchitherium whinnied, lowered its head, and sneezed onto the gritty road.

'Gently, Lass,' Dandi told her mare, savouring the growth of the chords that increased in volume as she approached. Her long nose twitched with pleasure as if she could feel the melody along her olfactory nerves.

Obediently, the baluchitherium slowed, turning aside to crop fern, although it kept an eye on the indigo stain. It liked things to have being or not to have being; these half-and-half objects disturbed it, though they could not impair its immense appetite.

Dandi climbed down her ladder onto the ground, glad to feel the ancient dust under her feet. She smoothed her hair and stretched as she listened to the music.

She spoke aloud to her mentor, half a world away, but he was not listening. His mind closed to her thoughts, and he muttered an obscure exposition that darkened what it sought to clarify.

'… useless to deny that it is well-nigh impossible to improve anything, however faulty, that has so much tradition behind it. And the origins of your bit of metricism are indeed embedded in such an antiquity that we must needs –'

'Tush, Mentor, come out of your black box and forget your hatred of my "metricism" a moment,' Dandi Lashadusa said, cutting her thought into his. 'Listen to the bit of "metricism" I've found here; look at where I have come to; let your argument rest.'

She turned her eyes around, scanning the tawny rocks near at hand, the brown line of the road, the distant black-and-white magnificence of ancient Oldorajo's town, doing this all for him, tiresome old fellow. Her mentor was blind, never left his cell in Aeterbroe to go farther than the sandy courtyard, hadn't physically left that green cathedral pile for over a century. Womanlike, she thought he needed change. Soul, how he rambled on! Even now, he was managing to ignore her and refute her.

'… for consider, Lashadusa woman, nobody can be found to father it. Nobody wrought or thought it, phrases of it merely *came* together. Even the old nations of men could not own it. None of them know who composed it. An element here from a Spanish pavan, an influence there of a French psalm tune, a flavour here of early English carol, a savour there of later German chorale. All primitive – ancient beyond ken. Nor are the faults of your bit of metricism confined to bastardy –'

'Stay in your black box then, if you won't see or listen,' Dandi said. She could not get into his mind; it was the mentor's privilege to lodge in her mind, and in the minds of those few other wards he had, scattered around Earth. Only the mentors had the power to inhabit another's mind – which made them rather tiring on occasions like this, when they would not get out. For over seventy centuries, Dandi's mentor had been persuading her to die into a dirge of his choosing (and composing). Let her die, yes, let her transubstantio-spatialise herself a thousand times!

His quarrel was not with her decision but with her taste, which he considered execrable.

Leaving the baluchitherium to crop, Dandi walked away from the musicolumn towards a hillock. Still fed by her steed's psyche, the column continued to play. Its music was of a simplicity, with a dominant-tonic recurrent bass part suggesting pessimism. To Dandi, a savant in musicolumnology, it yielded other data. She could tell to within a few years when its founder had died and also what sort of creature, generally speaking, he had been.

Climbing the hillock, Dandi looked about. To the south where the road led were low hills, lilac in the poor light. There lay her home. At last she was returning, after wanderings covering three hundred centuries and most of the globe.

Apart from the blind beauty of Oldorajo's town lying to the west, there was only one landmark she recognised. That was the Involute. It seemed to hang iridial above the ground a few leagues ahead; just to look on it made her feel she must go nearer.

Before summoning the baluchitherium, Dandi listened once more to the sounds of the musicolumn, making sure she had them fixed in her head. The pity was that her old fool wise man would not share it. She could still feel his sulks floating like sediment through her mind.

'Are you listening now, Mentor?'

'Eh? An interesting point is that back in 1556 Pre-Involutary, your same little tune may be discovered lurking in Knox's Anglo-Genevan Psalter, where it espoused the cause of the third psalm –'

'You dreary old fish! Wake yourself! How can you criticise my intended way of dying when you have such a fustian way of living?'

This time he heard her words. So close did he seem that his peevish pinching at the bridge of his snuffy old nose tickled hers, too.

'What are you doing *now*, Dandi?' he inquired.

'If you had been listening, you'd know. Here's where I am, on the last Ghinomon plain before Crotheria and home.' She swept the landscape again and he took it in, drank it almost greedily. Many mentors went blind early in life shut in their monastic underwater life; their most effective vision was conducted through the eyes of their wards.

His view of what she saw enriched hers. He knew the history, the myth behind this forsaken land. He could stock the tired old landscape with pageantry, delighting her and surprising her. Back and forward he went, painting her pictures: the Youdicans, the Lombards, the Ex-Europa Emissary, the Grites, the Risorgimento, the Involuters – and catchwords, costumes, customs, courtesans, pelted briefly through Dandi Lashadusa's mind. Ah, she thought admiringly, who could truly live without these priestly, beastly, erudite erratic mentors?

'Erratic?' he inquired, snatching at her lick of thought. 'A thousand years I live, for all that time to absent myself from the world, to eat mashed fish here with my brothers, learning history, studying rapport, sleeping with my bones on stones – a humble being, a being in a million, a mentor in a myriad, and your standards of judgement are so mundane you find no stronger label for me than erratic?! Fie, Lashadusa, bother me no more for fifty years!

The words squeaked in her head as if she spoke herself. She felt his old chops work phantomlike in hers, and half in anger half in laughter called aloud, 'I'll be dead by then!'

He snicked back hot and holy to reply, 'And another thing about your footloose swan song – in Marot and Beza's Genevan Psalter of 1551, Old Time, it was musical midwife to the one hundred and thirty-fourth psalm. Like you, it never seemed to settle!' Then he was gone.

'Pooh!' Dandi said. She whistled. 'Lass.'

Obediently her great rhinolike creature, eighteen feet high at the shoulder, ambled over. The musicolumn died as the mare left it, faded, sank to a whisper, silenced: only the purple stain remained, noiseless, in the lonely air. Lowering its great Oligocene head, Lass nuzzled its mistress's hand. She climbed the ladder onto the ridged plateau of its back.

They made towards the Involute, lulled by the simple and intricate feeling of being alive.

Night was settling in now. Hidden behind banks of mist, the sun prepared to set. But Venus was high, a gallant half-crescent four times as big as the moon had been before the moon, spiralling farther and farther from Earth, had shaken off its parent's clutch to go dance around the sun, a second Mercury. Even by that time Venus had been moved by gravito-traction into Earth's orbit, so that the two sister worlds circled each other as they circled the sun.

The stamp of that great event still lay everywhere, its tokens not only in the crescent in the sky. For Venus placed a strange spell on the hearts of man, and a more penetrating displacement in his genes. Even when its atmosphere was transformed into a muffled breathability, it remained an alien world; against logic, its opportunities, its possibilities, were its own. It shaped men, just as Earth had shaped them.

On Venus, men bred themselves anew.

And they bred the so-called Impures. They bred new plants, new fruits, new creatures – original ones, and duplications of creatures not seen on Earth for aeons past. From one line of these familiar strangers Dandi's baluchitherium was descended. So, for that matter, was Dandi.

The huge creature came now to the Involute, or as near as it cared to get. Again it began to crop at thistles, thrusting its nose through dewy spiders' webs and ground mist.

'Like you, I'm a vegetarian,' Dandi said, climbing down to the ground. A grove of low fruit trees grew nearby; she reached up into the branches, gathered, and ate, before turning to inspect the Involute. Already her spine tingled at the nearness of it; awe, loathing and love made a part-pleasant sensation near her heart.

The Involute was not beautiful. True, its colours changed with the changing light, yet the colours were fish-cold, for they belonged to another dimension. Though they reacted to dusk and dawn, Earth had no stronger power over them. They pricked the eyes. Perhaps, too, they were painful because they were the last signs of materialist man. Even Lass moved uneasily before that ill-defined lattice, the upper limits of which were lost in thickening gloom.

'Don't fear,' Dandi said. 'There's an explanation for this, old girl.' She added, 'There's an explanation for everything, if we can find it.'

She could feel all the personalities in the Involute. It was a frozen screen of personality. All over the old planet the structures stood, to shed their awe on those who were left behind. They were the essence of man. They were man – all that remained of him on Earth.

When the first flint, the first shell, was shaped into a weapon, that action shaped man. As he moulded and complicated his tools, so they moulded and complicated him. He became the first scientific animal. And at last, via information theory and great computers, he gained knowledge of all his parts. He formed the Laws of Integration, which reveal all beings as part of a pattern and show them their part in the pattern. There is only the pattern; the pattern is all the universe, creator and created. For the first time it became possible to duplicate that pattern artificially – the transubstantio-spatialisers were built.

Men left their strange hobbies on Earth and Venus and projected themselves into the pattern. Their entire personalities were merged with the texture of space itself. Through science, they reached immortality.

It was a one-way passage.

They did not return. Each Involute carried thousands or even millions of people. There they were, not dead, not living. How they exulted or wept in their transubstantiation, no one left could say. Only this could be said: man had gone, and a great emptiness was fallen over Earth.

'Your thoughts are heavy, Dandi Lashadusa. Get you home.' Her mentor was back in her mind. She caught the feeling of him moving around and around in his coral-formed cell.

'I must think of man,' she said.

'Your thoughts mean nothing, do nothing.'

'Man created us; I want to consider him in peace.'

'He only shaped a stream of life that was always entirely out of his control. Forget him. Get onto your mare and ride home.'

'Mentor –'

'Get home, woman. Moping does not become you. I want to hear no more of your swan song, for I've given you my final word on that. Use a theme of your own, not of man's. I've said it a million times, and I say it again.'

'I wasn't going to mention my music. I was only going to tell you that –'

'What then?' His thought was querulous. She felt his powerful tail tremble, disturbing the quiet water of his cell.

'I don't know –'

'Get home then.'

'I'm lonely.'

He shot her a picture from another of his wards before leaving her. Dandi had seen this ward before in similar dreamlike glimpses. It was a huge mole creature, still boring underground as it had been for the last hundred years. Occasionally it crawled through vast caves; once it swam in a subterranean lake; most of the time it just bored through rock. Its motivations were obscure to Dandi, although her mentor referred to it as 'a geologer'. Doubtless if the mole was vouchsafed occasional glimpses of Dandi and her musicolumnology, it would find her as baffling. At least the mentor's point was made: loneliness was psychological, not statistical.

Why, a million personalities glittered almost before her eyes!

She mounted the great baluchitherium mare and headed for home. Time and old monuments made glum company.

Twilight now, with just one streak of antique gold left in the sky, Venus sweetly bright, and stars peppering the purple. A fine evening in which to be alive, particularly with one's last bedtime close at hand.

And yes, for all her mentor said, she was going to turn into that old little piece derived from one of the tunes in the 1540 *Souter Liedekens*, that splendid source of Netherlands folk music. For a moment, Dandi Lashadusa chuckled almost as eruditely as her mentor. The sixteenth century, with the virtual death of plainsong and virtual birth of the violin, was most interesting to her. Ah, the richness of facts, the texture of man's brief history on Earth! Pure joy! Then she remembered herself.

After all, she was only a megatherium, a sloth as big as a small elephant, whose kind had been extinct for millions of years until man reconstituted a few of them in the Venusian experiments. Her modifications in the way of fingers and enlarged brain gave her no real qualification to think up to man's level.

Early next morning, they arrived at the ramparts of the town Crotheria, where Dandi lived. The ubiquitous goats thronged about them, some no bigger than hedgehogs, some almost as big as hippos – what madness in his last days had provoked man to so many variations on one undistinguished caprine theme? – as Lass and her mistress moved up the last slope and under the archway.

It was good to be back, to push among the trails fringed with bracken, among the palms, oaks and treeferns. Almost all the town was deeply green and private from the sun, curtained by swathes of Spanish moss. Here and there were houses – caves, pits, crude piles of boulders, or even genuine man-type buildings, grand in ruin. Dandi climbed down, walking ahead of her mount, her long hair curling in pleasure. The air was cool with the coo of doves or the occasional bleat of a merino.

As she explored familiar ways, though, disappointment overcame her. Her friends were all away, even the dreamy bison whose wallow lay at the corner of the street in which Dandi lived. Only pure animals were here, rooting happily and mindlessly in the lanes, beggars who owned the Earth. The Impures – descendants of the Venusian experimental stock – were all absent from Crotheria.

That was understandable. For obvious reasons man had increased the abilities of herbivores rather than carnivores. After the Involution, with man gone, these Impures had taken to his towns as they took to his ways, as far as this was possible to their natures. Both Dandi and Lass, and many of the others, consumed massive amounts of vegetable matter every day. Gradually a wider and wider circle of desolation grew about each town (the greenery in the town itself was sacrosanct), forcing a semi-nomadic life into its vegetarian inhabitants.

This thinning in its turn led to a decline in the birthrate. The travellers grew fewer, the towns greener and emptier; in time they had become little oases of forest studding the grassless plains.

'Rest here, Lass,' Dandi said at last, pausing by a bank of brightly flowering cycads. 'I'm going into my house.'

A giant beech grew before the stone façade of her home, so close that it was hard to determine whether it did not help support the ancient building. A crumbling balcony jutted from the first floor; reaching up, Dandi seized the balustrade and hauled herself onto it.

This was her normal way of entering her home, for the ground floor was taken over by goats and hogs, just as the third floor had been appropriated by doves and parakeets. Trampling over the greenery self-sown on the balcony, she moved into the front room. Dandi smiled. Here were old things, the broken furniture on which she liked to sleep, the vision screens on which nothing could be seen, the heavy manuscript books in which, guided by her know-all mentor, she wrote down the outpourings of the musicolumns she had visited all over the world.

She ambled through to the next room.

She paused, her peace of mind suddenly broken.

A brown bear stood there. One of its heavy hands was clenched over the hilt of a knife.

'I am no vulgar thief,' it said, curling its thick black lips over the syllables. 'I am an archaeologer. If this is your place, you must grant me permission to remove the man things. Obviously you have no idea of the worth of some of the equipment here. We bears require it. We must have it.'

It came towards her, panting doggy fashion, its jaws open. From under bristling eyebrows gleamed the lust to kill.

Dandi was frightened. Peaceful by nature, she feared the bears above all creatures for their fierceness and their ability to organise. The bears were few: they were the only creatures to show signs of wishing to emulate man's old aggressiveness.

She knew what the bears did. They hurled themselves through the Involutes to increase their power; by penetrating those patterns, they nourished their psychic drive, so the mentor said. It was forbidden. They were transgressors. They were killers.

'Mentor!' she screamed.

The bear hesitated. As far as he was concerned, the hulking creature before him was merely an obstacle in the way of progress, something to be thrust aside without hate. Killing would be pleasant but irrelevant; more important items remained to be done. Much of the equipment housed here could be used in the rebuilding of the world, the world of which bears had such high, haphazard dreams. Holding the knife threateningly, he moved forward.

The mentor was in Dandi's head, answering her cry, seeing through her eyes, though he had no sight of his own. He scanned the bear and took over her mind instantly, knifing himself into place like a guillotine.

No longer was he a blind old dolphin lurking in one cell of a cathedral pile of coral under tropical seas, a theologer, an inculcator of wisdom into feebler-minded beings. He was a killer more savage than the bear, keen to kill anything that might covet the vacant throne once held by men. The mere thought of men sent this mentor into sharklike fury at times.

Caught up in his fury, Dandi found herself advancing. For all the bear's strength, she could vanquish it. In the open, where she could have brought her heavy tail into action, it would have been an easy matter.

Here her weighty forearms must come into play. She felt them lift to her mentor's command as he planned to clout the bear to death.

The bear stepped back, awed by an opponent twice its size, suddenly unsure.

She advanced.

'No! Stop!' Dandi cried.

Instead of fighting the bear, she fought her mentor, hating his hate. Her mind twisted, her dim mind full of that steely, fishy one, as she blocked his resolution.

'I'm for peace!' she cried.

'Then kill the bear!'

'I'm for peace, not killing!'

She rocked back and forth. When she staggered into a wall, it shook; dust spread in the old room. The mentor's fury was terrible to feel.

'Get out quickly!' Dandi called to the bear.

Hesitating, it stared at her. Then it turned and made for the window. For a moment it hung with its shaggy hindquarters in the room. Momentarily she saw it for what it was, an old animal in an old world, without direction. It jumped. It was gone. Goats blared confusion on its retreat.

The mentor screamed. Insane with frustration, he hurled Dandi against the doorway with all the force of his mind.

Wood cracked and splintered. The lintel came crashing down. Brick and stone shifted, grumbled, fell. Powdered filth billowed up. With a great roar, one wall collapsed. Dandi struggled to get free. Her house was tumbling about her. It had never been intended to carry so much weight, so many centuries.

She reached the balcony and jumped clumsily to safety, just as the building avalanched in on itself, sending a cloud of plaster and powdered mortar into the overhanging trees.

For a horribly long while the world was full of dust, goat bleats and panic-stricken parakeets.

Heavily astride her baluchitherium once more, Dandi Lashadusa headed back to the empty region called Ghinomon. She fought her bitterness, trying to urge herself towards resignation.

All she had was destroyed – not that she set store by possessions: that was a man trait. Much more terrible was the knowledge that her mentor had left her for ever; she had transgressed too badly to be forgiven this time.

Suddenly she was lonely for his pernickety voice in her head, for the wisdom he fed her, for the scraps of dead knowledge he tossed her – yes, even for the love he gave her. She had never seen him, never could: yet no two beings could have been more intimate.

She also missed those other wards of his she would glimpse no more: the mole creature tunnelling in Earth's depths, the seal family that barked with laughter on a desolate coast, a senile gorilla that endlessly collected and classified spiders, an aurochs – seen only once, but then unforgettably – that lived with small creatures in an Arctic city it had helped build in the ice.

She was excommunicated.

Well, it was time for her to change, to disintegrate, to transubstantiate into a pattern not of flesh but music. That discipline at least the mentor had taught and could not take away.

'This will do, Lass,' she said.

Her giganic mount stopped obediently. Lovingly, she patted its neck. It was young; it would be free.

Following the dusty trail, she went ahead, alone. Somewhere afar a bird called. Coming to a mound of boulders, Dandi squatted among gorse, the points of which could not prick through her thick old coat. Already her selected music poured through her head, already it seemed to loosen the chemical bonds of her being.

Why should she not choose an old human tune? She was an anti-quarian. Things that were gone solaced her for things that were to come. In her dim way, she had always stood out against her mentor's absolute hatred of men. The thing to hate was hatred. Men in their finer moments had risen above hate. Her death psalm was an instance of that – a multiple instance, for it had been fingered and changed over the ages, as the mentor himself insisted, by men of a variety of races, all with their minds directed to worship rather than hate.

Locking herself into thought disciplines, Dandi began to dissolve. Man had needed machines to help him do it, to fit into the Involutes. She was a lesser animal: she could change herself into the humbler shape of a musicolumn. It was just a matter of *rearranging* – and without pain she formed into a pattern that was not a shaggy megatherium body, but an indigo column, hardly visible ...

For a long while Lass cropped thistle and cacti. Then she ambled forward to seek the hairy creature she fondly – and a little condescendingly – regarded as her equal. But of the sloth there was no sign.

Almost the only landmark was a violet-blue dye in the air. As the baluchitherium mare approached, a sweet old music grew in volume from the dye. It was a music almost as ancient as the landscape itself, and certainly as much travelled, a tune once known to men as Old Hundredth. And there were voices singing: 'All creatures that on Earth do dwell s ...'

Original Sinner

This was the order in which the A.S. *Intractible*'s hatches opened, after landing at Army Base, South City, Roinse, Mars. Firstly, the Second Aft Hatch, to emit a Leading Hand who ran in his suit across to the Control Bunker to collect Contact Assurances. Secondly (fifteen minutes later), Aft Hatch 'Q,' to emit three engineers who made a cursory survey of the jets before retiring to chat with the uniformed ground crew now appearing. Thirdly and fourthly, simultaneously, the Lower Midships Hatch (Personnel) to emit the Catering Officer who wanted to secure a supply of fresh bacon before the A.S. *Intractible* left again, and the Upper Midship Hatch (Cargo) to emit a heavy duty gangplank, from which Neptunian sulphosphates were trundled in covered trucks.

Fifthly, the Fore Control Hatch, to emit the pilot, who had brought the Army ship in from Orbit Epsilon, and the Captain, who was going to have a drink with the pilot. Sixthly, Warrant Officers' Hatch, from which a group of three officers emerged in civilian dress. Seventhly, the Personnel Duty Hatch (Personnel) to emit a platoon of Outer Planets Commando, who marched off the Army Base field in threes. Eighthly, the Personnel Duty Hatch (Stores), to emit a small vehicle carrying the equipment of the Commando platoon. Ninethly, the captain's Hatch, to emit the Trooping Officer and his A.D.C., heading in the direction of Roinse, the old city. Tenthly, the Heavy Cargo Hatch, amidships, from which various duty technicians in fatigue kit straggled, to climb over the ship and check its hull for faults.

Lastly, General Hatch (Ratings) swung open. By this time, two and a half hours had elapsed since landing.

'Isn't it just typical of the bleeding Army!' Wagner Hayes exclaimed, clattering down the gangplank. 'We've only got twenty-four hours here before we bat off for Earth again, and then they keep us mucking about with an FFI when we arrive. What did they think we could have picked up on that lousy hole Ganymede?'

'Don't forget we had a pay parade, too, Wag,' Dusty Miller said, chinking the credits in his pocket.

'They could have had that when we were space-borne if the ruddy RSM had been half sharp,' Wagner growled.

Leaving the ship with him were, besides Dusty, two slightly older men, Max Fleet and their bald unsmiling corporal, George Walters. The four came down onto the landing pad with a knot of other servicemen, all looking forward to a few hours' leave and a change from the rigorous confinement of the *Intractible*.

'You're always grumbling, young Wag,' George said. 'What are you going to do with yourself now you're out?'

'I'm certainly not going to get drunk, like you and Max!' Wagner exclaimed promptly. 'I've got more sense. Catch me wasting my money on booze!'

Backing up his friend, Dusty pointed across to one of the Base buildings in the direction of which they were walking.

'See that place, George?' he said. 'Wag and me are staying there, mate. Other Ranks' Hostel. We found it on the trip out. It's got everything; showers, ultra-violet, juke-boxes, local and Earth telly, terrific canteen ...'

'And a library,' Wagner said. 'A library bursting full of comics! I've never seen so many comics in my natural.'

'You did nothing but read comics on Ganymede,' Max Fleet said. 'Don't you ever want a change?'

'These are *up-to-date* comics, stupid,' Wagner said genially. 'Go and get sloshed with old George and keep your trap shut!'

They trudged companionably across the monotonous expanse of tarmac. It was good to be out of the confines of the ship; the air, as Max remarked to George, breathed well considering that it had once been artificially 'planted.'

'It's better in the hostel,' Wag explained. 'They maintain it there at full Earth pressure. I tell you, that place is a dream. It is; it's better than home! If you two drunken old reprobates had any sense –'

'Hallo! Here comes the bleeding padre!' Dusty said. 'You've had it, lads. From the right, pray!'

The four of them groaned in unison.

No doubt Padre Column heard them, but his smile was not affected. He included them all in the smile, the beefy Wagner with his open, boyish face, weedy Dusty with his peak haircut, dark and reserved Max, dough-faced corporal Walters with his parody of a monk's tonsure.

'Enjoy your leave, my friends,' the padre said. 'Try and regard this brief break in our journey home as an opportunity for spiritual refreshment. Remember that war is raging on Earth, and that as soon as we return there we shall be called upon to give of our very best.'

'Yes, sir, of course, sir,' Wagner and Dusty chorused together. George Walters looked sullen.

'You speak as if that was something to look forward to, sir,' he said.

'If we are to be tested, Walters, we must come to it with what fortitude we can muster,' Padre Column said. 'We must regard mortification as our common lot, I fear.'

'Come on, George, let's shove off!' Dusty said in an undertone, tugging at the corporal's sleeve; but George stood his ground.

'My wife was killed in the East Anglia Massacre last year,' he said distinctly. 'I doubt if I shall get back aboard the *Intractible* until two M.P.'s carry me aboard drunk.'

'Then you are a fool, Walters, and I only hope your younger companions will not follow your example.'

'Don't worry, sir,' Wagner said cheerfully; 'we wouldn't follow this old soak into the nearest cookhouse.'

So saying, he grabbed George's arm and moved him forcibly away. Dusty and Max Fleet, who had said nothing during this exchange, followed hurriedly. The padre stood watching them, lips pursed. A heated argument sprang up between Dusty, George and Wagner, lasting all the way to the Base gate. As usual, Max kept out of the controversy.

'You young fellows don't know what's good for you nowadays!' George said. 'When I was your age, I wasn't content to bash my bunk reading bloody comics – I was seeing a bit of life, knocking round the taverns with a few likely women.'

'No wonder you lost all your hair,' Dusty retorted. 'You'd better watch out, Max, or the corp will lead you down the primrose path into the dog house.'

'I'll watch it, Dusty,' Max said, as they reached the gate. He stood there with his hands in his pockets, suddenly aware that although he had spent almost all his tour of duty with these three men, they were not really his friends, nor ever could be. A momentary silence spread from him to the others, as if they too, at this moment of parting, had become aware for the first time of their own, separate identities.

'Well, we'll meet up again tomorrow evening, and see who looks in best shape then,' Wag said. 'Gentlemen of the ruddy ranks, Di-i-i-iss – wait for it! – di-i-i-iss – miss!'

But his tone was not as light as usual. Wag sounded slightly defensive. George, Max thought, had caught him on a sensitive spot with his remark about the rival attractions of comics and women.

Forgetting it at once, he turned away with George. As the two youngsters entered the air-conditioned hostel, he and George showed their passes and walked through the main gate into one day's liberty.

Roinse was partly a military town. When the terrific task of oxygenating the Martian atmosphere had been undertaken two generations back, the Army, in liaison with the Space Corps, had been in charge of the project. When the inter-racial wars had broken out on Earth, the military had tightened their grip here.

Yet mingled with the barracks and camps was a sizeable business city, also growing. As it grew its suburbs grew, bright and cheap and uniform, pathetic replicas of the square miles of suburb now being blown to bits all over Earth. There was another section of Roinse: the ancient Martian city, rock-hewn and ruinous, standing on the edge of the new built-up area. In the heart of the old alien city stood the village Roinse where the descendants of the original colonists lived, a proud and dwindling clique resenting all the more recent intruders.

Roinse, in short, was a muddled city – and an interesting one, heterogeneous as Rome, mysterious as Singapore.

George Walters and Max Fleet headed for the oldest part of town. The number of people in uniform thinned as they went, but George was still peevish and muttered about the folly of youth.

'I don't understand these kids,' he said. 'They're all the same today – rather watch a telegame over a bottle of squash than come out and have a real drink like a man.'

'Forget it, George,' Max said.

'Yes, let's forget it,' George agreed, taking the other's arm. 'Let the world go to pot eh? We'll show 'em! I feel like getting real soused tonight, Maxie, and forget the bloody war and everything.'

They passed into the shadow of a Martian building like a small hill. It might have been, in its prime, a cathedral or a railway station. The race that had built it was long gone; now their monument bore warning notices BEWARE OF FALLING ROCK. Many of its ancient cloisters had been adapted into stalls or shops by terrestrials. In one of the darkest corners stood the Flingabout Tavern. The two Earthmen went in, into an atmosphere of neon and noise.

Few customers were about. A juke-box blazed away in a corner; two couples danced in front of it. Girls in aprons bustled round, serving drinks and marsbergers. George eyed them appreciatively.

'This is living!' he exclaimed, rubbing his red hands. 'Maybe we pick up a couple of these tarts at closing time, eh, Max?'

'Maybe,' Max said.

They ordered Roinse Green wine in tankards.

'Here's to all those stinking, fruitless, useless months of our lives we wasted on Ganymede station!' Max said, raising his tankard.

Together they drank deep. George sighed with gratification, leaning back in his chair relaxedly, his fingers tapping on the table in time with the juke-box beat.

'This is living,' he repeated.

'Think of those poor kids with their faces buried in comics,' he said.

'I'll bet this place gets pretty wild after dark,' he said. He looked slightly bored.

'We can go somewhere else after another drink or two, if you want,' he said.

'Really paint the town,' he said.

'Show 'em old soldiers never die,' he said. Pause.

'You're quiet, Max,' he said.

Max drained off his tankard and stood up. His usually expressionless face puckered into a look of embarrassment.

'I'm sorry, George,' he said. 'There's someone I've got to go and see. I can't just sit here and get stewed on our one night free.'

'Now wait a minute!' George said, plonking down his tankard and getting up belligerently. 'Are you trying to walk out on me? Were we not going to make a day of it? Did we or didn't we not plan this bloody binge ever since we left Neptune?'

'I'm sorry,' Max repeated. 'I hate to let you down, George. There's someone I've got to see; I thought I could stay away but I can't.'

'It's Maggie, is it?'

Max sighed.

'Yes,' he said.

George sat down again, rubbing his bald head. 'Then you won't be wanting me with you.'

'Directly I leave this place, the women'll see you're alone and defenceless, and come swarming round you.'

'You're a swine,' George said. As Max went through the door, he was calling savagely for more drink.

Hands in pockets, shoulders hunched, Max walked through the old part of Roinse. The sun and the false satellite sun together cast double shadows everywhere. It was mid-summer. Only the white dust underfoot looked like winter.

I sometimes think that never blows so red
The rose as where some buried Caesar bled.

By the same token, the dust was white with the hopes and bodies of extinct Martians. An obvious thought, thought Max; but this was no age for subtlety. He walked rapidly until he came to an exchange store huddled against a mouldering pile of masonry. Over the door was one word only: DEACON. He entered without hesitation.

Maggie Deacon sat behind the counter, thumbing through a catalogue. She was lean and hard and green-gold, a typical Martian colonist woman. Her eyes were grey: she was not beautiful, except to Max.

As she stood up, he hardly recognised her. Her hair was red.

'Max!' she said. She pronounced it as if it was the sweetest word she ever spoke.

At the sound of her voice they were back where they had been before, two years ago when Max was on leave on his way to Ganymede in the troopship. He had forgotten she was a mutant of a type becoming not uncommon on Mars. Her hair colour changed with the seasons. Last visit, he had seen it in winter, when it was black; in the spring, it acquired a green tinge. Now, through the summer, it was a golden red. A few white hairs streaked it, adding to its brilliance.

The mutation was ugly, people said. Max felt otherwise. For him, it was a sign of the way she was different from all other women.

'Your husband?' Max asked, casting an eye towards the back of the shop. He was prompted to ask that first.

'He died only a week after you left,' she replied. 'Don't say anything about it. Just don't mention it.'

Max had met Maggie Deacon by chance. He had brought a ring into the shop to sell for drink money. They had looked at each other and recognised themselves for two of a kind: wary, hard, lonely, uncompromising, desperate. Deacon had lain in a back room issuing irate orders through the door, cursed with a spinal disease of long standing. Deacon had not mattered as Maggie and Max banished all that was barren in each other's lives.

Now Maggie came round the counter, wrapped her arms round Max's ribs and kissed him deeply. Finally taking her lips from his, she regarded him with satisfaction.

'The way you walk in so casually,' she said.

'You still remember me, Maggie,' he said.

Inside him, the luck and the love boiled up. Reaching out, he seized her roughly and drew her back into his arms, pressing his face into hers, devouring her.

'I'll close up the shop,' she said, when he released her. Their eyes were alight; they both looked ten years younger.

'There'll be a bed free now,' Max said.

She bolted and locked the flimsy door.

'We're not staying here now we can choose,' she said decisively. 'We need proper surroundings – besides, I don't get out enough.'

He followed her into the rear room. It was poor, tidy, dusty. The idea of criticising it, even mentally, never occurred to him; it was her place and he accepted it.

'How long?' she asked, brushing her hair, stooping to look in a tiny mirror.

'Till tomorrow, five in the afternoon.'

Silently, they faced up to the appalling briefness of it. She said not a word more on the subject, and he thanked God for her sense.

She bundled drink, food and a blanket into a basket. She straightened her skirt and was ready to go.

'We can climb to the top of the Cropolade,' she said. 'It'll be quiet there, and we'll be alone. I've got something to lie on.'

'Wherever you say, my love,' he said.

Flashingly, she smiled at him. Light-heartedness took them; they squeezed each other, excited as kids as she steered him to the back door.

'I wish you'd come tomorrow instead of today,' she said, as they emerged into a back alley, 'I meant to have a bath tonight.'

The Cropolade was another massive, meaningless, chunk of Martian architecture. The outskirts of the city ended round its feet; it was like a galleon aground on a reef. A large sand dune had worked against one side of it, forming a sweeping slope up which a track ran right onto the rocky shoulders of the Cropolade itself.

Max and Maggie lay close together on the top, beside a length of ruinous wall. Lights spattered the darkness below, but they disregarded them. Lights flecked the dark sky above, but they ignored them. Night had come, bringing the image of peace to them both.

She sat up and poured more wine.

'I'm feeling half tight,' he said, drinking avidly.

'Tell me about the half-tight thoughts you're thinking,' she murmured.

'Oh, there are too many of them. I'm thinking how I was a kid raised in a slum, no breeding, no education … yet right now I'm the happiest, luckiest man alive. And I'm thinking of all the things I've done and experienced in the universe – and of all those I haven't. And I know they're all valuable and should not be denied. And I know that through you I can find the best of everything.'

'I never would have guessed you had such a soft centre,' she teased.

He was annoyed. 'You're wrong there, mighty wrong! I may *think*, but I'm like rock inside … All hard, Maggie, all hard.'

She stroked his hair, asking him what else he was thinking.

'I'm thinking that we'll never find anybody better suited to each other than we are. That a day with you is better than a year anywhere else … That I ought to desert, skip the ship, and stay right here with you forever.'

Maggie sat up.

'You can't do that, Max. Mars is a small place. You'd never get away. Besides, it's wartime on Earth – they'd hunt you down and shoot you!'

'I was only thinking, love, only thinking. Lie down again. After being with you, the thought of the other fellows drives me crazy. If you knew how damned gormlessly *innocent* they are. Adult innocence makes me want to be sick.'

She had brought a small lamp. It hung above them on a stick, swaying slightly in a light breeze. The evening was chilly, and they snuggled closer.

'We'll stay here until it's time for you to – get back,' she said. 'We'll stay here till the very last moment.'

Neither of them spoke about the future. When they parted, it would be for good. Army other ranks never do the Outer journey twice. Besides, there was a war on on Earth; wars killed people.

They had both fallen asleep when the bright light played on them. Max sat up, feeling for a gun he did not have, knowing something was wrong. A pallid dawn glow sickened in the sky. Someone was calling him by name.

A vehicle had climbed the slope onto the top of the Cropolade. Its headlights seemed to souse them in blinding dry liquid.

'Max! Max Fleet!'

'Who is it?' Maggie asked. In the cruel illumination, her face was white, drawn, old. Glancing at her, Max was suddenly angry, frightened, full of hate. He jumped to his feet and advanced pugnaciously, clenching his fists.

'Who the ruddy hell are you?' he called.

'Max! It's me!'

He moved out of the beam and began to see again. A small duty truck stood there, its television antennae shimmering above it with reflected light. Young Wagner Hayes had jumped from the driver's seat and was coming towards Max.

Max told him to go away, using the strongest language he could muster.

'Don't muck about, Max,' Wagner said sharply. 'Get in the van, and we'll drive you back to the ship.'

'I'll get back to the ship when I'm ready.'

'You'll breeding well get back now, Maxy Boy! An urgent call's come through from Earth. There's an enemy offensive along the Greenland-Iceland axis or somewhere, and we're the joes who've got to go back and help squash it as soon as possible. Crisis on! Leave's cancelled.'

'Of all the dirty –'

Max broke off. Padre Column was approaching from the other side of the truck.

'What seems to be the trouble, Hayes?' he asked.

'It's Max here, padre –'

'My leave doesn't expire till five this afternoon!' Max exclaimed furiously. He wondered what Maggie was doing.

'On the contrary, it expired at midnight,' the padre said. 'Sorry, Fleet. The ship's siren sounded the Recall signal. I wonder you did not hear it up here. You're technically under arrest for overstaying leave.'

'How the hell did you find I was up here?'

The padre moved impatiently.

'Several trucks are out searching for you. All the troops are back aboard ship bar you and Corporal George Walters. We picked Walters up from a gutter. He was completely intoxicated; he is fast asleep in the back of the truck now. Before he passed out, he gave us the name of the woman you are with. We got her address and found someone who saw you both come up here. Now please get into the truck without any further trouble or foul language.'

*

He could see the weather-worn top-knot of the Cropolade all round and, further, the scattered lights of Roinse and, further still, the neutral and obnubilated blackness of Mars. He could see – yet it was as if he was blind. His senses rocked. He hardly felt the hand on his shoulder.

'You'll have to go, my dear; arguing will only make it worse,' she said. 'I know how it is. I understand.'

Choking, he turned to Maggie.

'Maggie, we'll never –'

'Leave that woman alone, Fleet, and come with us!' the padre said. He spoke quietly, but his words were loaded with contempt. Max turned on him.

'If you say one word against my Maggie, padre or no padre, you're going to get the biggest –'

'Haynes, get this man into the truck,' Padre Column said, sharply. 'If he is not intoxicated, his senses are besotted with something equally dangerous.'

'Come on, Maxy!' Wag said, advancing. He looked big. His baby face was screwed into the grimace of a man executing a painful duty. He put out a hand. Max hit him right on the mouth.

Wag stopped in surprise.

'Oh, well done!' Maggie exclaimed.

The padre and Wag charged together. Max put out a shower of blows. They seemed not to land. In a whirl of excitement – hardly any pain then – he realised he was being beaten. Wag was too big. He was being borne down, picked up ... he was still struggling, but he was being dumped into the truck. Confusion ...

Handcuffs clicked on his wrists and at once his mind cleared again.

'Maggie!' he bellowed. The sound was lost in the angry revving of the truck. Max half climbed to his feet and then fell over the unconscious George; when he had picked himself up again, the vehicle was already bumping downhill. Max did not call out any more. He sat on the floor of the truck, breathing hard.

When they reached the bottom of the long slope, Wag leant back and said, 'Sorry I had to hit you like that, Max.'

'It would be better to attend to your driving,' the padre said gently. This was enough to rouse Max again. He knelt up on the bumping floor. 'You're a fine one to say what's best!' he exclaimed bitterly. 'You and Wag and everyone – you're all the same! You say my senses are besotted; well, that's the way I like it. To suffer, to feel … What's it matter, whether it feels good or it hurts, if you're alive? You preach your bloody sermons against the snares of the senses. You must be mad! Everyone's senses are being starved, not surfeited. A race of fools, dullards, bores, is being raised – by you and your damned creed of the starvation of any natural urge. Why do you think George is lying here drunk? It's because he's reacting against your sort of living death!'

Sector Grey

Originality is far to seek in Era 124. Diversity is everywhere; originality nowhere. As a humorist put it, 'Every day someone somewhere is inventing gunpowder.'

All this chimes well with the Theory of Multigrade Superannuation, which allows for identical events occurring on different worlds at different times. Men evolve, family characteristics alter; the ancient mythic Adam remains unregenerate. Hence the persistence of aggression patterns that lead to war.

A volume such as this, which tries to scan Starswarm at one particular moment in time, must allow latitude for at least a campaign, if it is to be representative.

There are many conflicts to choose from.

Perhaps one of the most notable is now being waged in the strange formation known as the Alpha Wheel, beyond the Rift in Sector Grey. We have not the time, nor the sensory ability, to describe war on the largest scale it is ever likely to attain, fought bitterly between two races of telesensual beings.

We understand much more today about the Alpha Wheel than we did. The Wheel, quite simply, failed to develop. It remains a region only a light year and a half across, retaining within its borders many strange materials and even its own physical laws.

One instance of this: The disproportion in this embryo universe's chemical composition has resulted in an enormous quantity of free oxygen. Its abundance is so great that it fills what we would call interplanetary space, held there by the high gravitational and centrifugal forces of the system. Thus, the eight hundred planets that comprise the Wheel share one common atmosphere.

It is hard not to see a parallel between this oddity and the fact that the Jakkapic races, alone in Starswarm, are telesensual. As they share their ambient air, so they share certain sensory perceptions. And they have been at war, one planet with another, ever since man first made contact with them.

We know many men who are divided against themselves, for all that psyche-healing can do. The Jakkapic races suffer in the same way. Their wars are the more terrible because every blow struck against the enemy hurts the friend and the self equally.

The movements of Jakkapic machines are as predictable to an enemy as the movements of their troops. Their minds are shared; thus, their machines, being in essence but extensions of their minds, can never be secret. Deadlock in this murderous chess game would have been reached aeons ago, were it not for the element of mortality. Hearts and engines alike undergo failures. At the moment of failure, which is unpredictable, disorganisation occurs. Then the enemy strikes. The vast search systems that blink out across the blizzards of the Wheel are looking not for success but failure.

The hearts and engines that concern us here must be human ones. If we want a war in human terms, we have not far to go from the Wheel. The planet Drallab in the Eot system is also in Grey Sector.

There, a war has been raging for ten standard years. It is a mere tiff on a galactic scale, and is chiefly of interest because such is the rigid code of honour of the military juntas which rule Drallab that, although they are well launched into their Early Technological Age, they allow no weapon that cannot be carried by one man. Nation after Drallabian nation has exerted itself not to breaking the rule but to breeding stronger men to carry larger weapons. We shall see how the rule is circumvented in a different way, by the use of drugs.

Some of these drugs were superseded in Starswarm Central a thousand millennia ago. On Drallab, they are new, revolutionary. Every day someone somewhere is inventing gunpowder.

Sergeant Taylor lay in a hospital bed and dreamed a dream.

He was a certain colonel. He had inherited the rank from his father and his father's father. He had spent the first tender night of his life lying in the swamps of As-A-Merekass. Since he had survived being eaten by hydro-monitors and alligators, he was allowed to begin the military upbringing suitable to his family status. The parade ground had never been distant from his adolescence. All the women who had care of his earlier years possessed iron breasts and faces like army boots. The pulpy fruit of success would one day be his.

He was a certain colonel whose barracks during this war year were below ground. In the mess the Special Wing was making merry. The place was overcrowded, with long trestle tables full of food and wine and with soldiers and the women who had been invited to attend. Despite the Spartan aspect of the mess, the atmosphere was one of festival – that especially hectic kind of festival held by men whose motto is the old one: Eat, drink, and be merry, for tomorrow we die.

The colonel was eating and drinking, but he was not yet merry. Although it pleased him to see his men carousing, he was cut off from their merriment. He still knew what they had forgotten, that at any moment the summons might come. And then they would leave, collect their equipment, and go above to face whatever dark things had to be faced.

All this was a part of the colonel's profession, his life. He did not resent it, nor did he fear it; he felt only a mild attack of something like stage fright.

The faces around him had receded into a general blur. Now he focused on them, wondering idly who and how many would accompany him on the mission. He also glanced at the women.

Under duress of war, all the military had retreated underground. Conditions below were harsh, mitigated, however, by generous supplies of the new synthetic foods and drinks. After a decade of war, plankton brandy tastes as good as the real thing – when the real thing has ceased to exist. The women were not synthetic. They had forsaken the ruined towns above for the comparative safety of the subterranean garrison towns. In so doing, most of them had saved their lives only to lose their humanity. Now they fought and screamed over their men, caring little for what they won.

The colonel looked at them with both compassion and contempt. Whichever side won the war, the women had already lost it.

Then he saw a face that was neither laughing nor shouting.

It belonged to a woman sitting almost opposite him at the table. She was listening to a blurry-eyed, red-faced corporal, whose heavy arm lay over her shoulder as he spun a rambling tale of woe. Mary, the colonel thought; she must be called something simple and sweet like Mary.

Her face was ordinary enough, except that it bore none of the marks of viciousness and vulgarity so common in this age. Her hair was light brown, her eyes an enormous blue-grey. Her lips were not thin, though her face was.

Mary turned and saw the colonel regarding her. She smiled at him.

Moments of revelation in a man's life always come unexpectedly. The colonel had been an ordinary soldier; when Mary smiled, he became something more complex. He saw himself as he was – an old man in his middle twenties who had surrendered everything personal to a military machine. This sad, beautiful, ordinary face spoke of all he had missed, of all the richer side of life known only to a man and woman who experience each other through love.

It told him more. It told him that even now it was not too late for him. The face was a promise as well as a reproach.

All this and more ran through the colonel's mind, and some of it was reflected in his eyes. Mary, it was clear, understood something of his expression.

'Can you get away from him?' the colonel said, with a note of pleading in his voice.

Without looking at the soldier whose arm lay so heavily over her shoulders, Mary answered something. What she said was impossible to hear in the general hubbub. Seeing her pale lips move, in an agony at not hearing, the colonel called to her to repeat her sentence.

At that moment the duty siren sounded.

The uproar redoubled. Military police came pouring into the mess, pushing and kicking the drunks onto their feet and marching them out of the door.

The colonel rose to his feet. Leaning across the table and touching Mary's hand, he said, 'I must see you again and speak to you. If I survive this mission, I will be here tomorrow night. Will you meet me?'

A fleeting smile. 'I'll be here,' she said.

Hope flooded into him. Love, gratitude, all the secret springs of his nature poured forth into his veins. Then he marched towards the doors.

Beyond the doors, a tube truck waited. The Special Wing staggered or was pushed into it. When all were accounted for, the doors closed and the tube moved off, roaring into the tunnel on an upward gradient.

It stopped at Medical Bay, where orderlies with alcoholometers awaited them. Anyone who flipped the needle was instantly given an antitoxic drug. The colonel, though he had drunk little, had to submit to an injection. The alcohol in his blood was neutralised almost at once. Within five minutes everyone in the room was stone cold sober again. To wage war in its present form would not have been possible without drugs.

The party, quieter now and with set faces, climbed back into the tube. It rose on an ascending spiral of tunnel, depositing them next at Briefing. They were now on the surface. The air smelled less stale.

Accompanied by five under-officers and NCOs, the colonel entered Information Briefing. The rest of his men – or those picked for this particular mission – went to Morale Briefing. Here, animations would prepare them by direct and subliminal means for the hazards to come.

The colonel and his party faced a brigadier who began speaking as soon as they sat down.

'We have something fresh for you today. The enemy is trying a new move, and we have a new move to counteract it. The six of you will take only eighteen men with you on this mission. You will be lightly armed, and your safety will depend entirely on the element of surprise. When I tell you that if all goes well we expect to have you back here in ten hours, I do not want you to forget that those ten hours may vitally affect the whole outcome of the war.'

He went on to describe their objective. The picture was simple and clear as it built up in the colonel's mind. He discarded all details but the key ones. Where the forty-eighth parallel crossed the sea, the enemy was gathered in some strength in a stegor forest. Beyond the forest stood unscalable cliffs. On the clifftop, surrounded by the forest, was an old circular wooden building, five storeys high. On the top storey of this building, looking over the treetops, was a weather station. It commanded the narrow strait of sea that separated enemy from enemy.

The weather station watched for favourable winds. When they came, the signal would be given to gliders along the coast. The gliders would be launched and flown over enemy territory. They contained bacteria.

'We stand to have a major plague on our hands if this setup is not put out of action at once,' the brigadier said. 'Another force has been given the task of wiping out the gliders. We must also put the weather station out of action, and that is your job.

'A high-pressure area is building up over us now. Reports show that conditions should be ideal for an enemy launching in ten to twelve hours. We have to kill them before that.'

He then described the forces to be met with in the forest through which the attackers must go. The defences were heavy, but badly deployed. Only the paths through the forest were defended, since vehicular attack through the trees was impossible.

'This is where you and your men come in, Colonel. Our laboratories have just developed a new drug. As far as I can understand, it's the old hyperactivity pill carried to the ultimate. Unfortunately it's still rather in the experimental stage, but desperate situations call for desperate remedies ...'

With the briefing finished, the officers were joined by the men selected to accompany them. The twenty-four of them marched to the armoury, where they were equipped with weapons and combat suits.

Outside, in the open air, it was still night. In a land vehicle they rode over to an air strip, the ruins of an old surface town making no more than vague smudges in the darkness. They passed piles of defused enemy grenades. A vane awaited them. In ten minutes they were all aboard and strapped into position.

A medical man entered. He would administer the new drug when they reached the enemy forest; now he administered a preparatory tranquilliser orally, like a sacrament.

The vane climbed upward with a bound. Twenty-four men subsided into a drugged coma as they hurtled high into the stratosphere. Below, out of the bowl of night, the enemy forest swam.

Descending vertically, they landed in an acre of bracken beneath the shadow of the first trees. The sedation period ended as the hatch swung open.

'Let's keep it quiet, men,' the colonel said.

He checked his chronometer with the pilot's before leaving. It was dawn, and a chill breeze blew. The great cluster that contained Starswarm Central wheeled low in the sky.

The medico came around handing out boomerang-shaped capsules that fitted against the bottom teeth under the tongue.

'Don't bite on 'em until the colonel gives the word,' he said. 'And remember, don't worry about yourselves. Get back to your vane and we'll take care of the rest.'

'Famous last words,' someone muttered.

The medico hurried back to the vane. It would be off as soon as they were gone; the Special Wing had to rendezvous with another elsewhere when the mission was over. The party set off for the trees in single file; almost at once a heavy bore opened fire.

'Keep your heads down. It's after the vane, not us,' the colonel said.

Worries came sooner than expected. A strobolight came on, its nervous blink fluttering across the clearing, washing everything in its path with white. At the same time the colonel's helmet beeped, telling him a radio eye had spotted him.

'Down!' he roared.

The air crackled as they crawled into a hollow.

'We'll split into our five groups now,' the colonel said. 'One and Two to my left, Four and Five to my right. Seventy seconds from now, I'll blow my whistle; eat your pills and be off. Move!'

Twenty men moved. Four stayed with the colonel. Ignoring the racket in the clearing, he watched the smallest hand on his chronometer, his whistle in his left fist. As he expected, the fusillade had died as he blew his blast. He crunched his capsule and rose, the four men beside him.

They ran for the wood.

They were among the trees. The other four groups of five were also among the trees. Three of them were decoy groups. Only one of the other groups, Number Four, was actually due to reach the round building, approaching it by a different route from the colonel's.

As they entered the forest, the drug took effect. A slight dizziness seized the colonel, a singing started in his ears. Against this minor irritation, a vast comfort swept through his limbs. He began to breathe more rapidly, and then to think and move more rapidly. His rate of metabolism was accelerating.

Alarm filled him momentarily, although he had been briefed on what to expect. The alarm came from a deep and unplumbed part of him, a core that resented tampering with its personal rhythm. Coupled with it came a vivid picture of Mary's face, as if the colonel by submitting to this drug was somehow defiling her. Then the image and the alarm vanished.

Now he was sprinting, his men beside him. They flicked around dense bush, leaving a clearing behind. A searchlight burst into life, sweeping its beam among the tree trunks in a confusing pattern of light and shade. As it caught Group Three, the colonel opened fire.

He had acted fast, hardly realising he was firing. The guns they carried had special light-touch trigger actions to respond to their new tempo.

A burst of firing answered his shot, but it fell behind them. They were moving faster. They wove rapidly among the stegor trees. Dawn gave them light to see by. Opposition, as Briefing had forecast, was scattered. They ran without stopping. They passed camouflaged vehicles, tanks, tents, some containing sleeping men. All these they skirted. They shot anything that moved. A fifty per cent acceleration of perception and motion turned them into supermen.

Absolute calm ruled in the colonel's mind. He moved like a deadly machine. Sight and sound came through with ultra-clarity. He seemed to observe movement before it began. A world of noise surrounded him.

He heard the rapid hammer of his heart, his breathing, the breathing of his fellows, the rustle of their limbs inside their clothes. He heard the crackle of twigs beneath their feet, faint shouts in the forest, distant shots – presumably marking the whereabouts of another group. He seemed to hear everything.

They covered the first mile in five minutes, the second in under four. Occasionally the colonel glanced at his wrist compass, but a mystic sense seemed to keep him on course.

When an unexpected burst of firing from a flank killed one of the group, the other four raced on without pause. It was as if they could never stop running. The second mile was easy, and most of the third. Normally, the enemy was prepared for any eventuality: but that did not include a handful of men running. The idea was too laughable to be entertained. The colonel's group got through only because it was impossible.

Now they were almost at destination. Some sort of warning of their approach had been given. The trees were spaced more widely, kirry-mashies were being lined up, gun posts manned. As the light strengthened, it began to favour the enemy.

'Scatter!' the colonel shouted, as a gun barked ahead. His voice sounded curiously high in his own ears.

His men swerved apart, keeping each other in sight. They were moving like shadows now, limbs flickering, brains alight. They ran. They did not fire.

The gun posts opened up. Missing four phantoms, they kept up their chatter in preparation for the main body of men who never arrived. The phantoms plunged on, tormented most by the noise, which bit like acid into their eardrums.

Again the phantoms grouped in a last dash. Through the trees loomed a round wooden building. They were there!

The four fired together as a section of the enemy burst from a nearby hut. They shot a gunner dead as he swung his barrel at them. They hurled explosives into a sandbagged strongpoint. Then they were in the weather station.

It was as Briefing had described it. The colonel leading, they bounded up the creaking spiral stair. Doors burst open as they mounted. But the enemy moved with a curious sloth and died without firing a shot. In seconds they were at the top of the building.

His lungs pounding like pistons, the colonel flung open a door, the only door on this storey.

This was the weather room.

Apparatus had been piled up in disorderly fashion, bearing witness to the fact that the enemy had only recently moved in. But there was no mistaking the big weather charts on the walls, each showing its quota of isobar flags.

Several of the enemy were in the room. The firing nearby had alarmed them. Beyond them was a glimpse of cliff and grey sea. One man spoke into a phone; the others, except for a man sitting at the central coordinating desk, stared out of the windows anxiously. The desk man saw the colonel first.

Astonishment and fear came onto his face, slackening the muscles there, dropping his mouth open. He slid around in his seat, lifting his hand at the same time to reach out for a gas gun on the desk. To the colonel, he appeared to be moving in ultra slow motion, just as in ultra slow motion the other occupants of the room were turning to face their enemy.

Emitting a high squeal like a bat's, the colonel twitched his right index finger slightly. He saw the bullet speed home to its mark. Raising both hands to his chest, the man at the desk toppled off his stool and fell beside it.

One of the colonel's men tossed an incendiary explosive into the room. They were running back down the spiral stairs as it exploded. Again doors burst open on them, again they fired without thought. There was answering fire. One man squealed and plunged headfirst down the stairs. His three companions ran past him out into the wood.

Setting his new course, the colonel led his two surviving men towards their rendezvous. This was the easiest part of their mission; they came to the scattered enemy from an unexpected quarter and were gone before he realized it. Behind them, the weather station blazed, sending its flames high into the new day.

They had four miles to go this way. After the second mile, the maximum effect of the drug began to wear off. The colonel was aware that the abnormal clarity of his brain was changing into deadness. He ran on.

Sunshine broke through in splinters onto the floor of the forest. Each fragment was incredibly sharp and memorable. Each noise underfoot was unforgettable. A slight breeze in the treetops was a protracted bellow as of an ocean breaking on rock. His own breathing was an adamantine clamour for air. He heard his bones grind in their sockets, his muscles and sinews swishing in their blood.

At the end of the third mile, one of the colonel's two men collapsed without warning. His face was black, and he hit the ground with the sound of a felled tree, utterly burned out. The others never paused.

The colonel and his fellow reached the rendezvous. They lay twitching until the vane came for them. By then there were twelve twitching men to carry away, all that was left of the original party. Two medical orderlies hustled them rapidly into bunks, sinking needles into their arms.

*

Seemingly without interval, it was twelve hours later.

Again the colonel sat in the mess. Despite the fatigue in his limbs, he had willed himself to come here. He had a date with Mary.

The junketing was getting into full swing about him, as the nightly tide of debauchery and drunkenness rose. Many of these men, like the colonel himself, had faced death during the day; many more would be facing it tomorrow on one minor mission or another. Their duty was to survive; their health was kept in capsules.

The colonel sat at the end of one long table, close to the wall, keeping a chair empty next to him as the room filled. His ears echoed and ached with the noise about him. Wearily he looked round for Mary.

After half an hour had passed, he felt the first twinge of apprehension. He did not know her real name. The events of the day, the rigours of the mission, had obliterated the memory of her face. She had smiled, yes. She had looked ordinary enough, yes. But he knew not a thing about her except the hope she had stirred in him.

An hour passed, and still the chair beside him was empty. He sat on and on, submerged in noise. Probably she was somewhere with the drunk who had had his arm around her yesterday. Boom boom boom went the meaningless din, and the chair remained empty beside him.

It was after two in the morning. The mess was emptying again. Then it became suddenly clear. Mary would not come. She would never come. He was just a soldier, there would be an empty chair beside him all his life. No Mary would ever come. In his way of life, the Drallabian way of life, there was no room for Marys. He pressed his face into his hands, trying to bury himself in those hard palms.

This was Sgt Taylor's dream, and it woke him crying in his hospital bed.

He wept until the shouts of men in nearby beds brought him back to reality. Then he lay and marvelled about his dream, ignoring the pain of his shattered eardrums.

It was a wonderful mixture of reality and superreality. Every detail concerning the raid had been accurately reconstructed. Just like that, he had led his men to success a very few hours ago. The hyperactivity pills had behaved in the dream as in real life.

'What the hell was you dreaming about?' asked the fellow in the next bed. 'Some dame stand you up or something?'

Sgt Taylor nodded vaguely, seeing the man's lips move. Well, they had said there might be after-effects. Perhaps even now someone was inventing a drug to grow you new eardrums ...

Only in two details had his dream transcended reality.

He had never seen nor consciously looked for any Mary. Yet the authority of the dream was such that he knew that through all his life, through all the empty discipline and the empty debauchery, a Mary was what he had been seeking. He knew too that the dream predicted correctly: given the conditions of this war, there would never be a Mary for him. Women there were, but not women like Mary.

The other detail fitted with the first one ...

'Or maybe the way you was squealing, you was above ground playing soldier again, eh?' suggested the fellow in the next bed.

Sgt Taylor smiled meaninglessly and nodded at the moving lips. He was in a world of his own at present; and he liked it.

Yes, the other detail fitted with the first. In his dream he had promoted himself to colonel. It could be mere oneiric self-aggrandisement: but more likely it was something deeper than that, another slice of prediction matching the first.

Sgt Taylor was a soldier. He had been a soldier since birth, but now he was realising it all through. That made him soldier-plus. Mary was the softer side of life, the unfulfilled, the empty-chair side; now it was ruled out of being, so that he could only grow harder, tougher, more bitter, more callous. He was going to make a splendid soldier.

No love – but bags of promotion!

Sgt Taylor saw it all now, clear as a ray of sunlight. It was good to have shed his sentimental side in a dream. Shakily, he started to laugh, so that the man in the next bed stared at him again.

They should be able to think up some really bizarre missions for a man who was stone deaf ...

Stage-Struck!

The Wells Memorial Wing of the library was a long grey room, while by coincidence the under-librarian was a long grey man. His lips looked to be zipped as tightly together as the mouth of a miser's purse, his eyes were so deeply set in his face that they seemed puddles at the back of twin caves. There was, too, a greyness in his walk that suggested that existence on the Education Satellite was a burden to him. He looked – taking him all in all – a man at once bent and unbending, as if life, in offering too little, had been too much.

Nevertheless, he was smiling indulgently at the young student who so reverently looked through the magazines in his archives.

'I can tell you're fond of twentieth century literature,' he said.

'Indeed I am,' the student said. 'People say that just because it's five centuries old it holds no further interest, but that's all nonsense – particularly about all this prophetic literature, which was then at its richest.'

'Quite so, although personally I prefer the work of the earlier nineteenth century – that's my period. What are you studying in particular?'

The student was very young. With due sense of his own importance, he tapped the dusty magazines he held and said, 'I'm doing a research thesis of this type of prophetic literature – science fiction as it was called in its day – with a view to determining how nearly it was later fulfilled. Then when I'm fully qualified, I can go back in the Time Capsule and do actual field research.'

Meditatively, the under-librarian nodded.

'It needs careful training before one can make the mental adjustments necessary to travel to another age,' he said. 'I found this out to my own cost; there are more difficulties in it than just the technical ones.'

'You've extemporated, sir?' asked the student.

Nodding, the under-librarian picked up one of the magazines and opened it.

'Look here, here's a very perceptive story that will support your thesis: "Hide and Seek," by an author well known in his day. It's about a man in a spacesuit defeating a crack spaceship.'

'And this has since really happened?'

'Not exactly. But the same interestingly unlikely and uneven sort of contest has actually taken place.' The lined face for a moment relaxed into a glow of memory. 'I refer, of course, to the race between a space-ship and a stagecoach.'

'Er – I don't think I recall …' said the student, uncertain whether he was expected to do so or not.

'It was an incident in my personal history. Perhaps I may indulge myself by relating it to you. It must be two years since I last told it to anyone.'

'Er – will it take long?' asked the student. 'I have an appointment with my robotutor that I ought –'

This was nearly half a century ago (began the under-librarian inexorably), before the Time Capsules were as convenient and commodious as they are today. As you know, they are chiefly used today for all sorts of research into the past, but half a century ago this application was new, and it was a very raw and nervous young student of English literature who was ejected from his Capsule into the London of 1835.

You will naturally have heard of London. It was the capital city of a small island which disappeared under the sea in the Atlantic Shift of the late twenty-second century, and in 1835 it was one of the most important cities on the globe.

Picture then our young student, whom we will call Smith, making his way one raw November morning down Gracechurch Street to the *Spread Eagle*. He is in a panic. So much so that his young travelling companion, Bassy, can hardly keep up with him – although Bassy is in almost as great a panic. They have just emerged from the Capsule and are angry with each other and life.

The *Spread Eagle Inn* was a scene of much coming and going, a confusion and a profusion of people, bright or drab, but never a two alike. Everyone was making very good use of tongue and elbows, spitting freely, laughing, weeping, breathing the sharp air in and out – all the things universal education has rid us of. They filled the cobble street, they flocked under the archway, they jostled about the coachyard, adding their own flavour to the scents of cooking and horses. And the inn itself they crowded till the old structure bulged at its timbers. Round its galleries, in its rooms, in its parlours – bellowing for service – they milled, the Londoners of the pre-Victorian age.

'My God!' exclaimed Bassy. 'How do we get through this lot?'

Oh, the place was not really so crowded, but what makes a crowd is not its numbers so much as its individuals – and this was in the days before conformity. Some of these individuals now surrounded Smith and Bassy; a wizened boy selling lead pencils; a one-armed seaman hawking 'The Public and Private Life of Madame Vestris'; a Jew with a gold tooth pressing fifty-bladed penknives; an aged lady with a moustache crying nosegays; a scarecrow begging ale money; a rotund merchant under four capes offering ferrets for sale; a Spaniard displaying patent leather straps; a cripple advertising his sister; a placard boy advertising a play – with others of that ilk, besieging the travellers' ears in their attempts to reach their purses.

Twenty-fifth century sensibilities go down before this kind of assault. Smith and Bassy felt themselves sinking under the mob's determination.

What saved them was the cracked high note of a key bugle. Though this sound held no meaning for them, its effect on the crowd was magical. It began to flow like a tide, to part in the middle like a Red Sea, carrying the two travellers along with it. They were borne through the coach yard and into one of the tavern rooms.

Again the bugle sounded. Full tilt, a canary-bright coach rattled under the archway, its wheel hubs missing the near wall by inches. It drew to a splendid halt in the yard as stable boys ran out to hold its wheels and horses. A cheer went up from the onlookers, a sigh from the passengers, both holding the tableau only for a moment before the former group attempted to swarm onto the coach and the latter off it.

Bassy gazed at this scene in some delight until Smith pulled his sleeve. 'This is no time for sightseeing,' he said. And indeed it was not. In some eight hours, they would be cut off from their home epoch for ever. As I will presently explain, they were really in a mess.

They had been rushed into a small room of the *Spread Eagle*. Frankly inhospitable, it was the travellers' room, its bare plaster relieved only by the pencilled comments of earlier occupants. It contained benches, on which a beggar slept and a woman suckled twins, and a fireplace, the heat of which was barricaded in by four men standing round it with their stomachs to the flames.

One corner of the room was partitioned off; behind its flimsy barrier, a waiter of bleached aspect washed tankards and glasses in a bowl of something resembling gravy, wiped them on his apron, and passed them through a hatch into another room. Since he looked the least formidable creature present, Smith went across to him.

'We want to get to Birmingham,' he said. 'Can you tell us how it's done?'

The waiter fixed an eye on him, then squinted at him through the glass bottom of a tankard.

'It's done on foot by some, on nag's back by others, and I dassay by swimming up the canals by others,' he said, unsmiling.

'We're in a hurry. When does the next stage coach leave?'

'Stage struck, are you? You certainly don't sound like old stagers.' While indulging in this humour, the waiter never ceased his dipping and wiping act, for every ten seconds as regular as a cuckoo from a cuckoo clock, a snipey woman's face would pop through the hatch and cry savagely for glasses.

'Could you oblige me with a sensible answer, please?' Smith asked impatiently.

'Why, if it's sensible answers you want, cocker, you'd better ask at the booking office, hadn't you? You don't think I'd be doing this job if I had any sense, do you? *Coming*, you old bloodsucker!'

This last shouted reassurance was addressed to the proboscis which had just launched itself pecking through the hatch again. At the same time, the waiter jerked his left shoulder blade towards a rear door. Taking this as a sign, Smith and Bassy hurried through it, to find themselves in a long, low room, part of which was barricaded off to form a booking office.

When they had waited their turn behind an army subaltern and his lady, they confronted the clerk, a patriotically coloured gentleman with red cheeks, white hair and blue jowls.

He informed them that the *Tally-Ho!* would be leaving for Birmingham on the next quarter hour. Two outside seats were available, cost 3d per mile, or twenty seven shillings for the hundred and eight mile journey. Arrival, subject to acts of God or vagaries of horseflesh, seven and one half hours precisely after leaving the *Spread Eagle*.

Smith and Bassy gazed at each other in dismay.

'We'll hardly make it, even if they run to time. Why, that's not fifteen miles an hour!'

'It's the swiftest, safest, cheapest journey in the world. Take it or leave it, masters, *as* you please.'

In the end they took it. There was no option. Shrugging, the colourful clerk entered their names on the way-bill.

The yard had emptied considerably now, most of its previous occupants having dispersed after the last coach had arrived. Round the Birmingham coach, which had just been pulled from its stabling, was a swarm of ostlers, stable-boys, shoe-blacks, and other hangers-on, some of whom were harnessing – or interfering with the harnessing of – four recalcitrant black horses, while others loaded up luggage under the careful supervision of the guard. A small knot of passengers attended by a pair of porters had already assembled, stamping their feet or slapping themselves to keep warm.

All these preparations would ordinarily have delighted the hearts of the visitors from the future, had they not been only too aware that through their own foolishness this bit of the past might have to serve as their perpetual present.

At least there was no delay. Amid an orgy of tipping, the passengers were heaved aboard the stage, four of them inside, seven outside, Smith and Bassy being placed in the front, behind the box.

'Mind your ear'oles, one and all!' cried the guard, and blew a blast on the key bugle.

The coachman appeared, raising a cheer from the stable-boys and the freshly gathered crowd.

I wish you could have seen him! Young, dapper, well clad, under a mulberry-coloured many-caped benjamin and a fine, shining top hat. Birmingham Basil was a famous man on his ground, with a following as enthusiastic as any of your space jockeys of today.

He never mounted his box until he had inspected every buckle and rein of the team's harness, paying special attention to the coupling reins and curb-chains. Then he leapt lightly up, flung a rug round his kness, cracked the whip, and they were off!

A brave sight it was, the bright-painted coach with the coachmaster's name, William Chaplin, bold on the door, and the wheels and the harness twinkling, and the horses stepping high and fresh on their toes, and not a grain of dust anywhere! Tra-tra-tra went the key bugle, 'Watch your skulls, gents!' cried Basil to the outsiders, and they clipped smartly under the low arch of the *Spread Eagle* onto the stones of London.

Their pace even in the narrow alleys was spanking – yet what could Smith and Bassy do but despair to think that the spaceship they had to race to Birmingham could equal in one second the distance they could cover in one hour?

That spaceships should be required to take people back in time seemed a lot more novel fifty years ago than it does today. Then, the full implications of the Zope Pupa Equations had only just dawned. If I may indulge in a little background history, the facts were something like this.

By the beginning of the twenty-first century, interplanetary flight was a going but limited concern. It was only two centuries later, with the discovery of the unified field theory and the subsequent development of ships part-powered by anti-gravity, that vacuum-borne traffic really multiplied and interstellar travel was contemplated.

During the trial runs of starships – K-Capsules as the prototypes were called – out of the solar system and back, discrepancies in the unified field theory were observed. Professor Zope was the first to announce that time was as much a part of the true field as gravity, electricity, or magnetism, and that there existed right round the solar system a sort of neutral layer where, the other three factors reaching equilibrium, time itself became multi- instead of uni-directional.

These new facts did not remain merely academic marvels. T. X. Pupa, aided by Zope himself, produced those equations which postulate that having reached the neutral layer a spaceship may – under suitable motivation – choose its temporal value as readily as it does its velocital one to coast back to Earth on.

The suitable motivation, when turned from theory into technological fact, was the anticelerator. When fitted into a spaceship, the first Time Capsule was ready for its maiden voyage through time! Unfortunately, the bulk of the early anticelerators – 'time engines' in popular parlance – was so great that a Capsule, remotely controlled from a satellite, could only hold two passengers.

When Smith and Bassy made their journey, there were only six Capsules in operation, one of them belonging to UN University.

Their horrible mistake had been this: when the ship, after its journey through space and time, had landed them in London 1835, they had emerged excitedly; only when its doors had closed automatically behind them and it had vanished silently up into the pale dawn air, did they realise that they had left behind in the craft an essential piece of luggage.

The Capsule would return out of space for them in six months. But so that it did not fall into unlawful hands it would open its doors only to the signal of their psi-beacon. If it received no signal, it would return to UN University empty. And Smith and Bassy had left the psi-beacon behind!

'You fool!' Bassy gasped, his cheeks chalky white. 'How *could* you have left it behind?'

'*You* left it behind,' Smith said, growing very red. 'I thought you had it.'

'I was sure you had it.'

'You suicidal idiot!'

'You inept clot!'

They had scarcely fallen to blows when Smith remembered Melluish.

Melluish was a sound but stodgy economic historian who had graduated from UNU in the same year as Smith. Although Melluish's study of the Chartist movement and Smith's study of Charles Dickens gave them an interest in the same distant period of time, they had little else in common: except for the fact that Melluish also was using the University Capsule to do field research.

The Capsule, having shed Smith and Bassy, was batting out to the neutral layer, switching into the present, returning to Earth to collect Melluish, and then doing the journey over again to drop him and his partner Joseph in the past.

This operation would take the ship two weeks. And then Melluish would be landed in Birmingham 1835, nine hours after the time Smith stepped out in London. So Smith and Bassy had one chance of getting back to their proper period: by being at Melluish's point of arrival and catching his empty capsule back. All they had to do was race the ship to Birmingham. If they lost, it might well prove impossible to find Melluish and Joseph in the city or to establish contact with the future again.

Fortunately there was no problem about knowing exactly where to go in Birmingham. In a farewell drinking session, Smith, Melluish, Bassy and Joseph had exchanged all relevant details. Marsh Yard was Melluish's place of arrival, and 1700 hours his time – on that very day.

'And the stage is due in at quarter to five if we're lucky? We'll never make it!' Bassy sighed. 'Damn this confoundedly slow crate-on-wheels.'

By now they were out in the country and approaching the little hamlet of Ealing, the four horses trotting easily, and everyone easy except the two extemporates.

'What can we do but hope?' Smith exclaimed.

Falling to biting his lips, Bassy said, 'It's a damned pity the railway isn't open yet.'

'The London – Birmingham line won't be finished for another three years,' Smith said shortly. He was growing tired of Bassy's company.

Sitting beside Birmingham Basil on the box was a stout gentleman in a bright green cut-away coat and three mufflers who had been addressed as Sir Worsthorne Paine. His attention had gradually been diverted from the road to Bassy's complaints; turning, he seized the student by his coat.

'See here, my young buck,' he exclaimed. 'Your ignorance is making a proper fool of you. I don't know where you have sprung from, I'm sure, but evidently you haven't been at liberty to find out that you have the privilege of travelling by one of the most amazingly revolutionary inventions ever invented.'

'Let go of my lapel, you old meddler,' Bassy said, tugging his coat away. 'I probably know more about stagecoaches than you do. I'd rather travel by hearse.'

Sir Worsthorne's rubicund cheeks trembled with wrath and the movement of the vehicle.

'Why, you young pup, so you're conceited as well as ignorant! Let me tell you this – that thanks to the egregious Mr McAdam and Mr Thomas Telford, the roads in this country are the wonder of the Continent. So is its unrivalled coaching system. You and progress, sir, evidently ain't acquainted.'

'The Romans made better roads,' Bassy snapped, despite Smith's efforts to silence him.

'Oh? And I suppose you'll tell me they made better railways too, sir?' Sir Worsthorne exclaimed, blowing out his cheeks. 'Perhaps it chances you've not heard of the Parliamentary train from London to the Scottish capital that takes under twenty four hours for the journey? Perhaps you can name me another nation boasting a similar progressive institution?'

'Perhaps you can see why I grumble about this stage, then? The railways, primitive though they are, have already made these horse-drawn prisons virtually obsolete.'

The knight nearly exploded.

'Obsolete! Obsolete! You young shaver, do you not mind what the coaches have done for this country? They have revolutionised everyday life, they've brought the nation together! In my father's young day, London and Exeter were a fortnight's travel apart – now they're only seventeen hours apart. Gad, your sense of astonishment must be diminutive, unparalleled diminutive!'

Bassy's reply was drowned by the notes of the key bugle. Rounding a bend, the coach rolled into a small town and halted in front of an inn. The two extemporates – and every other onlooker – were treated to the spectacle of how rapidly a team could be changed. Four fresh horses were waiting. Their blankets were pulled off them and they were harnessed up as soon as the other animals, tired now, were led away. The guard, the horse-keepers, and ostlers worked together, while the innkeeper sallied forth to provide Birmingham Basil with a piping hot brandy and water. In two minutes the operation was complete and the *Tally-Ho* was covering ground again.

The quarrel did not resume. There was, Smith reflected, exhilaration in the ride. They rattled along most gamely, the agile guard tying the back wheel without climbing off when they went down steep hills. Much of the country – though it improved further on – was neglected and tumbledown after the recent troubles. Twice they passed a gibbet. On one occasion they saw a fox hunt, with the pack in full cry against the skyline and many of the huntsmen in top hats. Only when they plunged into a dense wood did Bassy grow restless again.

'Supposing we're held up by highwaymen?' he muttered to his companion. 'I don't see the coachman has any weapons with him.'

This remark was overheard by Sir Worsthorne, who had been ostentatiously maintaining a sulky silence.

'Highwaymen? Not a one's been seen on this territory since Regency days. We've no more need here for blunderbusses than we have for fiddles. What sort of wild country do you take yourself to be in? Russia? America? Come to think of it, you speak in an outlandish sort of voice. Not a Yankee, are you?'

'I'm as English as you are, you interfering old fool. Now mind your own business.'

This was too much for Sir Worsthorne. He turned dramatically to Birmingham Basil.

'Stop the coach, dragsman. Rein 'em in and let's have this settled once and for all.'

The coachman looked rebellious; but he knew he could rely on a generous tip from the knight, and drivers were ill paid, for all their responsibilities. As the team slowed and stopped, the occupants of the cab jumped down to see what was going on, while the other outsiders climbed over the luggage, the better to hear the altercation.

'Now,' roared Sir Worsthorne, standing up to face Bassy pugnaciously. 'I've travelled this ground many a time, yes, and driven the *Tally-Ho* myself when Basil allowed me, and never before have I met anybody like you for containing so much ignorance, spite and treasonableness under so nondescript an exterior. I, sir, am a knight and a justice of the peace and the owner of Gaydon Hill Hall in Warwickshire. I fought under the Iron Duke at Waterloo; I have shaken hands with Wilberforce; I backed the Reform Bill all along; and I've ridden a thousand-guinea hunter to hounds at Melton in my better days. Now sir, tell me what justification you have for *your* existence?'

'My friend is none too well,' Smith said quickly. 'He's had a bad shock.'

'Shock or not, he apologises to me here and now or he gets off and walks.'

'Since I've only stated facts, I see no reason to apologise,' Bassy said, standing up and looking stubborn. 'You're just a backward lot of bums, and that's the truth of it.'

That did it. A tremendous row developed, the other passengers joining in on Sir Worsthorne's side. Bassy had gone too far now to back down if he had wanted to. A minute more, and two of the other outsiders had grabbed him and hauled him bodily from the coach.

'Sorry, sir, but that's the way it must be,' Birmingham Basil said, cracking his whip and shaking the reins.

As they moved off, Smith stood up and called back, 'Don't forget – the south end of Marsh Yard at five o'clock! I'll do my best to hold the ship for you!'

With a lurch the coach was off. The figure of Bassy dwindled down the road until it was obscured by trees.

They made good time to Banbury, where the old knight left them. His own wap-john awaited him deferentially in his own drag, and he drove off in style as the other travellers hurried to make a quick but excellent meal of lamb pie at the inn. Twenty-five minutes later, they were starting off on the second half of the journey.

Although two more passengers had been taken on at Banbury, the box seat was half enpty, and Basil invited Smith to share it with him.

Smith had been sitting hunched in melancholy. In his head, clear as a diagram, he saw the Time Capsule and the stage coach racing each other – a race known only to him and the *hors de combat* Bassy, but nevertheless as much a race as if the ship were visible actually streaking through the sky overhead. Only grudgingly did he move next to Basil.

But Basil had a lively, enquiring mind, and was altogether a different type of man from the previous generations of coachman who had worked those routes in less enlightened days. He spoke philosophically of speed and its benefits, of politics and the state of the country, of his opinion of the King and even of Louis-Philippe, of the hazards of coaching and the boisterous charms of a certain Miss Hetty Hedges, a chambermaid at the *Spread Eagle*.

They bowled along, pausing only at tolls and stages. Relaxing, Smith began to respond to the conversation. He told how he was in England only for six months, how he hoped to meet the extraordinary de Quincey; and Landor, who should now be in the country; and have a chat about Shelley with Thomas Love Peacock; and perhaps even clear up some of that nasty business about Lord Byron and his half-sister; and above all interview that promising young parliamentary reporter of the *Morning Chronicle*, Charles Dickens.

But of none of these gentlemen had Birmingham Basil heard so that Smith was obliged to pursue other topics. Incautiously, he chatted about the future, and thus about electricity, atomic power, gravitics, and even extemporate travel. In fact he grew quite detailed about the wonders available to people living a few centuries ahead. With the exciting motion of the carriage – and above all with the excellent brandy that Basil pressed on him – he talked freely until interrupted by the notes of the guard's bugle sounding lustily across the countryside.

'All very interesting,' Basil said. 'You make me feel that working a four-in-hand may not after all be the best possible existence.'

Smith was too busy looking about him to answer.

Dark was falling as they clattered into Birmingham, a darkness in which the elements were aided by black and heavy smoke, belching from the chimneys of the industrial citadel. The glow of distant furnace fires, the ponderous waggons which toiled along the road, laden with iron or loaded with goods, the workers in the narrow thoroughfares – all these had their counterparts in noise; in the din of hammers, the rushing of steam, the dead heavy clanking of engines. All the air about them seemed laden with night and misery and cinders.

Both regret and fear settled in Smith's heart as they clattered through the dreary streets – then they were trotting past well- lighted shops and smart houses, and swinging into the yard of the *Old Royal Hotel*.

The time was five minutes to five.

Smith jumped down to the ground. His race was not yet run. He still had to reach Marsh Yard before the Capsule left; and how to get there he had no idea. Basil, seeing the bafflement on his face, pushed through the melee towards him

'You'll be wanting Marsh Yard,' he said. 'I heard what you called to that companion of yours we had to leave behind. It's only a couple of minutes from here. I'll show you the way. Somehow I feel quite an interest in your future.'

Grabbing up his portmanteau, Smith followed the coachman. They struggled through a knot of people out of the court, and then along a couple of ill-paved streets, through an alleyway, down a stinking lane, and into another dimlit street, into which Marsh Yard opened. All the time, Smith's twenty-fifth century heart went hammer, hammer, hammer, under his nineteenth century costume, while he lost sense of direction and time.

In Marsh Yard, a row of back-to-back houses were under construction. The place was deserted now, except for three people arguing in one corner. Behind them stood the Time Capsule; they were Melluish, Joseph and Bassy.

Smith ran towards them with a cry, forgetting all about Birmingham Basil.

'How did you get here so soon?' he demanded of Bassy.

'I had a lift from a wagoner to Banbury, and there I hired a fast post-chaise. I've been hanging about here for half-an-hour.'

'A fine mess you both made of things,' Melluish said angrily.

'It was Smith's fault.'

'Oh no, not at all! If you'd remembered –'

'If *you'd* remembered –'

'Stop arguing, both of you,' Melluish said, for he had just caught sight of the coachman. 'Smith, who's this fellow you brought with you, who is now covering us with a brace of pistols?'

The long grey under-librarian paused in his story for dramatic effect, whereupon the research student, who had listened all the while with reluctant interest, burst into laughter.

'Oh, wonderful!' he exclaimed. 'So that's how you got here to the present! I see it now. I had assumed that you were Mr Smith. But obviously you are someone even more remarkable! You are he who had his appetite wetted about the future and resolved to try it for himself; you are he who drew pistols on the extemporates; you, sir, are Birmingham Basil himself!'

The under-librarian looked baffled and vexed.

'Indeed, sir, I'm not. What gives you that absurd idea?'

It was the turn of the student to look baffled.

'I thought the point of your story lay that way. Then you *are* Smith?'

'That indiscreet fool? No, I am not, nor likely to be.'

'My mistake; I apologise. You prefaced the tale by saying this was an incident in your personal history. I presume then, sir, that you are none other than the unfortunate Bassy?'

The under-librarian ground his teeth.

'That ill-disciplined, ill-natured cur? No, damn you, I am not he, nor is he me.'

'Then I suppose you must be Melluish?' hazarded the student.

'Indeed I am not Melluish; the fellow has been dead these last ten years,' said the under-librarian angrily.

The student bit a carefully selected finger.

'Well, you can't possibly be the knight, Sir Worsthorne Who's-it ...'

'How right you are. I am Joseph, Melluish's companion. Not liking the look either of the nineteenth century in general nor of Basil's pistols in particular, I hopped back into the ship just before the doors closed and came straight back to the present. I spent ten minutes in the past all told.'

Uttering a cry of irritation and knocking the old science fiction magazines to the floor, the student demanded to know what became of the other extemporates.

'Why, Birmingham Basil had them arrested as Chartists and Dissenters. I got a rescue party sent back which had to atomise the prison to get them out. It all throws an interesting sidelight on the difficulties of time travel, doesn't it?'

Under an English Heaven

George Hutchinson phoned his brother Herbert at 12.15 on the first of July 1961.

'Herbert? That you? George here. I'm phoning from the *Mail*. We've just had a phone call from a bod out Newbury way. Guess what?'

'You tell me, laddie!'

'They've made it at last! An alien spaceship has landed just outside Newbury. I'm off to have a look at it as soon as possible. Get Helen and the kids rounded up and I'll collect you in ten minutes in the car. We'll be among the first to see the little green men.'

'Now look, George –'

'This is pukka, Herb, no kidding. History starts anew today. This is the most epoch-making day ever. Get your togs and I'll be round.'

He hung up. On his way out of the office, he barged into the News Editor.

'Keep this story under your hat, George,' Ralph Head advised. 'We'll have to confirm it before we do anything. It sounds like a lot of eyewash to me.'

'Okay,' George said abstractedly. 'But Gillwood phoned it in. He's always reliable, isn't he?'

Ralph took his pipe out of his mouth.

'Don't tell me you believe the Martians are here?!'

'Everyone knew they'd turn up sometime.'

'Well here's one provincial newspaper doesn't want 'em. I've got trouble enough with this shipyard business on my hands.'

George drove fast to the outskirts of town, turned up the drive of his brother's house and braked outside the front door. He entered the house clapping his hands and calling, 'Let's be having you.'

Helen met him in the passage, her apron on.

'What is all this nonsense you've been telling Herbert over the phone?'

'No nonsense, honey. A real big spaceship landed only thirty miles away. I'm going to take you all to see it. Isn't it the biggest thing you can imagine?'

'We can't possibly come, George. I'm just in the middle of getting the lunch!'

He levelled an imaginary pistol at his head and pulled the trigger.

'Lunch! You need to eat the day the world ends? Switch the gas off and let's go. Where's Herbert?'

'He's gone to get Frances from school.'

'Fine. Shed your apron and we'll drive along the road to meet them.'

'But Eric –'

'Look, Helen, Eric's at school all day. You needn't worry about him.'

'He'll be back at 4.15.'

'Well leave him a note in case we're late and tell him to watch the telly till we get back.'

She backed away, shaking her head.

'I've never seen you like this, George!'

'My God, I've never been like this! Now gather your traps like a good girl and let's get cracking.'

'And what do you suppose is going to happen to the baby?'

'Use your nous, pet! Shove it in the carry-cot and it can go in the back of the car.'

'Susan has to have a bottle at 2.15.'

'Helen … Helen … Where's your imagination, for heaven's sake? Go and get a bottle ready now.'

'It isn't so easy –'

The front door opened. Herbert came in, looking harassed. Frances, aged six, was with him, crying loudly. She let out renewed howls as she rushed into her mother's arms.

'Come on, Herbert,' George said, turning to his brother imploringly. 'Get these two girls into the car and let's be off.'

'Yes, let's move, love,' Herbert said. 'Into Uncle George's nice car, Francey.'

'You know I've got the fish on,' Helen said.

Through sobs, Frances turned a big red face to George.

'I gotta go to school this afternoon,' she said. 'Miss Angello would never forgive me if I missed my dancing.'

George squatted on his haunches and spread his hands in appeal.

'Look, sweetie, I want you to come with us. We're going to do some-thing so special, ever so special, better even than going to the zoo. This may be the most important day in your little life. Now you don't think your old uncle would tell you wrong, do you?'

'No ... But ... but it's forward kicking this afternoon.' And she dissolved into tears again.

'It's no good, George,' Helen said. 'We just can't come, and that's all about it.'

'You are a lot!' George said.

'Well it's no good being nasty, George. I mean how *can* we come?'

'May I have a drink of water?' George asked. He looked at his watch. It was 12.50. As Helen was filling the glass, baby Susan began to weep. Herbert hustled out into the back garden to rock the pram.

When he returned, George said briskly, 'One last appeal to your sense of proportion. The bloke that phoned this gen to the *Mail*, Ken Gillwood – you've met him, Herbert – he was in the "Gloucester Head" last month – he's reliable. Before phoning through, he drove out on his motor bike to check details. He says this thing can only be a spaceship. It looks like a zeppelin sitting on end, and must be all of eighty feet high. It's churned up the earth a bit and set light to a rick nearby. When Ken saw it at quarter to twelve there was no activity round it – no alien activity, that is, though the Newbury fire brigade had arrived to cope with the rick.

'Now, Herb, you used to belong to a UFO club, and Helen and you thought you saw a flying saucer over Reading station once –'

'It was Basingstoke, and it was when I was expecting Frances,' Helen said, as though that disposed of that.

'Okay, okay, we've all been young and foolish, but what I'm trying to say is that – no flattery – you're an intelligent couple, with open minds. You've always known that visitors from another planet *could* come. Now they *have* come. *I* don't doubt it, and you know how I used to scoff. Well, what I'm offering you is a free peep before half the country gets there or the police cordon the place off.

'So, last time of asking, are you coming?'

Helen and Herbert looked at each other.

'It's the children ...' Helen said.

'No, it's not that,' Herbert said, 'but look, George, have you considered it might be dangerous? You know as well as I do that if this thing has come from another planet, its crew will be armed with all sorts of super-weapons.'

George held up a hand.

'Enough, Herb. This is no time to be ignoble. You stay and mow the lawn in safety. I'm off.'

'– but there may be misunderstandings. The aliens may not want trouble any more than we do –'

'Okay, Herb, laddie. You're the family man. Get the front door sandbagged. I'm off.'

Sighing, he walked down the passage into the hall. As he went, he could hear Helen saying, 'Why don't you go, dear? There's nothing to stop you going.'

Ignoring them, George went out and climbed into his car. It was ten minutes past one. He had started up when Herbert came running to him.

'Perhaps I'll come,' he said. 'Helen'll stay and look after the kids.'

'Jump in,' George said briefly. He slid forward to the edge of the lawn, backed round to the garage and had the car facing towards the gate when Helen came running onto the porch.

'George ... George, look, if Herb's coming, I'd better come to. Do you mind?'

'Jump in,' George said.

'Well, hang on while I get things organised, for goodness' sake. I won't be a minute.'

*

114

She was not a minute. She was twenty-three minutes. The kitchen had to be seen to, the baby's bottle had to be prepared and put into a vacuum flask, a note had to be left for the baker. Frances had to be taken to a neighbour for her lunch and was left with strict instructions about crossing the road at the zebra crossing on her way to school. The front door key was hidden under the front door mat for Eric when he returned, and a note was left for him (pinned next to the baker's) explaining where everyone had gone and where the key was hidden. The washing was taken in off the line in case it rained.

Then Helen just slipped upstairs, changed her dress and put something on her face. She did well to manage it all in twenty-three minutes.

Coughing angrily as he flicked away the butt of his fourth successive cigarette, George helped her push the carry-cot into the back of the car. And then they were away. It was almost a quarter to two when they got onto the A4.

Checking with the address he had been given, George turned off onto a side road before they reached Newbury race course. The traffic here was thick and slow-moving.

'Do you think all these people have come to see ...' Herbert said, letting his voice fade away.

'Why not? They've had time enough to get here,' George said flippantly. The wait had made him cold, sardonic. Herbert, on the other hand, had become infected with excitement; or perhaps the sight of this line of cars had persuaded him that he was doing more than pursue a private delusion of his brother's.

'To think they actually landed in England!' he exclaimed. 'It's the greatest event since the birth of Christ ... Here, George, do you reckon there are any Russian spies about yet?'

'One in the car behind,' George said, referring to an Austin Countryman which was hooting imperiously.

They rounded a bend in the lane, and there – a field away, beyond a heavy summer hedge – the upper half of the alien ship was visible, its nose pointing like a blunt spire up to the cloudy English skies.

'That reminds me,' Helen said, horror-struck, 'I've asked the Vicar and Mrs Chadlington to tea this afternoon. In all the flap I quite forgot! You'll have to turn back, George.'

George laughed wildly.

Herbert nudged him before he could say anything silly. 'I just saw the vicar's car ahead,' he said. 'He must have forgotten too.'

The two men concentrated on the ship. It generated in their breasts the true thrill, the true wonder. That hull had nosed its way through unknown millions of miles of vacuum, to face Earth with a challenge – a hope – a threat – greater than any it had faced before. Standing silent in the rural landscape, it seemed to radiate a sense of its alien origins.

'What the hell's this?' George said.

The cars ahead were turning off the little side road into a dusty private road, to the gate of which George had now come. The gate was open, but a burly young man in a collarless shirt blocked the way. He held a cake tin bearing on the outside a crude picture of Windsor Castle and inside a pile of silver. Round his neck was a roughly written placard saying ENTRANCE FEE: ADULTS 1/- EACH, CARS 1/6, CHILDREN 6d.

'What the hell's this?' George repeated, sticking his head out of the window to say it to the burly young man.

'Entrance fee, shilling each, cars one and six, sir,' said the youth cheerfully.

'I can read, thank you. I'm questioning your right to rook me for going to look at that ship, which is certainly not your property.'

The youth grinned widely.

'I aren't charging you for looking at the ship, sir, I'm charging you for coming on my father's land. You can look from the road for nothing if you likes.'

'It's nothing but a damned swindle,' George said. 'You wait till the police come.'

'Oh, we lets them in for nothing, sir.'

'For heaven's sake, George, don't argue. Let's pay up and get in,' Herbert said.

With a bad grace, his temper not improved by more hooting from behind, George fished in his pocket and produced four and sixpence.

'Thank you, sir,' said the burly youth respectfully, 'and the babe in the back is another sixpence. We counts it as a child.'

'It *is* a child, you fool!'

'Then that'll be another sixpence, sir, if you please.'

Beyond speech, George paid up. They bumped down the dusty track and so into the field that contained the alien ship. Some thirty cars had already arrived and it was obvious there would soon be an overcrowding problem; the field was not large, and the half of it round the ship had been cordoned off by local police.

The fire engine sat in the far corner of the field beside a still-smouldering remnant of rick. Its crew were sipping cups of tea brought from the farmhouse, or sucking ices – George saw that an enterprising vendor was already on the scene, doing a brisk trade in iced lollies.

Leaving Susan to sleep peacefully in the back of the car, George, Herbert and Helen made their way over to the rope, standing as near as they could to the ship. They fell silent as they gazed at it.

'It's not really as big as I'd imagined it,' Herbert said disappointedly. 'Still, it's a beauty.'

'Yes, it's a beauty,' George breathed. They all took it in in awe.

'It makes me want to recite poetry,' Helen said. 'I can't find any words of my own. "Now God be thanked who matched us to His hour," you know ...'

Unboundedly grateful that at last they had reached a common and elevated mood, George said 'Funnily enough, I was thinking of a bit of Rupert Brooke too. What is it? Something about "... and gentleness, In hearts at peace, under an English heaven." But perhaps that's not very appropriate.'

They stared in silence again. Under this English heaven, the alien ship had acquired what appeared to be its first marking of the voyage: a white slash of bird dropping up by the nose. Otherwise its only other prominent feature was a round metal protrusion half way up its length, which they took to be a hatch. There were no ports visible. There was no sign of life.

George started looking about for other newspaper men. Cudliffe, who was officially covering for the *Mail*, had presumably come and gone with his photographer. As yet there seemed to be nobody about from the London dailies.

'Is your pal Gillwood still here?' Helen asked, divining George's thoughts.

'No. He's probably covering a Women's Institute meeting by now. God, the irony of it all! Something world-shattering like this and not a flaming soul who matters is about: just a gaggle of local cops and a few sightseers who couldn't care less. The thing landed at least three hours ago! If this was America, I bet the President would have been on the spot by now.'

'To say nothing of the heavy tanks,' added Herbert.

'Well, it's no use you men just criticising,' Helen said. 'All you ever do is talk. If this is your big moment, why not take it? Do something.'

'Such as?'

'You know as well as I do what they always do in the stories. Make some sort of signal or drawing to show them we're civilised.'

'We could try it,' Herbert said doubtfully. 'You mean, make a diagram of the solar system or demonstrate the square root of minus one?'

George snorted.

'You might just as well try to explain to them why some people call napkins "serviettes." The principle behind that is as fundamental to human nature as maths is, and who's to know what's fundamental to their nature – fundamental enough to be expressed in pictures anyhow. Beside, how do we know the aliens see along the same bit of the radiation spectrum as we do? The lack of ports would suggest they don't. But if they *do*, then it's no good doing a damn thing till they open a window to watch it.'

'Very logical, Mister Master Mind,' Helen said, smiling. 'Then how do you suggest we contact our visitors? And make it snappy because I think I can hear Susan crying.'

George leant on the rope barrier with both hands and said ponderously, 'There's no problem, Helen. You see, you and young Herb don't come to this with fresh minds. Mentally, fictionally, you've faced this wonderful arrival for years. Your UFO and SF magazines often tackle this very problem: How to contact the aliens. I say it's no problem.'

'Then why aren't we shaking hands with them right now?' Herbert asked.

'Don't make cheap jokes, Herb; they cost you too much. Look at it this way. This glorious ship is evidence of a great technological civilisation. This implies also a civilisation with as much goodwill as ours – any less and it would have blown itself to bits long before it got to making this ship. So then; intelligence plus civility equals reason. The boys in there are reasonable. More reasonable than we are.'

'I'd have granted you that without being argued into it.'

'I must go and see Susan and give her her bottle,' Helen said. 'I'm sure she's crying.'

She left as George continued his argument.

'If the aliens are reasonable and if they can detect us at all, then they will be able to detect that we are reasonable.'

'Why?'

'Use your loaf! Would a crowd of animals or savages behave like this English crowd? Would it put up barriers to keep itself away from what it has come to see? Would it pay tokens at the gate? Would it let itself be kept in order by only half a dozen bobbies if it were motivated by blood lust? You know jolly well it wouldn't! And another thing – look at the pattern of the English countryside, which we presume the aliens saw on their way down. Isn't its neatness and organisation a perfect example of the triumph of reason over nature?'

Herbert groaned, scratched his head, and ended up resting his hands on the rope in unconscious parody of his brother's pose.

'All this is obvious enough to you – and to me, of course. But why should it be obvious to really alien aliens?'

'Because they must be *reasonable* to be here at all, whether they look like elephants, octopuses or bloody sunflowers. And however stupid and bourgeois and conventional you may find the assembly here in this field, it too is governed by reason – so conspicuously so that it is probably more evident to the boys in the ship than it is to us. Ergo, we don't have to do a thing. We just wait until they've recovered from their journey and feel like communicating.'

'I wonder if you'd mind not leaning on the rope, sir? I'm afraid with the ground being so hard the supports aren't in very firm.'

The speaker was a policeman. He smiled at the brothers apologetically and they immediately straightened up.

'Sorry, constable,' George said. 'We're just so interested in this space-ship. Have you got any details about it you can tell us?'

'Can't really say as I have, sir,' the policeman said, obviously only too ready to stay and chat. 'Of course it's a nuisance, it being here, but just think if it had come down while the races were on. We have enough trouble with the traffic on the main road as it is.'

Herbert nodded gravely and said in a solemn voice, 'Is anyone being charged with obstruction?'

'Obstruction? Well, no, sir. We don't know who the thing belongs to, like, yet.'

'The Martians, would you say?'

The constable laughed delightedly, displaying enormous white teeth.

'You didn't really think it was a spaceship, did you, sir? Like on one of them television plays? It's a good job nobody believes them or we'd all be hiding in air raid shelters by now.'

'Where do you think it came from then?' George demanded sharply.

The constable dropped his voice. 'We reckon we got a pretty good idea where it come from, although no one's letting on yet. Now do you see that gent down by the hedge at the far end of the field, my side of the barrier? Sitting on a folding stool?'

They marked him well. He was young, spruce, self- contained, probably a university man.

'He came in a big Alvis saloon,' the policeman continued impressively. 'And there was two other men in with him. They're in the farmhouse now, goodness knows what doing. Well, they're from Harwell.'

'Likely enough,' George said. 'It's no distance from here.'

'More than likely: certain. They're from Harwell. It gives the whole game away, doesn't it?'

'How do you mean?'

The constable shook his head in pity for all persons unable to make deductions.

'Why, sir, this here machine belongs to them. They're up to all sorts of secret things at Harwell. I'll be surprised if it doesn't turn out to be worked by nuclear physics.'

And having thus blinded the two brothers by science, he passed heavily on. As George and Herbert looked at each other and smiled sorrowingly, Helen returned carrying a newly-fed Susan.

'I just heard a man in the crowd saying that your spaceship was made at Harwell, George,' she told him. 'Suppose it *is* an experimental plane or weapon …'

'Come on, Helen, you know better than that. You're talking like that copper. It's a mark of ignorance to be unable to believe the unlikely.'

'Well, I'd like to see inside first before I become too sure,' she said.

They stood about aimlessly, waiting for something to happen. From the spaceship itself there was no sign; the next diversion came from the other direction. The jib of a crane slid slowly between trees as it moved down the farm road. A great deal of shouting ensued. A small bulldozer appeared and demolished a stretch of bank, thus clearing a way for a procession of vehicles into the field.

First came an AERE Harwell Mutt with its blue and grey panels, followed by a civil ambulance. The crane was next, a twenty ton lorry-mounted affair that lurched into the field in a business-like way. Another large vehicle followed, an RAF super-articulated 'Queen Mary.' Close behind it were two lorries loaded with kit – winches, cables and canvas slings were visible in one – while the rear of this procession was brought up by an Army wireless truck.

'My God!' Herbert exclaimed, pointing to the two lorries. 'A Bomb Disposal unit! They're never going to load the ship onto that "Queen Mary," are they?'

It soon became obvious that they were.

'I just want to see what happens when they try to remove the charge,' commented George with grim relish.

The crane shaped up to the ship like a stork about to fight a torpid seal. Meanwhile, a ladder was stood against the hull, and an officer in dungarees shinned up it to tap smartly on the circular hatch – if hatch it was. As the echoes died across the field, an uneasy silence fell over the onlookers. The majority obviously feared massive retaliation, Helen with them.

'We've got the children to think of,' she said to her husband. 'The aliens aren't going to like this a bit. Let's get out.'

'Put Susie back in the car,' Herbert said, watching horrified as the officer, receiving no answer to his knock, produced oxy-acetylene equipment and proceeded to try and drill a hole in the hatch. George went pale around the gills. The crowd began to back away. Only the Harwell men stood their ground.

The little white flame had no effect on the metal. Eventually the officer, having achieved nothing, climbed down the ladder again; he was sweating as he retired to the lorry and dumped his kit.

*

Now the rest of the team got to work. They had been well drilled. The ship was hitched about with wire rope and secured. The hook of the crane was lowered and packed into position under the rope. At a signal, the cable tightened and the crane took most of the ship's weight. Block and tackle from one of the disposal lorries now took over control, swinging the ship's nose round and down until the crane was able to slide forward with the ship in position over the waiting 'Queen Mary.' As it was lowered down, the cable paid out too fast, so that the ship settled on the articulated vehicle with a noise like a herd of lust-maddened antelopes cantering over the Forth Bridge.

'Holy stars!' exclaimed Herbert. 'If the aliens don't interpret that as an act of aggression, they must be mad.'

Susan woke and started to cry.

'Perhaps they're all dead inside there,' George suggested. As he was speaking and Helen was trying to soothe the baby, their friend the policeman came up.

'There you are, sir,' he said. 'This rather confirms what I told you. I expect they'll take it back to Harwell now.'

'My God, Herb, perhaps they are going to take it to Harwell ...'

'Don't be daft, they'll probably take it to some Army depot and nobody will ever see who or what comes out of it,' Herbert said.

By this time, the space ship was being secured to the 'Queen Mary.'

George grabbed Helen and Herb by the arm.

'Listen, the powers that be may have a bright idea here, if they're going to cart the ship away to – well, say to Harwell. Anything they may want will then be on the spot. It'll be more convenient for the aliens too, and no doubt they are suspending judgment until they see where they're being taken.'

'You still think they're reasonable?' Herb said. 'And why are you pulling us along like this?'

'I'm getting you to the car. We're going to get out of here first before the rush starts.'

'Splendid!' Helen exclaimed. 'At last you're coming down to Earth. It's high time we were getting back.'

George cocked an eyebrow at her as he fished the car key out of his pocket. He nodded towards the 'Queen Mary,' which was already moving slowly across the field with its alien load.

'Honey, I'll get you home as soon as possible. But before that we're going to follow that ship and see where it's taken. I may seem to trust the aliens; maybe that's only because I don't know 'em. But I do know our authorities, and I wouldn't trust 'em further than I could throw 'em. Remember Belloc: "We knew no harm of Bonaparte but plenty of the squire"? If that damned ship disappears, it may disappear for good in a cloud of security.'

'Spoken like a newspaper man!' Herbert said. 'Pile in, Helen, and let's go!'

They piled in, slamming the doors as they started to bump across the field after the big articulated vehicle. Certainly, as George had planned, they were the first on the move, except for the crane, which bounded recklessly across the field. The 'Queen Mary' had by now negotiated the awkward opening and was heading down the farm road.

'What's that crazy devil doing?' George growled, as the crane driver slewed up to the opening. Next minute the other vehicle was stuck across the gap.

'Silly ass!' Herbert cried.

The crane driver backed, merely getting himself further stuck.

'Bloody amateur!' George bawled out of the window. 'Left hand down, man. Wajja think you're doing?'

But the crane was in trouble. Other civilian cars edged up to George as it manoeuvred. The Alvis came, honking impatiently. George joined in the chorus.

'He did it on purpose, George,' Helen said quietly. 'You're not meant to follow that ship.'

George turned his red face to her.

'Girl, you're right. We're framed, and neatly too, I must say. Hang on here, will you? I'm going to phone Ken Gillwood from the farmhouse and get him to follow the ship up on his motor bike. He should be at home by now.'

Flinging open the car door, George hurried between the other waiting cars and sprinted over the field. Climbing a bank, he pushed through the hedge at its thinnest point and jumped down into the lane.

The farmer's wife opened the door to his knock.

'I'm sorry, sir, the telephone's out of order today,' she said firmly. 'Such a shame, just when we need it.'

Before she shut the door in his face, George saw behind her one of the Harwell men, self-possessed and unsmiling.

Two days later, George phoned his brother from the *Mail* office again.

'Herbert? That you? George here. Get Helen and the kids rounded up and I'll collect you in ten minutes.'

'My God, George, not again!'

'Listen, Herb, this is really big! Ken Gillwood's just been on the blower. Guess what? You know I said we'd never hear of those aliens again? Well, I was wrong ...'

'Wouldn't be the first time. What's happened?'

'Something's just blown Harwell off the face of the Earth. Tell Helen to get the baby's bottle ready.'

Hen's Eyes

Mr Norman Fillbrook rubbed the end of his nose between thumb and index finger. The organ thus manipulated, having responded joyously to years of such treatment, was beautifully pliable, beautifully bulbous. Mr Fillbrook drew pleasure from rubbing his nose; his only pleasure at present.

His new superior in the Colonial Office (Mercury), Secretary Heathercote Thatch, was demonstrating his affinities with new brooms and, in the process of sweeping clean, had raised a cloud of dust about Mr Fillbrook's head that floated ominously there as if concealing from mortal view a damoclean sword of proven downward tendencies.

'I have been here in this establishment three weeks tomorrow, Mr Fillbrook, is that not so?' Mr Thatch said, looking monstrous and mottled from behind the barricades of his mustache.

'If you say so, sir.'

'Damn it, it's a fact whether I say so or not. You and I are going to have a clash of wills, Mr Fillbrook, if we are not careful.'

'I'm sorry, sir.'

'So am I. I'm a forgiving man, Mr Fillbrook, but this office has been grossly mismanaged. I'm not a man to let the sun go down on my wrath –'

'Here on Mercury it can't, sir.'

'Silence! – but I'm growing tired of deliberate obscurantism. Three weeks less a day I've been here and you have not put me in the picture yet.'

'Oh, sir ...' began Mr Fillbrook, a dreadful unease filling him. For Mr Thatch had picked up an earthgram from his desk and was scrutinising it with a glance sufficiently blazing to illuminate half the twilight zone. 'Oh, sir, I've been trying to break you in gradually. ... The department has become so large with all these immigrants from Earth and Venus. ... Is there something ...'

He halted in dread. Mr Thatch was waving the earthgram before him with the wounded dignity of a man trying to smother a fire with his best waistcoat.

'There *is* something, Fillbrook, yes. There is, to be precise, this earthgram. It comes, to amplify, from the Celestial Chuckle Ophthalmic Studios in Hong Kong, Earth. It deals, to specify, with the occular powers of one Hengist Mankiloe.'

Fillbrook gave what is termed 'a visible start'; its visibility was so great that Mr Thatch momentarily wondered if his Chief Assistant had not contracted the Greater Mercurian Nerverot. Thus deflected from his purpose, he asked in a calmer voice, 'Do I detect from that monstrous twitch that the name Celestial Chuckle has registered in your memory?'

Reaching blindly for the reassurance of his nose, Fillbrook said, 'No, sir, Mr Thatch, it was not that. It was just – the mention of Hengist Mankiloe's name.'

'And what importance may his ocular abilities hold for you, pray?'

'Mankiloe himself is in our Top Secret classification.'

'He is? Then I should have heard about him on the first day I arrived, not the twenty-first!'

'The twentieth, sir.'

'The twentieth then, you fool! Fetch me Mankiloe's dossier at once.'

'We don't have it at the moment. Inspector Thameson of Security has it.'

Mr Thatch's mustache bristled until he bore more than a passing resemblance to a bull peering over a thorn hedge.

'So? Letting a Top Secret dossier go out of this office, eh, Fillbrook? Men have done ten years in the curry mines for less.'

'I got the Inspector's signature, sir,' Fillbrook said, trying to take cover behind his nose.

'And I'll have his blood!'

'If you please, Mr Thatch, Mankiloe is rather a special case. This communication about his eyes –

'What have his eyes to do with it, man?'

'The gravitic plexuses – I mean plexi. No, I think plexuses is correct. That's what they're to do with.'

As he floundered, on the other side of the desk the record for the Reddest Faced Man on Mercury was broken by Mr Thatch with several blood vessels in hand.

'Optics! Plexi – I mean plexuses! Fillbrook, what do you think you're standing there saying? Are you pulling the wool over my eyes? What's this all about?'

Desperately, waving his hands with the vigour of a Lars Porsena doing his stuff on that bridge where even the ranks of Tuscany could scarce forbear to register approval, Fillbrook cried, 'It's the paintings, Mr Thatch, the paintings, you know. Of course I wouldn't dream of wooling – of pulling your wool, but this Mankiloe business is a very strange affair, very strange indeed. If I didn't tell you about it before, it was only because I thought you might laugh at me.'

Drawing himself up until he was practically levitating, Mr Thatch took firm control of himself and said in an icy voice, 'Have no fear of that; it is highly unlikely you will ever occasion me any merriment, Mr Fillbrook. But I must point out that your elucidations are merely dragging us further into the mud. Pull yourself together and tell me – *what* paintings are you referring to?'

'Why, the ones Inspector Thameson is holding.'

'Inspector Thameson again? What's the man doing, running a second-hand shop?'

'Not to my knowledge, sir –'

A bell pinged, interrupting them with its delicate chime as successfully as one mosquito can spoil a summer night's amour in a garden. Grunting, Thatch lumbered over to the communicator to see what it offered. He punched it and it put out its tongue of paper. Reading it with a brow of thunder and more than a hint of forked lightning, he passed it over to Fillbrook.

It came from one of the biggest stores in Wyndham, the domed city on Mercury in which the Colonial Office was established. It stated that two hundred and thirty yards of coarse second grade calico had been purchased some ten days before with a cheque drawn on a British bank. The cheque had proved un-negotiable; it was signed Hengist Mankiloe.

In an inspired attempt to avoid his superior's eyes, Fillbrook read the message through thirty-two times. So opaque a silence fell during this marathon performance, that when he did finally look up it was with the faint hope of finding that Mr Thatch had tiptoed out of the room and – for preference – tiptoed all the way back to Earth.

Alas, Mr Thatch had no intention of performing any such feat. He appeared, in fact, to be trying to qualify once more for the final round of the Most Crimson Man in the Universe championship. When he spoke, it was as if the massive slab of Old Red Sandstone which he so much resembled had given voice.

'The plot appears to thicken, Mr Fillbrook.'

'We have everything in hand, sir, Inspector Thameson and I. This communication was not entirely unexpected.'

'Mr Fillbrook. Optics, plexi, paintings, dud cheques, yards of drapery, a man called Mankiloe ... forgive me if I trespass on your treasured privacy, but WHAT THE DEVIL IS THIS ALL ABOUT?'

'O dear, not so loud, sir – the secretaries will hear you! It – It's the RODS, sir, the Research into Other Dimensions. These things all tie up ... there's a perfectly logical explanation.'

Secretary Thatch struggled for supremacy with a frog in his throat. Finally he said, 'There's been gross mismanagement in this department, Fillbrook. Your explanation must be not only perfect, not only logical – it must be forthcoming at once. I want no more dimensions than there is legislation to cover.'

'Then I think, sir, you ought to invite Inspector Thameson across. You might find Inspector Thameson's explanation more acceptable than mine.'

Thatch looked Fillbrook over from head to foot in grave irony, his eyebrows twitching up and down like two squirrels playing tag round an oak bole.

'It could hardly be less acceptable,' he said, adding in a voice fresh off a Plutonian glacier, 'Ring for Thameson immediately. I'll speak to him.'

*

Inspector Manson Thameson was an old Mercury hand. He had known Wyndham when it was a couple of air-inflated igloos. He was a small stout man with a bad complexion and ginger hair; but being a redhead with blackheads in no way spoilt his megalomaniac vision of Mercury as a fair planet and himself as its chief Sir Galahad.

Accordingly, he became piqued as the voice of the new Colonial Office Secretary barked in his ear when he lifted his receiver. Holding the instrument at arm's length hardly remedied matters; Thameson's arms were incredibly short.

'I can't come,' he said conversationally when there was a break in transmission. 'I'm busy. You come over here. I know you Colonial wallahs have nothing to do but sit on your reports all day.'

The sounds of a mature adult Thatch erupting were faithfully transmitted to him.

'Please yourself, of course,' Thameson said, and put the receiver down gently. 'We've other things to attend to.'

'Mmm of course we have, dawling,' said Diana Cashfare, adjusting herself more securely on her boss's knee. 'Who was it?'

Thameson ran his hand so amorously through her hair that she nearly screamed.

'Dawling, you've been getting so wonderfully blonde lately. ... What's that? Oh, some fellow from the Colonial Office. The new man, old Fillbrook's boss, Heathercote Thatch, you know. He won't bother us.'

Some few hundred milliseconds later, the door opened. Thatch entered.

The Matterhorn could not have put in an appearance with more dignity; nor would the Matterhorn have had the advantage of being attended by an obsequious Mr Fillbrook. Unfortunately the awe-inspiring effect of this visitation seemed lost on Inspector Thameson, who said, with only a cursory glance round, 'Stand back from this unfortunate woman. She is radioactive. I am searching her for Strontium 90 particles.'

Reluctantly concluding his topographical survey for the time, Thameson bustled the girl off-stage, and turned to put Secretary Thatch in his place.

This proved less easily done than said, and perhaps better left unsaid. At the end of quarter of an hour the two men were forced to acknowledge inwardly that if Thatch was an irresistible force personified then Thameson was an immovable object in human form. From then on they treated each other with the respect that grows between irreconcilables.

'So you've come to seek a little enlightenment on the Mankiloe affair,' Thameson said, when it was obvious they had sparred to a standstill.

'A little *explanation* ...' Thatch emended impatiently.

'Quite so, quite so, always glad to help a newcomer, Mr Thatch. It must be terrible to feel like a fish out of water. Well, first we'll go next door to the old police station.'

'Is that necessary?'

'Oh, it is necessary, sir,' Mr Fillbrook said, glad to be able to prove his existence verbally. 'You see the Inspector keeps his paintings in there.'

'So, you are an artist, Inspector?' Thatch said, surveying his opponent's carroty skull as if comprehending its significance for the first time.

'Fillbrook meant Mankiloe's paintings. You've heard of Mankiloe, I suppose?'

'He paints.' It was Thatch's bid at a punchy answer.

Shaking his head as if he had freshly taken on a wager to get one of his ears loose by Christmas, Thameson gathered up a bunch of keys and led the way outside.

Evidently hoping to remedy the ignorance of the air before him, he said, 'Hengist Mankiloe is a great painter. It may be that he is the greatest painter alive today. That hardly matters. What matters is that he still paints old-fashioned traditional style, with brush and canvas and pigment. His pictures fetch money – one of them would cover a colonial officer's salary for the thick end of three mercurian years.

'Mankiloe is known throughout the system – by anyone with any cultural pretensions. But how many people have any cultural pretensions these days? Not people like Mr Thatch and Mr Fillbrook.'

'Nonsense, Inspector, I know what I like and what I don't as well as the next man.'

'Well, that's true humility for you, when you consider the next man,' admitted Thameson, glancing at Fillbrook. 'But all I was saying is that

Mankiloe, who is a complete crook in just about every other way, has integrity when it comes to art. He won't compromise. He has remained his own man. That's why few people care for his work; it clashes with their piddling milk-fed vision of the world.'

'He sounds a detestable man.'

'It's possible to detest the man and admire the artist. Anyhow, it was because so many people on Earth found him detestable – or rather because he found so many of them destestable, that he came to Mercury. Since when he has been a thorn in my ample side. But it may be that he has also discovered another dimension; I for one would be delighted if it was an artist rather than one of these goddamned toffee-nosed scientists who did it.'

The signs that Thatch was winding himself up for a burst of controversy were three: a pavement-pulverising emphasis in his tread, a tendency to smoulder about the neckline, and an increased air-intake with high decibel yield. He was about to burst into argument if not flame when they reached the ancient shack which had housed all the Wyndham police in the dear dead days when Thameson was all the Wyndham police.

Unlocking the door, the Inspector led the way in.

The room was large and bare, with a great desk that resembled a medieval stocks in one corner, a clock whose hands – not of the best plastic – had curled into a derisory gesture, and various notices and rude epithets on the walls. Some of the latter, most of them questioning the legitimacy of the Wyndam police, were obscured by a row of canvases turned outwards along one wall so defiantly that Thatch shied towards them like a Turkish charger confronting the giaour.

Mankiloe's paintings were seven in number. Three were large, three or four feet wide by seven high; one was about four feet square; the others were smaller, going down to a rectangle nine inches wide by some twenty inches high.

'They're mere daubs!' Thatch exclaimed at once.

'Don't show your ignorance, man. Take a minute to look at them – they took days to paint.'

The canvases were recognisably on the same theme. The subjects they represented were a disquieting blend of abstract and surrealist, difficult to describe. In one, a recognisable stretch of Mercurian silicate desert merged into a curious distortion of towers where objects like plumes floated or lay. In another, things remotely like tractors, had tractors ever been built of woolly balls, distended themselves into a tranced brown twilight. In the third, the brown twilight was predominant; fluttering objects like falling books could be seen. In the fourth, behind a recognisable boulder, something: like an attenuated bus swathed in grey bunting was surrounded by wavering figures. In the fifth, the brown twilight was back, but punctuated by a curious object resembling the hull of a ship; but distortion and compression rendered its true shape unguessable.

The last two paintings bore an obvious relationship to each other. The smallest, the narrow rectangle, was of an inhuman figure; the other was, or appeared to be, a facial portrait of the figure.

It was difficult to be more explicit than that. The figure was golden, a hard unearthly gold, with three stilt-like legs and a polyhedric head. Either it was swathed in strips of cloth and armless, or it was naked and had several 'arms'. The distortion, fore-shortening, and blurring effects evident in the other pictures were, equally obtrusive here; they seemed to be less a freak technique than the artist's deliberate attempt to capture something uncapturable. In the painting of the head, blurring was again present. The polyhedric shape was clear enough; several planes rose into nodes which might have been taken for features.

The execution of all seven canvases was forceful. Here and there the paint protruded almost an inch from the rest, as if the artist had been forced to try to overcome the limitations of his medium.

'Extraordinary!' said Thatch.

Fillbrook turned to gaze in astonishment at his superior. In three weeks less a day this solitary breathed word was the only intimation he had had that Thatch could be impressed by the work of his fellow men. Like one quickly slipping a medical boot over an Achilles heel, Thatch added, 'Extraordinary rubbish, I should say. Now perhaps you'll tell me what all this has to do with an optician in Hong Kong and the fourth dimension.'

Tearing his gaze from the paintings and facing Thatch with the visible effort of a butler disentangling two flypapers, Inspector Thameson shook his body into a somewhat more spherical shape and said, 'No time for that. I'm just off to arrest a man.'

'Inspector, I came to see you expressly for the purpose of eliciting from you an explanation –'

'You may have heard of the man. His name is Hengist Mankiloe. Profession, artist. Whereabouts, out towards Brittling's Gap on the edge of the West Salt Desert not a hundred miles from here. Want to come along, boys?'

As he spoke, Thameson had begun towards the door like a one-man stampede, leaving his companions little chance to argue.

'We've no reason to go,' Fillbrook said feebly. He personally knew of explorers who after returning from the West Salt Desert had spent the rest of their days in a refrigerated asylum clinging to the conviction that they were Tournedos steaks *bien cuit*.

'We've every reason,' said Thatch, flinging his legs into gear. Even the Salt Deserts were preferable to self-accusations that he was pampering underlings. Puffing after the nearest upholder of the law, he asked, 'What made you decide so suddenly to arrest this man, Inspector?'

'I caught sight of that communication about the bouncing cheque Mankiloe tried to pass for the calico. It was stuck in your fist while you stood gawking at his paintings. It gives me the pretext I need for entering his caravan.'

'Caravan?'

'Don't ask so many questions. Fillbrook, tell your new boss about how there's no air on Mercury outside these domes, so that itinerants have to live in caravans.'

He bounded along under the polarised dome, a round determined man with a long indeterminate shadow. Behind him two stalwarts of empire strove to keep up and their dignity at the same time. They crossed Sun Avenue at a controlled canter and burst into the vehicle yard of the new Police HQ with some breath still in hand.

A sergeant came forward, listened to Thameson's instructions, and led him over to a waiting bubbletrack.

'Excellent,' Thameson said. 'Keep a watch for my automatic signal over UVHF, sergeant, but send a search party out for us if we are not back in this yard in twenty-four hours.'

'Very good, sir.'

At this exchange, both Fillbrook and Thatch quailed. Their eyes met, as far as that was possible across the natural hazard of Thatch's mustache. Something akin to mutual sympathy flickered there, like a shy fish in a large cold pond.

'Do you really think we ought to go, sir?' Fillbrook bleated.

The fish nose-dived into the murky depths.

'Duty, Fillbrook. I mean to get to the bottom of this,' snapped Thatch.

'Then get to the top of this,' urged Thameson, indicating the rung ladder up the side of the bubbletrack. The three men climbed up and into the vehicle. Last in, Thameson lowered the bubble over them and clamped it down. Settling himself in the high driver's seat, he gave a chummy wave to the sergeant and let her roll.

They headed down Sun Avenue and out through the West lock.

'It's enough to melt the ball-bearings off a brass monkey out here,' Thameson said cheerfully, and that the refrigerated air-conditioning was not proof against self-suggestion was shown by the beads of sweat which immediately blossomed forth on Fillbrook's forehead.

All around them stretched the landscape referred to not inappositely by a leading politician as 'the backside of the universe'. Even under a sun more glorious and unkempt than Thameson's hair, the land was a sterile grey, beautified only by natural slag-hills, an occasional gay bank of ash, or the alluring black of a sluggish lead stream.

'Now, with a bit of natural scenery about us, we can relax,' said Thameson, 'and I'll fill you in on the background to the Mankiloe case ...'

'If you are standing on your head again, Joe,' Hengist Mankiloe said in measured tones, 'I'll flay you alive and use your skin for my next canvas.'

He spoke without looking round or ceasing to slash a mixture of burnt umber and sienna into one tortured corner of a canvas.

Behind him, Joe came abruptly down, his feet sweeping through a parabola culminating in a loud crash on the floor that rocked the caravan. He dived for shelter as a palette knife skimmed above his head.

Mankiloe sighed. His aim was off when his spectacles were. He turned back to the painting and the view through the vision-port, where a thing like a distorted skyscraper lumbered about the middle distance. All this post-lunch shift he had worked at fever-pitch ... which reminded him ...

'Acne, old girl,' he said conversationally, although nobody was present in the compartment, 'I suppose you don't happen to be intending to roast us, do you? Do you mind telling me what the temperature is in here?'

'At twelve noon the longitude on the meridian approaches twelve point four two litres of prussic acid.'

Wrenching himself away from his easel, Mankiloe turned and kicked at a panel of Acne, the Automated Captain and Nurse (Electronic) which coped, or was supposed to cope, with the many problems of caravan life on the equivalent of a vacuum-packed furnace floor.

'What's the matter with you, girl? Can't get any sense out of you these days.'

'It's the cafard,' Acne explained. 'You bought this pile of junk sixth hand, I myself was third hand, you've never bothered to maintenance me, and now at last the square of the hypotenuse is equal to the sum of the square root of one is minus one.'

'Okay, Acne, forget it, but let's have the place ten degrees cooler, if you can manage it.'

'A drop in temperature precedes the precipitation of snow on the southern slopes of Aspasia was Pericles' mistress. Alexander was the horse of Bucephalus the G rat who –'

'ALL RIGHT, forget it! Babs!'

Babs appeared, lightly clad in a few beads and a suspicion of chiffon. This was her first trip and Mankiloe was going to make sure it was her last. She was a success in some vital respects, but her long sessions watching the Wyndham CV interfered with Mankiloe's work.

'What's the matter, Hen? Want some more beer?' she asked, with a smile that by exhibiting her teeth left nothing else to be exhibited.

Mankiloe waited patiently until her chiffon settled before replying. This body certainly knew how to dress for a warm climate.

'Yes please, love. And see that Joe's okay. Maybe he wants to go out. He has got the fidgets.'

'So have I, come to that.'

He patted her behind absentmindedly.

'You're lovely, Babs.'

'So are you, Hen.'

'Get that beer, love, eh?'

'Okay.'

She disappeared into the other compartment where they cooked, ate and slept. Dimly he heard her chatter to Joe. Sharply he heard her squeal in surprise. She came running back into the studio without the beer.

'Hen, Hen, there's something coming – a vehicle!'

'Head'n' this way, huh?' asked Hen, hamming it up with a mid-West accent. 'Kinda reckon it must be them pesky Injuns agin.' He put on his spectacles to look at her. 'You forgot the beer, Babs.'

'But they're nearly here, Hen. Who can it be?'

The lock bell rang.

'The sound of the doorbell ringing is equal to volume times mass of the gas,' Acne announced.

'Shut your great automated trap,' said Hen.

'It's not really her fault,' Babs said in a parenthesis. 'Joe will post his crusts into her.'

As Mankiloe moved over to the door, Joe skidded forward and got there first. 'I'll go, I'll go,' he cried.

They opened up. Three men, one nose, one Great Barrier Reef mustache, and one head of hair stood without, smouldering in the tinny confines of the caravan lock.

'You're trespassing on private property,' said Mankiloe mildly. 'Get out.'

'I know my Mercurian law as well as you do, Mankiloe,' Thameson replied, rolling forward as if he had been specially constructed to test the maximum load of caravan floors. 'We're police, and I have here a warrant for your arrest on which the ink is hardly dry. Anything you say may be taken either up or down in evidence.'

'That's a different kettle of fish; why didn't you say that in the first place?' Mankiloe asked defensively as he removed the paint brush from his mouth.

'He did,' said Thatch.

'I'll handle this,' said Thameson.

'Thank goodness,' said Fillbrook.

Thameson patted Joe's head.

'A nice kid you have here. Yours, Mankiloe?'

'Hell, does he look like mine?'

A friendly atmosphere having thus been established, they settled down to business. Babs appeared after a brief interval clad in something less revealing, chiefly because she had nothing *more* revealing, and served beer.

'First time I've ever sampled beer at boiling point,' said Thatch, mainly to keep his end up and his stomach down, for the bumpy ride over the desert had shaken his equilibrium.

'The sale of beer has been the subject of license ever since 1869, when brewers paid tax on every hundred barrels of Beerbohm, an essayist and stylist who rose to fame in the 1890s ...' said Acne.

'Pay no attention to her,' Mankiloe told his guests. 'Her beer-Beerbohm circuits appear to be shorting; they're probably adjacent. As for the temperature of the beer, I apologise. Our fridge and oven are also adjacent and there too Acne seems to be in some confusion. What can I do for you gentlemen?'

That Inspector Thameson was pulling himself together was externally evidenced only from a series of undulations of his sacrocostal area, as if in the battle to adjust himself, his ilium had become a second Ilium. The truth was, his preconceptions about artists were strong; he had expected a rebel painter like Mankiloe, this little wisp of a stoat of a man before him, to look slightly more capable of waving a banner at a barricade. However, since he was not one to take refuge in confused silence, he burst into confused speech.

'I have reason to suppose you have in your possession, Hengist Mankiloe, two hundred and thirty yards of fabric; to specify, coarse second grade calico.'

'Golly, did the cheque bounce?' groaned Mankiloe. He caught a wolf-like grin of satisfaction on Thatch's face and added, 'You can have it back intact if you like. This trip I decided to paint on hardboard instead.'

'That's right,' Babs said. 'He's pulled out all the panelling in the kitchen to paint on. That's how Joe is able to stuff crusts into Acne.'

Joe stood on his head in confirmation, Fillbrook stared at Babs in envy.

'If we can return the goods intact,' Thameson said, 'no doubt we can get this matter straightened out. I'll hold that rap over your head, Mankiloe, to ensure I get satisfactory answers to my main line of questions.'

'Ah ha, I didn't think you came all this way just for a few yards of canvas. Well?'

Scowling as when a kraken awakes with a hangover, Thatch said, 'We want to know what your paintings really represent.'

Thameson waved him into silence with his beer mug and assumed a judicial air.

'Supposing we lay a hypothesis before you, Mankiloe?'

'As you please.'

'All right. Supposing we – you and me and these gentlemen and even that half-clad young lady there – were standing all unknowing on the brink of a revolutionary discovery. Supposing you could be the instrument of that discovery. Supposing you knew you could, but because you were a bit antisocial you were holding out on the world and impeding progress.'

'Supposing your views and mine of what is progress did not coincide,' said Mankiloe sharply.

'Joe, you go and play in the other room before there's an argument,' Babs urged softly. She knew that progress and Mankiloe were as antithetical as prose style and communist manifestoes.

Inspector Thameson slapped his legs and took a new tack.

'Let me put a story to you, Mankiloe. Suppose we have a young artist. He's pretty good, becomes known to connoisseurs, but critics agree his subjects are pretty plebeian.

'Suppose this young artist, after a few chastening rubs with authority, decided Earth is over-civilised and heads out for a backwater like Mercury. Let's go on to suppose he buys an old space-sealed caravan sixth-hand, and in it makes various forays into the Twilight Zone of Mercury. And there he does a lot of paintings.'

They were all listening carefully. Even Fillbrook switched his gaze from Babs to Thameson with the sound of a rubber suction pad tearing off a steel wall.

Becoming somewhat histrionic under such rapt attention, Thameson rose and flung out a hand towards the nearest port.

'Look at that landscape simmering out there, gentlemen. That was what our hypothetical young artist had to paint. Dust, rock; debris. Fields of lava, no fields of grass. No trees – mountains of ash, but never a mountain ash. Blinding brightness, dense shadow, and a featureless plain that is plainly featureless.

'And yet – and yet, gentlemen –'

'Cut out the rhetoric, Thameson,' Thatch interposed testily.

'And yet, gentlemen and Mr Thatch, those are not the objects that our imaginary artist paints. Until now, he is an artist who has always depicted what he sees. He is not a surrealist; he is neither the exploiter nor the victim of his subconscious. He *paints what he sees*. And what does he see? Ha! Indescribable things, weird things – things you might say that could only belong to another dimension!'

He lowered his voice into a whisper and his bulk into a chair, pointed a finger at Mankiloe and proceeded.

'Now then. Some of these revolutionary paintings sell in London, where they come under the scrutiny of certain gentlemen of the Royal Society. These certain gentlemen, as it happens, are doing research into the findings of the First and Second Mercurian Geogravitic Expeditions which took place recently.

'The curious thing is that these paintings seem to link up in an odd way with the expeditions' findings, which were otherwise inexplicable. For one thing, the findings showed several considerable perturbations in magnetic and gravitic flow on the surface of Mercury; these perturbations were not static, but moved apparently at random over the Twilight Zone, just as our imaginary artist friend did.

'What was more, after careful inquiry the Royal Society gentlemen found that the movements of the major perturbation and our minor artist coincided.'

With a nervous gesture, Mankiloe pulled off his spectacles, mopping first them and then his countenance. Thameson noted the gesture and moved in his seat with such ponderous dignity that Acne was inspired to announce: 'Earth's greatest mountain range is the subterranean Mid-Atlantic range, which is over 7,000 miles long.'

'Silence! Proceed, Inspector Thameson,' ordered Thatch.

'I was about to. The next step in the inquiry was to place the whole matter into the capable, conscientious – never mind inspired – hands of a man actually on the spot, a highly talented individual we will call Inspector X.

'Now the Royal Society was fortunate in its man. Inspector X had not only a wide knowledge of matters scientific at his fingers; he also had a unique appreciation of things artistic. And he had imagination. With the comparative nearness of the sun, unusual stresses are formed on Mercury's surface that may form lesions in the fabric of space. It did not take the Inspector long to grasp that these gravitic plexuses, as the perturbations are called, might well be the gateways to other dimensions and other worlds.

'He got in touch with the RODS operative – Research Into Other Dimensions – and that gentleman confirmed the likelihood of the Inspector's supposition about the gateways.

'Obviously this artist fellow could see through these gateways. The question the wily Inspector next asked himself was – why should he alone be able to see through them? And the answer would seem to lie in the peculiar construction of the artist's eye.

'The artist, who was a little fellow like you, Mankiloe, wore specs just like you. So our Inspector cabled off to Earth to make a few inquiries. Eventually he got a highly satisfactory answer.

'It appears our artist had bummed around a bit before leaving Earth. He lit out for Mercury from the space port in Hong Kong, but before leaving there he had had a new pair of spectacles made in the Celestial Chuckle Ophthalmic Studios. These studios in due course forwarded details, forwarded exact details of a rare type of astigmatism from which the artist suffered, and which his spectacles were designed to alleviate.'

With a well-timed gesture the Inspector leapt forward and twitched the spectacles from Hengist Mankiloe's nose.

'And, gentlemen, here by more than coincidence is the very pair of glasses to which I refer.'

He waved them aloft.

'Notice that on the nose-piece or bridge is stamped the word "Ha-ha", the trade mark of the Hong Kong optician in question. So let us descend from fantasy to fact. *I*, gentlemen, am Inspector X. Hengist Mankiloe, you are the painter!'

Calmly, Mankiloe retrieved his spectacles and wedged them back into place.

'You have been ingenious, Inspector, you have been thorough, whereas I on the other hand am going to have another beer. But where does all this airy-fairy nonsense get you? Where does it get me?'

'It's going to get you into trouble if you don't watch your step,' Fillbrook said.

'Quiet, Fillbrook,' Thatch ordered. 'This needs handling with tact. *I'll* speak to him.'

He squared his shoulders and advanced on the painter.

'Listen, Mankiloe, we're going to let the Army Technical Wing have these astigmatism specifications. They're going to build big lenses with the same properties as your eyes. Obviously it just happens that your retina defects coincide with the degree of stress in the major gravitic plexus. But once we are equipped with these lenses, we'll be able to see what you see. How do you like that?'

'I dislike it intensely,' Mankiloe said. 'Just as I dislike you intensely.' He turned to the Inspector.

'Mind you, I'm admitting nothing, but suppose this were all true. Suppose these Army lenses were made and you people discovered this new dimension. Then what would you do?'

'Well, er … the question of colonisation would naturally arise …' The Inspector seemed ill at ease.

'Of course it would, and that would be my province,' Thatch said, coming to the fore again with the verve of a heavyweight back off diet on to red meat again. 'We'd go in with guns, prepared to meet any trouble the natives felt inclined to offer us.'

'The Strychnos Nux-Vomica is an Indian tree of the family Loganiacae. It contains strychnine, the formula for which is $C_{21}H_{20}O_2N_2$. Strymon, Struma Strutt, Struve, Strumica in Macedonia …' interposed Acne, pursuing her own line of reasoning.

'Shuddup!' said Babs, who had crept back in on the discussion carrying Joe.

A momentary silence fell in the caravan. Then Thameson thumped the half-finished painting on Mankiloe's easel.

'This weird object you're painting now, Mankiloe. Looks like a cross between a Victorian hat stand and a guillotine-maker's do-it-yourself kit. You didn't invent that. You can *see* it outside when you take your glasses off, can't you? Come clean, man!'

'Inspector, do you like my paintings?'

'Why, yes, I do. They take a bit of getting used to ... But – well, suppose this hat-stand affair was one of their trees?'

'Good guessing, Inspector. And suppose I told you several items you couldn't guess? Suppose I told you that once you could see into that other world you could walk into it. That it was a wonderland completely new – a dimension where nothing was the same as ours, where new standards of beauty and behaviour existed, where you could ever find things beyond imagining, fresh colours, different perspectives, and even alien qualities in your own body. So that everyone, even the most plebeian person, could just walk in and enjoy an overpoweringly intense aesthetic experience such as only a few rare visionaries have hitherto managed to qualify for ...'

'What a holiday centre it would make!' exclaimed Fillbrook, polishing his nose in excitement.

'Go on, Mankiloe,' said Thameson tensely.

'Don't tell them any more, Hen!' Babs said.

But Mankiloe had removed his glasses and was gazing out of the window like Keats sticking his head through a magic casement and casing the joint for fairy lands forlorn.

'And supposing that enchanting place were full of enchanting creatures, beings entirely outside our limited sphere of reference. Suppose these people were curious to look on, like a cross between an insect and an involved figure in a geometry book. Suppose they were golden, of a hard unearthly gold, and had dodecahedric heads, with only a blurred suspicion of features ... And suppose these people were as innocent as children and as powerful as devils.'

'Could they come and go into this world?'

'Yes, though with your everyday eyes you might not recognise them.'

'All right, Mankiloe,' Thatch said, in the manner of one who has endured shilly-shally long enough. 'Obviously this place, this dimension is ripe for exploitation. You've admitted it exists and –'

'I've admitted nothing!' Mankiloe said. 'I said "suppose" all the time. I'm an artist; I live in a world of suppose. You've come here on a wild goose chase, the bunch of you.'

'Not so fast, not so fast,' Thameson said. 'My friend didn't mean what he was saying about exploitation.'

142

'Or about going in armed? Or about establishing holiday centres? Rubbish! I tell you I know nothing! I paint what I imagine. Now take this wretched calico and get out of here.'

'You're lying to us, Mankiloe!'

Mankiloe laughed.

'Of course I'm not. I was kidding you along, that's all. Now I'm tired of the joke and I want to get on with my painting. There's the door. Kindly use it.'

Nonplussed, Thatch, Thameson, and Fillbrook fell back like factory owners confronted by a stray shop steward.

'Look, Mr Mankiloe, we have got all the facts,' Fillbrook said feebly.

'A few theories and a Chinese prescription – that's all you have! Take 'em and go.'

'We shall pursue this matter to the limit,' Thatch threatened.

'Not in my caravan you won't. Good-bye.'

Recognising defeat, Inspector Thameson picked up the bale of calico and passed it to Fillbrook to carry.

'You know, Mankiloe,' he said, pausing reluctantly by the air lock, 'I'm sorry you have to be like this. One of these pictures – a small one I hold back at Wyndham – it looks almost as if it might have been a child from a strange dimension – polyhedric head, golden skin, just as you said. I thought it was a beauty. I'm sorry – well, I'm sorry it's not true.'

'Good, day, Inspector. No charge for the beer.'

Defeated, the three men disappeared.

Mankiloe, Babs and Joe climbed into the blister to watch the bubble-track crawl off over the desert in a cloud of dust.

'Prothyle is hypothetical primitive matter from which all the chemical elements are supposed to be formed,' Acne said sadly.

'It's all hypothetical,' agreed Mankiloe. 'What those blighters will do, I mean.'

'Oh, Hen, I'm sure they won't rest with your explanation,' Babs said, obviously concerned.

'Probably not.' He removed his glasses and wiped his face wearily. Then he patted Joe's little golden dodecahedric head.

'We'd better go and tell your parents to get their solar annihilators ready,' he said.

Sector Azure

Even in a survey of contemporary Starswarm so brief as this it would be absurd not to look at the most used form of galactic transportation.

The mattermitters of Sector Yellow and the Burst, or the leisurely light-pushers that are popular in remote regions like sectors Grey or Violet, carry between them only fifteen per cent of the galaxy's traffic. Small ferry ships and freighters such as those operated by TransBurst Traders account for another eighteen per cent. The rest of the tonnage, goods or passenger, plunges through phase space in FTL (faster-than-light) ships.

The history of the starships is too well known for us to need to go into it here. Many civilisations go through phases in their development when their most typical transport is the oxcart, the stagecoach, or some kind of train. Particularly in their obsolescent stages, these forms of transport excite much affection.

But the FTL ships are most loved of all. They have taken many forms. Always they are just developing or becoming obsolete in some parts of Starswarm. We know that Dansson and the Fire Planets of Sector Diamond cut themselves off from the rest of the galaxy during Eras 83, 84 and 85, and forbade all movement by FTL to or from their planets.

Such post-technological epochs are common. They pass – indeed, under the Theory of Multigrade Superannuation, they must pass. Then the FTL ships roar back.

The following narrative deals with an incident in Sector Azure, where they are developing new (for them) braking systems for their ships. The story, however, does not concern technicalities. It shows what can happen to human character when influenced by new technologies.

If you will, you can regard it as a study in a new (for Azure) perversion. Or you may prefer to think of it as an example of the old (for Azure) problem of where a man should direct his love.

Murrag lay on the ground to await consummation. It was less than five minutes away, and it would fall from the air.

The alarms had sounded near and distant. Their echoes had died from the high hills of Region Six. Stretched full length on the edge of a grassy cliff, Murrag Harri adjusted the plugs in his ears and laid his fume mask ready by his side.

Everything was calm and silent now, the whole world silent. And in him there was a growing tension, as strange and ever delightful as the tensions of love.

He raised oculars to his eyes and peered into the valley, where lay the Flange, that wide and forbidden highway down which the starships blazed. Even from his elevation, he could hardly discern the other side of the Flange; it ran east-west right round the equator of Tandy Two, unbroken and unalterable, an undeviating – he'd forgotten the figure – ten, was it, or twelve, or fifteen miles wide. In the sunlight the innumerable facets of the Flange glittered and moved.

His glasses picked out the mountains on the south side of the Flange. Black and white they were, gnawed as clean as a dead man's ribs under the abrasion of total vacuum.

'I must bring Fay here before she goes back to Earth,' he said aloud. 'Wonderful, wonderful.' Assuming a different tone, he said, 'There is terror here on Tandy's equator, terror and sublimity. The most awesome place in Starswarm. Where vacuum and atmosphere kiss: and the kiss is a kiss of death! Yes. Remember that: "The kiss is a kiss of death."'

In his little leisure time Murrag was writing – he had been ever since I first met him – a book about Tandy Two as he experienced it. Yet he knew, he told me, that the sentences he formed there on the hill were too highly coloured, too big, too false. Under his excitement, more truthful images struggled to be born.

While they struggled, while he lay and wished he had brought Fay with him, the starship came in.

This! This was the moment, the fearsome apocalyptic moment! Unthinking, he dropped his oculars and ducked his head to the earth, clinging to it in desperate excitement with all his bones from his toes to his skull.

Tandy Two *lurched*.

The FTL ship burst into normal space on automatic control, invisible and unheard at first. Boring for the world like a metal fist swung at a defenceless heart, it was a gale of force. It was brutality ... but it skimmed the Flange as gently as a kiss brushes a lover's cheek.

Yet so mighty was that gentleness that for an instant a loop of fire was spun completely around Tandy Two. Over the Flange a mirage flickered: a curious elongated blur that only an educated retina could take for the after-image of a faster-than-light ship chasing to catch up with its object. Then a haze arose, obscuring the Flange. Cerenkov radiations flickered outward, distorting vision.

The transgravitic screens to the north of the Flange – on Murrag's side of it, and ranged along the valley beneath his perch – buckled but held, as they always held. The towering BGL pylons were bathed in amber. Atmosphere and vacuum roared at each other from either side of the invisible screens. But as ever, the wafer-thin geogravitics held them apart, held order and chaos separate.

A gale swept up the mountainsides.

The sun jerked wildly across the sky.

All this happened in one instant.

And in the next moment it was deepest night.

Murrag dug his hands out of the soft earth and stood up. His chest was soaked with sweat, his trousers were damp. Trembling, he clamped his fume mask over his face, guarding himself against the gases generated by the FTL's passage.

Tears still ran down his face as he limply turned to make his way back to the highland farm.

'Kiss of death, embrace of flame ...' he muttered to himself as he climbed aboard his tractor; but still the elusive image he wanted did not come.

In a fold of hills facing north lay the farmhouse, burrowed deeply into the granite just in case of accidents. Murrag's lights washed over it. Its outhouses were terraced below it, covered pen after covered pen, all full of Farmer Dourt's sheep, locked in as always during entry time; not a single animal could be allowed outside when an FTL came down.

Everything lay still as Murrag drove up in his tractor. Even the sheep were silent, crouching mutely under the jack-in-a-box dark. Not a bird flew, not an insect sparked into the lights; such life had almost died out during the hundred years the Flange had been in operation. The toxic gases hardly encouraged fecundity in nature.

Soon Tandy itself might rise to shine down on its earthlike second moon. The planet Tandy was a gas giant, a beautiful object when it rose into Tandy Two's skies, but uninhabitable and unapproachable.

Tandy One equally was not a place for human beings. But the second satellite, Tandy Two, was a gentle world with mild seasons and an oxygen-nitrogen atmosphere. People lived on Tandy Two, loved, hated, struggled, aspired there as on any of the multitudinous civilised planets in Sector Azure, but with this difference: that because there was something individual about Tandy Two, there was something individual about its problems.

The southern hemisphere of Tandy Two lay lifeless under vacuum; the northern existed mainly for the vast terminal towns of Blerion, Touchdown and Ma-Gee-Neh. Apart from the cities, there was nothing but grassland – grass and lakes and silicone desert stretching to the pole. And by courtesy an occasional sheep farm was allowed on the grasslands.

'What a satellite!' Murrag exclaimed, climbing from the tractor. Admiration sounded in his voice. He was a curious man, Murrag Harri – but I'll stick to fact and let you understand what you will.

He pushed through the spaced double doors that served the Dourt farmstead as a crude air lock when the gases were about. In the living-eating-cooking complex beyond, Col Dourt himself stood by the CV watching its colours absently. He looked up as Murrag removed his face mask.

'Good *evening*, Murrag,' he said with heavy jocularity. 'Great to see so nice a morning followed by so nice a night without so much as a sunset in between.'

'You should be used to it by now,' Murrag murmured, hanging his oculars with his jacket in the A-G cupboard. After being alone in the overwhelming presence of Tandy, it always took him a moment to adjust to people again.

'So I should, so I should. Fourteen earth years and I still see red to think how men have bollixed about with one of God's worlds. Thank heaven we'll be off this crazy moon in another three weeks! I can't wait to see Droxy, I'm telling you.'

'You'll miss the grasslands and the open spaces.'

'So you keep telling me. What do you think I am? One of my sheep! Just as soon —'

'But once you get away —'

'Just a minute, Murrag!' Dourt held up a brown hand as he cocked his eye at the CV. 'Here comes Touchdown to tell us if it's bedtime yet.'

Murrag halted on the way upstairs to his room. He came back to peer into the globe with the shepherd. Even Hoc the house dog glanced up momentarily at the assured face that appeared in the bright bowl.

'CVA Touchdown talking,' the face said, smiling at its unseen audience. 'The FTL ship *Droffoln* made a safe and successful entry on the Flange some three hundred and twenty miles outside Touchdown station. As you can see from this live shot, passengers are already being met by helicar and taken to the FTL port in Touchdown. The *Droffoln* comes from Ryvriss XIII in Sector Maroon. You are looking at a typical Ryvrissian now. He is, as you observe, octipedal.

'We will bring you news and interviews with passengers and crews when all the occupants of the FTL have undergone revival. At present they remain under light-freeze.

'We go now to Chronos-Touchdown for the revised time check.'

The assured face gave way to a shaggy one. Behind it, the untidy computing room of this astronomical department greeted viewers. The shaggy face smiled. 'As yet we have only a rough scheme for you. It will, as usual, take a little while to feed accurate figures into our pressors, and some reports have still to come in.

'Meanwhile, here is an approximate time check. The FTL ship entered Flange influence at roughly 1219 hours 47·66 seconds today, Seventeenday of Cowl Month. Impetus-absorption thrust Tandy through approximately 108·75 degrees axial revolution in approximately 200 milliseconds. So the time at the end of that very short period became roughly 1934 hours 47·66 seconds.

'Since that was about twenty-four and a half minutes ago, the time to which everyone in Touchdown zone should set their watches and clocks is … coming up … 1959 hours and 18 seconds … Now! I repeat, the time is now 1959 hours, one minute to eight o'clock at night, plus 18 seconds.

'It is still, of course, Seventeenday of Cowl.

'We shall be back to bring you more accurate information on the time in another two hours.'

Dourt snorted and switched the globe off. It slid obediently out of sight into the wall.

'Here I've just had my midday bite,' he growled, 'and there's Bes upstairs putting the kids to bed!'

'That's what happens on Tandy Two,' Murrag replied, edging from the room. Without wishing to seem rude, he was bored with Dourt's complaints, which occurred with little variation once a fortnight – whenever, in fact, an FTL ship arrived. He almost scuttled up the stairs.

'It may happen on Tandy Two,' Dourt said, not averse to having only Hoc to talk to, 'but that don't mean to say Col Dourt has to like it.' He squared his broad shoulders, thrust out his chest, and stuck his thumbs in his spunsteel jacket. 'I was born on Droxy, where a man gets twenty-four hours to his day – every day.'

Hoc thumped his tail idly as if in ironic applause.

As Murrag came upstairs, Tes marched past him on her way from the washing room. She was absolutely naked.

'High time the girl was taken to civilisation and learned the common rules of decency,' Murrag thought good-humouredly. The girl was several months past her thirteenth birthday. Perhaps it was as well the Dourt family were off back to Droxy in three weeks.

'Going to bed at this hour of the day!' Tes grunted, not deigning to look at her father's helper as she thudded past him.

'It's eight o'clock at night. The man on the CV has just said so,' Murrag replied.

'Poof!'

With that she disappeared into her room. Murrag entered into his room. He took the time changes in his stride; on Tandy now the changes had to be considered natural, for use can almost change the stamp of nature. Life on the farm was rigorous. Murrag, Dourt and his wife rose early and went to sleep early. Murrag planned to lie and think for an hour, possibly to write a page more of his book, and then to take a somnuliser and sleep till four the next morning.

His thinking had no time to grow elaborate and deep. The door burst open and Fay rushed in, squealing with exuberance.

'Did you see it? Did you see it?' she asked.

He had no need to ask to what she referred.

'I sat on the top of a cliff and watched it,' he said.

'You *are* lucky!' She did a pirouette, and pulled an ugly grimace at him. 'That's what I call my life-begins-at-forty face, Murrag; did it scare you? Oh, to see one of those starships actually plunk down in the Flange. Tell me all about it!'

Fay wore only vest and knickers. A tangle of arms and legs flashed as she jumped onto the bed beside him and began tugging his ears. She was Tes's younger sister and, six years old, the storm centre of the household.

'You're supposed to be in bed. Your mother will be after you, girl.'

'She's always after me. Tell me about the starships, and how they land, and –'

'When you've wrenched my ears off, I will.'

He was not easy with her leaning on him. Rising, he pointed out of his little window with its double panes. Since his room was at the front of the farmhouse, he had this view out across the valley. The girls slept in a room considered more safe, at the back of the house, tucked into solid granite ('the living granite', Dourt always called it), and without windows.

'Outside there now, Fay,' he said, as the little girl peered into the dark, 'are vapours that would make you ill if you inhaled them. They are breathed off by the Flange under the stress of absorbing the speed of the FTL ships. The geogravitic screens on this side of the Flange undergo terrific pressures and do very peculiar things. But the beautiful part is that when we wake in the morning the odours will all have blown away; Tandy itself, this marvellous moon we live on, will absorb them and send us a fresh supply of clean mountain air to breathe.'

'Do the mountains have air?'

'We call the air on the mountains "mountain air". That's all it means.'

As he sat down beside her, she asked, 'Do the vapours make it dark so quickly?'

'No they don't, Fay, and you know they don't. I've explained that before. The faster-than-light ships do that.'

'Are the vaster-than-light ships dark?'

'*Faster*-than-light. No, they're not dark. They come in from deep space so fast – at speeds above that of light, because those are the only speeds they can travel at – that they shoot right around Tandy one and a half times before the Flange can stop them, before its works can absorb the ship's momentum. And in so doing they twirl Tandy around a bit on its axis with them.'

'Like turntables?'

'That's what I told you, didn't I? If you ran very fast onto a light wooden turntable that was not moving, you would stop, but your motion would make the turntable turn – transference of energy, in other words. And this twirling sometimes moves us around from sunshine into darkness.'

'Like today. I bet you were scared out on the hillside when it suddenly got dark!'

He tickled her in the ribs.

'No I wasn't, because I was prepared for it. But that's why we have to get your Daddy's sheep all safely under cover before a ship comes – otherwise *they'd* all get scared and jump over precipices and things, and then your Daddy'd lose all his money and you wouldn't be able to go back to Droxy.'

Fay looked meditatively at him.

'Those vaster-than-light ships are rather a nuisance to us, aren't they?' she said.

Murrag roared with laughter.

'If you put it like that –' he began, when Mrs Dourt thrust her head around the door.

'There you are, Fay! I thought as much. Come and get into bed at once.'

Bes Dourt was a solid woman in her early forties, plain, very clean. She of them all was least at home on Tandy Two, yet she seldom grumbled about it; among all her many faults one could not include grumbling. She marched into Murrag's room and seized her younger daughter by the wrists.

'You're killing me!' Fay yelled in feigned agony. 'Murrag and I were discussing transparency of energy. Let me kiss him good night and then I'll come. He is a lovely man, and I wish he was coming to Droxy with us.'

She gave Murrag an explosive buss that rocked him backward. Then she rushed from the room. Bes paused before following; she winked at Murrag.

'Pity you don't like anyone else to carry on a bit more in that style, Mr Harri,' she said, and shut the door after her as she left.

It was something of a relief to him that her advances were now replaced by nothing more trying than innuendo. Murrag put his feet up on the bed and lay back.

He looked around the room with its spare plastic furniture. This would be home for only three weeks more: then he would move on to work for Farmer Cay in Region Five. Nothing would he miss – except Fay, who alone among all the people he knew shared his curiosity and his love for Tandy Two.

A phrase of hers floated back to him – 'the vaster-than-light ships'. Oddly appropriate name for craft existing in 'phase space', where their mass exceeded 'normal' infinity! His mind began to play with the little girl's phrase; reverie overcame him, so that in sinking down into a nest of his own thought he found, even amid the complexity gathered around him, a comforting simplicity, a simplicity he had learned to look for because it told him that to see clearly into his own inner nature, he had merely to crystallise the attraction Tandy Two held for him and all would be clear eternally; he would be a man free of shackles, or free at least to unlock them when he wished. So again, as on the cliff and as many times before, he plunged through the deceptions of the imagination towards that wished-for truthful image.

Perhaps his search itself was a delusion; but it led him to sleep.

Murrag and Dourt were out early in the cool hour before dawn. The air, as Murrag had predicted, was sweet to breathe again, washed by a light rain.

Hoc and the other dog – Pedo, the yard dog – ran with them as they whistled out the autocollics. Ten of them came pogoing into the open, light machines unfailingly obedient to the instructions from Dourt's throat mike. Although they had their limitations, they could herd sheep twice as quickly as live dogs. Murrag unlocked the doors of the great covered pens. The autocollies went in to get the sheep as he climbed aboard his tractor. The sheep poured forth, bleating into the open, and he and Dourt revved their engines and followed behind, watching as the flock fanned out towards the grasslands. They bumped along, keeping the autocollies constantly on course.

Dawn seeped through the eastern clouds, and the rain stopped. Filmy sun created miracles of chiaroscuro over valley and hill. By then they had the sheep split into four flocks, each established on a separate hillside. They returned to the farm in time to breakfast with the rest of the family.

'Do they get miserable wet days on Droxy like this?' Tes asked.

'Nothing wrong with today. Rain's holding off now,' her father said. Breakfast was not his best meal.

'It depends on what part of Droxy you live in, just as it does here, you silly girl,' said her mother.

'They haven't got any weather in the south half of Tandy,' Fay volunteered, talking around a mouthful, ''cuz it's had to be vacuumised so's the starships coming in at such a lick wouldn't hit any molecules of air and get wrecked, and without air you don't have weather – isn't that so, Murrag?'

Murrag agreed it was so.

'Shut up talking about the Flange. It's all you seem to think of these days, young lady,' Dourt growled.

'I never mentioned the Flange, Daddy. You did.'

'I'm not interested in arguing, Fay, so save your energy. You're getting too cheeky these days.'

She put both elbows on the plastic table and said with deliberate devilment, 'The Flange is just a huge device for absorbing FTL momentum, Daddy, as I suppose you know, don't you? Isn't it, Murrag?'

Her mother leaned forward and slapped her hard across the wrist.

'You like to sauce your Dad, don't you? Well, take that! And it's no good coming crying to me about it. It's your fault for being so saucy.'

But Fay had no intention of going crying to her mother. Bursting into tears, she flung down her spoon and fork and dashed upstairs, howling. A moment later her bedroom door slammed.

'Serve her *right!*' Tes muttered.

'You be quiet too,' her mother said angrily.

'Never get a peaceful meal now,' Dourt said.

Murrag Harri said nothing.

After the meal, as the two men went out to work again, Dourt said stiffly, 'If you don't mind, Harri, I'd rather you left young Fay alone till we leave here.'

'Oh? Why's that?'

The older man thrust him a suspicious glance, then looked away. 'Because she's my daughter and I say so.'

'Can't you give me a reason?'

A dying bird lay in the yard. Birds were as scarce as gold nuggets on Tandy Two. This one must have been overcome by the fumes generated in the previous day's entry. Its wings fluttered pitifully as the men approached. Dourt kicked it to one side.

'If you must know – because she's getting mad on the Flange. Flange, Flange, Flange, that's all we hear from the kid! She didn't know or care a thing about it till early this year, when you started telling her all about it. You're worse than Captain Roge when he calls, and he has an excuse because he works on the damn thing. So you keep quiet in the future. Bes and me will leave here with no regrets. Tes doesn't care either way. But we don't want Fay to keep thinking about this place and upsetting herself, thinking Droxy isn't her proper home, which it's going to be.'

This was a long speech for Dourt. The reasons he gave were good enough, but irritation made Murrag ask, 'Did Mrs Dourt get you to speak to me about this?'

Dourt stopped by the garage. He swung around and looked Murrag up and down, anger in his eye.

'You've been with me in Region Six nigh on four years, Harri. I was the man who gave you work when you wanted it, though I had not much need of you, nor much to pay you with. You've worked hard, I don't deny –'

'I can't see –'

'I'm talking, aren't I? When you came here you said you were – what was it – "in revolt against ultra-urbanised planets", you said you were a poet or something; you said – heck, you said a lot of stuff, dressed up in fine phrases. Remember you used to keep me and Bes up half the night listening sometimes, until we saw it was all just talk!'

'Look here, if you're –'

The farmer bunched his fists and stuck out his lower lip.

'You listen to me for a change. I've been wanting to say this for a long time. Poet indeed! We weren't taken in by your blather, you know. And luckily it had no effect on our Tes either. She's more like me than her sister – she's a quiet sensible girl. But Fay is a baby. She's silly as yet, and we reckon you're having a bad influence on her –'

'All right, you've had your say. Now I'll have mine. Leaving aside the question of whether you and your wife can understand any concept you weren't born with –'

'You be careful now, Harri, what you're saying about Bes. I'm on to you! I'm not so daft as you think. Let me tell you Bes has had about enough of you giving her the glad eye and making passes at her as if she was just some –'

'By God!' Murrag exploded in anger. 'She tells you that? The boot's on the other foot by a long chalk, and you'd better get that clear right away. If you think I'd touch – if I'd lay a hand –'

The mere thought of it took the edge off Murrag's wrath. It had the opposite effect on Dourt. He swung his left fist hard at Murrag's jaw. Murrag blocked it with his right forearm and counterattacked with his left. He caught Dourt glancingly on the ear as the farmer kicked out at him. Unable to step back in time, Murrag grabbed the steel-studded boot and wrenched it upward.

Dourt staggered back and fell heavily to the ground.

Murrag stood over him, all fury gone.

'If I had known how much you resented me all these years,' he said miserably, staring down at his employer's face, 'I'd not have stayed here. Don't worry, I'll say no more to Fay. Now let's go and get the tractors out, unless you want to sack me on the spot – and that's entirely up to you.'

As he helped the older man to his feet, Dourt muttered shamefacedly, 'I've not resented you, man, you know that perfectly well.'

Then they got the tractors out in silence.

*

The result of Dourt's fall was what he termed a 'bad back'. He was – and when he said it, he spoke with an air of surprise more appropriate to a discovery than cliché – not as young as he was. For a day or so he sat gloomily indoors by his CV, letting Murrag do the outside work, and brooding over his lot.

Tandy Two is a harder satellite to take than it seems at first – I know that after two five-year spells of duty on it. The density of its composition gives it a gravity of 1·35 Gs. And the fortnightly time hop when the FTLs enter takes a psychological toll. In the big towns, like Touchdown and Blerion, civilisation can compensate for these disadvantages. On the scattered sheep stations there are no compensations.

Moreover, Col Dourt had found his farming far less profitable than it had looked on paper from Droxy fourteen years ago. Tandy Two offered good grazing in a stellar sector full of ready-made mutton markets – twenty hundred over-urbanised planets within twice twenty light years. But his costs had been stiff, the costs of transport above all, and now he counted himself lucky to be able to get away with enough credits saved to buy a small shop on his old home planet. As it was, margins were narrow: he was reckoning on the sale of farm and stock to buy passage home for himself and his family.

Much of this I heard on my periodic tours through Region Six, when I generally managed a visit to the Dourts. I heard it all again the next time I called, thirteen days after the scuffle between Dourt and Murrag.

I looked in to see Bes, and found Dourt himself, sitting by a fire, looking surly. He had returned to work and wrenched his back again, and was having to rest it.

'It's the first time I've ever known you to be off work. Cheer up, you've only got a week to go before you'll be making tracks for home,' I said, removing my coat.

My truck was outside. Though only half a mile away by hill paths, the unit to which I was attached was at least ten miles off by the circuitous track around the mountains.

'Look how long the flaming journey back to Droxy takes when we do get off from Touchdown,' he complained. 'But with all my family I can't afford to travel FTL.'

He spoke as if the FTL ships were my responsibility, which in a sense they were.

'Even STLs are fast enough to make the subjective time of the journey no more than three or four months.'

'Don't start explaining,' he said. He waved his hand, dismissing the subject. 'You know I'm only a simple farmer. I don't grasp all the technical stuff about subjective time. I just want to get home.'

The two girls Fay and Tes came in after finishing their CV lessons. Tes was preparing lunch; eyeing me warily – she was a mistrustful creature – she told me that her mother was out helping Murrag with the flocks. Both girls came over to the farmer to join in the discussion; I coaxed Fay up onto my knee.

She wanted the whole business of how they would get home explained to her. 'You're a Flange maintenance officer, Captain Roge,' she said. 'Tell *me* all about it, and then I'll tell Daddy so's he can understand.'

'You don't have to understand,' her father said. 'We just take a ship that'll get us there eventually. That's all there is to it, thank God. The likes of us don't need to bother our heads about the technicalities.'

'I want to *know*,' Fay replied.

'It's *good* for us to listen,' Tes said, 'though *I* understand it all already. A child could understand it.'

'I'm a child and I don't understand it,' her sister said.

'The universe is full of civilised planets, and in a week's time you're all going to hop from one such to another such,' I began. And as I sought for simple words and vivid pictures to put my explanation across to them, the wonder of the universe overcame me as if for a moment I too was a child.

For the galaxy has grown up into a great and predominantly peaceful unit. Crime survives, but does not flourish. Evil lives, but knowledge keeps pace with it and fights it. Man prospers and grows kindlier rather than otherwise. Certainly our old vices are as green as ever, but we have devised sociological systems that contain them better than was the case in earlier eras.

Starships are our Starswarm's main connecting links.

Bridging all but the lesser distances are the FTL ships, travelling in super-universes at multiple-light velocities. Bridging the lesser distances go the STLs, the slower-than-light ships. The two sorts of travel are, like planetary economies, interdependent.

The FTL ship, that ultimate miracle of technology, has one disadvantage: it moves – as far as the 'normal' universe is concerned – at only two speeds: faster than light and stationary.

An FTL ship has to stop the moment it comes out of phase space and enters the quantitative fields of the normal universe. Hence the need for bodies such as Tandy Two, spread throughout the galaxy; they are the braking planets, or satellites.

An FTL cannot 'stop' in space. Instead, its velocities are absorbed by the braking planets, or, more accurately, by the impetus-absorbers of the Flanges that girdle such planets. The FTLs burst in and are reduced to zero velocity within a time limit of about 200 milliseconds – in which time they have circuited the Flange, gone completely around the planet, one and a half times.

STLs or mattermitters then disperse the passengers to local star systems much in the way that stratoliners land travellers who then disperse to nearby points by helicab.

Though STLs are slow, relativistic time contractions shorten the subjective journeys in them to tolerable limits of weeks or days.

So the universe ticks; not perfectly, but workably.

And this was what I told Dourt and his daughters.

'Well, I'd better go and finish getting your dinner, Daddy,' Tes said, after a pause.

He patted her bottom and chuckled with approval. 'That's it, girl,' he said. 'Food's more in our line than all this relativistic stuff. Give me a lamb cutlet any day.'

I had no answer. Nor had Fay, though I saw by her face that she was still thinking over what I had said, as she slid off my knee to go and help Tes. How much did it mean to her? How much does it all mean to any of us? Though Dourt had little time for theory, I also relished the thought of the lamb cutlet.

Before the food was ready, I took a turn outside with the farmer, who used his stick as support.

'You'll miss this view,' I said, gazing over the great mysterious body of Tandy whose contours were clad in green, freckled here and there with sheep. I must admit it, I am fonder of the beauties of women than of landscape; for all that, the prospect was fine. In the voluptuous downward curve between two hills, Tandy the primary was setting. Even by daylight the banded and beautiful reds swirling over its oblate surface were impressive.

Dourt looked about him, sniffing, admitting nothing. He appeared not to have heard what I said.

'Rain coming up from somewhere,' he observed.

In my turn I ignored him.

'You'll miss this view back on Earth,' I repeated.

'The view!' Dourt exclaimed and laughed. 'I'm not a clever man like you and young Murrag, Captain; I get simple satisfaction out of simple things, like being in the place where I was born.'

Although I happened to know he was born eight layers under the skyport in Burning, a Droxian manufacturing city, where they still metered your ration of fresh air, I made no answer. All he meant was that he valued his personal illusions, and there I was with him all the way. Convictions or illusions: what matter if all conviction is illusion, so long as we hang onto it? You would never shift Dourt from his, fool though he was in many ways.

I could never get under his skin as surely as I could with some people – Murrag, for instance, a more complicated creature altogether; but often the simplest person has a sort of characterless opacity about him. So it seemed with Dourt, and if I have drawn him flat and lumpy here, that was how I experienced him then.

To make talk between us, for his silence made me uneasy, I asked after Murrag.

Dourt had little to say. Instead he pointed with his stick to a tracked vehicle bumping towards us.

'That'll be Murrag with Bes now, coming home for a bit of grub,' he said.

He was mistaken. When the tractor drew nearer, we saw that only Bes was inside it.

As we strolled forward, she drove around the covered pens and pulled up beside us. Her face was flushed, and, I thought, angry looking, but she smiled when she saw me.

'Hullo, Captain Roge!' She climbed down and clasped my hand briefly. 'I was forgetting we'd be having your company today. Nice to see a strange face, though I'd hardly call yours that.' She turned straight to her husband and said, 'We got trouble on Pike's Brow. Two autocollies plunged straight down a crevasse. Murrag's up there with them now trying to get them out.'

'What were you doing up on Pike's Brow?' he demanded. 'I told you to keep number three flock over the other side while I was off work – you know it's tricky on Pike's with all that faulting, you silly woman. Why didn't you do as I told you?'

'It wouldn't have happened if my throat mike hadn't jammed. I couldn't call the autocollies off before they went down the hole.'

'Don't make excuses. I can't take a day off without something going wrong. I –'

'You've had six days off already, Col Dourt, so shut your mouth –'

'How's Harri managing?' I asked, thinking an interruption was necessary.

Mrs Dourt flashed me a look of gratitude. 'He's trying to get down the crevasse after the autocollies. Trouble is, they're still going and won't answer to orders, so they're working themselves down deeper and deeper. That's why I came back here, to switch off the juice; they work on maser-beamed power, you know.'

I heard Dourt's teeth grind. 'Then buck up and switch off, woman, before the creatures ruin themselves! You know they cost money. What're you waiting for?'

'What? For some old fool to stop arguing with me, of course. Let me by.'

She marched past us, an aggressive woman, rather plain, and yet to my taste pleasing, as though the thickness of her body bore some direct if mysterious relationship to the adversities of life. Going into the control shed, she killed the power and then came back to where we stood.

'I'll come with you, Mrs Dourt, and see what I can do to help,' I said. 'I don't need to get back to my outfit for another hour.'

A look of understanding moved across her face, and I climbed onto the tractor with her after a brief nod to Dourt.

There was some justification for this. If the situation was as she said it was, then the matter was one of urgency – the next FTL ship was due in under four hours, and forty thousand sheep had to be herded under lock and key before that. *Had to be:* or darkness would be on them, they would stampede and kill or injure themselves on the rocky slopes, and Dourt's hard-earned savings would be wiped out … that is, if the situation was as Bes said it was.

When we were out of sight of old Dourt and the farm, Bes stopped the tractor. We looked at each other. My whole system changed gear as we saw the greed in each other's eyes.

'How much of this story is a lie to get me alone and at your mercy?' I asked.

She put her hard broad hand over mine. 'None of it, Vasko. We'll have to shift back to Murrag as soon as possible, if he hasn't already broken his neck down the crevasse. But with Col hanging about the house, I couldn't have seen you alone if this opportunity hadn't turned up – and this'll be our last meeting, won't it?'

'Unless you change your mind and don't go to Droxy with him next week.'

'You know I can't do that, Vasko.'

I did know. I was safe. Not to put too fine a point on it, she'd have been a nuisance if she had stayed for my sake. There were dozens of women like Bes Dourt – one on nearly every hill farm I visited, bored, lonely, willing, only too happy to indulge in an affair with a Flange maintenance official. It was not as if I loved her.

'Then we'll make it really good this last time,' I said.

And there was the greed again, plain and undisguised and sweet. We almost fell out onto the grass. That's how these things should be: raw, unglamorised. That's the way it must be for me. Bes and I never made love. We coupled.

Afterwards, when we came to our senses, we were aware that we had been longer than we should have been. Scrambling back into the tractor, we headed fast and bumpy for Pike's Brow.

'I hope Murrag's all right,' I muttered, glancing at my arm watch.

She neither liked nor understood my perpetual interest in Murrag Harri.

'He's queer!' she sneered.

I didn't ask her to elaborate. I had heard it before, and the pattern behind it was obvious enough: Murrag disliked her hungry advances – and why not? She was plain, solid, coarse ... No, I do myself no justice saying all this, for Bes had a pure peasant honesty that in my eyes excused everything – or so I told myself.

At first when Murrag arrived at Dourt's farm, I had been jealous, afraid that he would spoil my innocent little game. When it was clear he would do no such thing, I grew interested in him for his own involved sake. Sometimes this had caused trouble between Bes and me – but enough of this; I am trying to tell Murrag's tale, not my own. If I digress, well, one life is very much tangled with the next.

We must have created some sort of a speed record to the foot of Pike's Brow. Then the terrain became so steep that we had to halt, leave the tractor, and go the rest of the way on foot.

Bending our backs, we climbed. Sheep moved reluctantly out of our path, eyeing us with the asinine division of feature that marks a Tandy sheep's face – all rabbity and timid about the eyes and nose, as arrogant as a camel about the lower lip.

Rain came on us with the unexpectedness it reserves for Region Six, as if a giant over the hump of the mountains had suddenly emptied his largest bucket across our path. I remembered Dourt's forecast as I turned up my collar. Still we climbed, watching little rivulets form among the short blades under our boots. I began to wish I hadn't volunteered for this.

At last we reached the crevasse. We scrambled along by its side towards the point where Murrag had climbed over into it, a point marked by the two live dogs, Hoc and Pedo, who sat patiently in the rain, barking at our approach.

The downpour was lessening. We stood, pulled our backbones painfully upright, and breathed the damp air deep before bothering about Murrag.

He was some twenty feet down into the crack, where it was so narrow that he could rest with his back on one side and his feet on the other. He was drenched from the water pouring over the edge; it splashed past him and gargled down into a ribbon of a stream about thirty feet beneath his boots.

One of the autocollies was wedged beside him, covered by mud. The other lay a short distance away and a little lower down, overturned but seemingly unharmed.

I noted the expression of Murrag's face. It was blank; he seemed to gaze into nothing, ignoring the rivulets that splashed around him.

'Murrag!' Bes called sharply. 'Wake up. We're back.'

He looked up at us. 'Hello,' he said. 'Hello, Vasko! I was just communing with the great earth mother. She's really swallowed me … It's funny, stuck down here in a fissure … like climbing between the lips of a whale.'

And there would have been more like that! Generally I had patience with his curious fancies, enjoyed them even, but not at such a moment, not with Bes standing there sneering, and the water running down my back, and a stitch in my side, and the time against us.

'It's raining,' I reminded him. 'In case you didn't notice, we're all wet through. For God's sake, stir yourself.'

He seemed to pull himself together, dashing wet hair back from his face. Peering upward rather stupidly, as if he were a fish, he said, 'Fine day for mountaineering, isn't it? If we're not careful, the earth under this autocollie will crumble and the machine may get wedged or damaged. As it is, it is still in working order. Fling me the rope down, Bes. You and Vasko can haul it up while I steady it.'

She stared blankly into my face. 'Damn it, I left the rope back in the tractor,' she said.

I remembered then. She unhooked it from her waist when we lay on the grass and in her haste had not bothered to tie it on again later, tossing it instead into the back of the vehicle.

'For God's sake go and get it then,' Murrag shouted impatiently, suddenly realising how long he had waited. 'I can't stay down here much longer.'

Again Bes looked at me. I gazed away down at the muddy boots.

'Go and get it for me, Vasko,' she urged.

'I'm out of breath,' I said, 'I've got the stitch.'

'Damn you!' she said. She started off down the hillside again without another word.

Murrag looked sharply at me; I did not return his stare.

It took her twenty-five minutes to return with the rope. In that time, the rain cleared entirely. I squatted by Pedo and Hoc, gazing over the dull and tumbled terrain. Murrag and I did not speak to each other.

The best part of another hour passed before we three bedraggled creatures managed to haul the autocollies up safely. We could have done the job in half the time, had we not been so careful to preserve them from harm; we all knew the balance of the Dourt finances, and the autocollie can cost anything from twenty percentages to five parapounds.

Panting, I looked at my arm watch.

In two hours less six minutes the next FTL was due for entry on Tandy Two. It was past the time I should have reported back to my unit for duty.

I told Murrag and Bes that I must be going – told them curtly, for after missing my lunch, getting a soaking, and nearly wrenching my arms off rescuing the dogs, I was none too sweet-humoured.

'You can't leave us *now*, Vasko,' Murrag said. 'The whole flock's in jeopardy, and not only this lot on the Brow. We've *got* to have every sheep under cover in two hours – and first of all someone must go back to the farm and switch the beam on again to get the dogs going. We need your help still.'

His eyes were as appealing as Bes's.

God, I thought, the way some people need people! He has his emotional requirements just as she has her physical ones. Hers are crashingly simple, his I don't understand; once these autocollie dogs were running again, they would see the sheep home in no time, without help.

Right then, I could not think of two people I would less like to be stuck on a mountain with. But all I said was, 'I'm a maintenance officer, Murrag, not a shepherd. I've made myself late for duty as it is. Since my truck's at the farm, I'll have to go back and collect it, so when I get there I'll tell Col to beam the juice to you – but from then on you're on your own.'

As I turned to go, Bes put her hand on my wrist. When I swung around on her, I saw her flinch from my expression.

'You can't just ditch us like this, Vasko,' she said.

'I'm ditching no one. I helped you drag the 'collies out, didn't I? I've got a job to do, and I'll be listed for reporting back late as it is. Now let me go.'

She dropped my hand.

I made off down the slope at a slow trot, digging my heels as I went. Now and again I slipped, falling back on the wet grass. Before I got to the level, I saw another tractor approaching.

Dourt was in it. He yelled to me as we drew nearer. 'I came to see what you lot were doing all this time. You've been taking so long I thought you'd all fallen down the hole with the 'collies.'

Briefly I told him what was happening, while he climbed slowly out of the tractor, clutching his back.

'I'm borrowing Bes's tractor to go back and switch on the juice, so that the autos can start herding as soon as possible,' I finished.

He fell to cursing, saying he was going to lose all his livestock, that they could never be driven under cover before the FTL arrived. I tried to reassure him before going over to the other vehicle.

As I climbed in he said, 'When you get there, tell Tes to come back here with the tractor. She can drive well enough, and we'll need her help. The more hands here the better. And tell her to bring the signal pistols. They'll get the sheep moving.'

'And Fay?'

'She'd only be in the way.'

Giving him a wave, I stood on the acceleration and rattled back to the farm. By now the sun was bright and the sky free of cloud, which did not stop my boots from squelching or my clothes from clinging to me like wet wallpaper.

The moment I reached the farm buildings I marched into the control shed, crossed to the appropriate board, and pushed the rheostat over. Power began its ancient song, the hum of content that sounds perpetually as if it is ascending the scale. Up on the pastures, the electronic dogs would be leaping into activity.

Everything appeared in order, though Col Dourt was not a man to keep his equipment spotless – and I reflected, not for the first time that day, that if he had cared to lay out an extra twenty parapounds or so he could have had switchboard-to-flock communication, which would have saved him valuable time on a day like this.

Well, it was not my concern.

In the living complex, Tes was alone. She stood in her slip, cutting out a dress for Droxy wear, and I surveyed her; she was developing well.

As usual, she seemed displeased to see me – baffling creatures, adolescent girls; you never know whether they are acting or not. I gave her her father's orders and told her to get out to Pike's Brow as soon as she could.

'And where's Fay?' I asked.

'It's none of your business, Captain Roge.'

As if she felt this was a bit too sharp, she added, 'And anyhow I don't know. This is one of my great not-knowing days.'

I sniffed. I was in a hurry, and it was, as she said, none of my business now, although I would have liked a farewell word with her younger sister. Nodding to Tes, I squelched out of the building, got into the maintenance truck, and began speeding back to my unit around the other side of the mountains. To perdition with all Dourts!

Murrag used to say that there wasn't a more interesting job than mine on all Tandy. Though he was prepared to talk for hours about his feelings – 'my Tandian tenebrosities', he sometimes called them – he was equally prepared to listen for hours while I explained in minute detail the working of the Flange and the problems of repair it posed. He learned from me any facts he filtered on to Fay.

Maintaining the Flange is a costly and complicated business, and would be even more so had we not costly and complicated machines with which to operate. Between FTL arrivals, my unit works ceaselessly over the strip – testing, checking, replacing, making good.

The complex nature of the Flange necessitates this.

To start with, there is the BGL – the Bonfiglioli Geogravitic Layer – marked by tall pylons, along the north of the Flange, which maintains all of Tandy Two's atmosphere within its stress; were this to contract more than a minimum leakage, the lives of everyone on the planet would be in jeopardy.

Before the BGL comes the 'fence', which prevents any creature from entering the Flange zone; after it come our equipment stores, bunkers, etc., before you get to the actual twelve-mile-wide Flange itself.

The Flange is a huge shock absorber, three storeys deep, girdling the planet. It has to absorb the biggest man-made shock of all time, though it is a delicate instrument with an upper surface of free-grooved pyr-glass needles. Its functioning depends first and foremost on the taubesi thermocouple, of which there is one to every square millimetre of surface; these detect an FTL ship before it re-enters normal space and activate the rest of the system immediately. The rest of the system is, briefly, an inertia vacuum. The FTL ship never actually makes contact with the Flange surface, of course, but its detectors mesh with the inertials and transfer velocities, stopping it in milliseconds – the figure varies according to planetary and ship's mass, but for Tandy Two it is generally in the order of 201·5 milliseconds.

The whole Flange is activated – switched on section by section of its entire twenty-five thousand miles length – two hours before an FTL ship arrives (only the computers beneath the strip know precisely when the starship will materialise from phase space). At that time, the various maintenance units give the whole system a final check, and the needlelike surface of the Flange looks first one way and then another, like stroked fur, as it searches for the breakthrough point I should have been back for that event.

I had come down to the valleys by now. Over to my left ran the graceful BGL pylons, with the Flange itself behind, already stretching itself like a self-activated rubber sheet; beyond it burned the dead half of Tandy, sealed off in vacuum, bleached dust-white in the sun. Less than a mile remained between me and the unit post. Then I saw Fay.

Her blue dress showed clearly against a tawny ground. She was several hundred yards ahead of me, not looking in my direction and running directly towards an electrified 'fence' that guards the BGL and the Flange itself.

'Fay!' I yelled. 'Come back!'

Instinctive stuff; I was enclosed in the truck; had she heard my cry it would only have speeded her on her way.

This was her last chance to see an FTL ship enter before she went back to Droxy. The absence of her father and mother had given her the chance to slip out, so she had taken it

'Fay!' I yelled as I drove, letting my lungs shout, because in my fear I could not stop them.

The fence was built of two components, an ordinary strand fence with a mild shock to keep sheep away, and then, some yards beyond, a trellis of high voltage designed simply and crudely to kill. Warning notices ran all the way between the two fences, one every three hundred and fifty yards – 125,714 of them right around the planet.

She dived through the strand fence without touching it.

Now I was level with her. Seeing me, she began running parallel between the two fences. Beyond her the eyes of the needles of the Flange turned first this way then that, restless and expectant.

I jumped from the truck before it stopped moving.

'You'll get killed, Fay!' I bellowed.

She turned then, her face half mischievous, half scared. She was running off-course towards the second fence as she turned. She called something to me – I could not make out, still cannot make out, what.

As I ducked under the sheep strand after her, she hit the other fence.

Fay! Ah, my Fay, my own sweet freeborn daughter! She was outlined in bright light, she was black as a cinder, the universe screamed and yapped like a dying dog. My face hit the dust shrieking as I fell. Noise, death, heat, slapped me down.

Then there was mind-devouring silence.

Peace rolled down like a steamroller, flattening everything, the eternal hush of damnation into which I wept as if the universe were a pocket handkerchief for my grief.

Fay, oh Fay, my own child!

Beyond the BGL, safe in vacuum, the Flange peered towards the heavens, twisting its spiked eyes. I rolled in the blistered dust without comprehension.

How long I lay there I have no idea.

Eventually the alarms roused me. They washed around me and through me until they, too, were gone, and the silence came back. When my hearing returned, I heard a throbbing in the silence. At first I could not place it, had no wish to place it, but at last I sat up and realised that the motor of my truck was still patiently turning over. I stood up shakily. The ill-coordinated action brought a measure of intelligence back to my system.

All I knew was that I had to return to the farm and tell Bes what had happened. Everything else was forgotten, even that the FTL ship was due at any time.

I got back somehow under the sheep fence, and into the cab. Somehow I kicked in the gears, and we lurched into action. *Fay, Fay, Fay,* my blood kept saying.

As I steered away from the Flange, from the burned ground to grass again, a figure presented itself before me. Blankly I stopped and climbed out to meet it, hardly knowing what I did.

It was Murrag, waving his arms like one possessed.

'Thanks to your aid we got the flocks under cover in time,' he said. 'So I came down here to see the FTL entry. You know, for me to see an entry – well, it's like watching creation.'

He stopped, eyeing me, his face full of a private emotion.

'It's like the creation, is it?' I said dumbly. My mouth felt puffy. *Fay, Fay, Fay.*

'Vasko, we've always been friends, so I don't have to mind what I say to you. You know that this event once a fortnight – it's ultimate excitement for me. I mean ... well, even something like sex palls beside watching an FTL entry.'

In the state I was in I could not grasp what he was saying. It came back to me long after, like finding a private letter behind the wainscoting of an empty house.

'And I've got the image of Tandy Two I was after, Vasko.' His eyes were alight, full of some inner fire. 'Tandy's a woman –'

There was no warning.

The FTL ship entered.

Cerenkov radiations belched outward, distorting our vision. For a second Murrag and I were embedded in amber. Tandy was girdled in a noose of flame, most of which expanded south safely into vacuum. The giant fist of impetus reaction struck us.

The sun plunged across the sky like a frightened horse.

As we fell, day turned to night.

For one of those long minutes that seemed a small eternity, I lay on the ground with Murrag face-down near by.

He moved before I did. When it penetrated my mind that he was slipping a fume mask on, I automatically did the same; without thinking, I had carried my mask from the vehicle with me.

He had switched on a flashlight. It lay on the ground as we sprouted bug-eyed jumbo faces, and splashed a great caricature of us up the mountainside. In the sky, the planet Tandy appeared, near full and bright, a phantom. As ever, it was impossible to believe it was not our moon rather than vice versa; facts have no power against the imagination.

Sitting there stupidly, I heard the words of an old poet scatter through my head, half of his verse missing.

O, moon of my delight who know'st no wane,
Something something once again.
How oft hereafter rising shall she look
Through this same garden after me – in vain!

But I had no time to connect up the missing words; if I had thought of it, I preferred it that way, thus emphasising my sense of loss. But no rational thought came.

All that came was the clash of two nightmares, Murrag's and mine. It seemed that I kept crying 'Fay is dead!' and that he kept crying 'Tandy Two's a woman!' We were fighting, struggling together while the ground steamed, I hating him because he did not care where I had expected him to care, he hating me because I had spoiled his vigil, ruined his climax.

My mind ran in shapes, not thoughts, until I realised that I had begun the fight. When I went limp, Murrag's fist caught me between the eyes.

I do not have to say what I felt then, slumped on the ground – the place I hated and Murrag loved – for this is supposed to be his story, not mine, although I have become entangled in it in the same directionless way I became entangled in Bes's life.

Murrag – you have to say it – could not feel like ordinary people. When I heard from him again, he did not even mention Fay; he had only used her to talk to about his obsession.

When, a week later, the STL ship *Monteith* departed for Droxy from Tandy, Col, Bes, and Tes Dourt travelled in it. So did I. I lay in the bunk in the medical bay, classified under some obscure technical label that meant I was dull of mind and unfit for further service.

The Dourts came to see me.

They were surprisingly cheerful. After all, they had made their money and were about to begin life anew. Even Bes never referred to Fay; I always said she was hard.

They brought me a letter from Murrag. It was elaborate, overwritten. Wrapped in his own discoveries, he clearly mourned as little for Fay as did the Dourts. His letter, in fact, displayed his usual sensitivity, and his blindness where other humans were concerned. I had no patience with it, though I later reread the final passages (which he has since used in his successful book, *To My Undeniable Tandy*).

'... Yilmoff's fifty-fourth era classic, *Theory of Images*, reveals how settings can hold deep psychic significances for men; we acquire early an Experience of place. When a planet exists with as distinct a personality – for the term in context is no exaggeration – as Tandy Two's, the significance is increased, the effect on the psyche deepened.

'I declare myself to be in love, in the true psychological sense of the word, with Tandy. She is my needful feminine, dwelling in my mind, filling it to the exclusion of others.

'So I give you my true portrait image of her: the planet-head of a girl, all sweet, rich hair north, but the south face a skull, and bound round her brow a ribbon of flame. This the portrait of my terrible lover.'

Make of this what you will. Crazy? I think not.

Only Murrag of all mankind has his mistress perpetually beneath him.

A Pleasure Shared

At seven thirty I rose and went over to the window and drew back the curtains. Outside lay another wintry London day – not nice.

Miss Colgrave was still in the chair where I had left her. I pulled her skirt down. Female flesh looks very unappetising before breakfast. I went through into the kitchen and made myself a cup of tea and poached an egg on the gas ring. While I did so I smoked a cigarette. I always enjoy a cigarette first thing in the morning.

I ate my breakfast in the bedroom, watching Miss Colgrave closely as I did so. At one point I rose to adjust the scarf round her neck, which looked unsightly. Miss Colgrave had not been a very respectable woman; she had paid the price of sin. But it would be a nuisance disposing of her.

First I would have to wrap her in a blanket, as I had done with Miss Robbins. This was also a nuisance, since I was rather short of blankets, and the worst of the winter was yet to come. I thought what a pity it was that the disposal of useless females like Miss Colgrave and Miss Robbins could not be made legal. After all, they were a blot on the community with their dirty habits.

For some while I thought about the blanket, enjoying another smoke as I did so. Then I decided I would go for a walk before doing anything. Miss Colgrave would not run away.

I went out on to the landing, locked my flat door, and proceeded downstairs. On the landing of the first floor, I met Mrs Meacher, dressed to go out. Mrs Meacher was a very proper little woman, and she liked me. Although she was young, I must say she was not as nosey as some.

'Good morning, Mr Cream,' she said. 'Not a very nice morning, is it?'

'At least it's not raining, Mrs Meacher.'

'No, well, there is that to be thankful for. And how's the sciatica this morning?'

I had sprained my back carrying Miss Robbins down to the coal cellar, and it had bothered me.

'Not too troublesome this morning, Mrs Meacher. We all have our crosses to bear, as Father used to say. And how's your rheumatism?'

'These stairs don't do it any good you know. I lay awake with it half the night. Still we mustn't grumble, must we?'

'Grumbling doesn't do any good, does it?'

'You didn't sleep too well, either, did you, Mr Cream? I mean I heard you walking about in the early part of the night, and several bumps. I got quite worried.'

Mrs Meacher was a very respectable young widow, but all women are curious. They do not keep themselves to themselves as men do. It is a fault that ought to be eradicated. However, I was very polite as usual; I explained I had been exercising my sciatica. Something made me add, 'You don't have a spare blanket, Mrs Meacher, that you could lend me?'

She looked a bit doubtful, and fiddled with her hat in the irritating way some women have.

'I might have one in the bottom of my wardrobe,' she said. 'I could spare you that. I'm in a bit of a hurry now. Perhaps you'd care to come in this afternoon for it. We could have a cup of tea together, if you like.'

'That would be nice, Mrs Meacher.'

'Yes, it would. I believe in people minding their own business, but it's nice to be neighbourly, isn't it, when your neighbours are the right sort.'

'Those are my sentiments, Mrs Meacher.'

She adjusted her hat. 'Half past four, then. I *respect* a man who doesn't drink, Mr Cream – not like that awful Mr Lawrence just moved in on the ground floor.'

'Public houses are the inventions of the devil, Mrs Meacher. Mother told me that, and I've never forgotten it. There's a lot of truth in it.'

She went downstairs, and I followed. I thought perhaps it would be a nice idea to ask her to have a cup of tea with me one afternoon – when I had my room clear, of course.

Mrs Meacher had bustled out of the front door before I got down into the dark hall. You could only see down there when the electric light was on. The bulb had fused, and our landlord had failed to replace it. He was a hard man who cared only about money – just the kind of man I despise.

'Cream!'

A door opened, and Lawrence appeared. He was a little fat man who walked about in slippers and shirt sleeves. I never let anybody see me without my jacket on. Careless in dress, careless in morals.

'Good morning, Mr Lawrence,' I said, trying to make him keep his distance.

'Here, Cream, I want a word with you. That was Flossie Meacher just went out, wasn't it?'

'No other women live in this establishment to my knowledge.'

'What about that pusher you had up in your room last night? I saw yer!'

To be accused thus of having women up in my room – as if I were some common little seducer! – by this vulgarian made me very angry. But he continued, 'Come in my room a moment. There's a thing or two you can help me on.'

'I am a busy man, Mr Lawrence.'

'Not too busy to help a chap, I hope. I know you're as thick as thieves with Flossie Meacher. You wouldn't want me to tell her about the pushers you have up in your room, would you?'

In this there was some truth. Though I had no great liking for Mrs Meacher, I did not wish to be lowered in her estimation. Making the best of a bad job, I stepped into Lawrence's untidy room.

The room contained an unmade bed, chairs, a table covered with beer and milk bottles, a pile of dirty clothes on the floor, and precious little else. Obviously the man lived a bohemian way of life I found distasteful; my parents had always brought me up to be tidy in all I did.

Lawrence offered me a cigarette.

'I'll smoke one of my own, thank you,' I said. I am a great believer in avoiding unnecessary germs. We both lit up – I condescended to share his match – and he said, 'Flossie Meacher don't think much of me, does she?'

'I have no idea of her opinions on the subject.'

'Oh yes, you have! I heard her telling you on the landing I was a dirty bastard. I stood here with my door ajar and heard every word you two said.'

'Mrs Meacher would not use foul language, Mr Lawrence.'

'Come off it, mate. Who do you think you are?'

Inspiration came to me at this point; I can think very quickly on occasions. It occurred to me that there would probably be other emergencies after Miss Colgrave, of a similar nature, and here I could turn this meeting to my future advantage.

'I merely came down, Mr Lawrence, to ask you if you could lend me a blanket. The nights are growing chilly.'

This disconcerted him. He looked very silly with his mouth open. I never open mine more than I can help, although my teeth are a good deal more attractive than his.

'I might have a spare blanket,' he said at last. 'But I was going to ask you about Flossie Meacher.'

'I will be pleased to tell you what I know in exchange for a blanket.'

'So that's the way it is! You're a funny cove, Cream, and no mistake … Well then, tell me this: is her husband, old Tom Meacher, dead?'

'I understand her husband passed away before she came to live in Institute Place.'

'Did he now? Poor old Tom! How did he peg out?'

'Mrs Meacher gave me to understand that her husband passed away due to pneumonia.'

'I see. I used to know old Tom Meacher. He used to have the occasional pint with me when I was working in Walthamstow. He was a brickie, same as me.'

I thought his coarse disgusting hands looked like a bricklayer's. I signified I was ready to receive the blanket and go.

'Not so fast. Here, sit down and have a beer with me like a civilised man.'

'Thank you, but to my knowledge civilised men do not touch beer. Certainly I never drink it.'

'You're a real snob, mate, aren't you?'

'Not at all. I will speak to anyone in any walk of life. I just have standards, that's all.'

'Standards … Ah well.' He shrugged his shoulders and went on. 'Tell me some more about Flossie. She's a proper martinet, isn't she?'

'She observes the decencies, if that's what you mean.'

'Comes to the same thing. People who observe decencies never got any time for anything else. I know she drove old Tom to drink, and then spent her life trying to keep him off it.'

'Mr Lawrence, Mrs Meacher's private life is entirely her own affair.'

'Ah, but it's not, you know. You see, I'm scheming to marry Flossie Meacher.'

Other people's lives can be so sordid that I really do not care to hear about them. But this man Lawrence's announcement surprised me to such an extent that I consented to sit by his table and listen while he told me a rambling tale. Several times I lost the thread of what he was saying, for it really was not particularly interesting.

He opened a bottle of beer for himself, as if he could not think without the nauseating stuff.

'I daresay you're wondering, Cream, why I should I want to marry a woman I know is a young battleaxe, eh? It's a funny story, really, I suppose. The years go by and things don't get no different ... I'm the sort of man who *needs* a harsh woman, Cream. I've always been the same ...'

I had been more fortunate. I had had a harsh mother to show me what the world was really like. That might have been the difference between this man and me; you could see even in the way we dressed which of us had had proper discipline as a child. I could still recall vividly the agony of having Mother clean my nails with the sharp file that dug down into the quick; in fact I think of it most times I bite my nails, even today.

'I was the youngest of seven kids, Cream. My parents were as kind as could be – never hurt a fly – and my brothers and sisters were kind too. We lived in a place out Dagenham way. Funny thing about their kindness – they never told me what to do, never told me a thing. You won't believe this, but I grew up in a proper maze, really lost, although there was lots of people all crowded round me all the time ...'

Oh, I believe it all right, Mr Lawrence, because you obviously are lost now. It just shows how breeding will tell. I was my parents' only child. I had their attention all the time, and as a result I have grown up neat and normal and sensible. Although Mother and Father passed away years ago, I often have the feeling they still watch over me. Well, I don't have to reproach myself for anything. I've grown up as they would wish. In fact I think I may say I'm stronger and just a little more respectable than they were. That was almost the last thing I said to Miss Colgrave, I remember, when I finally got her down into the chair. Disgraceful the way their bowel muscles lose control in those last moments. Father was so particular about such things; many's the whipping he gave me for wetting my bed; I know he would understand how I felt about Miss Colgrave.

'It was only when I was twelve anyone took any proper notice of me. Funny how it comes back to you, ain't it? I can see the broken railings round our back yard now ... It was when I was twelve I had my first girl friend. Sally, her name was, Sally Beeves. She was so pretty, she was. God, I can see her now! She had a little sister, Peggy. That pair made a dead set at me, Cream. They used to get me in the attic over the old garage her father ran. It'd turn your blood cold, Cream, if I told you all the things those girls did to me! Talk about torture. Why, one day, Sally got some rubber tubing ...'

Disgusting men like Lawrence can never talk about anything but women. If I took him upstairs and showed him Miss Colgrave, he might think a deal less of their breed.

And now he was telling me horrible things I did not want to hear. I could not keep my own thoughts separate from them. For a moment I thought in my anger how good it would be if the world were rid of Lawrence. But that was not my job; I had enough work on my hands. Besides, being a fastidious man, I heartily dislike scuffles, and Lawrence was probably stronger than me. When selecting my women, I always make sure they are physically small and on the weak side, so that we avoid any unseemly struggles. Besides, I have my heart to think of.

'Yet despite all she did to me, I loved Sally Beeves. You see, she was the first person ever to take real notice of me. The general family kindness wasn't enough. Honest, you may laugh, but I preferred Sally's cruelty. And sometimes when she made me cry, she'd kiss me, and then I'd swear to myself I'd marry her when I grew up ...'

Marriage. I might have known Lawrence's tedious tale would get round to *that*. Frankly, marriage is a subject I prefer to avoid. After Mother's death I foolishly married that woman Emily; if she had been alive to guide me I am sure I should never have done so.

Yet on the surface Emily seemed respectable enough. She was older than me and had some money of her own. She insisted we went for our honeymoon to Boulogne, which rather put me out, since I dislike travelling abroad where people cannot speak English. We crossed the Channel on the night ferry. We had hardly got into our cabin before she started making advances in a very obvious way I could not ignore.

I was more shocked and disappointed with Emily than I can say. On some pretext or other I got her up onto the boat deck and pushed her over the rail. It was easy and then I felt better.

Of course, later I felt sorry. I remember I suffered from one of my periodic bouts of diarrhoea. But her parents were so sympathetic when they heard of the accident, I soon got over it.

'As things turned out, Dad's business went bust, and we moved, so I never saw Sally again. And somehow after that, well, ordinary girls didn't have the same appeal. I have found other girls to treat me rough, but not in the same way as dear old Sally Beeves. Funny, isn't it? I mean I sometimes think I actually *prefer* being unhappy.

'Has it ever struck you, Cream, that we never really know ourselves, never mind other people?'

His life was a mess. Mine was so neat and self-contained. I had nothing in common with him, nothing at all. He was on his second bottle of beer already. Suddenly I stopped biting my nails and said, 'About that blanket, Mr Lawrence ...'

He said, 'I was getting round to asking you about Flossie upstairs. Don't you reckon she'd be the type for me, strict and hard? How old would you say she was?'

'I have never thought to enquire.'

'Make a guess, man.'

'About forty.'

'Ah. Thirty-eight or nine, I'd have said. And I'm forty-nine, so that wouldn't be so bad. Mind you, I like comforts with my miseries – does she strike you as having money, Cream?'

'She has her own furniture.'

'Ah. Well, old Meacher make a lot of money out of building in the fifties, before he died. Left her quite a tidy sum. I did hear ten thousand pounds mentioned. So she must be hanging on to it tight to be living in a dump like this.'

'Number Fourteen was perfectly respectable till you came here, Mr Lawrence.'

'Don't give me that! Have you ever been and had a sniff down the cellar? No, I don't suppose you have. It wouldn't be smart enough for the likes of you. It stinks as if they stored dead 'uns as well as lumber down there. Anyhow, the question is, has anyone else got his eye on our Flossie? And do you think she'd have me?'

'Since you force me to be honest, I don't think she'd even consider you, Mr Lawrence.'

'Then maybe you've got a surprise coming, *Mister* Cream. Nothing wrong with me when I'm sober ... Anyhow, what I want you to do is put in a good word for me. How about it?'

'I can't promise anything.'

'Go on, I'll give you a blanket. Two blankets.'

If the man wished to be foolish, I saw no reason why I should discourage him. I said I would do what I could. Eventually I accepted two very poor blankets from him and proceeded upstairs with them.

For an awful moment, I can't say why, I thought it was my mother in the chair. I had completely forgotten Miss Colgrave as I came in the door. This made me feel very bad, and I decided to go out for a coffee.

It seems a pity that people who do all they can to deserve to be happy should not be happy all the time.

I sat in a small cafe where I sometimes go, drinking a coffee. I had already decided not to work that day. They did not appreciate my efforts at the warehouse. I would turn up on the next day, and if they make trouble I should simply leave. Money was rather a worry; I hardly had enough for cigarettes. With some surprise I thought over what Lawrence had said about Mrs Meacher having ten thousand pounds.

A girl came in and sat at the next table to me. She was about my type, so I got talking to her. With these girls, you don't have to say much and they run on and on; they don't mind if you don't listen to them. This one said she was working at a nearby draper's and that she did photographic modelling in her spare time.

Ha ha, my girl, I thought, I know your sort. I hate photography and all art, because they all lead to the same thing. If I had my way, I'd burn all the picture galleries in the world. Then we might have less of all this immorality you read about. I've heard Father say that painters and authors were minions of the Devil, although he made an exception for some improving writers like Lloyd Douglas and Conan Doyle.

When I found out from this girl that she came to the cafe at the same time every day, I knew I could get in touch with her when I wished. I told her I was a director of a big blanket-manufacturing firm in the Midlands, and she agreed to pose naked for me if I required it. Then I left the cafe, after bidding her good morning.

On the occasions when I have disposal troubles on my mind, I often take long rambles round London. This I did now, although it was rather chilly. My stomach was a little upset, so that I was forced to visit various gentlemen's lavatories on my route. When I read some of the things written in the cubicles, they made me very ashamed and excited.

I watched some old buildings being pulled down. Demolition work always fascinates me, but my pleasure was spoilt by the racial people labouring on the site. These Jamaicans and other people should be sent back to Africa where they belong; there must be plenty of room for them there. Not that I believe in the colour bar. It's just that there isn't room for them here. I shouldn't want a daughter of mine to marry anybody at all racial.

Being able to amuse myself has always been one of my virtues. I'm never lonely, and I don't depend on other people. Father used to hate me playing with other boys; he said they might teach me dirty language. When I write filthy things on cubicle walls, it's always to make other boys ashamed. So when I saw by a jeweller's clock that it was half past four, I remembered I was invited to have tea with Mrs Meacher, and I directed my footsteps back towards Number Fourteen, Institution Place.

In the hall it was very dark. A slight smell drifted up from the cellar, dampish, mouldy, not unpleasant. Lawrence's door was ajar, but by the silence there I guessed he was out. As I began to ascend the stairs, a voice from above called my name. It was Mrs Meacher.

When I reached her landing, I observed she was looking distraught.

'I am afraid I am a little late for our tea party, Mrs Meacher,' I said politely.

'You'll have to prepare yourself for a shock, Mr Cream. Something awful has happened.'

I dislike awful things happening. They are apt to happen where women are. I said, 'I'm afraid I have to go out in a minute, Mrs Meacher.'

She became very wild.

'You can't go out. You can't leave me. Come in here, please! It's that Mr Lawrence. He's dead!'

In her excitement, she had taken hold of my arm and half dragged me into her room.

The place was in a disgraceful state. I saw at once that it was well furnished, even down to having a nice carpet on the floor, and lampshades and pictures and things. But a table and an armchair had been overturned. A tray with a cup and saucer and such lay on the carpet, with lump sugar spilling out in a curve. Some of these lumps were red, sucking up the blood that lay in pools or splashes here and there.

The cause of the blood lay in one corner under the window, bent double with his head hanging over a small work table. It was Lawrence.

Though his face was turned away from me, I recognised him by the pattern of his shirt, and the width of his fat back. The shirt was disfigured with blood. A pair of scissors stuck out of it. I saw at once that these scissors were the weapon used, and congratulated myself on the fact that the scarf I employed during my upsets with Miss Colgrave, Miss Robbins and the others, was so much less messy.

I sat down on an upright chair.

'Some water, please, Mrs Meacher. I feel quite faint at the sight of blood. You shouldn't have brought me in here.'

She fetched me the water. As I was drinking it, she began to talk.

'It wasn't deliberate, really it wasn't. I'm scared of men, I'm scared of men like that! He's a boozer, just like my husband was – just the same. You never know what they'll want next. But I never meant to kill him. I got so scared, you see. I could smell the drink on him. He scared me down in the dark hall, and then he followed me up here. I was scared out of my wits, really I was – but it wasn't deliberate.'

'I feel better for that,' I said, putting the glass down. It was a nice clean glass with a leaf pattern cut in it. 'You'd better tell me what happened, Mrs Meacher.'

She seemed to make an effort to calm herself, and sat down facing me so that she could not see Lawrence and the scissors.

'There's nothing much to tell, not really. Like I say, he followed me upstairs. He'd been drinking. I know the smell of beer all right, and you could tell by the way he acted. I couldn't get this door shut in time. I had to let him in, he was so insistent. Oh, I got all scared. And then he got down on his knees and – and he – oh, he asked me to *marry* him.'

'So you stabbed him with the scissors?'

'I lost my head. I kicked him and told him to get up. He begged me to kick him again. He seemed to get all excited. When he grabbed my skirt, I know what he was up to. Drunken, filthy brute! My sewing things were left out on the table. Without realising what I was doing, I took hold of my big pair of scissors and drove them into his back as he knelt there.'

I noticed with distaste that there were a few splashes of blood on her blouse and skirt.

Her eyes were wide as she added in a whisper, 'He took such a long time to die, Mr Cream. I thought he would never have done with blundering and falling round the room. I ran out until I heard he was quite still.'

'He didn't actually attack you, Mrs Meacher?'

'I've told you what he did. He grabbed my skirt. I felt his knuckles on my stockings!'

'He was touching your skirt in the process of proposing matrimony, I take it.'

'Mr Cream, he was *drunk*!'

I stood up.

'You realise I must report this to the police at once,' I said. 'I can't go getting myself mixed up in murder.'

She stood up too. She was shorter than me. Her eyes went very narrow.

'When he was still – moving about, I ran up to your room to see if you were in, to get you to come and help me. I knocked and ran straight in, Mr Cream. I saw that dead woman in that chair. You'd better *not* go to the police, Mr Cream! You'd better stay and help me get rid of this body, or someone's going to hear about that dead woman in that chair.'

With irritation, I recalled that although I had locked my door when I first left my room that morning, I had forgotten to do so later, after leaving Lawrence's blankets in there, owing to a temporary depression of spirts. It just shows you can't be too careful. I recalled the way Father used to tease Mother by saying that a woman would always find your secrets out.

'Well, what do you say to that?' Mrs Meacher asked.

'Naturally I will help you if I can.'

'The body?'

'I will help you dispose of the body.'

My stomach began to rumble the way it sometimes does in times of crisis.

'Excuse me, please,' I said, beginning to leave the room.

She followed me up instantly, in a very pugnacious manner I did not like at all.

'Where are you going?'

'To the toilet, Mrs Meacher,' I said with dignity.

It was a disgrace that the whole house had only the one toilet on the ground floor. While there, I had a chance to think things over more calmly. Lawrence would not be the sort of man anyone would want to trace. Who was there to care if he lived or died – except our landlord, who would ask no questions as long as he got his rent? Mrs Meacher could see to that.

Then we could have a little sort of double funeral. Both Miss Colgrave and Mr Lawrence could go down into the cellar, behind all that useless wood and junk, to join Miss Robbins, and the Irish girl. It would be nice to have help with the weight down all those wretched stairs. A pleasure shared is a pleasure doubled, as Mother used to say every Sunday when we went to chapel.

Thinking along those lines while I juggled with the chain until the cistern flushed, I had an idea. What Lawrence had said about Mrs Meacher's ten thousand pounds returned to my mind. It was a lot of money, and somehow I felt I deserved it.

She was a respectable woman – her reactions to Lawrence proved that. Besides if the worst came to the worst, she was smaller than me. Flossie. Flossie Meacher. Flossie – Cream.

As I proceeded back upstairs, I called out cheerfully, 'I'm just going to get a blanket. Don't worry. Leave everything to me, Flossie!'

Basis for Negotiation

The University of East Lincóln is a muddle of buildings. In the centre stands the theatrically baroque pile still called Gransby Manor, while round it lie the pencil-boxes of glass and cedar and cement that are our century's contribution to the treasury of world architecture. John Haines-Roberts and I walked round the grounds in agonised discussion, viewing our conglomeration of a college from all its meaningless angles.

When I tell you the date was July 1st, 1971, you will know what was the subject under discussion.

'I tell you I cannot just stay here, John, idle, isolated, ignorant,' I said. 'I must go to London and find out what the devil the government is doing.'

Most of the conversations that follow, I feel confident, are word for word what was said at the time. My memory is generally eidetic; in times of stress such as this, it records everything, so that I see John Haines-Roberts now, his head thrust forward from those heavy shoulders, as he replied, 'I will offer you no platitudes about considering your reputation at such a grave time. Nevertheless, Simon, you are a public figure, and were before your knighthood. You have a foot in both worlds, the academic and the world of affairs. Your work on the Humanities Council and the Pilgrim Trust has not been forgotten. You were MP for Bedford under Macleon. That has not been forgotten. At such a trying time, any untoward move by somebody of your stature may fatally prejudice the course of events, marring –'

'No, no, John, that's not it at all!' I stopped him with a curt movement of my hand. He talked that awful dead language of English newspaper leaders; with his evasions and euphemisms, his 'untoward moves' and 'trying times.' I could not bear to listen to him. He believed as I did on that one fundamental point, that the British Government had made the most fatal error any government could have done; but this apart we could have nothing in common. His woolly language only reflected the numbness of his intellect. At that terrible moment, one more prop fell away. I began to hate John. The man who had been my friend since I took the specially created chair of Moral History two years before suddenly became just another enemy of my country, and of me.

'We cannot discuss the problem in these terms,' I told him. He stopped, peering forward in that intense way of his. In the distance, I saw some undergraduates bunched together in the tepid sunshine and watching us with interest. 'The British have turned basely against their dearest friends and allies. Either this wounds you to the heart or it doesn't –'

'But the Americans can manage alone perfectly well –' he began, with all the patience and reason in the world in his voice. John Haines-Roberts was a saint; nothing in the world could ruffle him in debate. I knew he would be standing reasoning in some quiet corner of University College when the H-bombs fell.

'I'm sorry, John, I'm not prepared to go into it all again. The sands have run out – right out of the bottom of the glass. This is no time for talk. You don't think the Communists are standing talking, do you? I'm going to London.'

He saw I was making to go and laid a placatory hand on my sleeve.

'My dear fellow, you know I wish you well, but you have a reputation for being over-hasty. Never, never let action become a substitute for thought. You'll recall what that great and good man Wilberforce said when –'

'Damn Wilberforce!' I said. Turning away, I strode off. The undergraduates saw me coming and fanned out to intercept me on my way to Manor, pouring out questions.

'Is it true the Americans have cordoned off Holy Loch? Sir Simon, what do you think of the news about the International Brigade? Did you see C. P. Snow on TV, blasting poor old Minnie?' 'Minnie' was their nickname for Sir Alfred Menhennick, the Prime Minister.

Behind my back, John was still calling, 'Simon, my dear fellow. ...' To my audience, I said, 'Gentlemen, from this week onwards, only shame attaches to the name of England. You know how I feel on this subject. Please let me pass.'

Their faces were before me, troubled, angry, or snivelling. They began bombarding me with preposterous questions – 'Who do you think will win, America or China?' as if it were a boat-race staged for their delight.

'Let me through!' I repeated.

'Why don't you join up, if you feel so strongly?' 'We don't owe the Americans anything.' 'We'll still be here when they're one big hole in the ground.' And so on.

I said: 'You had the police in here last night. Rowdyism will get you nowhere. Why don't you go somewhere quietly and consult your history books if you have no consciences to consult?' I hated them, though I knew they half-sided with me.

'Consult our history books!' one of them exclaimed. 'He'll tell us to cultivate our gardens next!'

Angrily I pushed through them, making my way towards my rooms. That last remark echoed through my head; obviously many of them could not differentiate between my convictions and those of, say, Haines-Roberts. In the final judgement, he and I would be lumped together as men who sat by and let it happen – or, even worse, would be cheered as men who had not interfered.

With distaste I surveyed the comfortable room with Adam fireplace and white panelling that I had chosen in preference to an office in Whitehall, asking myself as I took in – through what a scornfully fresh vision! – the untidy bookcases and neat cocktail cabinet, if there was still time left to do something effective. How terribly often in the past must Englishmen have asked themselves that!

Momentarily I surveyed myself in the looking-glass. Grey-haired, long in the nose, clear of eye, neat in appearance. Not a don. More a retired soldier. Certainly – oh yes, my God, that certainly – a gentleman! A product of Harrow and Balliol and a Wiltshire estate. With the international situation what it was, it sounded more like a heresy than a heritage. Nothing is more vile (or more eloquent of guilt) than to hate everything one has been: to see that you have contaminated the things that have contaminated you.

Taking a deep breath, I began to phone my wife at home. When her voice came over the line, I closed my eyes.

'Jean, I can't bear inaction any longer. I'm going up to London to try to get through to Tertis.'

'Darling, we went over all this last night. You can't help by going to see Tertis – no, don't tell me you can't help by not going either. But it becomes more and more obvious each hour that public opinion here is with Minnie, and that your viewpoint ...'

By ceasing to listen to her meaning, I could concentrate on her voice. Her 'all' was pronounced 'arl,' her 'either' was an 'eether'; her tone had a soft firmness totally unlike the harshness of so many Englishwomen! – no, comparisons were worthless. It was stupid to think in categories. She was Jean Challington, my beloved wife. When I had first met her in New York, one fine September day in 1942, she had been Jean Gershein, daughter of a magazine publisher. At twenty-six, I was then playing my first useful role in affairs on the British Merchant Shipping Mission. Jean was the most Anglophile, as well as the most lovely, of creatures; I was the most Americanophile and adoring of men. That hasty wartime wedding at least was a success; no better Anglo-American agreement ever existed than our marriage.

This was the woman on whose breast I had wept the night before last, wept long and hard after the bleak TV announcement that in the interests of future world unity the British Government had declared its neutrality in the American-Chinese war. Last night I had wept again, when the USSR had come in on the side of the People's Republic and Sir Alfred Menhennick himself had smiled to viewers under his straggling moustache and reaffirmed our neutrality.

Now, with the phone in my hand and Jean's voice in my ear, I could not but recall Menhennick's hatefully assured delivery as he said, 'Let us in this darkest period of civilised history be the nation that stands firm and keeps its lamps alight. It is a difficult – perhaps you will agree that it is the most difficult – role that I and my government have elected to play. But we must never forget that throughout the quarter century of the Cold War, Great Britain's path has been the exacting and unrewarding one of intermediary.

'We must remember, too, that the United States, in facing Communist China, faces an enemy of its own creating. One of the most fatal failures of this century was the failure of the US to participate in world affairs during the twenties and thirties, when Britain and France strove almost single-handedly to preserve the peace. Despite constant warnings, the US at that time allowed their enemy Japan to grow strong on the spoils of an invaded China. As a consequence, the broken Chinese peoples had to restore their position as a world power by what means they could. It is not for us to condemn if in desperation they turned to Communism. That their experiment, their desperate experiment, worked must be its justification. At this fateful hour, it behoves us to think with every sympathy of the Chinese, embroiled yet again in another terrible conflict. ....'

The hypocrisy! The sheer bloody wicked hypocrisy, the lies, the distortions, the twists of logic, the contortions of history! My God, I could shoot Menhennick!

'Darling, I hadn't mentioned Menhennick,' Jean protested.

'Did I say that aloud?' I asked the phone.

'You weren't listening to a word I said.'

'I'll bet you were telling me to pack a clean shirt!'

'Nothing of the sort. I was saying that here in Lincoln there are some demonstrations in progress.'

'Tell me about them.'

'If you'll listen, honey. The best-organised procession carries a large banner saying, "Boot the Traitors out of Whitehall."'

'Good for them.'

'My, yes, good for them! The odd thing is, those boys look like exactly the same crowd we used to see marching from Aldermaston to Trafalgar Square shouting, "Ban the Bomb."'

'Probably they are. If you think with your emotions, slight glandular changes are sufficient to revise your entire outlook. In the Aldermaston days, they were afraid of being involved in war; now that Russia has come in on China's side, they're afraid that the US will be defeated, leaving us to be picked off by Big Brother afterwards. Which is precisely what will happen unless we do something positive now. What else goes on in Lincoln?'

Jean's voice became more cautious. 'Some anti-Americanism. The usual rabble with ill-printed posters saying, "Yanks, Go Home" and "Britain for the British." One of them spells Britain "B-R-I-T-I-A-N." So much for the ten thousand million pounds spent on education last year. ... It feels funny, Simon – to be an alien in what I thought was my own country.'

'It's not my country either till this is all put right. You know that, Jean. There's never been such a time of moral humiliation. I wish I'd been born anything but British.'

'Don't be silly, Simon.'

Foreseeing an argument, I changed the line of discussion.

'You've got Michael and Sheila and Adrian there with you?'

'Oh yes, and Mrs B. And a platoon or so of sheepish English soldiers drilling opposite the Post Office.'

'Fine. You won't be lonely. I'll be back as soon as I can.'

'Meaning just when?'

'Soonest possible, love. 'Bye. Be good.'

I put the phone down. I looked distractedly round the room. I put pipe and tobacco into one jacket pocket, opened a drawer, selected three clean handkerchiefs, and put them into the other pocket. I wondered if I would ever see the room – or Jean – again, and strove at the same time not to dismiss such speculations as simply dramatic.

London, I knew, could turn into a real trouble centre at any hour. Early news bulletins had spoken of rioting and arrests here and there, but these were mere five-finger exercises for what was to come.

Until now, the sheer momentousness of world events had deadened reactions. After a month of mounting tension, war between the US and China broke out. Then came Menhennick's unexpected tearing up of treaties and declaration of neutrality. Initially, his action came as a relief as well as a surprise; the great bulk of the electorate saw no further than the fact that an Armageddon of nuclear war had been avoided. The USSR's entry into hostilities was more a shock than a surprise, again postponing real thinking.

Now – as I foresaw the situation – a growing mass of people would come to see that if they were to have any hope for a tolerable future, it would be fulfilled only by throwing in our lot heart and soul with our allies, the Americans. We had behaved like vermin, deserting in an hour of need. Even Neville Chamberlain returning from Munich in 1938 to proclaim 'Peace in our time' had not brought the country into such disgrace as Minnie with his 'nation that keeps the lamps alight.'

Soon the English would realise that; and I wanted to be there when trouble broke.

As I was heading for the door, David Woolf entered, quickly and without knocking. David was University Lecturer in Nuclear Physics, with a good but troubled record from Harwell. Three years back, he had run for Parliament, but an ill-timed tariff campaign had spoilt his chances. Though his politics were opposed to mine, his astute and often pungent thinking was undeniably attractive. Tall and very thin, with a crop of unbrushed hair, he was still in his thirties and looked what he undoubtedly was: the sort of man who managed always to be unhappy and spread unhappiness. Despite this – despite our radically different upbringings – his father had been a sagger-magger's bottomer in a Staffordshire pottery – David and I saw much of each other.

'What is it?' I asked. 'I can't stop, David.'

'You're in trouble,' he said, clicking his fingers.

I had not seen him since the Chinese declaration of war forty-eight hours before. His face was drawn, his shirt dirty. If he had slept, clearly it had been in his clothes.

'What sort of trouble?' I asked. 'Aren't we all in trouble?'

'The Dean has you marked down as a dangerous man, and at times like this the Dean's kind can cause a hell of a lot of grief.'

'I know that.'

Dean Burroughs was a cousin of Peter Dawkinson, the reactionary old editor of the *Arbiter*, the newspaper as firmly entrenched behind out-dated attitudes as *The Times* had ever been at its worst period – and as powerful. Burroughs and I had been in opposition even before my first day at East Lincoln, back when I edited Garbitt's short-living independent *Zonal*.

'What you don't know is that the Dean has started vetting your phone calls,' David said. 'I was by the exchange just now. You made an outgoing call; Mrs Ferguson had it plugged through to old Putters, the Dean's fair-haired boy.'

'It was a private call to my wife,' I said furiously.

'Are you leaving or something? Don't mind my asking.'

'Yes, I'm leaving, though by God what you tell me makes me want to go and sort things out with Burroughs first. No, that luxury must wait; time's short. I must leave at once.'

'Then I warn you, Simon, that they may try to stop you.'

'Thanks for telling me.'

He hesitated, knowing I wanted him to move away from the door. For a moment we stood confronting each other. Then he spoke.

'Simon – I want to come with you.'

That did surprise me. The news about the phone did not; in the present tense atmosphere, it merely seemed in character, a small sample of a vast untrustworthiness. I accepted David's words as truth; David, though isolated from the rest of the teaching body by his political and sexual beliefs, had a way of knowing whatever was happening in the college before anyone else.

'Look, David, you don't know what I am doing.'

'Let me guess then. You are going to drive to London. You have influential friends there. You are going to get in contact with someone like Lord Boulton or Tertis, and you are going to throw in your lot with the group trying to overthrow the government.'

This was so good a guess that he read his answer in my face. I said, with some bitterness, 'Your politics are no secret to me. For years you have preached that we should disarm, that we should cease to behave like a first-rate power, with all the assumptions of a first-rate power, when we are really a second-rate power –'

He seized my arm, only to release it at once. Behind his spectacles, his eyes brimmed with anger.

'Don't be a bloody fool, Simon! We *are* a second-rate power, but now the moment of truth is upon us, isn't it? The bastards who misgovern us would not climb off their silly perches when they had a chance, when we were warning them. Now, *now,* they just *must* honour agreements. You know I've no time for America, but by God we owe it to them to stick by them: we owe it to ourselves! We mustn't behave like a fifth-rate power: that at least we're not.'

'So we've both arrived on the same side?'

From his pocket he produced a revolver.

'You could have worse allies than me, Simon. I don't go to Bisley every year for nothing. I'm prepared to use this when needed.'

'Put it away!'

Savagely he laughed.

'You're a gentleman, Simon! That's your trouble. It's the only really vital difference between us. You don't enjoy force! You're as like Minnie as makes no difference! In the ultimate analysis, his faults are yours – and it's a class fault.'

I grabbed his jacket, clenching a fist in his face and choking with rage.

'You dare say that! Even you've not opposed Minnie as bitterly as I. I hate all he stands for, hate it.'

'No you don't. You both belong to the same league of gentlemen – Balliol and all that. If it wasn't that your wife happened to be American, you'd feel as Minnie does. It's you blasted gentlemen putting the social order before the country that have got us into this bloody disgraceful muddle. ...' With an effort, he broke off and pushed my hand roughly away, saying, 'And I'm in danger of doing the same thing myself. Sir Simon, my apologies. Our country has disgraced us before the world. Please let me come to London with you. I'm prepared to do anything to boot out the Nationalist party. That's what I came here to say.'

He put out his hand; I shook it.

We were round at the car port getting my Wolseley out when Spinks, the head porter, came thudding up at the double.

'Excuse me, Sir Simon, but the Dean wants you very urgently, sir. Matter of importance, sir.'

'All right, Spinks. I'll just drive the car round to the front of Manor and go in that way. He's in his rooms, I take it?'

His round heavy face was troubled.

'You will go straight in to him *now,* sir, won't you? He did stress as it was urgent.'

'Quite so, Spinks. Thank you for delivering the message.'

I drove round to the front of Manor, accelerated, and in next to no time we were speeding down the drive. David Woolf sat beside me, peering anxiously back at the huddle of buildings.

'Relax,' I said, knowing it would anger him. 'Nobody's going to shoot us.'

'The war's forty-eight hours old – I wonder how many people have been shot already?'

Not answering, I switched on the car radio as we struck the main road. I tried the three channels, General, Popular, and Motorway. On the first, a theatre organ played *Roses of Picardy*. On the second, a plummy woman's voice said, '… when to my bitter disappointment I found that all the jars of strawberry jam had gone mouldy; however, this tragedy –' On the third, a disc jockey announced, 'That was *My Blue Heaven*, and while we're on the subject of colour, here are Reggy Palmer and his Regiment in a colourful arrangement of another old favourite, *Chinatown*.'

'I wonder they didn't censor that one out for reasons of political expediency,' David said sourly.

We stayed with the jocular jockey, hoping to catch a news bulletin, as I drove south. Avoiding Lincoln, we entered the newly opened M13 at Hykeham and increased speed. Noticing the number of Army vehicles heading south with us, David started to comment when the news came through.

'This morning has been punctuated by disturbances and demonstrations in most of the larger towns throughout Britain. Some arrests have been made. In Norwich, a man was fined twenty pounds for defacing the Town Hall. The Sovereign's visit to Glasgow has been postponed until a later date.'

'Royalty!' David grunted.

'Tautology!' I grunted.

'The Soviet Ambassador to Britain said today that the Soviet peoples greatly sympathised with the wisdom shown by the British in remaining neutral. They themselves had been drawn into the conflict with the deepest reluctance, and then only because vital interests were at stake. M. Kasinferov went on to say that he was sure that guided by our example the rest of Europe would remain neutral, thus saving itself from what could only be complete annihilation.'

'Bloody flatterers,' David growled.

'Concealed threats,' I growled.

'In the United States of America, our neutrality has been generally condemned, although as one Washington correspondent points out, "Had Britain not torn up her treaties with us, she might well have been obliterated by now." Discussions over the immediate evacuation of US air, naval, and military bases in this country are taking place in Whitehall. A government spokesman said they were proceeding in what he described as "a fairly cordial atmosphere."'

'How English can you get?' David asked.

'They're probably tearing each other's throats out,' I said, instinctively pressing my foot down on the accelerator. I looked at my watch; an idea had occurred to me. From the dashboard, the gentlemanly voice continued in the same tones it had used in happier years to describe the Chelsea flower show.

'Last night saw little aerial activity, though reliable US sources report aerial reconnaissance from points as far apart as the Arctic Circle and Hawaii. Formosa is still under heavy bombardment from shore batteries. Units of the British Fleet stand ready to assume defensive action in Singapore harbour. The fighting between Chinese Airborne forces and units of the Indonesian army in Northern Central Sumatra and near Jakarta in Java still continues. Peking yesterday reported the evacuation of Medan in Sumatra, but Indonesian sources later denied this, whilst admitting that the city was "almost uninhabitable" by now. The landing of US troops near Palembang continues. So far only conventional weapons are being used on all fronts.'

'So far ... so far,' David said. 'They're only limbering up yet.'

That was where all the trouble had begun, in Sumatra, little more than a month ago. Peking had protested that the large population of overseas Chinese there were being victimised. Jakarta had denied it. A bunch of bandits shot a prominent Indonesian citizen in the Kesawan, Medan. President Molkasto protested. Tempers flared. Fighting broke out. The UN were called in. The USSR protested against this unwarranted interference in national affairs. A plane full of US experts was shot down near Bali, possibly by accident. The slanging started. Three weeks later, the People's Republic declared 'a crusade of succour': war.

'David, we're going to London via Oxford,' I said.

He looked curiously at me.

'What the hell for? It's a long way round. I thought you were in a hurry?'

'The motorway will take us as far as Bicester. The delay won't be too great. As you know, I'm a Fellow of Saints; I want to call in there and have a word with Norman, if possible.'

His reaction was predictable. Among the less informed on his side of the political arena, Saints had an undeserved reputation for being a sort of shadow Establishment from which the country was governed.

This legend had been fostered by the fact that Saints, as a compromise between Princeton's Institute for Advanced Studies and Oxford's own All Souls, naturally contained the influential among its members.

'Who is Norman?' David inquired. 'Do you mean Norman Parmettio, the Contemporary Welfare chap?'

'If you like to put it like that, yes, "the Contemporary Welfare chap." He's in his eighties now, but still active, a sage and lovable man. He drafted the Cultural Agreement of '69 with Russia, you know. He's seen academic and public service, including working as an aide to old Sir Winston at Yalta in the forties.'

'Too old! What do you want to see *him* for?'

'He's an absolutely trustworthy man, David. You forget how out of touch I am. We can't just drive into London knowing absolutely nothing of what is going on behind the scenes. Norman will put us in the picture as to what's happening in the Foreign Office and to who's changed sides in the last forty-eight hours.'

'Touché. Carry on. You know I only came for the ride – but for God's sake let something happen. My stomach's turning over all the time; I have a presentiment of evil. I'm sick!'

'So's the whole confounded country.'

We felt sicker before we reached Bicester. Another news bulletin gave us more details of local events. International news, as I had suspected, was being heavily censored; there was no mention of what was happening in Europe, or of what the Commonwealth was saying or doing.

Several members of the government had resigned – the predictable ones like Hand, Chapman, and Desmond Cooney, with a few unexpecteds such as poor old Vinton and Sep Greene. Martial law had been proclaimed in Liverpool and Glasgow. In the interests of public safety, a curfew would operate tonight and until further notice in the following cities: London, etc. … Airline services between Britain and the US and Britain and the USSR were temporarily suspended. The LCC were all out at Lords for 114.

At Fogmere Park we ran into trouble. There was a big USAF base at Fogmere. You could see the planes and runways from the road at one point. A knot of people perhaps a hundred strong – a fair number for such a country spot – filled the road. Several cars were parked on the verges, some with men standing on top of them. Banners waved, many of them bearing the usual disarmament symbol. One florid individual was haranguing the crowd through a megaphone.

'This'll take your mind off your stomach,' I told David, rolling forward at 20 mph and sounding my horn. I glanced sideways at him. He sat rigid with his fists clenched in his lap – presumably nursing his presentiment of evil.

The crowd that had been facing the other way turned to look at us, parting instinctively to clear the road. The fellow with the megaphone, a big man with a red face and black moustache, dressed in a loud tweedy suit – how often one saw his type about the country! – bore down on us and tried to open my door.

'It's locked, old fellow,' I said, rolling down my window. 'Looking for a lift to somewhere?'

He got his big fingers over the top of the window and poked the moustache in for me to inspect. His eyes went hotly from me to David and back to me.

'Where do you two think you are going?' he asked.

'Straight down this road. Kindly get your face out of the way. You are being obstructive.'

He was running to keep up with us. I could hear the crowd shouting without being able to grasp what they were saying.

'Don't annoy him,' David said anxiously.

'I want to talk to you,' the heavy man said. 'Slow down, will you. Where are you going? What's the ruddy hurry?'

His head was outside the car door. The window closed electrically, catching his fingers. He roared in anger, dropping the megaphone to clasp his bruised knuckles. As we surged forward, it became apparent why the crowd had gathered. Beyond them had been established a check-point with a black-and-white bar across the road and the legend: 'UNITED STATES AIR COMMAND. HALT.' Behind sandbags were armed men and a couple of hefty tanks, besides several light vehicles, including a British Army Signals truck. It all appeared very efficient in the colourless sunshine.

As I halted at the barrier, two Americans in uniform stepped forward, a corporal and a sergeant, one on either side of the Wolseley. Again my window came down. The sergeant looked round and amiable. I thrust my face out before he could get his in.

'What's happening here, Sergeant?'

'US Air Command check point. Just a formality to check for weapons. We have to stop all vehicles.' This in an East Coast accent: Maine, I guessed.

'Have to? Whose orders?'

'Look, my orders, sir. It's only a formality. We don't want trouble.'

'It's we English, unfortunately, who don't want trouble, Sergeant, but I'm curious to know by whose authority you have closed a main British road.'

The crowd behind, divided in loyalty as in understanding, called, 'Lock 'em up!' and 'Let 'em go!' indiscriminately.

The corporal on David's side of the car, a yellow-complexioned fellow I had already marked as a trouble-maker, since his type was prevalent in the British Army, said, 'You Limey copsuckers, you'd always argue rather than act.'

'Simon, don't be difficult; tell him what he wants to know and let's get on,' David implored. Turning to the corporal, he added, 'Don't make any mistake, we're really on your side.'

'Oh, no you ain't, Mac. You're just a neutral. You ain't on anyone's side.'

'A very apposite answer, if I may say so,' I replied. 'I still wish to know by whose orders you have erected this barrier across the highway.'

'Let's not argue, mister. Let's just say it's necessary, or I wouldn't be here wasting my time,' said the sergeant patiently. A British Army officer, a dapper captain, was coming from behind the barrier towards us. I beckoned to him and repeated my question.

Instinctively he summed me up, just as I summed him up the moment he spoke. Under his Sandhurst veneer I recognised the Birmingham middle-class accent, just as I saw he had identified my Balliol honk, accentuated for the occasion. The moment would be lost on our American sergeant, a breed without many subtleties.

'There's been a spot of trouble, sir,' the captain said, very politely. 'A small private van passed along the road a couple of hours ago and machine-gunned the American planes over on the runway. So we are just taking precautions to see that such a breach of neutrality doesn't happen again.'

'Captain, I am a friend of Lord Waters, the Lord Lieutenant of the county. Who has sanctioned this road block?'

'We naturally have official permission, sir, which I could show you.'

'Get 'em moving, Captain, before we all die of boredom,' urged the sergeant. Two other cars had arrived behind us and were hooting.

'Do you mind me asking, sir, have you any weapons in the car?'

'No, Captain. No bombs, no machine-guns.'

'Splendid. Carry on to the next check-point, sir, and try to keep moving all the time.'

'I will try,' I assured him earnestly, and we rolled under the barrier arm as it lifted. A mile down the road was the other point, stopping vehicles coming from Oxford; it let us through without comment.

'Rather a comic incident that, eh?' I said.

David's face was wooden.

'Your sort loves to make trouble and humiliate people, doesn't it?' he said.

'Not at all. You can't have every Tom, Dick and Harry blocking the roads, or where would we be? I just asked a question I was perfectly entitled to ask.'

'It comes to the same thing in the end.'

'It's people like you who fail to ask pertinent questions that get misled. Your party, for instance.'

'You dare mention parties after the tragic mistakes *yours* has made this last week?' He was furious. Debate always made his temper rise.

Quietly I said, 'You know I know my party has behaved indefensibly, David – quite indefensibly. But your party's unreal dreams of collective security without armament, of nuclear disarmament in a nuclear age, have hampered the country's striking power so effectively that our shame must also be yours. Remember the TSR 2? When you were the ones who pulled our teeth, how could you expect us to bite? What curb could we offer the Red powers? At least these traitors like Minnie and Northleech can plead they had no alternative but to act badly.'

'Christ, you wriggle on the hook as deftly as they do! What about the torn-up treaties? What about the promises? What about the Anglo-American alliance? All hot air, I suppose?'

'Here's Oxford,' I said, as we came on to the top of the Banbury Road.

We were stopped again, this time by an exotic crowd of RAF Regiment, Army, Civil Defence, and police, with a couple of AA men for luck. Plus a cheerful bunch of civilians doing good business with an ice-cream van.

'Sorry, sir, can't go through Oxford unless you've got a good reason for it.' This was a well-scrubbed corporal with a tommy-gun over his shoulder, ambling up to the car.

'Such as? I am a fellow of Saints and am on my way there now.'

'Better make it next week instead, sir. There's been a bit of trouble in the town. A fire or two and some hooliganism. We're trying to keep the city centre clear. Try the by-pass, sir, if you were thinking of going through. Keep moving and you won't get into no trouble.'

He wasn't to be budged.

'There's a phone box over there,' David pointed. 'Try phoning Norman.'

'Good idea. Thanks, Corporal.'

'Thank you, sir. Nice day, anyhow, isn't it?'

'Yes, lovely. Except for the LCC, eh?'

'What, sir? Oh yes, quite, sir. They didn't put up much of a show, did they?'

We left him beaming as I drove over to the side of the road. David laughed with an angry face.

'You love playing the decent chap and you love playing the cad, Simon. Which are you really?'

'The common man, David, *l'homme moyen sensuel*. In other words, a bit of both. Buy yourself an ice-cream while I'm phoning.'

I got through to Saints straight away and recognised the head porter's voice at once, strained as it was through thickets of phlegm. Legend has it they built the college round him.

'That you, Dibbs? Challington here. Would you put me through to Professor Norman Parmettio.'

'Hello, sir, nice to hear your voice. We haven't seen you here for months. You used to be so frequent.'

'Pressure of work, I fear. Is the professor there?'

'Well, we had a bit of trouble last night, sir.'

'Trouble? What sort of trouble?'

'Well, sir, we had to have the fire brigade round, sir. Some young hooligans threw petrol bombs over the east wall, sir. Terrible it was, sir. Fortunately I was all right in here. I phoned the police and the fire brigade and anyone I could think of. Proper scaring it was. I've never seen nothing like it.'

'Indeed, anyone killed?'

'Not to speak of, sir. But the east wing's ruined. Your old room gone, sir, and part of the chapel. By a miracle of good fortune my lodge was preserved, but –'

'It seems impossible such things could happen in Oxford, Dibbs. The time is out of joint. Where's Professor Parmettio?'

'Those are my feelings exactly, sir. There you have it. Terrible it was. As for the professor, bless his soul, he committed suicide the day before yesterday, an hour or so after the Prime Minister spoke about us British being neutral and keeping the lamps alight. At least he missed the fire and all the fuss –'

'Parmettio dead? Do you say he's dead?'

'No, he committed suicide, sir, up in his bedroom. Left a note to say his country had dishonoured him and that he was taking the only possible course open to him. A fine old fellow he was, sir. ....'

As I climbed back into the car, David dropped a newspaper he was scanning.

'You're as pale as a ghost, Simon. What's the matter?'

'How's your presentiment of evil, David? Norman's dead. Committed suicide – couldn't bear the dishonour. Poor dear old Norman! The porter told me and put me on to the Warden.'

'On to Starling? He's a true blue government man. What did he have to say?'

'He's not so true blue as we thought; frankly I feel sorry for him. He sounded like a sick man over the phone. He told me that several of the clearer-thinking younger Fellows, Thorn-Davis, Shell, Geoffrey Alderton, and one or two more, tried to charter a private plane to fly to America. Foolish, I suppose, but quite understandable. They were apparently arrested at the aerodrome and haven't been heard of since. Starling went round and saw the local superintendent of police in person but couldn't get a word out of the man. He was almost weeping as he told me. And then –'

'Then?'

'Starling was cut off.'

We sat in silence.

At last David said, 'I'm sorry if I sounded stupid before. It's all a bit nastier than we thought.'

'No nastier than we had a right to expect. We'd better get to London while we still have the chance.'

'You think all potential trouble-makers are being arrested?'

'What else? And I'd hazard that by now you and I are on the list. Got that gun of yours ready?'

He had bought a local paper from a vendor while I was phoning. As we drove off I caught sight of its headlines: RUSSIAN NUCLEAR SATELLITE IN ORBIT: Ultimate Weapon, Moscow Claims; For Emergency Only.

At one point, David leant over and switched the radio on, but they were playing *Roses of Picardy* again.

We drove into and through the outskirts of London without being stopped. By noon we were crawling through Hammersmith, moving in fits and starts through dense traffic.

'How about stopping for a drink and some sandwiches?' David asked. 'We don't really know when we'll eat again, do we?'

'Good idea. There's a pub over there that looks likely.'

London was far from normal. In the centre of town we would see processions and meetings. Here were only people in small groups, hanging about or strolling. Some of the smaller shops were closed. Never had I seen such a large percentage of the population with their eyes buried in newspapers, not even at the time of the Suez crisis, back in '56 – when the Americans had failed to support us, came the treacherous thought to my brain. Momentarily irritated with myself, I ushered David into the pub.

As I ordered drinks, I saw him cast his eye over the men present. One of them next to him, a man in voluble conversation with his mate, mistaking the intent of David's look, leant towards him and said, 'You agree, don't you, mate?'

I could not be sure what David replied in the general hubbub, but I heard the other fellow say, 'Why should we go to war for a lot of black men in Sumatra? I'd never even heard of Sumatra till last week! I reckon the government did right. Old Minnie has my vote every time. Let the blighters fight their own battles.'

At last I got served. Carrying a tray with a Guinness and a pale ale and expensive chicken sandwiches over to David's table, I was in time to hear David say, 'I can't see that neutrality *is* a way of saving our skins.'

The two men, who worked, or so I surmised, at the big cake factory nearby, were on him with glee.

'You mean you think it would be *safer* to have declared war on the Chinks and Ruskies?'

'I mean that once global war breaks out, safety axiomatically disappears.'

'Never mind axiomatically, mate! As long as we aren't in it, it's not global, is it? 'Ere, Bill, there's a bloke here thinks we ought to be fighting for the bloody Yanks!' They motioned to a couple of their mates, and soon there was a ring of them round our table. David's nervousness increased.

'If they wants a war, let them have it, I say,' Bill opined. His cheeks were heavy with woe and drink-fat. 'It's none of our business.'

'But that's precisely what it is, Bill,' I said. 'You've heard of NATO, the North Atlantic Treaty Organisation, I expect?'

Howls of derision greeted this. The first speaker – Harry, I believe he was – leant over our table and said, 'Are you honestly going to sit there and tell me that you want to see this country blown to bits just because the Americans have come a cropper in Sumatra?'

'That's not a proper question. But if you are trying to ask me whether I support the democratic way of life, then I must answer yes –'

'Democracy! Wrap up!'

'– because I believe, like many another Englishman, that it is better to die fighting than die under Communist bombs or whips.'

'That's all bloody propaganda!'

'Who's he think he is?'

'Go and join the Army!'

'You're a right one,' Bill said to me. 'What have the Yanks done for you to make you so fond of them?'

'You ought to ask yourself that,' David said angrily. 'You're old enough to remember the last war – yes, and the war before that! How do you think we'd have managed without American aid then?'

'Okay then,' Bill said in gloomy triumph. 'Then we'll hang on for three years and *then* we'll come in to help them, the way they did with us before!'

This sally drew a howl of laughter, and they turned away from us, losing interest and going back to a game of shove-ha'penny.

'Bill certainly averted a nasty moment,' David said with rancour. He drank deeply into his Guinness. 'Thank God for this poisonous British ability to laugh at themselves.'

'And at others.'

We drank up, ate our sandwiches, and rose to go.

'See you on the Russian Steppes – scrubbing them!' Harry called. Their laughter followed us into the sunshine.

We drove down the Mall and so to the Foreign Office, where I hoped to see Tertis. We had passed the marchers and the speakers, the ragged and the angry; but the prevalent mood was distastefully light-hearted. Although many of the shops had closed, cafés and pubs were open, and people were treating the whole thing as a grand unplanned holiday, lying in the parks caressing each other or buying each other ice-cream.

All this angered David much more than it did me; he had always been the one with faith in the masses.

I thought of the cities I knew thousands of miles away, their grandeurs and their shortcomings: Washington, New York, San Francisco (my favourite American city), Chicago, Kansas City, and others I had never had the opportunity to visit. Yes, and I thought of Moscow and Leningrad, Baku and Tiflis, each of which I had visited on trade missions in the fifties; and of the teeming cities of the Orient, Canton, Shanghai, Peking with its factories and Ming tombs, Amoy, all cities I had not visited and now never would visit.

What was happening in them now? Were they being crushed to the ground even while London lazed in the sun? I looked up to the sky, half expecting to see – I knew not what.

'Not yet,' David said grimly, interpreting my look. 'But it will come.'

We parked the car with difficulty and made our way to the FO.

On the drive down from Oxford, after hearing of Norman Parmettio's death, my mind had become clear. If it were possible to help overthrow Minnie's government, I would help. If I were needed to take part in a new government, in whatsoever capacity, again I would help. Throughout the fifties and the early sixties, when the Cold War had shown signs of thawing (largely because of the then Russian leader Khrushchev's love-hate affair with the West) I had remained convinced that Communism was a declared enemy. Nothing I had written or spoken publicly had wavered from that belief. My record was clean. There were not so very many like me left in Britain. If I were needed, I would serve.

Although I did not know if Tertis was accessible, he was my best line of approach. I had worked with him often; we knew and trusted each other. If he were not available, I would try elsewhere, probably with the Athenaeum as first call.

At the doors of the FO, David and I were stopped. We had to give our names, after which I was allowed to write a note for a messenger to take up to Tertis. The messenger was gone for a long while; only when fifteen minutes had elapsed did he return and request us to follow him.

Leo Tertis was assistant head of the Military Relations Department formed in the sixties and lately of growing importance. We walked down a corridor I remembered well, with messengers lounging by doorways and chandeliers hanging overhead. Nobody knocks on doors in the FO, the assumption, I suppose, being that anyone admitted to the building in the first place will be birds of a feather. When our messenger indicated the second room of the Department, I walked straight in.

Tertis was there, five years my junior and at fifty a curiously youthful figure with plump pale cheeks, almost white hair and dark eyebrows. He looked, not unexpectedly, exceedingly grave and very tired. A vacuum flask of coffee stood on his desk; though the window was open, a smell of stale cigarette smoke pervaded the room.

He had been sitting talking to a short plump man. As David and I entered, he broke off, rose, and came round the desk to shake my hand. I introduced David; Tertis eyed him appraisingly.

'David Woolf; I remember the name. You stood for Fleetwood in the by-election, didn't you?' he asked.

'I did.'

'Then you're a unilateralist. What are you doing here with Sir Simon?'

Give David his due, he hardly hesitated before replying, 'I've seen the error of my ways.'

'You're too late, my boy,' Tertis said grimly, turning away to add, 'I won't pretend I'm particularly glad to meet either of you just now, but while you're here you'd better be introduced to the Minister of Economic Affairs, Mr Edgar Northleech.'

I had already recognised the plump man as Northleech. For me he represented one of the country's worst enemies, a crony of Menhennick's, and one of the prime movers for increased appeasement towards the USSR since the retirement of Macmillan had allowed his sort to get into power. Northleech moved heavily towards us now, his white hair flowing round his head, paunch well out, beaming through his spectacles as he extended his hand. David took it; I did not.

Moving round to Tertis, I said, 'We don't have to tell each other where we stand. What can I do to help, Leo?'

'I'll give you the true picture in a moment; it's bad. Friend Northleech, like your friend Woolf here, is busy changing sides. These are men of straw, Simon, blowing with the wind. I would rather ditch them than use them.'

Northleech came into the conversation saying, in the rambling manner he maintained even when angry, 'The ability to change should not be despised. I can help you, Tertis. I can get you to Menhennick; he's ready to discuss anything; pressure of events makes him feel he may have been misled.'

'Misled!' David exclaimed. 'We don't want to *talk* to you and Minnie. We want to shoot you. Don't you realise that revolution or civil war is brewing up and down the country? Misled, be damned!'

'Enough of that talk, Mr Woolf,' said Northleech. 'We have the situation in hand, you know. Anybody can be misled.'

'It's the duty of men in office not to be misled. You've failed in your duty – abysmally. The Communist bloc's intentions have been clear since the forties.'

Red in the face, Northleech pointed a fat and shaking finger at David and said, 'That comes well from a unilateralist and a homosexual!'

'Leave personalities out of this! At least I and my party acted from our convictions. We advocated national disarmament as a first step towards general international disarmament. We advocated neutrality because as a neutral power Britain could weld other neutrals into a powerful enough group to break the deadly *status quo* of Big Two power ideologies that have frozen the world since the close of World War II. But your people, Northleech – yes, and I include you in this, Simon, and you, Mr Tertis – what were you up to all the time?'

Tertis banged furiously on his desk.

'That's enough,' he said. 'If you wish to remain in here, hold your tongue.'

But David went straight on, levelling one finger like a firearm at the three of us.

'Your sort had no real thought for world peace, or even for the country. You were after preserving the social structure to which you belonged, just as Halifax, Baldwin, Chamberlain, and the other hangers-on did in. the thirties. You're the damned middle-class powermongers, with no knowledge of Russian or Chinese language and culture, or of what goes on in their dangerous skulls. It's your unspoken assumptions that have ruined Britain, not Communism or Socialism or all the other isms put together – your assumption that the best thing that can happen to anyone is that he can become a conformist and a gentleman, your assumption that your own narrow way of life is the only fit way of life. What happened to the workers? Once they got an education – *your* type of education, with a smattering of Shakespeare and a veneer of BBC accent – then they too were hell-bent on becoming gentlemen, poor carbon-copy gentlemen.'

'Paranoia!' I exclaimed.

'Why?' he demanded explosively, turning on me. 'Because I don't subscribe to your conventions? Don't worry, you had nearly everyone else subscribing. You fools, you've ended by deluding yourselves. That's why we're all on the brink of disaster: you said to yourselves, "Oh, the Chinese leaders are gentlemen. Treat them like gentlemen and they'll behave like gentlemen!" Look where it's got you.'

'You're a very foolish young man,' Northleech said. 'There is no historical basis for your remarks. If we have in this country a rule by gentlemen, as you claim, then it is simply because the hoi-polloi have proved themselves unfit to rule. Besides, there is no conspiracy. Sir Simon and I went to the same public school, but we never had one opinion in common, then or since.'

'Except the unspoken assumption that you were both of leader material!'

'Bringing you to the FO has gone to your head, David,' I said. 'Your speech would have been more effective delivered to rabble in Trafalgar Square.'

'It may be yet. I'd still like to know why Northleech should be here, rather than with Minnie, palling up to the Chinese.'

With a brow of thunder, Tertis said, 'If you'd had the courtesy to keep quiet when you came in here, you would have heard why the Minister is here. It's too late for your type of speechifying, Mr Woolf, just as it's too late for a lot else. Edgar, you'd better tell them why you came.'

Northleech cleared his throat, glanced anxiously at Tertis, removed his spectacles to polish them furiously as he said, 'It is no longer possible to keep peace with the People's Republic. Three hours ago – probably at about the time you were leaving your university – the first nuclear weapon of World War III was detonated. A "clean" one-megaton bomb was dropped on Hong Kong. It fell at about six in the evening, local time, when the maximum number of people was about in the streets. We are as yet unable to obtain coherent accounts of the extent of the destruction.'

In the silence that followed, Tertis's internal phone rang. He picked it up, listened, said, 'Bring him in.'

Looking up at us, he said wearily, 'Our country is fatally split, gentlemen. That's the curse of it: when we come to discuss any detail, the opinions on it are infinite, and one man's vote is as good as another's. Perhaps it's the democratic system itself that has brought us to this humiliating position; I don't know. But I must ask you now to put personal considerations aside if you wish to remain here. We are about to be visited by General Schuller, Deputy Supreme Commander of NATO.'

This I scarcely heard. I was still overwhelmed by the news of the Hong Kong catastrophe and trying to assess its meaning. As a result, I had one of the briefest and most significant exchanges that ever passed between two men.

I asked Northleech, 'Then I suppose we are now actually at war with Communist China?'

Northleech said, 'No. Their Ambassador has apologised. He claims the bomb was dropped by accident.'

There seemed to me no possible reply ever to this, but David asked, 'And you believed him?'

'It seemed politic to do so,' Northleech said stonily.

'Politic! My gods alive, there's a term being used appositely for once!' David broke into ragged laughter.

Hopelessness came up and overwhelmed me. The terrible betrayal all round was at last revealing itself, and not a man in the country was innocent. Faintly, I said to Tertis, 'You were going to put us in the picture. What of the countries of the Commonwealth?'

A. deep voice from the door said, 'Canada declared war on the common enemy two hours after the US did so. It was expedient for the defence of the North American continent. Australia entered the war as soon as Sydney got news of the Hong Kong disaster. Your government promptly tore up the SEATO agreement. Seems the one thing it *is* efficient at is the gagging of news.'

General Schuller did not introduce himself. He marched into the room and planted himself by Tertis. He was brusque and angry and had cut himself shaving with an old-fashioned razor that morning. His German-American accent was thick and nasal. Dark, handsome, very neat and bemedalled, he dominated the room with compressed fury.

'Well, Tertis, here I am. Who are these men? We were to be alone, as I understood it'

Tertis stood up, listing us without introducing us. I felt like an undergraduate again under that black stare. The General made no comment, save for a snort when Northleech's identity was made known to him. Plainly he dismissed David and me from his calculations. David, with his sensitive nature, would not stand for this. Stepping forward, he produced his revolver and said, 'I am an enemy of your enemies. I'm prepared to shoot any traitors, sir.'

Schuller never paused.

'Shoot Northleech,' he ordered.

As my body seemed to freeze, so the tableau did. Even Northleech only cringed without moving from where he stood. David Woolf remained absolutely immobile. Then he returned the gun to his pocket and spoke contemptuously, in perfect command of himself.

'I kill from conviction, not to pass a personality quiz.'

Schuller grunted again, outwardly unmoved, but from that moment the first impact of his personality was weakened.

'I won't mince matters,' he said, swinging his head so that he spoke directly to Tertis. 'Britain has never added anything to the power of America. Rather, it's been a liability, a weak partner to be helped along, mind without muscle. Get it?'

'There to aid your muscle without mind,' I interposed tartly, but he continued without condescending to notice the interruption.

'We could have done without Britain as a partner once. But because she needed us, we've got bases and personnel and war material over here to defend our friends. Now at the eleventh hour – no, by Jesus, nearer half-past midnight! – your Prime Minister announces that Britain is to be neutral. Egged on by Red threats and encouragement, he says America must withdraw from these Isles. Right?

'It so happens it is no longer strategy for us to withdraw. We cannot withdraw. We are not going to withdraw. What's going to happen now, Tertis?'

Without hesitation, Tertis said, 'As things are now, with the present government, we shall fight you to turn you out.'

'Get in the picture, man! You *are* fighting us. Norfolk's a battleground right now. Outside Glasgow, the RAF is bombing our installations.'

'I don't believe it!' I said.

'You'd bloody better believe it, *Sir* Simon, because it's happening right enough.'

'I believe it, General,' Northleech said. 'You presumably want to know what can be done to change the situation?'

'No. I'm going to tell *you* what can be done.'

'You need our help, General. Don't interfere with our offering it to you. What are the alternatives as you see them?'

'The alternatives are brutal. Either you get Minnie Menhennick and his boys out of the way and replace him by a reliable anti-Red government, or – or London is going to be destroyed and this island will become an American forward base. You've got till sundown to act. We can't let you have any further time.'

Put the way he put it, it sounded all wrong. Without American interference, we would have set our house in order anyway. Made to do it under threats, we would become inglorious traitors. After all, what future was there for Britain in a nuclear war? Suddenly before my eyes rose a picture of our cities all in ruins, women and children dying, even as they were dying now in Hong Kong ... and it could happen within five minutes of our declaration of war. All the same, Schuller's view was understandable, inevitable even. I just wished it could have been put by someone less obviously a gunman.

Dismissing that hopeless argument *ad hominem*, I asked Northleech, 'Where is Minnie? Can you get us to him? Is he at Chequers, or No. 10, or where?'

'He's in London, in an underground HQ. I could get us there in twenty minutes in my car, if you're sure it's the right thing. ...'

'It's too late to *talk*. We have to act,' General Schuller said. 'Yes, let's for God's sake go in your car. My Thunderbird might be a little kind of conspicuous.'

'I'm staying here,' Tertis said. He was the least rattled of any of us. 'Though I'm under suspicion, I can be more use by keeping in touch at this end. My boss feels as I do, and there are plenty more in responsible positions who will back a change of government. You're comparatively unknown, Simon, but they'd accept you for PM in the emergency. You go with the Minister.'

As the others moved towards the door, I shook Tertis by the hand and said, 'I'll do whatever I can.'

'One word of warning,' he said. 'The country is now under martial law. Conscription for Civil Defence starts tomorrow, and you, Simon, have been officially declared an agitator – by the Dean of your college, so I hear. There's a warrant out for your arrest, so mind how you go.'

'It should improve my reputation if I stand for office,' I said. 'And David?'

Tertis nodded.

'They want him too.'

I turned round just too late to see what happened then. David had evidently gone first into the corridor. Northleech was frozen in the threshold with General Schuller close behind. Shouts came from along the corridor, shouts and the sound of running feet.

David pulled out that wretched revolver and fired twice, backing into the room as he did so. Someone screamed and the running stopped.

Belatedly, one shot was fired in reply. It splintered through the door, which David had shut by then.

Gasping, he looked round at me and said, 'They're after us, Simon. Now what the hell do we do?'

'Rubbish,' Schuller growled. 'They're after me: who else? What is this, a trap or something? Northleech, Tertis, get that desk across the door before they rush us.'

He strode across the room as Tertis and Northleech went into action. He wrenched open the side door leading into the third room of Tertis's department. This was the secretaries' room. There were three of them, nice fresh young fellows all looking rather identical with identical suits and their hands raised above their heads. The General had brought two majors and a signalman with him, to wait for him in this outer office. The majors had already attended to the secretaries, while the signalman worked at his walkie-talkie, speaking into it in unhurried code.

'Nice fast work, Farnes and Able,' General Schuller said, striding into the third room and adding to the secretaries, 'Sorry about this, boys, but if I'm in a trap you'll have to play hostage.'

'They're after Woolf and Sir Simon, General, not you,' Tertis said, following Schuller. 'Let me go out into the corridor and explain to them.'

'You'll stay where you are. I'm sorry not to trust you, Tertis, but right now the British aren't my favourite nation. I'm taking no chances with anyone. Farnes and Able, bring those three hostages into the other room. Get the desk in too and barricade the side door with it. Look slippy. Operator, get Green Devil One on the air.'

'Right to hand, sir,' the operator said, looking up and handing a scramblerphone to Schuller.

Both majors carried light machine-guns. The one addressed as Farnes covered Tertis, David, Northleech and me, while Able directed the three secretaries. The latter worked efficiently, dragging in the desk, even smiling as they did so; for them this seemed just a break in FO routine. I wondered whether they were displaying British nonchalance or if they genuinely did not grasp the seriousness of the situation.

For myself, I expected a grenade to come through the door at any moment, until it occurred to me that the guards outside were holding their fire in case they injured the General. Everything happened in such rapid succession that it was difficult to think clearly. Although I did not know in what tone Dean Burroughs had reported my hurried exit from East Lincoln, it seemed likely that he would have exaggerated enough for the group in the corridor to regard me as a potential killer.

The General handed the scramblerphone back to his operator, informing the majors as he did so, 'They're going to have a whirlybird at this window in two minutes minus.'

Instinctively we all glanced over at Tertis's long windows with the balcony looking out across Horse Guards' Parade.

Later it occurred to me that here was a moment for clear thought – the first since the General had entered the room. He filled it by striding from one desk to the other with his jaw forward, saying with heavy sarcasm, 'And now, my friend Tertis, we'll test out your theory that the guards outside aren't gunning for me at all. Farnes, throw this guy David Woolf out into the corridor.'

You understand there were ten of us in the room. The place was comparatively crowded. I saw David's face shift as he ducked and moved. He looked rat-like: both frightened and frightening.

'You can't do this, Schuller. I'm on your side. Take me in the helicopter with you!'

He dodged behind Northleech, who whinnied with fright, and behind Schuller, pulling out his gun as he went. The crazy scheme no doubt was to hold Schuller at pistol-point until we were all safe in the copter. Doubtless David fell between self-preservation and patriotism and saw this idea as offering more hope than being pushed out into the corridor.

'Hold still, General, I won't harm –' he began, his voice shrill. But Farnes moved too. He sprang two paces across the room, dropped to one knee, and fired an automatic, one short and deafening burst.

The long window splintered and fell in. Northleech dropped next – through sheer panic reaction. For a second, dazed, I thought David had not been hit. Then dark blood gouted out of three holes in his shirt, spreading fast.

General Schuller swung round on him. David closed his eyes and fired one shot. Schuller blundered forward on to him. The two men fell together, breaking a chair as they went. Appalled, the two majors ran forward.

In moments of extreme crisis, a governing mechanism seems to take over from the rational centres of the brain. Without reflecting at all on what I was doing, I went to the outer door, pushed aside the desk that barricaded it, and threw it open.

Behind an open doorway opposite, armed men watched from cover. I saw their weapons come up. Down the corridor one way, another group had gathered, dark suits mingling with khaki.

'General Schuller has been assassinated! Help!' I called.

Framed in the doorway with smoke drifting past me, I must have looked a wild enough figure. But it was that pregnant cry 'Assassination,' echoing down the corridors of the Foreign Office, that brought them all running. As they came, I turned and beckoned Northleech.

In the excitement, the two of us left unnoticed. My last glimpse into the room caught a sudden shadow falling over it. Schuller's helicopter was arriving – on time, but too late. We ran down the corridor, Northleech puffing hard. As we descended the grand staircase, more shots rang out. Another fool had gone trigger-happy. Long bursts of automatic fire indicated that the helicopter was returning as good as it got.

We met several people. To all of them I uttered my formula and they scattered. Even at the door, where a no-nonsense captain in the South Wales Borderers moved to block our escape, I said, 'Captain, General Schuller has been assassinated and you people will have to answer for it. See you get reinforcements and surround the building. Nobody whatsoever must leave until further orders. Clear?'

'I'm not in charge here, sir –'

'Then consider yourself so immediately. Get half a dozen men up on the second floor at once.'

He jumped to it and we were through.

'My car!' Northleech puffed. 'It's got a radio link. I must speak to Whitehall as we go. Over this way.'

He headed towards the Chiefs' Park and I followed, blinking in the sunshine.

'We're going to Menhennick?' I asked.

'Yes.'

His car was one of the new JC wagons, with a chauffeur lounging near who threw open the rear door smartly as we approached.

'The Tower, James – fast,' Northleech ordered.

We climbed in and I asked, 'You mean to say Menhennick's in the Tower of London? How singularly appropriate.'

'Underneath it.'

Northleech was just recovering his breath. As we rolled forward he opaqued the bullet-proof glass so that we could see out and not be seen. At the press of a button, a small bar slid out at knee level. At the press of another, his radiophone opened before him. We were of course completely sound-proofed off from the driver.

The screen before the Minister lit. A severe matron appeared, with behind her a crowded Whitehall room where people came and went.

'Give me Bawtrey, General Intelligence,' Northleech said, still puffing slightly.

'There may be a moment's delay, Minister. Routine is a little disturbed at present.'

'Fast as you can, miss. Emergency.'

She turned away. Northleech stabbed a finger at the screen.

'I'll give her "routine disturbed." Look, there's some bugger walking round that room with a cup of tea in his hand. Do you wonder the country's going to the dogs!'

I bit off the obvious answer that it was people like him who helped it go. He poured us some drinks, looked more cheerful, and began to grumble, all the while tapping one knee impatiently and staring at the screen before him.

'Sorry we had to leave Leo Tertis with his hands full like that. ... Expedient, however. Look, Simon, I don't want you to feel disappointed, but Tertis was flannelling you in there.'

'In what way?'

'This incredible stuff about the possibility of your becoming PM No offence, but it just shows how far poor old Tertis's judgement is awry'. I urged the Foreign Secretary to get him into something safe like Housing years ago. ... I mean, for PM we need a man of experience, a young man, a man in the public eye, a man who knows the ropes, knows where to turn for guidance.'

'To you for instance?'

'I'll serve as long as the public need me, Simon. I'm an old warhorse.'

'You're a bloody pacifist, Edgar. Appeasement's the be-all and end-all of your philosophy.'

He looked broodingly at me, entirely without taking offence.

'You don't really want to see this grand little country blown to bits just to gratify your ambition, do you?'

'My record –'

'Bugger your record! You can't help being what you are, I know. You've never held office and you can't see the reason for being guided by necessity occasionally. There's none of the sticker about you, Simon, that's what's lacking. In my young days, I had the fortune to be guided by the great Lord Halifax –'

'You know what I think of Halifax!'

'I don't care what you think. You don't think enough. That's the world's trouble. Look at Schuller: the action school, as much brain power as a bull. Need never have been killed if he'd spent thirty seconds cogitating instead of emoting. *Non cogitavit ergo fuit.* Same with Woolf – an anarchist and subversive like all his kind. He had no idea he was shooting Schuller; it was simple father-hatred squeezed the trigger.'

'Package reasoning! There was a lifetime's conviction behind that bullet of David's. He had a reasoned hatred of big and noisy men who use their position to make more noise –'

'Putting you through,' said the panel. Simultaneously, a bearded man in shirt sleeves with a cup at his elbow and a pile of flimsies in his fist blinked into being on the screen.

'Hello, Bawtrey,' Northleech said, with a parade of affability. 'What's happening since I called you last?'

'Everything,' Bawtrey said, taking a swig from his cup. 'What do you want to know, Minister?'

'Relevant events of the last two hours. Hong Kong?'

'Nothing fresh. No new H-bombs dropped. First casualty estimate, one hundred fifty thousand dead, wounded, and missing. Singapore on general alert, Aussie fleet engaging Chinese warships off New Guinea. Three Russian nuclear subs detected and destroyed off Alaska coast –'

'What else? Washington?'

'Contact with America is just about defunct,' Bawtrey said, looking at us under his eyebrows. 'They're tearing their hair here, Minister. Not a peep from Washington, New York, Ottawa, Toronto – the whole blessed continent might just as well have disappeared. All cables are reported temporarily out of order, and all wavelengths blanketed with unusually strong interference.'

Northleech and I looked at each other.

'How long has this been the case?' Northleech asked.

Bawtrey glanced at his watch.

'I've been on shift two hours. Two and a half hours, at a guess. There may be something through in a few minutes. Meanwhile, hang on, here's something else of interest.'

As he was speaking, Bawtrey leafed through his flimsies. 'The first space battle is now in progress. US Orbiters attacking the Red nuclear satellite, meeting opposition from Tsiolkos and China bugs.'

'Europe?'

'Mobilisation in France, Italy, and the Scandinavian countries. Every man in Western Germany at the frontier, Reuter reports. Same in Turkey, Greece. Main impression seems to be that they're waiting to see what Great Britain decides.'

As the man talked, I stared out of the window. We moved with unconscionable slowness, though Northleech's driver took short cuts when he could. Trafalgar Square was crowded, and not only with soap-box orators. A figure in a white cassock was holding a service on the steps of St Martin's-in-the-Fields. Down the Strand, traffic was entirely at a standstill. We detoured round Covent Garden, to squeeze into a Fleet Street almost as crowded.

In contrast to the sightseers round the Park, people here looked grave. Outside a Civil Defence recruitment booth, both men and women queued. The military was out in strength; a column of light tanks added to the traffic congestion. I thought of the other grey old capitals of Europe, members of the same dying yet grand order, all teetering on the brink of annihilation.

Bawtrey shuffled up another piece of paper as we approached Ludgate Circus.

'Dame reaffirms Sark's neutrality,' he read disgustedly, screwing it up. 'And here's one more in your line, Minister. Deputy Supreme Commander of NATO, General Gavin T. Schuller, was assassinated within the last twenty-five minutes by David Woolf, described as a member of the British Communist Party. Members of the Special Police shot Woolf before he could escape. Fighting is still –'

He paused. Someone visible to us only as a torso tapped Bawtrey's shoulder and handed him a fresh communiqué. He read it out slowly, squinting now and again at Northleech as he did so.

'Here's one for the general circuits. Sounds like big stuff. Seems they finally got through to Washington and Ottawa. This one's datelined Washington and reads: "Mr Martin Mumford, President of the United States, will make a special address to the world at 1500 hours, British Summer Time, today." That's in about twenty-eight minutes' time. "This address will transcend in importance any previous statement ever made by a US President." Hm, some billing. "It is of the utmost importance that the largest possible audience in all countries sees and hears the President speak." Sounds as if the Martians have stepped in, doesn't it?'

'That will be all, thank you, Bawtrey,' Northleech said, obviously disapproving such facetiousness. As he switched off, the bearded man picked up his cup, swigged it and faded into nothing. The set folded neatly back into its compartment

The traffic thinned; we accelerated along the last stretch of the way, and the Tower swung into sight ahead. The bright dress uniforms had gone. Light tanks had replaced the sentry-boxes. Everything was handled efficiently. Northleech produced a pass for the guard officer, which was okayed. Nevertheless, we and the driver had to climb out and be searched for firearms, while two plain-clothes men simultaneously examined our vehicle.

They gave us clearance in about forty-five seconds, saluting us as we drove on under Byward Tower with a guard riding beside the driver.

We drove over to the Queen's House and climbed out. I followed Northleech inside. Another guard stationed by a wooden staircase was replacing the receiver on a handphone as we entered; the main gate had warned him we were about to arrive. He flicked over a switch normally concealed behind oak panelling.

The wooden staircase hinged at the sixth step up, yawning open to reveal a flight of carpeted stone stairs descending underground. Motioning to me, Northleech started down them, his untidy white hair fluttering round his head in the warm updraught of air.

I recognised that smell of canned air, sweet with disinfectant. It reminded me of the underground HQ of my department in Hyde Park during World War II. This was a much more elaborate and larger subterranean system. At the bottom of the stairs was a chain of three airlocks giving one on to each other, their indicators all at a neutral green. They opened on to a large circular space, well-lit but almost deserted. Here stood a magazine and paper stall, a tobacconist's, and a café, all open. Piped music played softly. I noticed other stairs leading down into this foyer.

Without hesitation, Northleech led over to a central block of lifts, a row of perhaps a dozen of varying sizes, each with an ancient male attendant waiting by the doors. We entered the nearest.

'Level X,' Northleech said crisply.

Glancing at me with a sly humour, he remarked, 'You see the government hasn't been entirely unprepared for emergencies.'

'Every man for himself,' I replied.

It was an express lift. I climbed out at the bottom feeling slightly sick. For a second we had been in free fall.

Here was a maze of corridors, with many people moving fast with set faces. After some slight confusion and a word or two of barked argument, Northleech got us into an anteroom, where a smartly formidable secretary left us, returning in two minutes.

While he was out of the room, Northleech said, 'I know this man, this secretary. Obviously Menhennick is still in full control. We'll have to watch our step until we see how the land lies. Agreed?'

'It seems inevitable.'

'Keep it that way. We don't want trouble if it can be avoided.'

'Spoken in character, Minister.'

'Don't be a bloody fool, Simon. You're out of your depth and you know it.'

The secretary, returning, said, 'The PM's with the Indian Premier and other Commonwealth gentlemen. You may go in, but don't intrude.'

We went in.

We did not intrude.

The room was impressive. Some fifty men were gathered there, many of them leading diplomats. Waiters with trays unobtrusively served drinks. On the surface it appeared incongruously peaceful. I recognised Mr Turdilal, the Indian Premier, at once. He stood on a raised platform with Minnie slightly behind him. Minnie looked worn and shrunken; his face reminded me of the ill look I had seen on the face of Sir Anthony Eden at the time of Suez.

Turdilal seemed incongruously cheerful. He was in full spate as we entered, waving a relaxed right hand in time with his phrases.

'... and furthermore, gentlemen, you need no reminding from me that India has always stood for the peace of the world. We are an old nation and we have always stood for peace. That is why we are standing now at this terribly black hour of international conflict solidly behind the British government and most of the other members of the Commonwealth for neutrality. We —'

'What about the invasion of Indonesia?' a voice called.

Turdilal smiled a charming smile.

'What about the invasion, indeed, my South American friend? Carnage added to carnage does not equal peace, my friend. We are not Gadarene swine, may I remind you. Your country is also on friendly terms with Indonesia, but you are not hurrying to bear arms on their behalf. No. You are wise. Instead you are stepping up armament production to sell to China, I guess.'

Ugly murmurs greeted this, but Turdilal flowed on.

'South America must remain neutral. And that is what I am saying also about Britain and the Commonwealth. Someone must rebuild out of the ashes. That is a harder task than creating the ashes. So I for one applaud Mr Menhennick's stand against the pressure of power politics.'

A hubbub arose as he finished, angry cries mingling with cheers and the odd handclap.

Minnie came forward, clapped Turdilal weakly on the back, and held up his hand for silence. When it came, he rubbed the hand over his moustache and said, 'Thank you for your support, gentlemen. I realise our country is in an invidious position, I realise it only too well. But we have been in an invidious position for a quarter of a century now, ever since the perfection of this deadly nuclear power and the emergence of the two great powers. Rest assured, I have done all in my power to keep our beloved country safe. Rest assured, I shall not stand down —'

'Shame!' I cried.

'– until I feel the nation has no more need for me. ...'

'Go, in God's name, go!' I shouted.

Two Ghana ministers looked angrily round and said, 'Keep silence while he speaks,' and a waiter pressed a large whisky into my hand.

'I will say no more now,' Minnie continued, looking at his watch. 'In two minutes, the American President, Mr Mumford, is speaking to the world via Telstar II. We can see it on the wall screen here. I do not know what he is to say, but doubtless it will be of grave import. Just at present our contacts with Washington are disturbed; however, I have been reliably informed that a very few hours ago the American continent was subjected to intense nuclear bombardment on both her seaboards.'

A ripple of amusement that grew with the beginning of his last sentence was killed stone dead by the end of it. A terrible silence, a chill, settled over everyone present – myself, of course, included. Everyone present had their differences with the United States, yet in that moment friction died and love came uppermost. Many faces were full of shame. We all stood motionless.

Not a word was spoken until the big wall screen lit. The time was three o'clock.

The Global Viewing sign came on, a spinning world with the illuminated orbits of the TV relay stations surrounding it. How long, I wondered, before they were shot down and TV shrank again into a petty national plaything instead of the transnational communication it had become?

A voice said, 'Here is the President of the United States of America, Mr Martin Wainwright Mumford.'

He sat composedly at a desk bare of everything bar one sheet of paper. He wore a neat suit. Behind him hung the American flag. He looked young, determined, and under enormous strain. He launched into what he had to say without preliminaries; he spoke without rhetoric.

'I invited everyone in the world to see and hear me because what I have to say is of personal importance to you all.

'Only a few hours ago, the enemies of the United States launched their mightiest weapons upon us. Intercontinental ballistic missiles carrying nuclear warheads descended on all our major cities almost simultaneously. Their destructive forces when unleashed on their targets were so great that no nation could have survived the blow.

'Happily, all those missiles were checked some miles up in the atmosphere.

'The United States of America now possesses a sure defence against the hideous and hitherto all-conquering weapon of nuclear bombing.

'This defence is of such a nature that it could only be given thorough trial under actual test conditions. We have had to undergo that test, and we have survived. Had the defence failed, I should not be here talking to you now.

'The defence takes the form of a shield, which we call the geogravitic flux. In theory, this form of defence has been known for some time, but its consumption of energy seemed so vast as to render it impracticable. However, our scientists and technologists have perfected a way whereby the shield – which now covers all of North America, our Canadian allies as well as ourselves – the shield draws its power from the nuclear powers it destroys. The greater the force exerted against it, the more greatly the shield is able to resist.

'You will see that we are in consequence impregnable. What is more, we shall remain impregnable for a long time. We have this new defence. Our enemies have new weapons. We were subjected not only to nuclear attack; we were bombarded by a type of anti-matter bomb infinitely more terrible than the nuclear bomb, which must now be regarded as old-fashioned. Our shield effectively repelled all comers.'

Almost furtively, I glanced about me. Every face was fixed in fascination on that grave face looming on the screen. An immense pressure of triumph was building up as the President continued his address.

'I confess that this nation – as yet – has no anti-matter bomb. We have been concentrating on methods of defence rather than offence. But we have literally at our finger-tips the mighty power of the atom. So far we have unleashed no retaliatory bombs in reply to the brutal attack of our enemies.

'It is my hope that retaliation will not be necessary. America and Canada cannot be conquered; but we could bring our enemies to their knees two hours from now. We could destroy them utterly, as they well know. We do not desire to take this ultimate step. The collapse of the two vast Communist countries would involve the rest of the free world in decades of rehabilitation too costly to be visualised. So we are stepping forward, laying our cards on the table, and inviting our enemies to make peace with the Free World at once.

'This is an unprecedented step to take. We live in unprecedented times; God grant us unprecedented courage to meet it.

'Such a step would not have been possible had not our friends the British, and the other North Atlantic countries who look to them for leadership, decided to remain neutral. Had they not so decided, then beyond doubt they would have suffered the same terrible bombardment inflicted on us. Without the geogravitic shield, they would never have survived, and we should have been forced to carry out total war to avenge their destruction.

'So I say again, we whole-heartedly and unreservedly offer a fresh chance to make peace. On behalf of my government and people, I invite the leaders of the Communist bloc to meet me personally on neutral ground in London. I give them forty-eight hours to make a just peace. After that time, if they have not shown themselves more than willing to build a lasting agreement – they know what the consequences will have to be.

'They will be shown no mercy then, as they have shown us no mercy. But the United America offers them more than mercy now.'

Mumford's image disappeared. At once a subdued uproar broke out in the hall. Like many of the others, I was weeping with an un-British lack of restraint.

Next to the hall was a canteen. As I was eating there a few minutes later, Northleech approached, talking to a secretary. By his manner, I saw he bubbled with excitement. No doubt he was, in his own phrase, being guided by necessity. He broke off his conversation to speak to me.

'Look here, Sir Simon, this wonderful gesture of Mumford's has put a different complexion on matters. I will see to it personally that the warrant for your arrest is cancelled straightaway.'

'Thank you. Then I can get back to East Lincoln to see how my wife is. Though I shall have to tender my resignation to the Dean.'

'Understandable, quite. Well, that must remain your worry; I can't interfere there, naturally.'

'Naturally.'

'Though the Dean may not accept it. His anti-American views were always too clear. Since you'll no doubt return there as something of a hero, he may feel that by keeping you on he will gain popularity for himself. I'm sure I should feel like that, in his boots.'

I looked down at my plate to conceal my distaste.

'I'm sure you would,' I said. 'But I'm sick of appeasement in all its forms. A new breeze is blowing from now on, and I'm coming back into politics.'

A spark of anger fired in the old boy. He rapped on my table, making my spoon rattle against the plate.

'Before you do that, you'd better learn to distinguish between negotiation and appeasement.'

'I can already. You're a great appeaser, Minister; Mumford is a great negotiator. The difference is in the position from which you talk: a position of weakness or a position of strength. Mumford's is one of strength, yours and Minnie's one of weakness – and chiefly moral weakness.'

He cleared his throat. His wattle had turned a dusky red. In a low voice he said, 'Stop kicking a man when he's down. You saw for yourself how shaken poor old Alfred Menhennick was. He can't resign quickly enough.'

There had never been better news. I only wished Jean – and David Woolf – could have shared it with me. Then, sobering my excitement, came the thought that we would have to turn out all of Minnie's sympathisers before the peace contingent arrived from America. When I spoke, the secretary flinched at the poison in my voice.

'Your own position is none too happy, Edgar. Mumford may have granted Britain a face-saver for general consumption, but you well know how Washington must really be feeling about us. Aren't we revealed, every one of us, as a set of cowardly turncoats – not only to the US but to the world? You might alleviate the situation slightly by resigning with Minnie, as quickly and publicly as possible – or perferably by falling on your sword.'

He gripped the back of his chair.

'I remember this sort of holier-than-thou cant from you in the Sixth Form,' he said. 'I'm a politician, not a Roman. I've no time for your sort of dramatics. It's true the world, and the Americans in particular, are going to need a lot of explanations, but I'm not going to quit now – I'm going to give them those explanations. Now more than ever the country needs experienced leaders.'

Only for a moment did his face grow ugly; then he smiled with his mouth alone. The secretary aped the gesture of ill-omen.

Conversation Piece

Mister, this may be a funny place to say such a thing, but I've always held that if a man can't get on with society, that's his fault, not society's, and I still stick to that – and I'm a man who's seen our society from top as well as bottom.

No, you've always got to blame yourself. Not but what troubles don't come up and hit you unexpectedly. Yet even those troubles can have their roots in some flaw in your own character, timidity or concupiscence or whatever; we don't do any good by hiding the fact. I could give you an instance.

It was last Christmas Day – Christmas 2061, only a month back, though as far as I'm concerned it might be a century ago – that Randy Kellylarge was charged with murder.

Nowadays, in our finely adjusted society, murder's the rarest of crimes, and you might think Kellylarge would be an exceptional man. Well, I never met him, but I've concluded that far from being remarkable he was just a weakling, and that what's more he deserved all he got.

Of course, as far as the actual murder was concerned, as the marrijudicator admitted afterwards, while deducting twenty whole points from Kellylarge's Ability A card, there was provocation. Heck, here you and I stand in this lousy queue; I may as well tell you about it.

Seems Kellylarge had undergone a pretty trying day on the game preserve. The zambuck, or whatever those deer are with curly horns, had been stampeding, and three of them went over a precipice. That's a mark against anyone's Proficiency C, as you can imagine. Costs about forty mahounits a day to maintain, does one zambuck – you don't want to lose any.

So Kellylarge was not too agreeable that evening when he got into the marrena. His proxi sensed this and said she would take him for a spin. They'd just had new batteries and A-G plates installed, and the bug went like a boom.

Kellylarge's proxi was a pleasant-looking blonde girl called Ida Cassilis. She had, besides the usual female curves, the usual female range of moods. An exciting girl, generous, and full of life – far too good for Kellylarge. This evening she was reckless, driving like jazz through the city. Why? Well, she had a new green wisp of scarf on, and probably she wanted to see it flutter in the wind. You know women, stranger; in a word, unpredictable.

Yes, as you say, that's what marrenas are for – to see how well a man responds to such womanliness.

Anyhow, Ida gears in on a levelway, U-turns, and is A-Ging up a flyup in the city centre before you can say 'World President.' She bats out on to a level above the rooftops without signalling, and they run slap into an oncoming biwheel, pflatt!

Of course Kellylarge and Ida were strapped; they weren't hurt, although the bug was a write-off. Since its A-Gs were still functioning, it hung there in the air, slightly lop-sided and six feet off the level. He jumped down. He called to Ida to jump down into his arms. She couldn't; she was scared. He persisted. She got hysterical. He couldn't get up to her again. Big scene.

The biwheel, being roboted, had staggered on after dropping an audibuoy to mark the spot of the accident. A passing tellicopter picked up the audibuoy signal before the militia did, homing in on it in time to catch the big scene. I saw it myself. I was passing through McKenna Concourse when it came up on the public globe and stopped to watch.

Certainly it looked funny to an onlooker, with him down there shouting and her up there shouting back – was his neck red! Anyhow Kellylarge didn't find it amusing. Ida looked nice even in that absurd position.

When the militia had rescued her, they caught the pneumat back to his flat, where a good old row started. Kellylarge said he had wanted to go out for a quiet ride, Ida said of course he had: his flat was small enough to give anyone claustrophobia.

That really hurt Kellylarge, slap in his pride. I don't know if you understand the social stratifications here in the United African Republics, stranger, but the situation is roughly like this. Now that the last slice of the Amazon Basin has gone under the plough, these big wildlife reserves we run here – particularly the Kasai Park, which is the most highly organised – are the last stretches of undeveloped land in the world. In consequence, they're worth a mint of money. Countries like Common Europe and the United States of Both Americas, that are almost entirely covered by urbanism, send their executives here to untense among the animals, and pay through the nails for the privilege. Kellylarge was sent here on leave in this way, and at the same time he was carrying on his marriage trials here in Manono.

His social ratings stood at about 30 : 60 : 75 : 80. Low on Ability even then you see.

In a small town like this – we only cover an area of twenty-five square miles, but we're growing – accommodation is short all round. Same thing all over UAfR, but particularly bad here. So we allow floor space in ratio to social ratings. A real crack 95 : 95 : 95 : 95 man would be allowed maybe as much as fifty square feet to live in, and so down on a sliding scale. Poor old Kellylarge only rated twenty-six square feet.

You know what that means – shared amenity rooms. Being an insecure sort of individual, Kellylarge took this personally. No social sense! Funny how often Common Europe breeds that type nowadays.

Don't shuffle like that, chum. The queue's beginning to move, and I'll get on with the tale.

'You damned hutch-dweller!' Ida called him. Not that I don't think twenty-six square is enough for any man – particularly a punk like Kellylarge – but you know how these proxi queens live! They're privileged, rightly so, to my mind, considering the ardours of their jobs.

'Call me that again if you dare,' Kellylarge said, moving towards her.

'I called you a damned little hutch-dweller,' Ida said. 'You come home stinking of animals, and then you expect me to stay cooped up in here with –'

He jumped her. He had his hands round her throat and was choking the life out of her before they could get to him. Boy, I'm anti-social, I know, or I wouldn't be in this queue, but why don't they show that sort of stuff on the tellyglobes? Wishywashy, that's what the world's become. With fifty thousand million people around, naturally they're scared of violence.

Anyhow, the flat door burst open, and in rushed the marrijudicator, a man called Ben Manjaro, his continuity girl, and a couple of the marriage ministry boys.

They pulled Kellylarge off Ida and clapped a stun on him.

'You're a murderer, Kellylarge!' Ben Manjaro said, mopping his brow.

'You didn't give me time,' Kellylarge said.

'You know the law, Kellylarge – only the intent to murder has to be proved. Prevention is better than the crime. That's twenty points off your Ability A, and you know it.'

'Please not that, sir. I can't face the disgrace. Why, if I drop twenty I shall lose my job with Eldorado Els. You know this was just a test – I'd never treat my real wife like that!'

'No? Well, with your new rating you'll never get the chance. With a 10 : 60 : 75 : 80, you don't think they'll let you marry your intended, do you? You're all washed up, Kellylarge.'

Kellylarge staggered back, white as a shirt, robbed of the power of speech. And at that point, Ida got up and made *her* speech!

Eh? No, thanks, chum, I'd never dare to smoke here, and I'd advise you not to either. You must come from Common Europe – cigarettes may be lit on the streets there, but you're in a smokeless zone here, which includes reefers and cigarettes.

As I was saying, Ida Cassilis started letting fly at the marrijudicator then.

Manjaro let her have her say. Any lesser breed would have been knocked right down the rating hierarchy on the spot. Still, you know what proxies are. Since they stopped marriage being a lottery and took to testing men for matrimonial suitability the proxi girls have become more glamorous than drama stars; so the marrijudicator stood with his mouth open, letting Ida have her say.

That's what comes of paying people on a scale outside the ratings. They get too much those girls, and for what? For just acting a part, that's all. Does that make them better than us? Does that qualify them for dual consumption quotas? Okay, buster you're right – it does. But it shouldn't.

I'm all mixed up. I admire the proxies really, but look at it historically. (You can see I'm an educated man, even if I do stand here flattening my feet with you abil-nils.) Once you start getting whole regions of the world covered with two- or three-level cities, you get population troubles, even with planktrition to ease feeding, right? You have to breed inhibitions, right? To keep Billy Blank from elbowing his neighbour or stepping into someone else's centimetre of space, right? That was how we progressed from world peace to the concept of Personal Peace.

To have that, you want nice quiet docile kids growing up everywhere like those flowers they used to have that you see in the period globies. Okay, then that means systematised mating – husband and wife well adjusted, no trouble, no friction, all nice and quiet and docile. Heck, it's not as difficult as it sounds. They don't have to be happy, just so long as they don't quarrel.

It took some organising at first. Not that there were protests, I don't mean; we've been lucky the way we've been able to trim calorie intake so that those old civic liberties so-called – all that medieval ritual of voting and stuff – became a nuisance and were abolished. But the trouble was to pass the right legislation.

Probably you remember how World President Soepoena took a hand in polishing some of the final clauses himself. What it boiled down to in the end is two main laws: that it is criminal to bear children out of wedlock – since the Church flung in its hand with the State, that went through easily enough – and that marriage can only be permitted where the couples have undergone tests to prove they aren't suffering from violent tendencies or any other retrogressive emotions.

Under the newly established Ministry of Marriage, the marrenas were set up, with proxies and all, to carry out these tests, and of course Kellylarge had to go through the hoop like anyone else. His intended was some girl who worked on the Zuyderzee collective as a gametophyticists' assistant, a nice quiet little creature who had already passed her tests. She'd never have been capable of jumping off on the slanging spree that Ida did.

'You're just a log of cog!' Ida told Manjaro. 'Why didn't you stay outside and let Randy murder me? Maybe we'd both have been happier! I'm sick and tired of this job. Look at all I had to put the poor boy through today – faking that stupid bug accident on the upper levels, needling him about his floor quota, and all that! Do you wonder he got angry at me? Who can blame him?!'

'The question is not one of blame but of classification,' snapped the marrijudicator. Manjaro was a big man, swelling now like bagpipes, the likeness increased by a tartan flush on his face caused by an amalgam there of blue vein and red flush. 'Kellylarge has proved himself unfit for modern marriage, and it's no further concern of yours.'

'So much the worse for modern marriage!'

'You mustn't say that,' Kellylarge interrupted. 'I just forgot myself, Ida, and I'm sorry, but don't get yourself into trouble for my sake.'

'You stay out of this, Randy, you darned fool. You've put your foot in it far enough as it is.'

'What do you mean, put my foot in it? I'm trying to apologise, aren't I? Is this Christmas or isn't it, when people of goodwill are nice to each other?'

'What's Christmas to do with it? Don't be old-fashioned! No wonder you only qualify for enough floor-space for a chipmunk.'

'Why. you cow, I wish I *had* really got you down there and got my hands round that damned white delicate delicious neck –'

'Just because you've been fraternising with animals you think –'

Ben Manjaro seized her by one white delicate delicious wrist and swung her away from Kellylarge.

'Now see here, Miss Cassilis,' he said sternly, 'just you cool down, you've been through these tests with a thousand men before. Many of them muffed their tests, and you never gave a chirp. Why all the excitement this time over a lousy 30 : 60 : 75 : 80?'

She stamped with anger, swished her arm free, swirled her hair. It must have been a marvellous sight.

'Because he's not just a 30 : 60 : 75 : 80. He's not just a cog like all the rest of them. He's Randy Kellylarge, and he's the first man ever to offer me violence.'

'Ida, I said I'm sorry –'

'You keep *out* of this!!'

'Okay, Miss Cassilis, he offered you violence. Is that any reason why you should offer violence back?'

'Yes it is. I *love* him!'

'But Ida –'

'Don't keep interrupting, you lovely crazy hunk of maladjusted manhood, you!' she cried, and flung herself upon him with an orgy of kisses.

You know the old saying about the course of true love never running counter to one's rating. It didn't hold true in this case. There was a real dust-up, I tell you, the reverberations of which were heard in the highest quarters, and it wasn't long before things started moving – talking of which, I detect a sluggish shuffle at the head of this dead-and-alive queue. We're on our way, feller!

This row, you'll recall, took place on Christmas Day. By the middle of Boxing Day, both Ida Cassilis and Randy Kellylarge were in trouble – and both were giving trouble back. Let's take this girl Ida first, because she is definitely the more interesting of the two.

Manjaro stood just so much maladjustment from her, and then he hit back.

'Miss Cassilis, carrying on like this in front of witnesses will do you no good,' he warned her.

The gesture she made at the marriage ministry boys showed exactly what she thought of them. Indicating Kellylarge, she said, 'Can't you see why I'm upset? For heaven's sake, what's going to happen to this poor boy? One man in a thousand with spirit, and you inflict this brutal punishment on him.'

Manjaro sighed heavily.

'Brutal nothing. The law's the law, whether you kid yourself you're in love or whether you don't. Calm down before I get irritable, Miss Cassilis, and stop trying to buck against the status quo.'

'To hell with the status quo, Mr Manjaro! I'm fed up with it. It stinks! Oh, for a man with spirit, with fire, with daring!'

Manjaro went tartan-faced again.

'You've gone just too far, you trumped-up little proxi. As of now, you're fired from the marriage ministry. Now get out of here, the lot of you!'

Well, Ida wasn't the girl to sit down under that; she organised all the other proxies to go on strike on her behalf.

*

I've always argued that these proxies get far too many privileges, and nothing will ever make me change my mind. Yet you can see that they hold a unique position of power in our well-organised society. I mean, through their pretty hands go all the men who ever aspire to marriage, so that they are for ever indulged, for ever having men trying to court them nicely. Then again, they have to play up and be more cantankerous than a normal woman, just to make the tests rigorous enough, and you can't tell me this does not make them something of a race apart.

So the proxies staged a strike. They refused to test any more men till Ida was reinstated. As a result – pouff! – no more marriages! World President Soepoena sent them an address all about working for the greatest integration of the greatest number. Made no difference. The girls stuck to their guns.

As for Kellylarge, he went back to the Kasai Park preserve like a beaten dog. Knowledge of his derating had preceded him, but the authorities there left him alone. They knew that as soon as his company got the news it would jerk him back to Europe. He had just a few hours left before his leave was cancelled.

What did he do? He headed into the bush, where he had struck up a relationship with some sort of gazelle – a gerenuk, I believe it was. During his range work, he had found this animal with its foot wedged between two boulders. Kellylarge rescued it, and they'd been close ever since; the way I heard it, Kellylarge saw Boxing Day in with his gerenuk.

Came morning and he had to face up to reality. As he reported back to the lodge, the beam came through from his company, and there was Kellylarge's boss glaring at him from a private globe.

'Kellylarge, your leave's cancelled,' that individual said. 'Your marrena report's just in. As a result, you're reclassified. From date you're working as assistant artificer with our subsidiary firm in the Lofoten Islands. Report there by midnight tonight, General European Time.'

Huh! Kellylarge was a lunk, a clot, a real abil-nil, I grant you, but he had his feelings the same as the rest of us, and you can imagine how his feelings were. For one thing, he'd never see his intended again; with his new rating, they could not even meet, let alone marry.

Don't get restless, stranger, we're nearly at the top of the queue. And then, zippo, the old free trip to Callisto! Yes, I've heard all those rumours about it being just a penal colony. Don't believe a word of it; it's this intense secrecy about deportees Earthside that gives rise to the ugly talk. We're being shipped out there as misfits, right? Right, then on a frontier world we'll have a chance to fit. Anyhow, back to Kellylarge.

No sooner had he had this kick in the teeth from his company, than Ida came through on the beam to him. Most of what I'm telling you is more or less common knowledge, but some of it I heard from a friend at Beam Central. Unfortunately, Ida came through on scramble, so we don't know what was said – but we can guess.

For sure she told Kellylarge that the strike had now succeeded. The proxies had won their point, Ida was reinstated, mainly through the intercession of one of the other girls, who had tested World President Soepoena's brother before his marriage; she got the President personally interested in Ida's case. He brought pressure to bear on the marriage ministry, so that Ida was reinstated.

And no doubt when Kellylarge heard that, he saw a way to save himself from the Lofoten Islands. Probably he was in love with Ida I don't know, but who wouldn't be with an item like her? So he proposed marriage then and there, and she turned him down flat. A proxi marry a 10 : 60 : 75 : 80? Not likely?

So he broke loose in despair. Beat it into the bush, back to this gerenuk. Poor lunk! You know how close a man and a critter can be, now this law is passed and we don't have to hunt 'em. Kellylarge hid out on the ranges among the acacias for two working weeks before they caught him. Only last week that was; they say he had grown very thin.

Still, who cares what happened to Kellylarge? He was just a small cog in a big big machine. What happened to Ida Cassilis was much more interesting. World President Soepoena unfortunately had his interest in her aroused by the strike. He sent for her secretly, and, well, they knew each other for rebels, and they fell in love with each other.

That was awkward, I tell you, with the World President forced to be celibate by church-state law. They married, anonymously and secretly, in Chile, in a little chapel five thousand metres above sea level. My God, there was a fool for you! It lasted only twenty-four hours before some dirty spy found out – and, well, the law is the law.

But Kellylarge: small time! A failure. He's probably standing in some wretched deportee queue now, just as we are! What's that, stranger?

I said I'm Randy Kellylarge, butch. How I've stood here listening to you spiel for so long I'll never know.

For your information, you have the tale all wrong at several crucial points, despite all your prying. Just in case you intend to blab my private business all over Callisto, let me tell you that when Ida Cassilis beamed me at Kasai, she proposed to me. I didn't propose to her: I turned her down, if you must know.

I turned her down because I thought she was a maladjusted monster. She had none of the qualities I look for in a woman. I preferred the peace and sweetness of being with my poor little Gerenuk. Ida was a hateful creature, gross, unspiritual, and only attracted to me because of my unfortunate lapse into violence …

Anyhow, what's all this to you?

You ask *me* that? Kellylarge, if we could remove our deportee chains and masks you'd know. Up to last week, I was World President Soepoena.

Danger: Religion!

The four of us must have made a strange group, plodding manfully through nowhere.

Royal Meacher, my brother, led the way. His long arms and bony hands fought the wind for possession of his cloak, the shabby mantle that stayed about him no more certainly than his authority.

Next the breeze from the north plucked at the figure of Turton, our man Turton, poor old Turton, the mutant whose third arm and all but useless third leg combined with his black coat to give him from behind something of the appearance of a beetle. Over his shoulder, Turton carried Candida in an attitude of maximum discomfort

Candida still dripped. Her hair hung down like frayed ribbon. Her left ear jogged up and down the central seam of Turton's coat; her right eye seemed to peep sightlessly back at me. Candida is Royal's fourth wife.

I am Royal's younger brother, Sheridan. I felt defeated by Candida's stare. I kept hoping that the jig-jog of Turton's walk would jog the eye shut; and so I supposed it might have done had her head not been hanging upside down.

We walked towards the north, into the molars of the wind.

The road on which we walked was narrow and absolutely straight. It appeared to lead nowhere, for despite the wind a miasmal mist rose from the damp about us. The road ran along a dyke, the sides of which, being but newly constructed, were of bare earth. This dyke divided a stretch of sea. We had sea on both sides of us.

On our right, the water was appreciably less placid than the water on our left, for it was still the sea proper. On the left, that body of water had already been cut from its parent by a mole which lay ahead of us. Soon the water on our right would undergo the same fate.

Beyond it, almost as far as our vision extended in that direction, we could see another dyke extending parallel with ours. The sea was being parcelled into squares. In time, as the work of reclamation proceeded, the squares would be drained; the sea would dwindle into puddles; the puddles would become mud; the mud would become soil; the soil would become vegetables; and the vegetables – oh, yes! – the vegetables would be eaten and become flesh; ghosts of future people grew in the two halves of sea, the one with ripples and one with waves.

Treading steadily on in the drips from Candida's hair and clothes, I looked back over my shoulder.

The vast funeral pyre we had left had shrunk now: the kiln was a tiny black pipe topped by flame. No more did we feel its heat or smell the smell of ignited bodies, but the effluvia lingered in our memories, Royal still spoke of it, rambling in and out of quotation as his habit was, addressing the wind.

'You note how the parsimonious Dutch reclaim both their land and their dead in one operation. And those grisly corpses, maligned by sea and radiation, will make excellent fertiliser from their ashes. How convenient, how concise! Occam's razor cuts precious fine, friends: the obscene fagends of one chemical reaction go to start another. "Marvellous is the plan by which this best of worlds is wisely planned." Forty thousand dead Dutchmen should guarantee us a good cabbage crop in five years, eh Turton?'

The bent old man, with Candida's head nodding idiot agreement, said, 'Back before the last two wars, they used to grow tulips and flowers here, according to the stoker at the kiln.'

Dark was coming in now, the mist thickening, the sulky captive sea falling motionless as the wind died Beyond the outline of my brother's back I could see a light; with gratitude I mouthed its ugly name: Noordoostburg-op-Langedijk.

'That mouldy towerful of cadavers would seem to be less appropriately applied to tulips than cabbages, Turton,' Royal said. 'And what more suitable envoi to the indignity of their deaths? Recollect your Browne: "To be gnawed out of our graves, to have our skulls made drinking bowls, and our bones turned into pipes, to delight and sport our enemies –" how does it go? – "are tragical abominations escaped in burning burials." Since Browne's time, we've grown a lot more ingenious! Nuclear destruction and incineration need not be the end of our troubles. We can still be spread as mulch for the genus brassica ...'

'Cabbages it was, cabbages or tulips,' old Turton said vaguely, but Royal was not to be deflected. He talked on as we trudged on. I was not listening. I wanted only to get off this eternal earthwork, safe into civilisation and warmth.

When we reached Noordoostburg-op-Langedijk, a mere platform joined by dyke and mole to the distant land, we went into its only café. Turton laid Candida down on a bench. He unbent his beetle back and stretched his arms (but the third never stretched straight) with groans of relief. The café manager came forward hurridly.

'I regret I cannot introduce you properly to my wife. She is religious and has passed into a coma,' Royal said, staring the man out.

'Sir, this lady is not dead?' the manager asked.

'Merely religious.'

'Sir, she is so wet!' the manager said.

'A property she shares with the confounded stretch of water into which she fell when the coma overtook her. Will you kindly bring us three soups; my wife, as you see, will not partake.'

Dubiously, the manager backed away.

Turton followed him to the counter.

'You see, the lady's very susceptible to anything religious. We came over with the party from Edinburgh specially to see the cremation down the road, and Mrs Meacher was overcome by the sight. Or perhaps it was the smell, I don't know, or the sound of the bodies bubbling in the incinerator. Anyhow, before anyone could stop her, backwards she went – splash! – and –'

'Turton!' Royal called sharply.

'I was just trying to borrow a towel,' Turton said.

After that, we ate our soup in silence. A puddle collected under Candida's clothing.

'Say something, Sheridan,' Royal demanded, rapping his spoon on the table at me.

'I wonder if there were fish in those fields,' I said.

He made his usual gesture of disgust and turned away. Fortunately I did not have to say anything more, for at that moment the rest of our party came in for soup; the incineration ceremony had finished just after we left; we had left only because of Candida.

Soup and rationed chocolate were all that the café offered. When the party had finished up their bowls, we went outside. I draped Candida over Turton's shoulder and followed.

The weather was showing its talents. Since the wind had fallen, rain had begun to fall. It fell on the concrete, in the polder, into the sour sea. It fell on to the buzz-jet. We all packed into it, jostling and pushing. Somehow, Royal managed to get in away from the rain first. Turton and I were last aboard, but Turton had been wet already.

This buzz-jet was just a missile left over from the last war and converted. Perhaps it was uncomfortable, yet it could move; we headed north-west across the sea and over northern England, where not a light showed from the stricken lands; in a quarter of an hour the lights of Edinburgh showed blearily through the wet dark.

Our craft was a government one. Private transport of any variety was a thing of the past. Mainly it was fuel shortage that had brought the situation about; but when the last war ended at the beginning of 2041, the government passed laws forbidding the private ownership of transport – not that they were not increasingly eager to hire their own vehicles out as production improved.

At Turnhouse airport we climbed out and made our way with the crowd to a bus shelter. A bus came after a few minutes; it was too full to take us; we waited and caught the next one; it crawled with us into town, while we stood like cattle in a truck.

That sort of thing takes the edge off what otherwise had been a very enjoyable day's sightseeing. We had had several such excursions to celebrate my demobilisation from the army.

Since the war, Edinburgh had become the capital city of Europe, chiefly because the others had been obliterated or made uninhabitable by radiation or the after-effects of bacterial warfare. Some of the old Scottish families were proud of this promotion of their city; others felt that this greatness had been thrust upon them; but most of them took advantage of the shining hour by thrusting up rents to astronomical heights. The thousands of refugees, evacuated and displaced people who poured into the city found themselves held to ransom for living space.

When we climbed out of the bus at the city centre, I became separated from the others by the crowd, that cursed anonymous crowd speaking all the tongues of Europe. I brushed off a hand that clutched at my sleeve; it came again, detaining me more forcibly. Irritably, I looked round, and my eyes met the eyes of a square dark man; in that instance, I took in no more detail, beyond saying to myself that his was a great gothic cathedral of a face.

'You are Sheridan Meacher, fellow of Edinburgh University, Lecturer in History?' he asked.

I dislike being recognised at bus stops.

'European History,' I said.

The expression on his face was not readable; weary triumph, perhaps? He motioned to me to follow him. At that moment, the crowd surged forward, so that he and I were born out of it and into a side street.

'I want you to come with me,' he said.

'I don't know you. What do you want?'

He wore a black and white uniform. That did not endear him to me. I had seen enough of uniform in those weary war years underground.

'Mr Meacher, you are in trouble. I have a room not five minutes away from here; will you please come with me to it and discuss the situation with me? I assure you I will offer you no personal harm, if that is why you hesitate.'

'What sort of trouble? I know of no trouble?'

'Let us go and discuss it.'

I could look after myself with this fellow; with that knowledge, I shrugged my shoulders and followed him. We went together down a couple of backstreets, towards the Grassmarket, and in at a grimy door. The man with the gothic face preceded me up a winding stair. At one point, a door opened, a dim-lit hag's face peeped out at us, and then the door slammed again, leaving us in the gloom.

He paused on a landing and felt in his pocket. He said, 'I shouldn't think a house like this has changed much since Dr Johnson visited Edinburgh.' Then in an altered tone, he added, 'I mean – you did have a Dr Johnson, Samuel Johnson, didn't you?'

Not understanding his phrasing – yet I had not taken him for other than an Englishman – I said, 'Of course I know of Johnson: he visited this city to stay with his friend Boswell in – about 1773, I would say.'

In the dark he sighed with relief. Sliding a key into a lock, he said, 'Of course, of course, I was just forgetting that the road from London to Edinburgh was open by that date. Forgive me.'

He opened a door, switched on a light and ushered me into his room. I went in a half daze, for his remark had shaken me. What could the man mean? Edinburgh and London had been connected – though often tenuously – for a long time before Johnson's visit. I was beginning to form ideas about this gothic stranger – and all of them were later proved wrong.

His room was bare and nondescript, a typical lodging room with a combo toilet in one corner, in another a hand generator in case the main electricity supply failed, and a screen standing on the far side of the room with a bed behind it. He went across to the window to draw the curtains before turning to confront me.

'I should introduce myself, Mr Meacher. My name is Apostolic Rastell, Captain Apostolic Rastell of the Matrix Investigation Corps.'

I inclined my head and waited; the world was full of sinister-sounding establishments these days, and although I had never heard of the Matrix Investigation Corps, I did not intend to put myself at a disadvantage by saying so. We stood looking at each other, summing one another up. Captain Rastell was a considerable man, untidy perhaps, but prepossessing, strongly built with being bulky, a man perhaps still in his twenties, and with that extraordinary face that looked as if it could have regarded the end of the world undismayed. He smiled and moved behind his screen, to emerge dragging an object like a trunk. This he stood on its end.

The trunk was locked with some sort of a combination lock. Rastell worked it, staring at me somewhat grimly as he listened to the tumblers click.

'You had better look at the inside of this before I offer any explanation,' he said.

He opened the trunk. What I saw there drew me impulsively forward. I took a good look, and a horrible faintness overcame me. I staggered and he caught me, holding me as I recovered.

Inside the trunk was a small chair, a stool with a backrest. It was fringed with various instruments that reminded me vaguely of the drills and other accessories that stand by a dentist's chair. But it was what lay behind the chair that caught me off guard.

I saw myself reflected from a screen that covered the back of the trunk; the anonymous room was also reflected there, if reflected is the word, its dimensions cramped and twisted, so that it looked as if the figures of Rastell and myself stood on the outside rather than the inside of a cube. The effect was as if I peered into a distorting mirror; but this was no mirror – for I found myself staring distractedly at my own profile!

'What is it?'

'You are an intelligent man, Mr Meacher, and since I am in a hurry I hope that already this sight has suggested to you that there are departments of life which are a mystery to you, and into which you have not peered or cared to peer. There are other earths than this one of yours, Mr Meacher; I come from such a one, and I invite you to follow me back to it now.'

I backed away without dignity, sitting down on a chair and staring up at him. It would be tedious here, and a little shameful, to recount the terrors, hopes and suppositions that fled through my mind. After a moment, I calmed myself enough to listen to what he was saying. It went something like this:

'You are not a philosopher, Mr Meacher, but perhaps you know nevertheless that many men spend large parts of their lives waiting for a challenge; they prepare themselves for it, though they may not guess what it is until the moment comes. I hope you are such a man, for I have neither the time nor the patience for lengthy explanation. In the matrix from which I come, we had a dramatist last century called Jean Paul Sartre; in one of his plays, a man says to another, "Do you mean to say that you would judge the whole of someone's life by one single action?" and the other asks simply, "Why not?" So I ask you, Mr Meacher, will you come with me?'

'Why should I?'

'You must ask yourself that.' In the circumstances, what monstrous assumptions behind that remark!

'You will come? Excellent!' he said, coming forward and taking my arm. Unthinkingly, I had risen, and he had taken my rising for assent. Perhaps it was.

What is the nature of the authority that one man can have over another? Unprotesting, I allowed myself to be led over to the seat in his – let me use his own term – his portal. He saw me settled there and said, 'This is nothing that you are unprepared for; you may be astonished, but you are not surprised. It will be news for you, but probably nothing upon which you have not privately speculated, when I tell you that the earth as you know it is merely a three dimensional appearance – an outcrop, a geologist would call it – of a multi-dimensional universe. To comprehend the multi-dimensional universe is beyond man's power, and perhaps always will be; one impediment being that his senses register each of its dimensions as a three-dimensional reality.'

'Rastell, for God's sake, I don't know what you are saying!'

'The violence of your denial persuades me otherwise. Let me put it this way, with an analogy with which you may be familiar. A two-dimensional creature lives on a strip of paper. A bubble – that is, a three-dimensional object – passes through the paper. How does the two-dimensional creature perceive the bubble? First as a point, which expands to a circle that at its maximum is the circumference of the bubble; the bubble is then half-way through the paper; the circle then begins to contract until –'

'Yes, yes, I understand all that, but you are trying to imply that this two-dimensional creature can climb onto the bubble, which is –'

'Listen, all that stops the creature climbing onto the bubble is its attitude of mind, its system of logic. Its mind needs a twist through ninety degrees – and so does yours. Join the creature's strip of paper up at both ends and you get a lively representation of your mind: a closed circle! Yon can't perceive the other matrices. But I can make you perceive them. A twist of the paper gives you a Mobius strip, and you get a one-sided object. I'm going to give you an injection, now, Mr Meacher, that will have a roughly similar effect on your perceptions, only you will gain a dimension instead of losing it.'

It was crazy! He must somehow have hypnotised me – fascinated me certainly! – to make me go as far as that with him. I jumped up from the chair.

'Leave me alone, Rastell! I don't know what you are saying, and I don't want to. I don't want any part of it. I was mad to come here and listen to – Rastell!'

His name came from my lips as a shriek. He had put out his hand as if to steady me, and plunged the tip of a small hypodermic into the vein of my left wrist. A warm and prickly sensation began to course up my arm.

As I swung towards him, I brought my right fist up, aiming a blow instinctively at his face. He ducked, putting out a hand to steady me as, carried off balance, I staggered forward.

'I'd sit down if I were you, Meacher. You have nicomiotine in your veins, and if you are unused to it, any exertion may make you sick. Sit down, man.'

My gaze fixed on his face, with its tall lines, and the extraordinarily sensible relationship between its various features. I saw that face, graven on to my sight, as a central point, a cardinal fact, a reference from which the whole universe might be mapped; for the influence of time and event lay in that face, until it in its turn influenced time and event, and in that linkage I saw symbolised the whole wheel of life that governs men. Yes, I knew – even at the time I knew – that already I was gliding under the influence of the drug Rastell had given me. It made no difference. Truth is truth, whether you find it or it finds you.

When I sat down in the seat, it was with a motion that held the same magic dualism. For the act might have seemed a submission to Rastell's will; yet I knew it was more vitally a demonstration of my will, as inside the universe of my body a part of me called my will had brought into play a thousand minute responses, as blood and tissue co-operated in the act. And at the same time that this dramatic and cosmic act was in process, I was hearing the voice of Rastell, booming at me from a distance.

'In this matrix of yours, I understand you passed through what is now referred to as the Tobacco Age, when many people – this applied particularly to the first half of last century – were slaves to the tobacco habit. It was the age of the cigarette. Cigarettes were not the romantic objects portrayed by our historical novelists; they were killers, for the nicotine contained in them, though beneficial to the brain in small quant- ites, is death to the lungs when scattered over them in large quantities. However, before the cigarette finally went out of production towards the end of the sixties – how are you feeling, Meacher? – it won't take long – before the downfall of the cigarette firms, they developed nico- miotine. Because the firms were in general bad odour, the new drug lay neglected for fifty years; in fact in this matrix of yours it is neglected still, as far as I can ascertain.'

He took my wrist and felt my pulse, which laboured beneath my skin like a man struggling to free himself from imprisonment in a sack. Sunk in a whole ocean of feeling, I said nothing: I could see the benefit of remaining unconscious all one's life. Then one could be free to pursue the real things.

'You probably won't know this, Meacher, but nicotine used to retard the passing of urine. It set in motion a chain of reactions which released a substance called vasopressin from the pituitary gland into the blood- stream; when the vasopressin reached the kidney, the excretion of water taken by the mouth was suppressed. Nicomiotine releases noradrenaline from the hypothalamus and from the tegmentum of the midbrain, which is the part of the brain that controls consciousness and the functions of the consciousness; at the same time, the drug builds up miodrenaline in the peripheral blood vessels. This results in what we call an "atten- tion transfer". The result – I'm simplifying here, Meacher, because you probably aren't taking this in normally – the result is a dislocation of consciousness, necessary to switch over from one matrix to another. The flow of attention is, to revert to my former analogy, given a Möbius twist and tagged onto the next matrix.

'The seat on which you sit is in a circuit which can be tuned to various vibratory levels, each of which corresponds to a matrix. I move this lever here, and you and the portal will slip easily through into the matrix from which I have come. Don't think of it as going through a barrier; rather, you are avoiding a barrier.

'The effects of this technique can also be achieved by long mental discipline; it was this that the yogi were unwittingly reaching out for when they – ah, you are sliding through now, Meacher. Don't be alarmed.'

I was not alarmed. I was standing outside my own shell and seeing that to all of us come moments of calm and detachment; that stillness might be the secret that only a handful of men in any generation stumbles on. And at the same long-drawn moment of time I was aware that my left foot had disintegrated.

No dismay assailed me. For the right foot had disintegrated too, and the wisdom and symmetry of this event merely pleased me. Everything was disintegrating into mist – not that I took it seriously, although for a moment I was frightened by the basilisk stare of my jacket buttons, staring up unwinkingly at me, so that I was reminded of those lines of Rimbaud's about 'the coat buttons that are eyes of wild creatures glaring at you from the end of the corridors'. Then buttons and Rimbaud and I were gone into mist!

A feeling of sickness preceded me into Rastell's matrix.

I sat up shivering in the seat, my head suddenly clear and my body temperature low. The drug had built up to a certain pitch and then abandoned me. It was as if a passionate love affair had been ended by an unexpected desertion, a betraying letter. In my misery, I looked about me and saw a room very like the room I had left. It was the same shape, it had the same doors and windows, with the same prospect out of the window; but the curtains were not drawn, and it was light outside. I fancied the furniture was slightly different, but had not taken in the other room clearly enough to be positive. One thing I was sure of: the other room had not contained a little ugly man dressed in a one-piece denim suit and standing motionless by the door, staring at me.

Disappointment, anger, fear, ran through me. Uncertainty, too. How could I be sure that I had not roused from a long unconsciousness, that this was not a trick of some kind? Where was the wretched Rastell? I got to my feet and ran behind the screen at the other side of the room. Fortunately, there was a basin fitted to the wall. Nausea hit me as soon as I moved. When I had been sick, I felt a little better.

As I emerged shakily from behind the screen, I found Rastell there.

'You'll soon feel better,' he said. 'The first time's always the worst. Now we'll have to get a move on. Can you walk all right? We'll catch a cab in the strect.'

'Where are we, Rastell? This is still Edinburgh, isn't it? What's happened?'

He snapped his fingers impatiently, but answered in a quiet voice.

'You have left the Edinburgh of AA688, which is how we designate your home matrix. We are now in the Edinburgh of AA541. In many vital respects, it much resembles the matrix you have left. In some ways you will find it identical. Only the workings of chance have brought divergences from what you at first will think of as the norm. As you adjust to inter-matrix living, you'll realise that the norm does not exist. Let's move.'

'I don't understand what you are saying. Are you saying that I may find my brother and his wife here?'

'Why not? It's quite possible that you may find yourself here – here and in a thousand other matrices. It seems to be a property of matter to imitate itself in all matrices and of chance to modify the imitations.'

He said this as if repeating some sort of received idea, walking as he did so to the shabby fellow, who, all this time, had stood patiently unmoving by the door. Despite my confusion, I saw this fellow wore a bracelet over his denims below one knee; from the bracelet radiated four short arms that seemed to bite into his flesh, Rastell produced a key from his pocket and thrust it into a lock in the bracelet. The four arms fell outwards, and hung loosely from their hinges on the bracelet's rim. The man rubbed his leg and hobbled round the room, restoring his circulation. He kept his eye on both Rastell and me, but especially on me, without looking at either of us directly, and without speaking.

'Who is this man? What are you doing?' I asked.

'He might have tried to escape if I had not locked him still,' Rastell said. He produced a bottle from under his tunic. 'They still have whisky in this matrix, Meacher, you'll be glad to hear; have a good pull – it will help you take control of yourself.'

Gratefully, I drank the warming stuff down from the bottle.

'I'm in control of myself, Rastell. But this talk of matter imitating itself in all matrices – it's like a vision of hell. For God's sake, how many matrices are there?'

'There is not time to go into all that now. You shall have the answers if you help us. As yet, in any case, we have uncovered more questions than answers. Verification of the existence of the multi-matrix universe was only made some twenty years ago; the Matrix Investigation Corps was only established fifteen years ago, in 2027, the year the Fourth World War broke out in your matrix. In this matrix, the war did not take place.'

'Rastell, I'm sorry, you must return me to my old world. I want no part of this.'

'You are a part of it. Dibbs, help Mr Meacher to the door.'

Dibbs was the voiceless one. He came towards me, keeping his eyes to the ground, but looking nastily alert as he advanced. I backed towards the door. Rastell grabbed my arm and pulled me round, not unkindly.

'You don't want to be mauled by a slave. Pull yourself together and let's get along. I know it's a shock at first, but you are a man of intelligence; you'll adjust.'

I knocked his hand away.

'It's because I'm a man of intelligence that I reject all this. How many of these matrix worlds are there?'

The Corps measures consciousness in dees. Spaced three dees apart from each other lies an infinity of matrices ... Yes, an infinity, Meacher, and I see the word does little to reassure you. Only a few dozen worlds are known as yet. Some are so like this that only by a few details – the taste maybe of the whisky, or the name of a Sunday newspaper – do they differ at all; others – we found one, Meacher, where the earth was in an – an improperly created state, just a ball of turbulent rivers of mud, lying under permanent cloud.'

He opened the door as he was speaking, and we went together down the winding stair, and out into the street by a grimy door.

It had been evening when I went into that house, or a house like it. Now it was an iron grey day, with a daylight forged to match the stones of the city. Oh yes, this was Edinburgh all right, unmistakeably Edinburgh, and unmistakeably not the Edinburgh I knew.

The buildings looked the same, though a slight strangeness in the pattern they presented made me think that some of them were altered in ways I did not recollect. The people looked different, and dressed differently.

Gone were the shabby and talkative crowds among which Royal and I had travelled only a short while before. The streets were almost empty, and those that travelled on them were easily observed to fall into two classes. Some men and women there were who travelled the streets with their heads held high, who walked briskly, who smiled and saluted each other; they were well dressed, in what I thought of then as a 'futuristic' style, with wide plain collars and short cloaks of what looked like a stiff leather or plastic. Many of the men wore swords.

There was another class of man. They did not greet each other; they moved through the streets with no grace in their carriage, for whether they walked or loped – as many of them did – they kept their heads down and looked about only furtively from under their brows. Like Dibbs, they all wore denims, like him they bore the bracelets below one knee, and like him they bore a yellow disc on their backs, between their shoulder blades.

I had plenty of time to observe these people for Rastell, as he had promised, had got us a cab, and in this we set off in the direction of Waverley Station.

The cab amazed me. It would have held four men at a pinch, and it was worked by manpower. Three denimed men – I was already, I think, referring to them mentally as the slave class – were chained to a seat behind the cab; Dibbs climbed up with them to make a fourth; together they worked away at foot pedals, and that was the way we moved, propelled by four sweating wretches!

In the streets ran several similar cabs, and even sedan chairs, which are well suited to the uneven nature of Edinburgh's topography. There were also men riding horseback, and the occasional conventional lorry. I saw no buses or private cars. Remembering how the latter class of vehicle had been forbidden in my own matrix, I asked Rastell about it.

'We happen to have more manpower than we have fuels,' he said. 'And unlike your wretchedly proletarian matrix, here most free men have leisure and find no need to hurry everywhere.'

'You impressed on me the need for hurry.'

'We are hurrying because the balance of this matrix is in a state of crisis. Civilisation is threatened, and must be saved. You and others like you from other matrices are being brought here because we need the perspective that an extra-matricial can give. Because your culture is inferior to ours does not mean that your abilities may not be valuable.'

'Inferior? What do you mean, inferior? You look to be a couple of centuries behind us, with your antiquated sedans and these anachronistic pedal cabs.'

'You don't measure progress just by materialist standards, Meacher, I hope?' Up came his gothic eyebrows as he spoke.

'Indeed I don't. I measure it by personal liberty, and from the bare glimpse I have had of your culture – your matrix, you have here nothing better than a slave state.'

'This *is* nothing better than a slave state. You are a historian aren't you, a man capable of judging not simply by the parochial standards of his own time? What race became great without slave labour, including the British Empire? Was not classical Greece a community of slave states? Who but slaves left all the lasting monuments of the world? In any case, you are prejudging. We have here a subject population which is a different thing from slavery.'

'Is it to the people concerned?'

'Oh, for Church's sake, be silent, Meacher! You do nothing but verbalise.'

'Why invoke the church about it?'

'Because I am a member of the Church. Take care not to blaspheme, Meacher. During your stay here, you will naturally be subject to our laws, and the Church keeps a firmer hold over its rights than it does in your matrix.'

I fell gloomily silent. We had laboured up onto George IV Bridge. Two of the slaves, working at the furthest extent of their chains, had jumped down from the back of the cab and pushed us over that stretch of the way. Having crossed the bridge, we began to go steeply down by The Mound, braking and freewheeling alternately, though a flywheel removed most of the unpleasant jerkiness from this method of progress. Edinburgh Castle, grandly high on our left, looked unchanged to me, but in the more modern part of the town before us I saw much change, without being able to identify any particular bit of it with certainty; for Royal, Candida and I had not lived very long in Edinburgh.

Whistles sounded ahead. I took no notice, until Rastell stiffened and drew a revolver from his pocket. Ahead, by the steps of the Assembly Hall, a cab had crashed and turned over on to its side. The three slaves attached to it could be seen – we had them in sight just round the bend – wrenching at their chains, trying to detach them from the cab. A passenger had survived the crash. He had his head out of the window and was blowing a whistle.

'The subs have allowed another crash – this is a favourite spot,' Rastell said. 'They get too negligent.'

'It's a difficult corner. How can you tell they allowed it to happen?'

Giving me no answer, Rastell half opened the door of our cab and leant out to shout at our slaves.

'Hey, you subs, stop this cab at once. I want to get out. Dibbs, jump down!'

We squealed to a halt on the slope. When Rastell jumped out, I did the same. The air was cold. I was stiff and uneasy, very aware that I was so far from home that the distance could not be measured in miles. I looked about, and Dibbs and the three pedallers watched me with their eyebrows.

'Better follow me, Meacher,' Rastell called. He had begun to run towards the wrecked cab. One of the slaves there had wrenched his chain from its anchorage in the flimsy metal of the cab. Moving forward, he swung the loose end of the chain and brought it across the head of the passenger. The whistling stopped in mid-note. The passenger sagged to one side, and then slid out of our sight into the cab. By that time, the slave had jumped on to the top of the cab and turned to face Rastell. Other whistles began to shrill. A siren wailed.

When the slave on the cab saw that Rastell carried a gun, his expression changed. I saw his look of dismay as he motioned to his fellows who were still captive and jumped down behind the cab. His fellows stood there trembling, no longer trying to get away.

Rastell did not fire. A car came tearing up the hill with sirens wailing and bucked to a halt between Rastell and the upturned cab. Black and white uniformed men jumped out. They wore swords and carried guns. On the roof of the car was a winking sign that read CHURCH POLICE. Rastell hurried over to them. I stayed where I was, half in the shelter of our cab, undecided, not wanting any part of anything. Dibbs and his fellows subs stood where they were, not moving, not speaking.

A crowd was collecting by the steps of the Assembly Hall, a crowd composed of the ruling class. The sub who had broken loose was kicked into the back of the police car. While the others indulged in argument I had time to look at the police car more carefully. It was an old vehicle, driven, I felt sure, by an internal combustion engine, a powerful beast, but without the streamlining that is characteristic of the cars I grew up with. It had a double door set in either side, and another, through which the wretched sub was pushed, at the back. Its windows were narrow, pointed, and grouped into pairs, in the style of windows in the Early English churches; even the windscreen had been divided into six in this way. The whole thing was elaborately painted in white and light blue and yellow. Why not, I thought, when you have plenty of time and slave labour is cheap?

Rastell was returning, though the debate round the steps of the Assembly Hall was still on.

'Let's get on,' Rastell said. He signalled curtly to Dibbs and the subs. We all climbed aboard and resumed our journey. I looked at the crowd about the church police car as we passed it. With a start, I thought I recognised one of the hangers-on in the crowd. He looked much like my brother Royal; then I told myself that my nerves were being irresponsible.

'There's too much of that sort of incident,' Rastell said. 'This trouble flared up all at once a few years ago. They must have a leader.'

'I'd guess they also had a cause. What will happen to the man who broke free from the cab and coshed the passenger?'

'That sub?' He looked at me, his lips curving in a smile not entirely free from malice. 'He struck a churchgoer. I was not the only witness. He'll be hanged at the castle next week. What else could we do with him? He'll be granted last rites.'

The grand stretch of Princess Street, a street fit for any capital, was changed, although many of the buildings were as I knew them. Their rather commercial gaiety had gone. They presented a drab uniformity now. Their windows were unwashed; the goods displayed for sale in the shop windows looked uninviting. I peered eagerly at them as we thudded by at a stiff walking pace. The big car showrooms had gone, the shops were not piled with the gadgets I knew. On the pavements, greater variety was in evidence. Many people were about, looking cheerful as they shopped. Few slaves in sight, and I now observed that among the free some looked far less prosperous than others. Sedans, pedal-cabs, four-wheel bicycles and little electrically powered cars moved busily along. I was sorry when we halted before a large grey building and Rastell signalled me to alight.

'This is the headquarters of my chapter,' he said, as we pushed through the doors with Dibbs following.

'I believe it's a block of offices in my matrix.'

'On the contrary, it is the Commission for Nuclear Rearmament. Are you forgetting already how war-oriented your matrix is?' He relented then, and said in less ironic tones, 'However, you'll probably find us too religious. It's a matter of viewpoint really.'

The place was bustling. The foyer reminded me of an old-fashioned hotel; its furniture was cumbrous and oddly designed, reminding me of the styles of Elizabeth II's era, fifty years ago or more, except that everything was so colourless.

Rastell marched over to a noticeboard and scanned it

'We have half-an-hour before the next history briefing for extra-matricials. I'll see you are found a room where you can wash and rest. I have one or two people I ought to see. We'll meet again, shortly, at the briefing.'

He signalled a passing servant, a girl dressed not in denims but in a curious black and white pantaloon. I felt anxious at leaving Rastell, my one contact with my own matrix. He interpreted my expression, and arched one of his eyebrows.

'This sub girl will take good care of you, Meacher. Under the dispensation, she will serve you in any way you may require.'

As he disappeared, I thought, not an unlikeable devil, given better circumstances. I followed the sub girl, noting the yellow disc between her shoulder blades. She led me up one flight of stairs and along a corridor, and opened a door for me. When I was inside, she followed, locked the door, and handed me the key. Despite myself, I began to get ideas. In that awful dress, she looked foolish, and her face was pasty, but she was young and with good features.

'What's your name?'

She pointed to a button on her dress. On it was the name Ann.

'You are Ann? Can't you talk?'

She shook her head. A sensation like cold needles prickled in my chest; it occurred to me that I had not heard a word from Dibbs or from the slaves by the upturned cab. Moving towards her, I touched her chin.

'Open your mouth, Ann.'

Meekly, she let her jaw hang. No, her tongue was there, as well as several teeth that needed stopping or pulling. The helplessness of the creature overwhelmed me.

'Why can't you speak, Ann?'

She closed her jaw and lifted up her chin. On the whiteness of her neck ran an ugly red scar. Uncheckably, the tears sprang to my eyes. I clasped her thin shoulders and let anger burn over me.

'Is this done to all slaves?' Shake of head. 'To some – to most of them?' Nod. 'Some sort of punishment?' Nod. 'Hurt you?' Nod. So remote! 'Are there other men like me, from other matrices, along this corridor? Blank look. 'I mean other strangers from other places like me?' Nod. 'Take me to one of them.'

I gave her the key. She unlocked the door and we went into the corridor. At the door of the room next to mine she stopped. Her key fitted that lock, and the door swung open.

A fellow with a thatch of wispy yellow hair and stubble all round a great leg of jaw sat at a table eating. He ate with a spoon, furiously. Though he looked up as I came in, he did not interrupt the ladling of food into his mouth.

'You're an extra-matricial?' I asked. He made noises of assent into his stew.

'So am I. My name's Sheridan Meacher. We can't agree to give these people any help to bolster up their regime. Their entire system is evil, and must be destroyed. I'm trying to get people to help me.'

He put his spoon down. He stood up. He leant over the table.

'What's evil about the system here, jack?'

I showed him Ann's scars, explaining what they were. He laughed.

'You want to come and have a look at my home matrix,' he said. 'Ever since an unsuccessful revolution ten years ago, the Chinese have employed all scholars in chain gangs. They're busy making roads across the Cairngorms.'

'The Chinese? What have they to do with it?'

'Didn't they win the third world war in your matrix?'

'Win it! They didn't even fight it!'

'Well, then, you're just lucky, jack, and if I were you I'd be inclined to keep my trap shut.'

Before I had backed out of his room, he was again spooning stew
into his mouth.

In the next room was a little plump man, red in the face and bald of
head, who jumped quickly back from his sub girl as I entered.

'I'm extra-matricial like you,' I told him, 'and I don't like what I
have seen here so far. I hope you feel that these people should not be
encouraged in any way.'

'We've rather got to make the best of things now we're here, that's
my feeling,' he said, coming forward to look at me. 'What don't you like
about this place?'

'I've only just arrived, but this system of slavery – it alone is enough
to convince me that I can't possibly support the ruling regime. You
must feel the same.'

He scratched his bald head.

'You could have worse than slavery, you know. At least slavery guar-
antees that a part of the population lives about the level of animals. In
the Britain of my matrix – and I expect you have found the same – the
standard of living has been declining ever since the beginning of the
century, so much so that some people are beginning to whisper that
communism may not after all be the solution we –'

'Communism in Britain? Since when?'

'You sound so surprised, anyone would have thought I said democracy. After the success of the General Strike of 1929, the first communist
government was established under the leadership of Sir Harold Pollitt.'

'All right, thanks very much. Just tell me this – will you back me in
opposing this regime of slavery?'

'Well, I don't oppose you in opposing it, comrade, but first I'd want
to know a little more –'

I slammed the door on him. I had backed out so hurriedly, I jumped
into another man moving rapidly down the corridor. Brought up short,
we regarded each other. He was young and dark, about my weight and
height, with a high bridge to his nose, and I liked the look of him
immediately.

'You're an extra-matricial?'

He smiled and held out his hand. When I held out mine, he grasped
my elbow instead; so I grasped his elbow.

'My name is Mark Claud Gale. I'm on an errand of revolt, and you look like a possible conscript. None of these spineless fellows will back me up, but I'm not going to give this government any help –'

'Ah, count me with you all the way, Mart. Well met! I am Sherry Meacher, and I also am recruiting. If we stick together and defy the regime, others may follow our example, and we will see that we are returned to our own matrix. And then perhaps the slaves –'

The brazen tongue of a bell interrupted me.

'Time for the historical briefing,' Mark said. 'Let's go and learn what we can, Sherry; the knowledge may be of use to us later. By my shrine, but this is an adventure!'

This aspect of the matter had not struck me before, but to have this dependable ally heartened me immensely, and I felt ready for anything. A heady and pleasurable excitement filled me. I could not wait to get to the briefing, and to hear, to listen, to be assaulted and insulted by a barrage of new facts that – only a day ago! – would have seemed the wildest fantasy.

A pair of dark-clothed church police appeared at the head of the stairs and began ushering us down. The bald man from communist Britain (but for all I knew there were a million communist Britains) tagged on with us, but did not speak. Ann disappeared as we pressed downstairs. Counting heads, I noted there were twenty-two of us. As we filed into a hall at the back of the foyer, we found another thirty-odd people awaiting us; from the variety of clothes they were wearing, it was apparent that they were also extra-matricials.

We sat at long tables on benches, and looked at the head table, which stood on a dais and contained three men, each with a secretary, and church police standing behind them. One of the three men was Rastell; he gave no sign of having noticed me, and I wondered if I should even have occasion to speak to him again.

A bell sounded, and one of the men on the dais, a white-haired man of good bearing, rose to his feet.

'Gentlemen and sinners, you are welcome in this peaceful matrix. We thank you for coming here to offer us help and wisdom. I am the Lieutenant Deacon Administered Bligh, and with me are two members of my committee. Captain Apostolic Rastell is now going to give you a brief history of this matrix, so that you may have a correct perspective. A sub will come round distributing pens and paper to all who wish to make notes.'

Rastell rose, bowed slightly to Bligh and went straight into his talk.

He spoke for almost two hours. From the body of the hall, hardly a whisper came. We listened fascinated to the history of a world like ours, and yet so hauntingly unlike. Rastell's version was heavily trimmed by propaganda, yet the man's own personality enlivened even the heaviest passage of dialectic.

A few instances of the strange things Rastell told us must suffice. In this matrix, the concept of nationality has not risen (AA688 Rastell had called it, and I had committed the number to memory), German and Italian nationality had not been achieved until the second half of the nineteenth century, but the other great European countries had achieved unity several centuries earlier. In this matrix in which I now found myself, the kings of England and France had been less successful in their struggle against the feudal lords; one reason for this was, I gathered, that the church had looked less favourably on the concept of earthly kingdoms.

England had only become a united kingdom in 1914, at the time of the French-German war, in which Britain was neutral and the United States of America sold armaments to both sides. In the first world war of 1939, the alignment of power was as I knew it, with a Nazi Germany fighting against Britain and France and, later, America and Russia entering as their allies, while Japan fought on the same side as Germany. Japan, however, had been Christianised. The Americans, having been less attracted to a less heavily industrialised Europe, had turned their attention and their missionaries to Japan earlier than they had done in my matrix.

This led to a crisis in the conduct of the war. American and British scientists developed an atomic bomb. Before using this weapon against the Japanese and German enemy, the forty-fifth president of the United States, Benedict H. Denning, consulted with the Convocation of Churches. The Convocation was a powerful group. It not only forbade the use of such a weapon against nominally Christian countries; it gradually took over jurisdiction of the weapon. The war lasted until 1948, by which time the Church was completely in control of all nuclear power development.

A long and hard war had vitiated both the US and her allies. At the end of the conflict, weak governments fell and a strong church rose as a challenging power. Its rule had spread to other countries, particularly to Europe, which was occupied after the war, not by armed forces but by battalions of churchmen.

Since that date, almost a century ago, mother church had kept the fruits and the secrets of nuclear power under her voluminous skirts. The exhaustion of natural resources had necessitated the employment of subject populations, but there had been no war since 1948. The rule of religion poured out its benefits on to all mankind. What Rastell did not mention were any negative or suppressive results of this rule.

Some of these suppressions were obvious enough. With an autocratic central control and the lack of incentives that wars provide, scientific and technological developments had dropped away. World populations, on the other hand, had risen steeply – Rastell mentioned at one point that, after the amalgamation of the Grand Christian Church of 1979, methods of contraception were universally discouraged. The new populations were born into slavery.

'We have been able to turn away from materialism because we have a large subject population to perform the menial tasks of the world for us,' Rastell said. It struck me at the time that this was a neat way of saying that almost every nation without mechanical labour is forced to use slaves.

From what he said, and from what he omitted, it became apparent that almost the only scientific development since the 1960s was the portals and transmatricial travel. The church had not encouraged space travel. No doubt they would have been shocked to learn of the Battle of Venus in the Fifth World War, in which I had taken part.

When Rastell had finished speaking, a stunned silence lay over the hall. It had grown dusk while he talked; now lights came reluctantly on as we returned to awareness of our own situation. I could see by the faces about me that to many of the extra-matricials, Rastell's material had been more astonishing than I found it.

What amazed me most was the way the church had departed from what it represented in my matrix. Rather glibly, I decided that it was the possession of nuclear power that had worked the change. Such a possession would have needed strong men to control it, and obviously the strong men had ousted the meek. Another case of absolute power corrupting absolutely. So I said to myself, with the church cast as villain of the piece. Then Administered Bligh rose again, and made me doubt my own reasoning.

'Now that you have a perspective with which to work,' he said, 'we can proceed to place before you the problem with which we are faced. As most of you will know, you were brought here to give us your help. All of you are students of history in some form or other. A meal is going to be served to you right away; afterwards, we shall explain the problem in detail and invite your advice; but now I will put it to you in general terms, so that you can consider it while you eat.

'We try to instil into our subject population the eternal truth that life in this world is always accompanied by sorrow, alike for those that lead and those that are led, and that they must expect to find their rewards for virtue in the hereafter. But subs do not learn. Several times they have risen against their masters. Now – I will tell you frankly, gentlemen – we are faced with a much more serious revolt. The subs have captured the capital; London is in their hands. The question we are going to ask you with all its ramifications, is this: will leniency or harshness be the most effective way of dealing with them? In giving us your answers, you must bear in mind the parallels with your own times.'

He sat down. Already plates were clattering. Subs of both sexes poured forth from doors at the far end of the hall, bearing food.

The little bald man from communist Britain was sitting next to me.

'An interesting poser, that,' he said. 'Leniency is always striking to the uninformed mind, if it is properly stage managed.'

'These people are dogs, spineless hypocrites,' Mark told him. 'And you must come from a nasty boot-licking culture if you can seriously give their problem a minute's thought. Don't you agree, Sherry?'

He had a merry, honest face. It banished my doubts.

'It cheers me immensely to hear that they are having trouble in London. There are about fifty extra-matricials here, Mark. Quite a few of them must feel as we do and will refuse to help this regime. Let's find them and get them together –'

Mark held up his hand

'No, Sherry. Listen!' He leant forward to speak confidentially. Bald Head also leant forward to catch his words. Mark put his palm over the man's nose and pushed him away.

'Go and play in the bushes, smoothpate,' he said. To me he said, 'Two's never a crowd. An undisciplined bunch of men is nothing but a pain in the kilt. I know, I've had experience. In my own matrix, I'm History Instructor in one of our military schools. I've served all over the world – I only got back from legion duty in Kashmir a week before these people caught me. Believe me, these people are used to dealing with slaves, not free men; the two of us can get away with murder.'

'What are you planning?' I had a nasty feeling that I had let myself in for more trouble than I had bargained for.

'First we test their resourcefulness. At the same time we get weapons. Can you fight, Sherry? You look to me like a warrior.'

'I fought in World War V, on Earth and Venus.'

'All these world wars! My matrix is completely different – we only have local campaigns. Much more sensible! When we have time, we must talk and talk – and listen, of course. Just now, we must get to the kitchens. Kitchens are always well stocked with weapons, even if these curs are vegetarians.'

He did not wait for my agreement. He had slipped from the bench and. was off, bent double so that he could not be seen from the dais. I did the only possible thing. Glad in my heart to be committed, I followed.

Double swing doors of heavy wood led into the kitchens. We barged in. It was a huge place, and gave an impression of darkness rather than dirt, but all the equipment looked to me incredibly old-fashioned.

There was an overseer with a short whip in his hand who saw us at once and came towards us. He had a long raw face and sandy eyebrows – yes, an Edinburgh type, I thought, even as I cast about and noted that there was only one other overseer in the whole place, to watch over the activities of perhaps thirty slaves. A plan formed in my mind.

'Leave this one to me,' I told Mark.

As the overseer came up, with a 'What do you gentlemen want, pray?' on his lips, I swung up a metal tray from a table at my right hand. The edge of it caught him clean across the bridge of his nose, and he dropped as if dead. Startled, I saw he had a yellow disc between his shoulder blades.

'I'll get the other blighter,' Mark said, clapping my shoulder as he passed.

There were thick-handled mops standing in buckets against one wall. I seized one and ran it through the handles of the doors into the hall. That would settle them for a minute or two. Another pair of swing doors led to a scullery; I fixed them in the same way. One other door led from the kitchen, a wide door that gave onto a courtyard. Pushing a great wooden table, I smashed it against the door and jammed it shut.

Turning, I saw that Mark had settled with his overseer. By now the slaves had grasped that something had happened. They dropped their various tasks and stood gaping at us. Grabbing a butcher's knife that lay on a bench, I jumped onto the bench and spoke to them.

'Men, you can be free! It is a man's right to be free! Arm yourselves and help us fight those who oppress you. You are not alone. If you can help us, others will help you. Now is the time for revenge. Arm yourselves! Fight for your freedom! Fight for your lives!'

I saw Mark turn to me in amazement and horror. Even more surprising to me was the response of the subs. They knotted together in fear, gazing at me as if I was about to kill them. Taken off balance, I waved my arms and shouted. A hammering at the hall doors roused them. Crying, they rushed for it, and began to try and tear away my mop, each impeding the other in their anxiety.

Jumping down among them, I pushed them back. They were flimsy and frightened.

'I'm trying to help you! Don't let them in – they'll kill you. You know they'll kill you. Barricade the doors with the tables!'

All they did was shrink back. A few uttered a sort of un-vocalised cry. Mark roughly grabbed my arm.

'Sherry, by my shrine you're crazy! These are slaves! Scum! They are useless to us. They won't fight – slaves never do unless they have tasted better days. Leave them. Arm yourself and let's get out of here.'

'But Mark, the whole idea –'

He shoved a great bunched fist under my jaw, swinging it without touching me in time with his words.

'The idea is to overturn this church regime. I know where my duty lies – with the free, not with the servile. Forget these slaves! Grab a bigger knife and move.'

'But we can't leave these people –'

'You liberal fool, we can and we will!' He ran across to a long lead sink and pulled a heavy chopping knife from it, tossing it to me. As I caught it, he bellowed again at me to move. By now, the hammering on the kitchen door had grown in volume. They were seriously alarmed, and would be breaking in in a minute. The slaves cowered in a group nearby, watching Mark and me anxiously. I turned and ran after Mark.

He pointed to a heavy goods lift in one corner. We ran to it.

'It only leads upstairs.'

'That'll do. Get in, and haul.'

We jumped into the cumbrous contraption. It could be manhandled from inside by the ropes that supported it.

'Hey, stop!'

At the shout, both Mark and I turned. The overseer I had laid out with the tray was staggering towards us.

'Let me join you,' he said. 'I'd sooner die than carry on as I am. I'll fight on your side.'

'You're an overseer. We don't want you!' I said.

'No, wait,' Mark said. 'He is a promoted slave, isn't that right, fellow? They generally have plenty of fight in them because they've learnt the difference between better and worse. Climb in, man. You can show us the layout of this place.'

The overseer climbed in beside us, and helped to haul away on the ropes. We creaked up into darkness. As we bent to the task, Mark said, 'We want church police uniforms as quickly as possible. Then we can walk out of the building with any luck.'

'Should be easy enough,' grunted the overseer. 'Friends, whether we meet death or daylight, my name's Andy, and I'm glad to be of your company.'

'We're Mark and Sherry, and that tray was not delivered in anger.'

'Man, I'd thought you'd cleft my skull in two pieces. I must work off my sorrow on a churchgoer as soon as possible.'

He hadn't long to wait before he did that. As we emerged onto the ill-lit first floor landing, a portly man in gaiters and some sort of ecclesiastical garb was passing the hatch-way. As he turned, saw us, and opened his mouth, I leapt out at him. He gave a shout before I could bring him to the ground, and almost immediately a police officer appeared. I'll never forget his look of horrified surprise as he rounded the corner and came upon three wild men. He went for his gun far too late. Andy was there, sinking a steel blade through his jacket, through his chest, into his heart He died with the look of surprise still frozen onto his face.

'Ah, blood of the bull, neatly done, my noble lads!' Mark exclaimed. He pulled open a nearby door, and we dragged the two bodies into the room. A wood fire burned in an old-fashioned grate. It looked as if the occupant of the room might be back fairly shortly.

'We've got two good sets of clothing here,' I said 'You two climb into them if they'll fit. I'll see what goes on outside. I'm sure you wouldn't want anyone to catch you with your trousers down.'

The portly man in gaiters was unconscious. Mark gagged him before beginning to strip off his clothes.

Prowling in the corridor, I could hear a din from below. It seemed to be rising from the lift shaft. I knew we were in the thick of trouble, and the knowledge only delighted and excited me. As I got to the head of the stairs, I heard a footstep on them, and knew someone was almost at the top of them, ascending rapidly but quietly. A sort of broom cupboard on wheels stood by me; hurridly I slid behind it, into the shadows, not sure whether I had exposed myself to view or not.

Whoever it was had gained the landing. A sort of fury to attack – based perhaps on fear – overcame me. I heaved the cupboard away from the wall and flung myself out. Falling, the cupboard struck the newcomer, sending him spinning against the wall. I was at his throat before I realised it was Rastell.

'Mark!' I called. He appeared almost at once, and we dragged Rastell into our room and shut the door. Mark drew his knife.

'Don't kill him, Mark. I know him.'

'Know him? He's our enemy, Sherry. Let me skewer him and you can wear his uniform. It's about your size.'

'Aye, skewer him, or I will,' Andy said.

'Leave him alone,' I said. 'We'll strip him and leave him tied up here, but I won't see him killed.'

'Well, look sharp,' said Mark, and he and Andy lowered their knives.

Rastell's face had turned an ashy shade of white. He made no protest as I pulled off his jacket and trousers. I hated to see him look so craven.

'Remember what you said, Rastell? "Men spend large parts of their lives awaiting a challenge." Well, here it is!'

Ha did not answer a word. As I tugged his garments onto myself, I tutned to Mark.

'What's the plan?'

'These people aren't efficient, or they'd never have failed to post guards over us in the hall. After all, they had no particular reason to. think we should be friendly. But they can get mobilised against us more quickly than we can gather a force together against them. So we must leave Edinburgh.'

'There is a police car outside. We could steal that and join the rebellion in London, if either of you can drive,' Andy said. He was over by the window, peering out at the back of the building.

'In my matrix, transport is publicly owned, and I'm no driver,' I said.

'In mine, one learns to drive as part of the initiation rites at puberty,' Mark said. Going to stare down at the car with Andy, he said, 'We'll try it. Hurry up and get those clothes on, Sherry. But we won't try for London. We must leave Edinburgh the way we came – by the portal machines. The one that brought me here was up on Arthur's Seat, and there were others beside it. We can drive there straight away. Once we get back to our own worlds – Andy, you can come to mine with me – we can muster aid there, and then reappear in London, armed and properly prepared to fight. My government would welcome the chance.'

I was not sure whether mine would, vitiated as the nation's resources were after a long thermonuclear war, but in outline the plan was a good one. It was no time for argument. Having buttoned up Rastell's tunic over my chest, I ripped a length of cord from the blind on the window and tied Rastell to the bars at the back of the cumbersome sofa. As I finished doing this, something creaked in the corridor. We all three turned to the door at once.

'It's the lift going down!' Andy exclaimed. 'Come on, Sherry, they're onto us.'

With a whoop, Mark grabbed up a heavy rug that lay before the fire. Burying his hands in it, he seized the fire-basket out of the fireplace and ran with it blazing and smoking out of the room. He flung it, and burning logs, basket, and rug went flying down the lift shaft after the lift. Hardly pausing, he ran to the top of the stairs with us after him. We raced down together.

A half dozen church police, revolvers at the ready, came charging along the lower corridor. We met them at the bottom of the stairs. Before Mark could do anything rash, I gripped his arm and called to the police, pointing wildly back up the stairs as I did so, 'Quickly, they're up there – second floor! Cover them while we go and get the hoses!'

Cheering, the police burst past us. The look of delight on Andy's face! As we ran to a rear exit, we could hear screams from the direction of the kitchen. I wondered if the lift was on fire, or if the slaves were being beaten for failing to stop us.

We broke out into a courtyard, under surveillance from a hundred windows. Although it was dark, several slaves were about, unloading meat from a van, lighting their way with long waxy torches. Nearer to us stood the car we had seen from the upper window; a policeman in the black and white uniform sat at the wheel, holding a paper, but looking uneasily about. As I wrenched open his door, he flung the paper in my face and fumbled for his gun. Yelling like a savage, I threw all my weight on him, knocking him sideways across the seat, springing on top of him. Andy had piled into the back seat. His hands came over to grasp the wretched man round the neck. At the same moment, the gun exploded.

Its noise, breaking only a foot away from my ear, seemed almost enough by itself to kill me, though the bullet tore through the roof. The man was struggling violently under me, but for the present I could do nothing; all fight had gone from me. I lay across the policeman while Andy choked the life out of him.

As they were struggling, Mark had started the car. His hands ran all over the controls as he tested their functions. It bucked as he cursed it, and then moved forward. In a daze I saw what happened next.

Two police officers came dashing out of a doorway slightly ahead. The revolver shot had brought them. They were armed only with swords. Without pausing, they both jumped on to the running board on the near side of the car. Unfortunately some of the narrow windows were open, and so they clung there. One managed to draw his sword, thrusting it in at Andy, who still struggled with my man. He let go and grasped the wrist that held the sword. As if in slow motion, as we slowly rolled forward,

I saw the other hanger-on unsheath his sword and bring it through the window, preparing to settle Andy before he settled me. I could do nothing. The concussion of the explosion so near my head still left me dazed. I just slumped there, looking at the well-tended sword blade as it stabbed towards Andy.

Gathering speed, Mark slewed the wheel. We headed for the meat van. Slaves shrieked and scattered. Mark swerved again, missing the other vehicle by inches. A flaring torch splashed over our front windows. Agony distorted the faces of our two hangers-on. Their heads twisted, their mouths gaped open, their swords dropped, as they were crushed between the two vehicles and fell away from our sight.

Andy was patting us both on the back and cheering. He produced a small flask of whisky – which he found in the hip pocket of the trousers he had commandeered – and made me take a sizeable swig. My throat burned and I felt better.

The fellow I was half-lying on was unconscious. Together, Andy and I dragged him over into the back seat.

'This is a crazy car to drive,' Mark said, but he was doing well. We were clear on to the streets now. There was no sign of alarm here, and Mark was driving slowly, so as not to excite attention. The streets were ill-lit, and little traffic was about. I had no idea of the time, but it could not have been later than eight o'clock, yet hardly a soul could be seen. The slaves, I thought, probably had a curfew; the rest were probably in bed or at prayers.

'It'll be wonderful to get another place to live,' Andy said. 'And while I think of it, slow down, Mark, and turn right here up Hanover Street. There's a big government store at the top here. Peace Militant it's called, that supplies only to officials, I've heard. One of the fellows in the kitchen had to work here once on a time. If we can get in there, for sure it'll be shut, and we can break in and find some of these portals.'

Mark shifted gear, and we growled uphill. Off Princes Street, lights were few and far between. At the top of the road we found the store. It was a great solid granite block with little pinchpenny ecclesiastical windows in which goods darkly lay. A board above a barred door said Peace Militant. Andy groaned.

At that moment I was taking another mouthful of his whisky. I turned to see what was the matter. The man he had half strangled had revived and thrust a knife between his ribs. He was just withdrawing it as I turned. Dim light shone on the blade, and by that same tawdry glow I saw his teeth as he growled and came at me. I was already at him with the bottle.

The heel of it caught him in the eye. Involuntarily, he brought his hand up, and I grasped his wrist and wrenched the knife from his grip. He yelped. My fury was back. Climbing over the seat at him, I bore him down into the darkness, while the knife – his own knife! – sunk down and carried him into a night from which there would never be a dawn.

I found Mark was shaking me.

'You did a good job, boy, but once is enough. Leave him. Come on, we've got to get into the shop quickly before they catch up with us.'

'He's killed Andy. Andy's dead!'

'I'm sorry about it too. Weeping won't help it. Andy's dog's meat now. Come on, Sherry, you're a real warrior. Let's move.'

We got out on the pavement. With an elbow, Mark stove in a window, and we climbed through. As simple as that! That terrible feeling of excitement was on me.

We began tramping through the store.

The ground floor yielded nothing, though we separated and searched. We were about to go upstairs when I found a notice board on which was a floor directory. In the light filtering in from outside, I read a line that ran: Basement: Tropical Plants, Gardens, Café, Library, Extra-matricial Equipment. Mark and I took the stairs at a run.

Below ground, we thought it safe enough to switch on a couple of lights. Here was the first evidence that this civilisation had some sort of aesthetic sense. Heating was on, and in the warmth basked a tropical garden. Flowering trees and shrubs, a line of banana plants, gaudy hibiscus, rioted here in carefully tended disorder. The centrepiece was a pool on which lilies floated and the lights were reflected back in dark water. Beyond the pool, the café had been arranged with tables and chairs out on a terrace overlooking the pool. Attractive, I thought, and we pushed past the chairs and came to the next department. Here stood a dozen portals, made in several different sizes and models.

We both cheered, dropped our knives, and got to work.

This was something about which we knew nothing. There was much to be learnt before we could return to our own worlds. To my relief, we found that the portals we came across first were primed for immediate sale and contained phials of nicomiotine as well as other drugs. There were manuals of instruction provided, and we sat down to master their contents with what patience we had.

The business of returning to one's own matrix turned out to be fairly simple. One had a preliminary injection of a fluid with a complicated name which seemed to be a kind of tranquilliser, followed by a jab of nicomiotine in the stated quantity according to one's size, age, ration, and then sat in the portal seat, the vibratory rate of which could be adjusted to matrix numbers shown on a dial. When the drugs took and the body's vibratory rate reached the correct pitch the return was effected.

'These people may have established a loathsome social order, but this invention is something to their credit,' I said. 'And if they would only educate and liberate their slaves. I can't help admiring any matrix that has escaped with no more than one world war.'

'We've had no world wars,' Mark growled.

'Then you look at it differently, but for the slaves –'

'Sherry, you keep talking about these slaves. I'm tired of the subject. By the Phrygian birth, forget all about them. In every matrix there must be conquerors and conquered, dogs and masters. It's a law of human nature.'

I dropped the instruction manual and stared into his face.

'What are you saying? We have only done what we have done, fought as we have, for the sake of the poor wretches enslaved here. What else did we fight for?'

He was crouching beside me. His face had set hard. His words fell from his lips like little graven images.

'I have done nothing for the slaves. What I have done has been against the church.'

'As far as that goes, I'm pretty startled by its conduct too. In my matrix, the Christian Church is a power for good. Though I don't belong to it myself –'

'Death to the Christian Church! It's the Christian Church I fight against!' He jumped to his feet. I leapt up too, my own anger woken by his words, and we stood glaring at each other.

'You're crazy, Mark. We may not agree with the church, but it has been the established church in Britain now for centuries. To start –'

'Not in my Britain! It's not established in my Britain. Christianity is the faith of dogs and underlings where I come from. When Rastell started to tell us his history, he talked about the Roman Empire being established in the East by Constantine the Great, and he said that Constantine, followed by an emperor he called Theodosius, established Christianity as the official creed of the Empire. Did it happen that way in your matrix?'

'Yes, just as Rastell said.'

'Well, it didn't happen in mine. I know of this man you call Constantine; we call him Flavius Constantinus. Of Theodosius I have not heard. Constantinus was killed by his father-in-law, Maximian, and never became emperor. Maxentius the Great became emperor after Diocletian.'

I was puzzled now, as well as angry. Gibbon no doubt would have been delighted to hear of this setback fox Christianity, but its implications left me baffled.

'All this was seventeen centuries ago. What has it to do with us?'

'Everything, my friend – everything. In your matrix and in this one Christianity was imposed on the West by two misguided emperors. In mine it was stamped out, though it still survives among the barbarians and slaves whom we rule in the East, and the True Religion was fostered, and grew.'

'The True Religion?'

'By my shrine, Sherry, have you never heard of the soldier's god? Then bow down before the name of Mithras!'

I saw it then, saw above all my criminal stupidity in thinking that because we seemed to have a common purpose we might have a common past. This man, with whom I had spent the fiercest hour of my life, was an enemy. How much of an enemy, I thought I saw before he did, and there lay my only advantage. He was less clear now about conditions in my matrix than I was about his. I saw that he would go back to his matrix and probably bring back a legion of warriors to tumble the unwarlike regime here. Though I wanted slavery abolished, I did not want that! The thought of inter-matricial war and conquest was horrifying; knowledge of the portals must never get back to his Mithraic world. The conclusion was obvious; I had to kill Mark Claud Gale!

He saw it in my eyes before I reached him. He was quick, Mark! As he stopped to grasp his knife, I kicked it flying and caught his shoulder with my knee. He fell, taking me with him, his fingers digging into my calf. A personal wrestle was what I did not want; he was probably in better condition than I. A weapon was what I wanted. As his right hand came up to grasp me, I planted my free knee on his windpipe and wrenched his am down hard over it, at the same time pulling myself loose from his grasp. Jumping up, I ran into the artificial garden.

Behind the café were rows of garden tools on display. He hurled a can at me before I reached them. The can struck my shoulder and bounced through the front of the café in a shower of glass. I turned; he was almost on me. I kicked one of the light tables between us and backed off to the racks. Feeling the shaft of one of the tools behind me, I brought it forward, flinging my weight with it as if it were a lance. I had hold of a rake. It struck Mark in the thigh as he jumped aside.

I had time to make another lunge, but he had the other end of the rake. Next moment, we were struggling face against face. He brought his skull down hard against my nose. Pain and fury burst like a volcanic eruption over me. I had him by the throat, jabbing him in the groin with my knee. He hooked a leg round my other leg, jerked it. As I fell, I stamped on his toe. For a moment he doubled in pain and the back of his neck was unprotected. Even as I chopped the side of my hand down on it, I felt the weakness of my blow. I was dizzy from the pain in my nose.

We broke apart. The rake lay between us. Gathering my strength, I turned, brought another tool from the rack behind, and swung it in a circle. He had stopped to grab the rake. Changing his mind, he backed away, and I ran at him with the tool upraised. It was a fool's move. He ducked and let me have it in the stomach with a swinging left. I broke the shaft over his shoulders and we fell backwards into the ornamental pool.

The water was warm, but the shock of it helped me to keep my senses. It was about three feet deep. I floundered to my feet, beating off slimy lily stalks, still grasping one end of the tool. I was bellowing for breath like a hungry sea lion. Mark took longer to come up. From the way he moved, from the way his left arm hung limp and he clutched his left shoulder, I knew I had broken something useful. He turned away from me and headed for the opposite bank, where banana trees and tall grasses grew.

Compassion rose in me. I had no heart to go on. Had he not been my ally? But in that moment of weakness, he turned and looked at me. I understood that look. We were enemies, and he was going for a weapon with which to kill me. There would be plenty about: pruning knives, shears, blades of all kinds. I could not let him get away.

He dragged himself up onto the bank, using only one arm.

The broken half of the garden tool in my hand was the business end of some sort of edging implement, with a sharp crescent shaped blade. I threw it hard.

He staggered and grasped at the banana tree. He missed. He tried to reach the shaft in his back with his good hand, but failed. He fell back into the pool, disappearing among reeds. There was a good deal of threshing about in the water, but it stopped at last. I climbed out of the pool and headed drunkenly for the portals.

It was useless to ask me how I got through the vanishing routine. I don't know. Somehow I did all that was necessary, injected myself, tuned the portal. As I sat in the seat, I could hear noises outside, distant and meaningless, and the sound of a door being broken in, and the squeal of whistles. Then the Möbius effect overcame me and – I was sprawling on a crowded nightclub floor with three half-naked dancers shrieking their heads off. I was back home!

To say the authorities were interested is seriously to understate. One thing I could not tell them and it saved a lot of trouble. I could not remember the classification number of the matrix from which I had escaped. There could be no going back there, except by accident. Rastell's world was safe among a myriad others.

This fortunate bit of ignorance saved me from a severe moral problem. Supposing we could have got back easily to Rastell's world, had we any right to intervene on behalf of the slaves? In any one world, there's enough trouble in circulation, without looking for it in others.

Candida says we have moral obligations to all matrices. I say we have a moral obligation not to judge other people's standards by our own. Royal refuses to believe my whole experience. We are still arguing. It's a freedom not to be despised.

The Green Leaves of Space

The flowers of the geranium were bright red. Dr Robert Mays carried the plant out of the potting house and through into his conservatory, to place it on a bench in the sun. The bold tones of the flower contrasted richly with the foliage of the alien plants behind it.

As Dr Mays set the geranium down, his house robot – always referred to as 'Mrs Hooper' – appeared at the door.

'I have admitted two young humans to your living-room, sir. Their names are Harry and Ann Gillett. They have luggage with them, sir.'

'I'll come and see them, Mrs Hooper. The Gilletts will be on the spaceship with me when we start for Damonn tomorrow, so they will be staying the night. You'd better prepare a room for them.'

'Very good, sir.'

Dr Robert Mays straightened his back and brushed grains of soil out of his beard. He was a noted exobotanist, at thirty-four perhaps the most famous of the men who studied the wonders of plant life on other planets. In the last month or two, he had also become the centre of a controversy about the future of Damonn. The resultant publicity had given him a wariness that was visible in his bearing as he walked into the living-room to meet the Gilletts.

Harry and Ann Gillett were standing before the large window, gazing out of it at the vista of London. In this year of 2263, London was a spacious and clean city. From Dr Mays's window, one caught a prospect of the glittering white cliff's of Wembley, with the blocks of Ealing, Hendon and Willesden farther away, and beyond them again a multitude of other blocks, gold-tipped Acton and the tall spire of Pancras. The city units were separated by green parkland, and joined by a gleaming complex of bridges and aerial roads.

'You can see the space station from here, if you know where to look,' Dr Mays said, pointing south towards distant Richmond. 'We take off from there in the *John Russell* tomorrow afternoon.'

'You have a splendid view, Dr Mays,' Ann said, as she shook his hand.

'The view's better out in space – particularly as I'm not very popular on Earth just now.'

She dropped her gaze and looked nervously at her husband. The gesture made Dr Mays feel uneasy; it would be difficult if these two, who would work with him on Damonn for six months, were opposed to his plans for the planet. Yet they looked reassuring – Harry, a stocky and keen-featured young man, Ann, very smart and pretty, and not more than twenty. Both of them obviously of the up-and-coming generation.

'You'd better come into the conservatory and look at the Damonnian plant life I brought back with me last trip,' Dr Mays said.

They both became excited.

'We've heard a lot about the plant life of Damonn,' Harry said. 'From the telloid stories about Devil Vegetation to your own articles in *Nature*.'

'Can the plants really think, Dr Mays?' Ann asked.

'That's a very large question. I hope to give you a large answer on Damonn. Not all forms of plant life there are equally developed.'

'But some of it is hostile to man?'

'You'd better ask some of the plants themselves,' Dr Mays said, pausing dramatically on the threshold of the conservatory and gesturing in. Then he uttered an exclamation and ran to where he had left the geranium.

The geranium was no longer in its pot. The pot lay on the bench on its side, soil spilling from it. Behind it, towering above it, one of the alien plants was in motion.

This particular plant was a species of Damonnian climber with broad and shield-shaped leaves. At rest, these leaves were almost black, but now they had begun to change colour. Superficially, the plant might have been mistaken for an earth species, until one saw that it was locked to its supporting stake, and that its long-fingered roots lowered themselves into or withdrew themselves from their nutrient solution at will.

Dr Mays followed the motion of the leaves and saw his geranium. It was being passed upwards, tossed from one cupped leaf to the next. When it reached a leaf too light to hold it, it fell, tumbled on to the bench, and rolled off at Ann Gillett's feet in a flutter of petals. Ann backed hastily away.

Harry seized her arm and struck a defensive attitude.

Without thinking, Dr Mays laughed.

'It won't hurt you! You'd better get used to a few vegetable tricks – we're going to be surrounded by such things on Damonn.'

Harry didn't see the joke.

'You seem over-confident about these plants, Dr Mays. Yet in your articles you admit that some have a terrific array of stings and barbs. Why should anyone expect anything but hostility from a sentient plant?'

'That's man-thinking. These are vegetables, not pygmies with blow-guns. Watch this chap – he was only curious about the geranium.'

The climber's leaves were changing colour. Softly, swiftly, the dark green turned to red. Patchily, the whole plant turned into a hue that was a very good imitation of the geranium. Three other plants along the bench copied it. Harry and Ann stared at them fascinated. Dr Mays strode down to the other end of the conservatory, and through a door into a small hothouse.

'Come and see my tropical varieties!' he called.

They spent an hour there, gathering some idea of the kind of plant they might meet in the equatorial zones of Damonn. The plant that particularly fascinated Ann and Harry was what Dr Mays called his 'butterfly net'. It scuttled to the far end of its leash, trying to get away from them as they approached, a crablike plant, that used its thick roots as legs and concealed its body with smooth oval leaves.

'This is an insect-eater. Watch it catch its prey,' Dr Mays told them.

Along one side of the hothouse ran various breeding boxes. Some cabbage white butterflies fluttered in one of them. Dipping into the box, Mays caught a butterfly in a pair of tongs, brought it close to his butterfly net plant, and released it.

The top of the plant's 'body' snapped open. White strands, each terminating in a sucker, sailed out and fastened on the butterfly as it circled towards the light. The insect was dragged into the body, and the lid closed on it.

'A simple mechanism – but effective,' Dr Mays said. 'Now watch what happens when I put my face near.'

He thrust his head towards the plant. Laboriously, it climbed the stick to which it was secured, in an effort to get away, but the head still moved nearer. Again the lid came open; the white strands sailed outwards and spread, each landing on the face of the exobotanist. Ann gasped, but Harry motioned her to be silent.

The whole plant, except for its roots, underwent rapid colour changes. Then the strands were withdrawn into their hiding-place, and within a minute, the last tremulous hue had fled.

'Surely it might have hurt you – poisoned you!' Ann exclaimed.

Dr Mays shook his head.

'Not a chance – though that was something I only discovered by accident. It's no more likely to attack me than a cat is to attack a cabbage. It's a question of what constitutes its natural prey. Don't forget that on Damonn there are many plants and many insects, but no mammals, no large animals of any kind. Evolution took a different path from its path on Earth. That's why I say that the plant life can never be an enemy of man – only man of it.'

'Yet it killed men from the first Damonn Exploratory Expedition,' Harry said. 'Wrapped stalks round their necks, thrust tendrils down their gullets.'

'Perhaps that was an attempt to find how man speaks,' Dr Mays said. 'But we can talk of that tomorrow. After all, we shall have a whole week on the *John Russell* together, before we confront the Damonnian vegetation.'

Next day, the *John Russell* rose from the launching-pad and headed into the heavens. Twenty hours later, clear of the plane of the solar system, the Overdrive engines came on, and the ship entered hyperspace. Through the viewports, the stars instantly became long bars of light split into their spectral colours; this optical illusion, caused by the ship's acceleration beyond the speed of light, made the passengers feel that they journeyed through a cage with an infinity of bars.

'How does Jhim like hyperspace?' Ann asked Dr Mays.

'Nothing worries Jhim, provided he gets his sugar ration,' the exobotanist said, patting. Jhim, who sat stolidly on his shoulder, gazing at the spectacle beyond the ship.

'Jhim's certainly a remarkable creature,' Harry said.

'He's only just come out of a fortnight's hibernation,' Dr Mays told them. 'Every two months, Jhim takes a fortnight's sleep, burrowing underground to do so. I brought him aboard in his earthbox. Isn't that so, Jhim?'

'That's right, boss. Anything you say grows.' The creature nodded sleepily.

'He gets his words mixed up,' Dr Mays said, as the other two laughed.

Jhim was an old friend of Dr Mays. When the exobotanist discovered him, Jhim was one of the many life forms on Kakakakaxo, a world in the Crab Nebula. Kakakakaxo moved in an eccentric orbit round its sun; when it was nearest, at perihelion, its life forms became semi-animal, able to move about and often to hunt prey; while at aphelion, when Kakakakaxo was farthest from its sun and the climate became severely cold, the life forms burrowed below ground and turned semi-plant, drawing nourishment direct from the soil.

'In fact,' Harry observed, when Dr Mays explained all this to them, 'Jhim is a cross between a parrot and a carrot!'

'Don't be rude. People who live in grass houses shouldn't throw stains,' Jhim said, shaking a gaudy wing and waving one of its six paws at Harry.

Laughing, they moved into Dr Mays's cabin to talk of more serious things. First, Harry insisted on taking a phototec of Jhim. He set up his apparatus, and within five minutes presented Dr Mays with a translucent six-inch cube, in the middle of which glowed a 3D image of Jhim.

'It's perfect,' Dr Mays said. 'Work of this standard is what we need on Damonn. If I didn't know so before, I know now that the government sent me the right man.'

Harry Gillett had risen to be head phototect at Commonwealth University. In the art of phototecture, he had few rivals anywhere in the galaxy. On the day that he married Ann, one of the leading young exopainters of her day, an unbeatable team had been created. On Damonn they would record as much as they could of the native life for the next edition of the *Galactic Encyclopaedia*, and for other works of reference.

'I hope nobody will obstruct our work on Damonn,' Dr Mays said, when they had seated themselves and the two men had lighted mesca-hales. 'You may have heard that I have been making myself unpopular lately with the Galactic Council.' When he saw they made no answer to that, he continued. 'Although I am employed by the Council, I quarrel with its attitude towards the colonisation of newly discovered planets. It is far too ruthless. Any suitable Earth-type planet is immediately thrown open to colonists, who wreck the natural order in ten years or less.'

'What else can the Council do, Dr Mays?' Harry asked. 'It was fixed over half a century ago that population density should not exceed four hundred people per square mile, and while the population continues to rise, the overspill must find homes on other planets.'

'There are better solutions to that problem than to desecrate other worlds.'

'Desecrate!' Ann Gillett exclaimed. 'The pioneers and colonists are terribly brave people who generally have to fight a strange environment before they can settle down and create civilisation. You call that desecration?'

Dr Mays nodded his head vigorously.

'Yes, I call that desecration, however savage the planet is.'

'We've never yet found a planet,' Harry said, 'with any form of life that can rival man and man's ability to create civilisation. Why shouldn't we move in and make ourselves comfortable?'

The exobotanist leant forward and pointed a finger at Harry.

'Supposing a race of aliens with our sciences had discovered Earth back in the Carboniferous Age. Supposing they had adopted your attitude. Supposing they had "colonised" our planet. Supposing they had drained the swamps, cleared the forests, dammed the rivers, built roads – done all the things the Council is planning to do to Damonn. Supposing all that had happened, then ask yourself this question: would *we* be here now? Would mankind have evolved at all? Would any of the species of Earth creature we know have been given a chance to evolve over the long centuries, beyond perhaps the humble slug and the woodlouse? You know the answer: a decided No.'

During Dr Mays's last speech, Harry had become red in the face.

'What if all you say is true?' he asked. 'What do you want to do in a case like Damonn? – Sit about for three hundred million years and see if anything interesting evolves? No! Man's the only intelligent form of life we know of. Why should we need other kinds? There'd probably only be trouble with them if we found them.'

'We shall never find them, the way we blunder along,' Dr Mays said soberly. He gestured out at the immensity of hyperspace beyond his viewport. 'Look out there, Mr Gillett. The universe is a large and lonely place. Man's a young race yet, riding among the stars like a kid on his first motor-cycle. Don't you think the day will come – perhaps not for millions of years – when we are going to want other company, other sorts of life, that can supplement our limited senses with senses of their own?'

Ann stood up before Harry could reply.

'Travelling on other planets must make you very far-sighted, Dr Mays,' she said. 'But in peering ahead you should be careful you don't fall over the facts at your feet. I think Harry and I will go to bed before we all say things we may regret later. Don't forget the three of us have to work as a team.'

'Good-night, ladies,' Jhim called. 'And I wish you pheasant dreams.'

When the Gilletts had gone, Dr Robert Mays sat in a chair, too restless to retire. He felt that he had made a fool of himself. Moodily, he picked up the brochure concerning the flight which the space line, Allied Astronautics, placed by every bedside on the ship. The brochure took the form of a phototec cube, with a button set in its opaque rear wall. As he pressed the button, the images in the brochure changed, now with an image of one of the line's new ships, now with a view of one of the cabins, now with a list of the directors of the line.

At the last item, Dr Mays stopped. He looked more closely at the directors' names. The Chairman was Sir Hilary Gillett.

Dr Mays's heart gave an extra beat. Sir Hilary would be Harry's uncle. And Allied Astronautics were the firm who would get the contract to transport colonists from Earth to Damonn unless Dr Mays could carry through his plans for that unfortunate planet. The contract would be worth several billion credits over a period of twenty years. In the circumstances, it was hardly likely that he could expect support from Ann and Harry!

He put the brochure down beside him, and sat staring into the future.

The flight to Damonn was uneventful, except for a failure of the environment machinery. This was the small laboratory amidships where the used air was recycled, its moisture content removed, and fresh oxygen-nitrogen mixture pumped back over the ship's ventilators. For several hours, both passengers and crew lay on their bunks and laboured to breathe increasingly foul air, while two engineers and a chemist fought to remedy the fault. After that unpleasant experience, everyone was correspondingly keener to arrive at Damonn as soon as possible.

By ship's chronometers, they broke out of hyperspace seven days after entering it. Owing to the phenomenon called relativity, time in hyperspace had crawled by comparison with Earth time; during their seven-day voyage, four months had passed on Earth.

Time meant nothing to the stars. They hung unchangingly in the mighty dark of space. And two of them grew into bright suns; they were known as B79 Alpha and Beta, the binary suns about which Damonn revolved. Presently the green disk of Damonn was visible, swelling like some incredible fruit from a mote to a great globe.

Touchdown was the name of the first township on Damonn. It lay in the bend of a river that fifty miles further down its course flowed into a mighty ocean covering half the world. It was with gratitude that Ann, Harry, Dr Mays, and the other passengers – not forgetting Jhim – climbed out and stretched their legs.

'This is better than face flight!' Jhim exclaimed, as he circled above Dr Mays's head, landed on his shoulder, and scuttled down his back to the ground.

During the journey, they had all been inoculated against hostile micro-organisms in Damonn's atmosphere. They could now breathe the fresh air with impunity, and enjoy it.

Transport was still in short supply on Touchdown. Ann, Harry and Dr Mays walked to the prefabricated building that served as government offices. All arrangements were simple; within five minutes they had shed their luggage in an outer office and had been shown in to see Governor Phillips. He shook hands perfunctorily and motioned them into chairs.

'I don't pretend I'm glad to see you back, Dr Mays,' he said. 'However, I've been instructed to give you some assistance in your surveys, so that

I shall do. Forestry Department have laid on a hovercar that is yours when you need it.'

'Thank you, Governor. I'm grateful.'

'Then show your gratitude please by refraining from spreading propaganda. Your project for preserving Damonn in its natural state has its sympathisers even here, and I don't want any trouble. I'm committed to a hard job and a strict timetable, and nothing must go wrong.'

'We are here to work, not talk, Governor,' Harry reminded him.

The governor turned his big head and inspected Harry.

'Keep on feeling like that, young man. I know Damonn is a pretty planet, but we aren't here to be sentimental. Nor are we going to spoil everything. Remember that this idea of preserving Damonn as it is is just a romantic fancy. There aren't any natives, there aren't any animals. All we're doing is lopping off the confounded plant life – and Damonn has too much of that to be healthy!'

He moved to a map of the planet that hung on the wall behind his desk, and thumped it.

'See this pink square here? That's the land we are clearing first. Two hundred square miles of it, absolutely impassable at present, but potentially useful agricultural land. In three months' time, the reclamation team will have finished there and can move on to another area. Then we're ready for eighty thousand colonists in the first area. It's man's work we're doing here, Mays.'

'And whose work are you undoing?'

'Don't go mystical on me, Mays. Mr Gillett, you and your wife are welcome here, but get on with your work. This is a tough world. It's a fine place to work. It's not a good place to stand around and try to argue.'

As they emerged into the sunlight, Dr Mays said, 'You see now the sort of bigotry I'm up against.'

'But just look at the planet the Governor's up against,' Ann said.

They were standing near the perimeter of the town, marked here by a high wire fence. Beyond it, the ground had not been cleared. The vegetation grew tall, although not particularly close together. It was mainly of the very dark green that Ann and Harry had observed in the exobotanist's specimens. Two factors rendered it sinister. Patches of colour moved over the plants in fugitive fashion, vanished, appeared again; and the vegetation moved, though there was no wind to move it. It rustled and stirred as if a horde of creatures awaited in ambush there.

'Is it – does it always writhe like that?' Ann asked.

Dr Mays raised an eyebrow and gazed at her mockingly.

'Only when people are about,' he said.

Touchdown boasted no hotels as yet. Dr Mays and his companions left their luggage at the government rest house, where cubicles had been allotted them, and set to work immediately. Harry in particular was keen to get started.

As they walked over to Forestry Department to collect the promised hovercar, the exobotanist outlined his plans.

'If the entire biosphere of this planet is to be ruined, as Phillips and his friends intend, then we must have as complete a record as possible of as many forms of Damonn's life as possible. We'll fly out to the farthest reclamation camp, see what's going on there, and then aim to keep always one jump ahead of them. In that way we can work by hops right up to the north pole. Then we survey the south continent, which is absolutely virgin ground. Have you got all the equipment you need, Harry?'

Ann laughed.

'I couldn't pile a thing more on to him or he'd collapse,' she said.

'He'd collapse if I sat on his shadow,' Jhim cackled, trotting along beside them.

Harry was so loaded with apparatus that Dr Mays helped him with the heavier items. They found the hovercar without any trouble, signed for it with the Department, and loaded it up. Five minutes later, they were in the air and heading north.

Both of Damonn's suns, Alpha and Beta, were in the sky, with Beta sinking towards the western horizon. It looked like a large fuzzy ball, perhaps three times the size of Earth's sun, and emitting appreciably less light. As Dr Mays explained, this star was a red giant, and several hundred million miles away. The nearer star, and the one round which Damonn revolved, was Alpha, a blinding blue-white dwarf sun only some sixty million miles distant and at present almost at zenith in the sky, shining through thin cloud.

'A good plant-growing world,' the exobotanist said, squinting up at the sky. 'Though how the colonists will take to the heavy rainfall, I don't know.'

When the sun was obscured, half an hour later, it was not by cloud but smoke. They rose higher, passing over a whole bank of it. Below them, a forest fire blazed, its fire front clearly visible as they flew beyond it.

'You see that! That's how the vandals clear the land,' Dr Mays said.

'It seems a pretty efficient way of doing it,' Harry said dryly.

'And what follows? They divide the ground into fields, they build houses. The rain comes, the wind blows. All that delicate topsoil, so long sheltered by the jungles, gets blown away. In five years, this whole continent will be a dust bowl.'

'They're aware of all those factors. They'll guard against them.'

'Certainly, certainly. I'm not saying they're fools, Harry. But they're greedy. They won't take *enough* safeguards, they'll cut corners and costs, because they're greedy for quick profits. I tell you this'll be desert in a few years.'

The reclamation outpost was in sight. They lapsed into silence as the hovercar sank. Ann was looking at the forest towards which the fire was heading. Pulses of dim colour were flowing outwards from the danger centre, and all the vegetation was in movement. Then her view was obscured as rain came sliding in from the south.

It was at that moment the time bomb exploded.

Acrid smoke billowed round them. Ann screamed. The cabin glass shattered and rain came spurting in. Dr Mays fought with the controls, but they were useless. The dark vegetation came plunging up to meet them. They struck it with tremendous force, and darkness closed round them.

Ann was roused by the sound of her own coughing. She opened her eyes to find thick smoke swirling about her. She was sprawled on the floor of the wrecked hovercar. Harry and Dr Mays lay near her; Harry had a wound on his head.

With the smell of burning vegetation in her nostrils, Ann tried to lift her head, and at once she saw the plants. Large and black, but flecked with livid colours, one of them loomed over the car, bending forward and pressing its leaves against the wreck. It was like an immense fleshy fir tree. Its limbs came through the broken windows. They extended towards her and touched her. Even as she was attempting to scream, she fainted.

When she came to, she was upside-down and being pulled out of the wreckage. As she rose into the air, she had a clear view of the forest fire, unquenched by the rain. The noise from it struck her in a dull roar; the heat painted the sky crimson. And then she found herself being passed up into the higher branches of the tree, just as the geranium had been passed in Dr Mays's conservatory, back on Earth. She struggled frantically.

Something gaudy fluttered by her cheek. It was Jhim, calling to her.

'Keep still! Keep still! Let sleeping ducks lie! The plants say they can save us.'

As Ann twisted round to look at the little creature, she caught sight of the two men. They were both in the grip of the vegetation. Dr Mays was swathed in it, and had already been lifted from the wrecked machine. Harry was just being pulled out. Through the swirling smoke, Ann saw her husband dragged free and placed on the back of an astounding object.

The trees were passing her from one to another, away from the direction of the fire. She knew now that the vegetation was acting in unison to save her and Harry and Dr Mays. Tossed high in the dark foliage, she saw Harry more clearly. He had been placed on the back of a giant vegetable. Dr Mays had recovered consciousness and was leaning over Harry.

The two men were being carried along on one of the biggest life forms on the planet, the kind that Dr Mays had heard referred to by explorers as a soil-sucker. Unlike the tree-like plants that were passing Ann along to safety, the soil-suckers were able to move from location to location – after the fashion of Dr Mays's butterfly net plant, but on a much larger scale.

This soil-sucker was over 20 feet long, and broad in the body. It plodded through the forest, its fastest pace a slow walk, moving caterpillar fashion, drawing itself up and then extending again, so that the two men were given an uncomfortable ride. Once it stopped and let down the double row of suckers that had given it its name; the suckers drank up water and mud from a stream. The soil-sucker, in fact, was like a flower that carries its own private flower bed inside it. Dr Mays lolled in a bed of mauve petals each a foot long.

As he was bandaging Harry's brow, the phototect roused and opened his eyes.

'The crash,' he whispered. 'What happened? The hovercar. ...'

'We were sabotaged, Harry. You can see that various groups have a strong financial interest in exploiting this planet to the uttermost. They want me out of the way, and are ruthless enough to have tried to do so without worrying whether you and Ann were killed.'

'Was Ann. ...'

He did not finish his question. Relief filled him when Dr Mays pointed to her in the rocking treetops. Though she looked rather green, she managed to give him a reassuring wave. Harry sat up, and Dr Mays explained what was happening.

By now the rain was stopping, the smoke had thinned, and the fire was falling behind them, though its crimson stain still flooded the sky behind them.

Jhim came down on to Dr Mays's shoulder, hopping about restlessly.

'The plants call my name,' he said. 'All the forest is a voice crawling to me.'

The trees petered out on the margins of savannah land. Ann was lowered to the ground, and the soil-sucker stopped. Harry and Dr Mays slid off its back and ran over to Ann. She was dizzy and breathless, but otherwise unharmed. All round them, other types of vegetable capable of movement were emerging from the forest and crawling into the long grass to safety.

'I don't want a ride like that again,' Ann gasped. 'But what is happening to the soil-sucker?' They looked behind them. Bands of colour were passing over the mass of tousled petals. It began to move slowly away.

'I feel we ought to thank it,' Harry said. Then he caught the exobotanist's eyes. 'They have intelligence, haven't they?'

'Why not?' Dr Mays said. 'They've had millions of years evolving without any opposition from animal life. It is hardly extraordinary that they should have developed intelligence.'

He paused. Jhim was flying off with the soil-sucker, settling on its back. The exobotanist called to it, but the creature did not obey. Instead it called, 'The plants know me, so I go. Good-bye, Doctor! A rolling stain gathers no morse.'

Dr Mays shaded his eyes and stared after the disappearing Jhim and the soil-sucker.

'Jhim has found friends,' he said quietly to Harry. 'You were right. He can communicate with them. He'll be better with them than with me. I've long been convinced that the colour changes we have observed are an elaborate form of language; that's a point I have come back to study, though I'd say we've just had conclusive proof of it.'

Harry suddenly burst into a rage that astonished Ann even more than the exobotanist.

'All right, all right! What's the good of standing in the middle of this wilderness and discussing things so calmly? Things aren't half as simple as you think, Dr Mays. Let's give our mouths a rest and get our legs in action!'

Laying a hand on his arm, Ann asked, 'What's all that about? I suppose you're furious because you've lost your equipment?'

Harry began to flush round the neck. 'I'm sorry, Ann. I'm mad at myself. I've been such a fool, and I've expected you to be a fool with me. Dr Mays, I have an uncle – he's the chairman of Allied Astronautics – who stands to gain very considerably from the colonisation of Damonn; consequently, I stand to gain too; and I've let this prejudice me against your cause. I hope that you will let me now aid you in your fight against exploiting Damonn.'

They shook hands, and Dr Mays patted the phototect awkwardly on the shoulder.

'You mustn't think of me purely as an idealist,' he said. 'We stand to gain more ultimately from studying Damonn than ruining it. On the voyage here in the *John Russell*, when the environment machinery went wrong, I was thinking that an intelligent plant would do the job so much better – remove the carbon dioxide from the air, exhale oxygen, and advise when anything went wrong. Do you think these plants would take to space travel?'

'There's an idea, Harry,' Ann said. 'We'd better lay it before your uncle.'

'First catch the uncle,' Harry said, smiling. As he began to walk, the others fell in beside him. Skirting the area of the blaze, they began to head towards the reclamation camp.

Flickering in the grass about them, little coloured signals of hope were passed back to the secret vegetable intelligence that ruled all Damonn.

Sector Green

Kakakakaxo is presently being colonised by ten thousand men, women and children from the depressed worlds of the Rift.

Craig Hodges has every reason for being concerned about these populations and their depredations on 'new' planets. Fortunately, Starswarm Birthstrike has the matter very much under control. This galaxy-wide organisation educates the planets of the federation in new methods of mental contraception.

Although this operation is costly, it proves less expensive – and exacts less toll on human sensibilities – than the business of establishing colonists on virgin planets.

Birthstrike is undoubtedly the chief factor causing a slowdown in the rate of galactic expansion. With its enlightened use practised on some eleven and a half thousand worlds, overcrowding is not the problem it was even two eras ago.

We are apt to forget that the methods of mental contraception were formulated on the watery world of Banya Ban, in Sector Green, over fifty eras ago. That they have taken so long to spread is hardly surprising to anyone familiar with the Theory of Multigrade Superannuation, which has some sensible things to say about ideas being acceptable only to the group in which they emerge.

Banya Ban has changed almost as much as Droxy and Dansson in the last fifty eras. It is a world of immense inventiveness coupled with little drive. These characteristics are evident as much in Banya Ban's literature as its life, as the following brief chronicle shows.

I

The way of telling time in Mudland was ingenious. Double A had a row of sticks stuck in the mud in the blackness before his eyes. With his great spongy hands that sometimes would have nothing to do with him, he gripped the sticks one by one, counting as he went, sometimes in numbers, sometimes in such abstractions as lyre birds, rusty screws, pokers, or seaweed.

He would go on grimly, hand over fist against time, until the beastly old comfort of degradation fogged his brain and he would forget what he was trying to do. The long liverish gouts of mental indigestion that were his thought processes would take over from his counting. And when later he came to think back to the moment when the takeover occurred, he would know that that had been the moment when it had been the present. Then he could guess how far ahead or behind of the present he was, and could give this factor a suitable name – though lately he had decided that all factors could be classified under the generic term Standard, and accordingly he named the present time Standard 0'Clock.

Standard 0'Clock he pictured as a big red soldier with moustaches sweeping around the roseate blankness of his face. Every so often, say on payday, it would chime, with pretty little cuckoos popping out of all orifices. As an additional touch of humour, Double A would make 0'Clock's pendulum wag.

By this genial ruse, he was slowly abolishing time, turning himself into the first professor of a benighted quantum. As yet the experiments were not entirely successful, for ever and anon his groping would communicate itself to his hands, and back they'd come to him, slithering through the mud, tame as you please. Sometimes he bit them; they tasted unpleasant; nor did they respond.

'You are intellect,' he thought they said. 'But we are the tools of intellect. Treat us well, and without salt.'

II

Another experiment concerned the darkness.

Even sprawling in the mud with his legs amputated unfortunately represented a compromise. Double A had to admit there was nothing final in his degradation, since he had begun to – no, nobody could force him to use the term 'enjoy the mud', but on the other hand nobody could stop him using the term 'ambivelling the finny claws (clause?)', with the understanding that in certain contexts it might be interpreted as approximately synonymous with 'enjoying the mud'.

Anyhow, heretofore it remained to be continued that everywhere was compromise. The darkness compromised with itself and with him. The darkness was sweet and warm and wet.

When Double A realised that the darkness was not utter, that the abstraction utterness was beyond it, he became furious, drumming imaginary heels in the mud, urinating into it with some force and splendour, and calling loudly for dark optics.

The optics were a failure, for they became covered in mud, so that he could not see through them to observe whether or not the darkness increased. So they came and fitted him with a pair of ebony contacts, and with this game condescension on their part, Double A hoped he had at last reached a point of noncompromise.

Not so! He had eyelids that pressed on the lenses, drawing merry patterns on the night side of his eyeballs. Pattern and darkness cannot exist together, so again he was defeated by myopic little Lord Compromise, knee-high to a pin and stale as rats' whiskers, but still Big Reeking Lord of Creation. Well, he was not defeated yet. He had filled in Application Number Six Oh Five Bark Oomph Eight Eight Tate Potato Ten in sticks and sandbars and the old presumption factor for the privilege of Person Double A, sir, late of the Standard O'Clock Regiment, sir, to undergo total partial and complete Amputation of Two Vermicularform Appendages in the possession of the aforesaid Double A and known henceforth as his Eyelids.

Meanwhile, until the application was accepted and the scalpels served, he tried his cruel experiments on the darkness.

He shouted, whispered, spoke, gave voice, uttered, named names, broke wind, cracked jokes, split infinitives, passed participles, and in short and *in toto* interminably talked, orated, chattered, chatted, and generally performed vocal gymnastics against the darkness. Soon he had it cowering in a corner. It was less well-equipped orally than Double A, and he let it know with a rollicking 'Fathom five thy liar fathers, all his crones have quarrels made, Rifle, rifle, fiddle-faddle, hey', and other such decompositions of a literary-religio-medico-philosophico-nature.

So the powers of darkness had no powers against the powers of screech.

'Loot there be light!' boomed Double A: and there was blight. Through the thundering murk, packed tight with syllables and salty with syllogisms, he could see the dim, mud-bound form of Gasm.

'Let there be night!' boomed Double A. But he was too late, had lost his chance, had carried his experiment beyond the pale. For in the pallor and squalor, Gasm remained revoltingly *there*, whether invisible or visible. And his bareness in the thereness made a whereness tight as harness.

III

So began the true history of Mudland. It was now possible to have not only experiments, which belonged to the old intellect arpeggio, but character conflict, which pings right out of the middle register of the jolly old emotion chasuble, not to mention the corking old horseplay archipelago. Amoebas, editors and lovers are elements in that vast orchestra of classifiable objects to whom or for whom character conflict is ambrosia.

Double A went carefully into the business of having a C.C. with Gasm. To begin with, of course, he did not know whether he himself had a C.: or, of course squared, since we are thinking scientifically, whether Gasm had a C. Without the first C., could there be the second? Could one have a C.-less C.?

Alas for scientific inquiry. During the o'clock sticks that passed while Double A was beating his way patiently through this thicket of thorny questions, jealousy crept up on him unawares.

Despite the shouting and the ebony contacts, with which the twin polarities of his counternegotiations with the pseudo-dark were almost kept at near-maximum in the fairly brave semistruggle against compromise, Gasm remained ingloriously visible, lolling in the muck no more than a measurable distance away.

Gasm's amputations were identical with Double A's: to wit, the surgical removal under local anaesthetic and with two aspirin of that assemblage of ganglions, flesh, blood, bone, toenail, hair and kneecap referred to hereafter as Legs. In this, no cause for jealousy existed. Indeed, they had been scrupulously democratic: one vote, one head; one head, two legs; two heads, four legs. Their surgeons were paragons of the old equality regimen. No cause for Double A's jealousy.

But. It was within his power to *imagine* that Gasm's amputations were other than they were. He could quite easily (and with practice he could perfectly easily) visualise Gasm as having had not two legs but one leg and one arm removed. And that amputation was more interesting than Double A's own amputation, or the fact that he had fins.

So the serpent came even to the muddy paradise of Mudland, writhing between the two bellowing bodies. C.C. became reality.

IV

Double A abandoned all the other experiments to concentrate on beating and catechising Gasm. Gradually Mudland lost its identity and was transformed into Beating and Catechising, or B & C. The new regime was tiring for Double A, physically and especially mentally, since during the entire procedure he was compelled to ask himself why he should be doing what he was, and indeed *if* he was doing what he was, rather than resting contentedly in the mud with his hands.

The catechism was stylised, ranging over several topics and octaves as Double A yelled the questions and Gasm screamed the answers.

'What is your name?'

'My name is Gasm.'

'Name some of the other names you might have been called instead.'

'I might have been called Plus or Shob or Droo or Harm or Finney or Cusp.'

'And by what strange inheritance does it come about that you house your consciousness among the interstices of lungs, aorta, blood, corpuscles, follicles, sacro-iliac, ribs and prebendary skull?'

'Because I would walk erect if I could walk erect among the glorious company of the higher vertebrates, who have grown from mere swamps, dinosaurs and dodos. Those that came before were dirty brates or shirty brates; but we are the vertebrates.'

'How many are pervertebrates?'

'Why, sir, thirtebrates.'

'What comes after us?'

'After us the deluge.'

'How big is the deluge.'

'Huge.'

'How deluge is the deluge?'

'Deluge, deluger, delugest.'

'Conjugate and decline.'

'I decline to conjuge.'

'And what comes after the vertebrates?'

'Nothing comes after the vertebrates, because we are the highest form of civilisation.'

'Name the signs whereby the height of our civilisation may be determined.'

'The heights whereby the determination of our sign may be civilised are seven in number. The subjugation of the body. The resurrection of the skyscraper. The perpetuation of the speeches. The annihilation of the species. The glorification of the nates. The somnivolence of the conscience. The omnivorousness of sex. The conclusion of the Thousand Years War. The condensation of milk. The conversation of idiots. The confiscation of monks —'

'Stop, stop! Name next the basic concept upon which this civilisation is based.'

'The interests of producer and consumer are identical.'

'What is the justification of war?'

'War is its own justification.'

'Let us sing a sesquipedalian love-song in octogenarian voices.'

At this point they humped themselves in the mud and sang the following tuneless ditty:

'No constant factor in beauty is discernible.

Although the road that evolution treads is not returnable,

It has some curious twists in it, as every shape and size

And shade of female breast attestifies.

Pendulous or cumulus, pear-shaped, oval, tumulus,

Each one displays its beauty of depravity

In syncline, incline, outcropping or cavity.

Yet from Droxy to Feroxi

The bosom's lines are only signs

Of all the pectoral muscles' tussles

With a fairly constant factor, namely gravity.'

They fell back into the mud, each lambasting his mate's nates.

V

Of course for a time it was difficult to be certain of everything or anything. The uncertainties became almost infinite, but among the most noteworthy were: the uncertainty as to whether the catechisings actually took place in any wider arena of reality than Double A's mind; the uncertainty as to whether the beatings took place in any wider arena of reality than Double A's mind; the uncertainty as to whether, if the beatings actually took place, they took place with sticks.

For it became increasingly obvious that neither Double A nor Gasm had hands with which to wield sticks. Yet on the other appendage, evidence existed tending to show that some sort of punishment had been undergone. Gasm no longer resembled a human. He had grown positively torpedo-shaped. He possessed fins.

The idea of fins, Double A found to his surprise, was not a surprise to him. Fins had been uppermost in his mind for some time. Fins, indeed, induced in him a whole watery way of thinking; he was flooded with new surmises, while some of the old ones proved themselves a washout. The idea, for example, that he had ever worn dark glass optics or ebony contacts – absurd!

He groped for an explanation. Yes, he had suffered hallucinations. Yes, the whole progression of thought was unravelling and clarifying itself now. He had suffered from hallucinations. Something had been wrong in his mind. His optic centres had been off-centre. With something like clarity, he became able to map the area of disturbance.

It occurred to him that he might some time investigate this cell or tank in which he and Gasm found themselves. Doors and windows had it none. Perhaps, like him, it had undergone some vast sea change.

Emitting a long liquid sigh, Double A ascended slowly off the floor. As he rose, he glanced upward. Two men floated on the ceiling, gazing down at him.

VI

Double A floated back to his former patch of mud only to find his hands gone. Nothing could have compensated him for the loss except the growth of a long, strong tail.

His long, strong tail induced him to make another experiment – no more nor less than the attempt to foster the illusion that the tail was real by pretending there was a portion of his brain capable of activating the tail. More easily done than thought. With no more than an imaginary flick of the imaginary appendage, he was sailing above Gasm on a controlled course, ducking under but on the whole successfully ignoring the two men floating above.

From then on he called himself Doublay and had no more truck with time or hands or ghosts of hands and time. Though the mud was good, being above it was better, especially when Gasm could follow. They grew new talents – or did they find them?

Now the questions were no sooner asked than forgotten, for by a mutual miracle of understanding, Doublay and Gasm began to believe themselves to be fish.

And then they began to dream about hunting down the alien invaders.

VII

The main item in the laboratory was the great tank. It was sixty feet square and twenty feet high; it was half full of sea water. A metal catwalk with rails around it ran along the top edge of the tank; the balcony was reached by a metal stair. Both stair and catwalk were covered with deep rubber, and the men that walked there wore rubber shoes, to ensure maximum quiet.

The whole place was dimly lit.

Two men, whose names were Rabents and Coblison, stood on the catwalk, looking through infra-red goggles down into the tank. Though they spoke almost in whispers, their voices nevertheless held a note of triumph.

'This time I think we have succeeded, Dr Coblinson,' the younger man was saying. 'In the last forty-eight hours, both specimens have shown less lethargy and more awareness of their form and purpose.'

Coblison nodded.

'Their recovery has been remarkably fast, all things considered. The surgical techniques have been so many and so varied. Though I played a major part in the operations myself, I am still overcome by wonder to think that it has been possible to transfer at least half of a human brain into such a vastly different metabolic environment.'

He gazed down at the two shadowy forms swimming around the tank.

Compassion moving him, he said, 'Who knows what terrible traumata those brave souls have had to undergo? What fantasies of amputation, of life, birth and death, or not knowing what species they were.'

Sensing his mood, and disliking it, Rabents said briskly, 'They're over it now. They can communicate with each other – the underwater mikes pick up their language. They've adjusted well. Now they're raring to go.'

'Maybe, maybe. I still wonder if we had the right –'

Rabents gestured impatiently, guessing Coblison spoke only to be reassured. He knew how proud the old man secretly was and answered him in the perfunctory way he might have answered one of the newspapermen who would be around later.

'The security of Banya Ban demanded this drastic experiment. It's a year since that alien Flaran ship "landed" in our Western Ocean. Our submarines have investigated its remains on the ocean bed and found proof that the ship landed where it did *under control*, and was only destroyed when the aliens left it.

'You know these Flarans, Dr Coblison – they're fish people, aquatics. The ocean is their element, and undoubtedly they have been responsible for the floods extending along our seacoast and inundating the pleasure islands of Indura. The popular press is right to demand that we fight back.'

'My dear Rabents, I don't doubt they're right, but –'

'How can there be any "buts"? We've failed to make contact with the aliens. They have eluded the most careful probes. Nor is there any 'but' about their hostile intent. Before they upset our entire oceanic ecology, we must find them out and gain the information about them without which they cannot be fought. Here are our spies, here in this tank. They have post-hypnotic training. Soon, when they're fit, they can be released into the sea to go and get that information and return with it to us. There are no "buts", only imperatives, in this equation.'

Slowly the two men descended the metal stairway, the giant tank on their left glistening with condensation.

'Yes, it's as you say,' the other agreed wearily. 'I would so much like to know, though, the sensations passing through the shards of human brain embedded in fish bodies.'

'It doesn't really matter – so long as they're successful,' the first said firmly.

In the tank, in the twilight, the two giant sea creatures swam restlessly back and forth, readying themselves for their mission.

Sector Vermilion

The most simple statement you can make is also the most profound: Time passes. A million centuries – give or take a dozen – have elapsed since the human family began to move from one planet to another.

Directly, little is known about the first primitive men or the worlds they conquered. Indirectly, we know a great deal. The classical Theory of Multigrade Superannuation helps us.

The Theory was formulated in Starswarm Era 80, and with it we, forty-four eras later, can deduce more about both past and present than we should otherwise be able to do.

The fifth postulate of the Theory states that 'the progress factors that intelligent beings cause, as well as the factors stimulating their intelligence, are both independent of the universal progression factor, within certain limits'. These limits are defined in the remaining postulates, but the statement as it stands is adequate.

Put simply, it means this: The Universe is similar to a cosmic clock; the civilisations of man are not mere cogs but infinitely smaller clocks, ticking in their own right.

Shorn of its intellectual clothes, the idea stands forth naked and exciting. It means that at any one time, the inhabited solar systems of Starswarm – our galaxy – will exhibit all the characteristics through which a civilisation can pass.

So it is fitting that in this anniversary of star flight we should survey a handful of the myriad civilisations, all contemporary in one sense, all isolated in another, that go to make up our galactic cluster. Perhaps we may find a hint that will show us why the ancients launched their frail metal spores into the expanses of space.

Our first survey comes from the remote part of Starswarm designated as Sector Vermilion. There, far from the accepted routes of our interstellar societies, you will find a culture with some unity that embraces two hundred and fifteen thousand planets.

Among those planets is Abrogun – a planet with a long history, tenanted now by only a few hermit-like families. Among those families ...

I

A giant rising from the fjord, from the grey arm of sea in the fjord, could have peered over the crown of its sheer cliffs and discovered Endehabven there on the edge, sprawling at the very start of the island.

Derek Flamifew/Ende saw much of this sprawl from his high window; indeed, a growing restlessness, apprehensions of a quarrel, forced him to see everything with particular clarity, just as a landscape takes on an intense actinic visibility before a thunderstorm. Although he was warmseeing with his face, yet his eye vision wandered over the estate.

All was bleakly neat at Endehabven – as I should know, for its neatness is my care. The gardens are made to support evergreens and shrubs that never flower; this is My Lady's whim, who likes a sobriety to match the furrowed brow of the coastline. The building, gaunt Endehabven itself, is tall and lank and severe; earlier ages would have found its structure impossible: its thousand built-in paragravity units ensure that column, buttress, arch and wall support masonry the mass of which is largely an illusion.

Between the building and the fjord, where the garden contrives itself into a parade, stood My Lady's laboratory and My Lady's pets – and, indeed, My Lady herself at this time, her long hands busy with the minicoypu and the squeaking atoshkies. I stood with her, attending the animals' cages or passing her instruments or stirring the tanks, doing always what she asked. And the eyes of Derek Ende looked down on us; no, they looked down on her only.

Derek Flamifew/Ende stood with his face over the receptor bowl, reading the message from Star One. It played lightly over his countenance and over the boscises of his forehead. Though he stared down across that achingly familiar stage of his life outside, he still warmsaw the communication clearly. When it was finished, he negated the receptor, pressed his face to it, and flexed his message back.

'I will do as you message, Star One. I will go at once to Festi XV in the Veil Nebula and enter liaison with the being you call the Cliff. If possible, I will also obey your order to take some of its substance to Pyrylyn. Thank you for your greetings; I return them in good faith. Goodbye.'

He straightened and massaged his face: warmlooking over great light distances was always tiring, as if the sensitive muscles of the countenance knew that they delivered up their tiny electrostatic charges to parsecs of vacuum and were appalled. Slowly his boscises also relaxed, as slowly he gathered together his gear. It would be a long flight to the Veil, and the task that was set him would daunt the stoutest heart. Yet it was for another reason he lingered; before he could be away, he had to say a farewell to his mistress.

Dilating the door, he stepped out into the corridor, walked along it with a steady tread – feet covering mosaics of a pattern learned long ago in his childhood – and walked into the paragravity shaft. Moments later, he was leaving the main hall, approaching My Lady as she stood gaunt, with her rodents scuttling at breast level before her and Vatya Jokatt's heights rising behind her, grey with the impurities of distance.

'Go indoors and fetch me the box of name rings, Hols,' she said to me; so I passed him, My Lord, as he went to her. He noticed me no more than he noticed any of the other parthenos, fixing his sights on her.

When I returned, she had not turned towards him, though he was speaking urgently to her.

'You know I have my duty to perform, Mistress,' I heard him saying. 'Nobody else but a normal-born Abrogunnan can be entrusted with this sort of task.'

'This sort of task! The galaxy is loaded inexhaustibly with such tasks! You can excuse yourself for ever with such excursions.'

He said to her remote back, pleadingly: 'You can't talk of them like that. You know of the nature of the Cliff – I told you all about it. You know this isn't an excursion: it requires all the courage I have. And you know that in this sector of Starswarm only Abrogunnans, for some reason, have such courage ... Don't you, Mistress?'

Although I had come up to them, threading my subservient way between cage and tank, they noticed me not enough even to lower their voices. My Lady stood gazing at the grey heights inland, her countenance as formidable as they; one boscis twitched as she said, 'You think you are so mighty and brave, don't you?'

Knowing the power of sympathetic magic, she never spoke his name when she was angry; it was as if she wished him to disappear.

'It isn't that,' he said humbly. 'Please be reasonable, Mistress; you know I must go; a man cannot be forever at home. Don't be angry.'

She turned to him at last.

Her face was high and stern; it did not receive. Her warm-vision was closed and seldom used. Yet she had a beauty of some dreadful kind I cannot describe, if kneading together weariness and knowledge can create beauty. Her eyes were as grey and distant as the frieze of the snow-covered volcano behind her. She was a century older than Derek, though the difference showed not in her skin – which would stay fresh yet a thousand years – but in her authority.

'I'm not angry. I'm only hurt. You know how you have the power to hurt me.'

'Mistress –' he said, taking a step towards her.

'Don't touch me,' she said. 'Go if you must, but don't make a mockery of it by touching me.'

He took her elbow. She held one of the minicoypus quiet in the crook of her arm – animals were always docile at her touch – and strained it closer.

'I don't mean to hurt you, Mistress. You know we owe allegiance to Star One; I must work for them, or how else do we hold this estate? Let me go for once with an affectionate parting.'

'Affection! You go off and leave me alone with a handful of miserable parthenos and you talk of affection! Don't pretend you don't rejoice to get away from me. You're tired of me, aren't you?'

Wearily he said, as if nothing else would come, 'It's not that –'

'You see! You don't even attempt to sound sincere. Why don't you go? It doesn't matter what happens to me.'

'Oh, if you could only hear your own self-pity!'

Now she had a tear on the icy slope of one cheek. Turning, she flashed it for his inspection.

'Who else should pity me? You don't, or you wouldn't go away from me as you do. Suppose you get killed by this Cliff, what will happen to me?'

'I shall be back, Mistress,' he said. 'Never fear.'

'It's easy to say. Why don't you have the courage to admit that you're only too glad to leave me?'

'Because I'm not going to be provoked into a quarrel.'

'Pah! You sound like a child again. You won't answer, will you? Instead you're going to run away, evading your responsibilities.'

'I'm not running away!'

'Of course you are, whatever you pretend. You're just immature.'

'I'm not, I'm not! And I'm not running away! It takes real courage to do what I'm going to do.'

'You think so well of yourself!'

He turned away then, petulantly, without dignity. He began to head towards the landing platform. He began to run.

'Derek!' she called.

He did not answer.

She took the squatting minicoypu by the scruff of its neck. Angrily she flung it into a nearby tank of water. It turned into a fish and swam down into the depths.

II

Derek journeyed towards the Veil Nebula in his fast light-pusher. Lonely it sailed, a great fin shaped like an archer's bow, barnacled all over with the photon cells that sucked its motive power from the dense and dusty currencies of space. Midway along the trailing edge was the blister in which Derek lay, senseless over most of his voyage, which stretched a quarter way across the light-centuries of Vermilion Sector.

He awoke in the therapeutic bed, called to another day that was no day by gentle machine hands that eased the stiffness from his muscles. Soup gurgled in a retort, bubbling up towards a nipple only two inches from his mouth. He drank. He slept again, tired from his long inactivity.

When he woke again, he climbed slowly from the bed and exercised. Then he moved forward to the controls. My friend Jon was there.

'How is everything?' Derek asked him.

'Everything is in order, My Lord,' Jon replied. 'We are swinging into the orbit of Festi XV now.' He gave Derek the coordinates and retired to eat. Jon's job was the loneliest any partheno could have. We are hatched according to strictly controlled formulae, without the inbred organisations of DNA that assure true Abrogunnans their amazing longevity; five more long hauls and Jon will be old and worn out, fit only for the transmuter.

Derek sat at the controls. Did he see, superimposed on the face of Festi, the face he loved and feared? I think he did. I think there were no swirling clouds for him that could erase the clouding of her brow.

Whatever he saw, he settled the lightpusher into a fast low orbit about the desolate planet. The sun Festi was little more than a blazing point some eight hundred million miles away. Like the riding light of a ship it bobbed above a turbulent sea of cloud as they went in.

For a long while, Derek sat with his face in a receptor bowl, checking ground heats far below. Since he was dealing with temperatures approaching absolute zero, this was not simple; yet when the Cliff moved into a position directly below, there was no mistaking its bulk; it stood out as clearly on his senses as if outlined on a radar screen.

'There she goes!' Derek exclaimed.

Jon had come forward again. He fed the time coordinates into the lightpusher's brain, waited, and read off the time when the Cliff would be below them once more.

Nodding, Derek began to prepare to jump. Without haste, he assumed his special suit, checking each item as he took it up, opening the para-gravs until he floated and then closing them again, clicking down every snap-fastener until he was entirely encased.

'395 seconds to next zenith, My Lord,' Jon said.

'You know all about collecting me?'

'Yes, sir.'

'I shall not activate the radio beacon till I'm back in orbit.'

'I fully understand, sir.'

'Right. I'll be moving.'

A little animated prison, he walked ponderously into the air lock.

Three minutes before they were next above the Cliff, Derek opened the outer door and dived into the sea of cloud. A brief blast of his suit jets set him free from the lightpusher's orbit. Cloud engulfed him as he fell.

The twenty surly planets that swung round Festi held only an infinitesimal fraction of the mysteries of the Starswarm. Every globe in the universe huddled its own secret purpose to itself. On some, as on Abrogun, the purpose manifested itself in a form of being that could shape itself, burst into the space lanes, and rough-hew its aims in a civilised, extra-planetary environment. On others, the purpose remained aloof and dark; only human beings, weaving their obscure patterns of will and compulsion, challenged those alien beings to wrest from them new knowledge that might be added to the store of old.

All knowledge has its influence. Over the millennia since interstellar flight had become practicable, mankind was insensibly moulded by its own findings; together with its lost innocence, its genetic stability disappeared. As man fell like rain over other planets, so his family lost its original hereditary design; each centre of civilisation bred new ways of thought, of feeling, of shape, – of – life itself. In Sector Vermilion, the man who dived headfirst to meet an entity called the Cliff was human more in his sufferings than his appearance.

The Cliff had destroyed all the few spaceships or light-pushers landing on its desolate globe. After long study from safe orbits, the wise men of Star One evolved the theory that the Cliff attacked any considerable source of power, as a man will swat a buzzing fly. Derek Ende, alone with no power but his suit motors, would be safe – or so the theory went.

Riding down on the paragravs, he sank more and more slowly into planetary night. The last of the cloud was whipped from about his shoulders, and a high wind thrummed and whistled around the supporters of his suit. Beneath him, the ground loomed. So as not to be blown across it, he speeded his rate of fall; next moment he sprawled full length on Festi XV. For a while he lay there, resting and letting his suit cool.

The darkness was not complete. Though almost no solar light touched this continent, green flares grew from the ground, illumining its barren contours. Wishing to accustom his eyes to the gloom, he did not switch on his head, shoulder, stomach or hand lights.

Something like a stream of fire flowed to his left. Because its radiance was poor and guttering, it confused itself with its own shadows, so that the smoke it gave off, distorted into bars by the bulk of the 4G planet, appeared to roll along its course like burning tumbleweed.

Further off were larger sources of fire, most probably impure ethane and methane, burning with a sound that came like frying steak to Derek's ears, spouting upward with an energy that licked the lowering cloud race with blue light. At another point, a geyser of flame blazing on an eminence wrapped itself in a thickly swirling pall of smoke, a pall that spread upward as slowly as porridge. Elsewhere, a pillar of white fire burned without motion or smoke; it stood to the right of where Derek lay, like a floodlit sword in its perfection.

He nodded approval to himself. His drop had been successfully placed. This was the Region of Fire, where the Cliff lived.

To lie there was pleasant enough, to gaze on a scene never closely viewed by man fulfilment enough – until he realised that a wide segment of landscape offered not the slightest glimmer of illumination. He looked into it with a keen warmsight, and found it was the Cliff.

The immense bulk of the thing blotted out all light from the ground and rose to eclipse the cloud over its crest.

At the mere sight of it, Derek's primary and secondary hearts began to beat out a hastening pulse of awe. Stretched flat on the ground, his paragravs keeping him level to 1G, he peered ahead at it; he swallowed to clear his choked throat; his eyes strained through the mosaic of dull light in an endeavour to define the Cliff.

One thing was sure: it was huge! He cursed the fact that although photosistors allowed him to use his warmsight on objects beyond the suit he wore, this sense was distorted by the eternal firework display. Then in a moment of good seeing he had an accurate fix: the Cliff was still some distance away! From first observations, he had thought it to be no more than a hundred paces distant.

Now he realised how large it was. It was enormous!

Momentarily he gloated. The only sort of tasks worth being set were impossible ones. Star One's astrophysicists held the notion that the Cliff was in some sense aware; they required Derek to take them a sample of its flesh. How do you carve a being the size of a small moon?

All the time he lay there, the wind jarred along the veins and supporters of his suit. Gradually it occurred to Derek that the vibration he felt from this constant motion was changed. It carried a new note and a new strength. He looked about, placed his gloved hand outstretched on the ground.

The wind was no longer vibrating. It was the earth that shook, Festi itself that trembled. The Cliff was moving!

When he looked back up at it with both his senses, he saw which way it headed. Jarring steadily, the Cliff bore down on him.

'If it has intelligence, then it will reason – if it has detected me – that I am too small to offer it harm. So it will offer me none, and I have nothing to fear,' Derek told himself. The logic did not reassure him.

An absorbent pseudopod, activated by a simple humidity gland in the brow of his helmet, slid across his forehead and removed the sweat that had formed there.

Visibility fluttered like a rag in a cellar. The forward surge of the Cliff was still something Derek sensed rather than saw. Now the masses of cloud blotted the thing's crest, as it in its turn eclipsed the fountains of fire. To the jar of its approach even the marrow of Derek's bones raised a response.

Something else also responded.

The legs of Derek's suit began to move. The arms moved. The body wriggled.

Puzzled, Derek stiffened his legs. Irresistibly, the knees of the suit hinged, forcing his own to do likewise. And not only his knees, but his arms too, stiffly though he braced them on the ground before him, were made to bend to the whim of the suit. He could not keep still without breaking his bones.

Thoroughly alarmed, he lay there flexing contortedly to keep rhythm with his suit, performing the gestures of an idiot.

As if it had suddenly learned to crawl, the suit began to move forward. It shuffled over the ground; Derek inside went willy-nilly with it.

One ironic thought struck him. Not only was the mountain coming to Mohammed; Mohammed was perforce going to the mountain ...

III

Nothing he did checked his progress; he was no longer master of his movements; his will was useless. With the realisation rode a sense of relief. His Mistress could hardly blame him for anything that happened now.

Through the darkness he went on hands and knees, blundering in the direction of the oncoming Cliff, prisoner in an animated prison.

The only constructive thought that came to him was that his suit had somehow become subject to the Cliff: how, he did not know or try to guess. He crawled. He was almost relaxed now, letting his limbs move limply with the suit movements.

Smoke furled him about. The vibrations ceased, telling him that the Cliff was stationary again. Raising his head, he could see nothing but smoke – produced perhaps by the Cliff's mass as it scraped over the ground. When the blur parted, he glimpsed only darkness. The thing was directly ahead!

He blundered on. Abruptly he began to climb, still involuntarily aping the movements of his suit.

Beneath him was a doughy substance, tough yet yielding. The suit worked its way heavily upward at an angle of something like sixty-five degrees; the stiffeners creaked, the paragravs throbbed. He was ascending the Cliff.

By this time there was no doubt in Derek's mind that the thing possessed what might be termed volition, if not consciousness. It also possessed a power no man could claim; it could impart that volition to an inanimate object like the suit. Helpless inside it, he carried his considerations a stage further. This power to impart volition seemed to have a limited range; otherwise the Cliff surely would not have bothered to move its gigantic mass at all, but would have forced the suit to traverse all the distance between them. If this reasoning were sound, then the lightpusher was safe from capture in orbit.

The movement of his arms distracted him. His suit was tunnelling. Giving it no aid, he lay and let his hands make swimming motions. If it was going to bore into the Cliff, then he could only conclude he was about to be digested: yet he stilled his impulse to struggle, knowing that struggle was fruitless.

Thrusting against the doughy stuff, the suit burrowed into it and made a sibilant little world of movement and friction that ceased the moment it stopped, leaving Derek embedded in the most solid kind of isolation.

To ward off growing claustrophobia, he attempted to switch on his headlight; his suit arms remained so stiff he could not bend them enough to reach the toggle. All he could do was lie there in his shell and stare into the featureless darkness of the Cliff.

But the darkness was not entirely featureless. His ears detected a constant *slither* along the outside surfaces of his suit. His warmsight discerned a meaningless pattern beyond his helmet. Though he focused his boscises, he could make no sense of the pattern; it had neither symmetry nor meaning for him ...

Yet for his body it seemed to have some meaning. Derek felt his limbs tremble, was aware of pulses and phantom impressions within himself that he had not known before. The realisation percolated through to him that he was in touch with powers of which he had no cognisance; conversely, that something was in touch with him that had no cognisance of his powers.

An immense heaviness overcame him. The forces of life laboured within him. He sensed more vividly than before the vast bulk of the Cliff. Though it was dwarfed by the mass of Festi XV, it was as large as a good-sized asteroid ... He could picture an asteroid, formed from a jetting explosion of gas on the face of Festi the sun. Half-solid, half-molten, the matter swung about its parent in an eccentric orbit. Cooling under an interplay of pressures, its interior crystallised into a unique form. Thus, with its surface semi-plastic, it existed for many millions of years, gradually accumulating an electrostatic charge that poised ... and waited ... and brewed the life acids about its crystalline heart.

Festi was a stable system, but once in every so many thousands of millions of years the giant first, second, and third planets achieved perihelion with the sun and with each other simultaneously. This happened coincidentally with the asteroid's nearest approach; it was wrenched from its orbit and all but grazed the three lined-up planets. Vast electrical and gravitational forces were unleashed. The asteroid glowed: and woke to consciousness. Life was not born on it: it was born to life, born in one cataclysmic clash!

Before it had more than savoured the sad-sharp-sweet sensation of consciousness, it was in trouble. Plunging away from the sun on its new course, it found itself snared in the gravitational pull of the 4G planet, Festi XV. It knew no shaping force but gravity; gravity was to it all that oxygen was to cellular life on Abrogun; though it had no wish to exchange its flight for captivity, it was too puny to resist. For the first time, the asteroid recognised that its consciousness had a use, for it could to some extent control the environment outside itself. Rather than risk being broken up in Festi's orbit, it sped inward, and by retarding its own fall performed its first act of volition, an act that brought it down shaken but entire on the surface of the planet.

For an immeasurable period, this asteroid – the Cliff – lay in the shallow crater formed by its impact, speculating without thought. It knew nothing except the inorganic scene about it, and could visualise nothing else but that scene it knew well. Gradually it came to some kind of terms with the scene. Formed by gravity, it used gravity as unconsciously as a man uses breath; it began to move other things, and it began to move itself.

That it should be other than alone in the universe had never occurred to the Cliff. Now that it knew there was other life, it accepted the fact. The other life was not as it was; that it accepted. The other life had its own requirements; that it accepted. Of questions, of doubt, it did not know. It had a need; so did the other life; they should both be accommodated, for accommodation was the adjustment to pressure, and that response was one it comprehended.

Derek Ende's suit began to move again under external volition. Carefully it worked its way backward. It was ejected from the Cliff. It lay still.

Derek himself lay still. He was barely conscious. In a half-daze, he pieced together what had happened.

The Cliff had communicated with him; if he ever doubted that, the evidence of it lay clutched in the crook of his left arm.

'Yet it did not – yet it could not communicate with me!' he murmured. But it had communicated: he was still faint with the burden of it.

The Cliff had nothing like a brain. It had not 'recognised' Derek's brain. Instead, it had communicated with the only part of him it could recognise; it had communicated directly to his cell organisation, and in particular probably to those cytoplasmic structures, the mitochondria, the power sources of the cell. His brain had been bypassed, but his own cells had taken in the information offered.

He recognised his feeling of weakness. The Cliff had drained him of power. Even that could not drain his feeling of triumph; for the Cliff had taken information even as it gave it. The Cliff had learned that other life existed in other parts of the universe.

Without hesitation, without debate, it had given a fragment of itself to be taken to those other parts of the universe. Derek's mission was completed.

In the Cliff's gesture, Derek read one of the deepest urges of living things: the urge to make an impression on another living thing. Smiling wryly, he pulled himself to his feet.

Derek was alone in the Region of Fire. An infrequent mournful flame still confronted its surrounding dark, but the Cliff had disappeared. He had lain on the threshold of consciousness longer than he thought. He looked at his chronometer and found that it was time he moved towards his rendezvous with the lightpusher. Stepping up his suit temperature to combat the cold beginning to seep through his bones, he revved up the paragrav unit and rose. The noisome clouds came down and engulfed him; Festi was lost to view. Soon he had risen beyond cloud or atmosphere.

Under Jon's direction, the space craft homed onto Derek's radio beacon. After a few tricky minutes, they matched velocities and Derek climbed aboard.

'Are you all right?' the partheno asked, as his master staggered into a flight seat.

'Yes – just weak. I'll tell you all about it as I do a report on spool for Pyrylyn. They'll be pleased with us.'

He produced a yellow-grey blob of matter that had expanded to the size of a large turkey and held it out to Jon.

'Don't touch this with uncovered hands. Put it in one of the low-temperature lockers under 4Gs. It's a little souvenir from Festi XV.'

IV

The Eyebright in Pynnati, one of the planet Pyrylyn's capital cities, was where you went to enjoy yourself on the most lavish scale possible. This was where Derek Ende's hosts took him, with Jon in self-effacing attendance.

They lay in a nest of couches that slowly revolved, giving them a full view of other dance and couch parties. The room itself moved. Its walls were transparent; through them could be seen an ever-changing view as the room slid up and down and about the great metal framework of the Eyebright. First they were on the outside of the structure, with the brilliant night lights of Pynnati winking up at them as if intimately involved in their delight. Then they slipped inward in the slow evagination of the building, to be surrounded by other pleasure rooms, their revellers clearly visible as they moved grandly up or down or along.

Uneasily, Derek lay on his couch. A vision of his Mistress's face was before him; he could imagine how she would treat all this harmless festivity: with cool contempt. His own pleasure was consequently reduced to ashes.

'I suppose you'll be moving back to Abrogun as soon as possible?'

'Eh?' Derek grunted.

'I said, I suppose you would soon be going home again.' The speaker was Belix Ix Sappose, Chief Administrator of Star One; as Derek's host of the evening, he lay next to him.

'I'm sorry, Belix, yes – I shall have to.'

'No "have to" about it. You have discovered an entirely new life form, as I have already reported to Starswarm Central; we can now attempt communication with the Festi XV entity, with goodness knows what extension of knowledge. The government can easily show its gratitude by awarding you any post here you care to name; I am not without influence in that respect, as you are aware. I don't imagine that Abrogun in its present state of political paralysis has much to offer a man of your calibre. Your matriarchal system is much to blame.'

Derek thought of what Abrogun had to offer; he was bound to it. These decadent people did not understand how a human contract could be binding.

'Well, what do you say, Ende? I do not speak idly.' Belix Ix Sappose tapped his antler system impatiently.

'Er ... Oh, they will discover a great deal from the Cliff. That doesn't concern me. My part of the work is over. I'm a field worker, not an intellectual.'

'You don't reply to my suggestion.'

He looked at Belix with only slight vexation. Belix was an unglaat, one of a species that had done as much as any to bring about the peaceful concourse of the galaxy. His backbone branched into an elaborate antler system, from which six sloe-dark eyes surveyed Derek with unblinking irritation. Other members of the party, including Jupkey, Belix's female, were also looking at him.

'I must return,' Derek said. What had Belix said? Offered some sort of post? Restlessly he shifted on his couch, under pressure as always when surrounded by people he knew none too well.

'You are bored, Ende.'

'No, not at all. My apologies, Belix. I'm overcome as always by the luxury of Eyebright. I was watching the nude dancers.'

'May I signal you a woman?'

'No, thank you.'

'A boy, perhaps?'

'No, thank you.'

'Ever tried the flowering asexuals from the Cephids?'

'Not at present, thank you.'

'Then perhaps you will excuse us if Jupkey and I remove our clothes and join the dance,' Belix said stiffly.

As they moved out onto the dance floor to greet the strepent trumpets, Derek heard Jupkey say something of which he caught only the words 'arrogant Abrogunnan'. His eyes met Jon's; he saw that the partheno had overheard the phrase, too.

To conceal his mortification, Derek rose and began to pace around the room. He shouldered his way through knots of naked dancers, ignoring their complaints.

At one of the doors, a staircase was floating by. He stepped onto it to escape from the crowds.

Four young women were passing down the stairs. They were gaily dressed, with sonant-stones pulsing on their costumes. Their faces were filled with happiness as they laughed and chattered. Derek stopped and beheld the girls. One of them he recognized. Instinctively he called her name: 'Eva!'

She had already seen him. Waving her companions on, she came back to him, dancing up the intervening steps.

'So the hero of Abrogun climbs once more the golden stairs of Pynnati! Well, Derek Ende, your eyes are as dark as ever, and your brow as high!'

As he looked at her, the trumpets were in tune for him for the first time that evening, and his delight rose up in his throat.

'Eva! … Your eyes as bright as ever … and you have no man with you.'

'The powers of coincidence work on your behalf.' She laughed – yes, he remembered that sound! – and then said more seriously, 'I heard you were here with Belix Sappose and his female; so I was making the grandly foolish gesture of coming to see you. You remember how devoted I am to grandly foolish gestures.'

'So foolish?'

'So devoted! But you have less ability to change, Derek Ende, than has the core of Pyrylyn. To suppose otherwise is foolish; to know how unalterable you are and still to see you is doubly foolish.'

He took her hand, beginning to lead her up the staircase; the rooms moving by them on either side were blurs to his eyes.

'Must you still bring up that old charge, Eva?'

'It lies between us; I do not have to touch it. I fear your unchangeability because I am a butterfly against your grey castle.'

'You are beautiful, Eva, so beautiful! And may a butterfly not rest unharmed on a castle wall?' He fitted into her allusive way of speech with difficulty.

'Walls! I cannot bear your walls, Derek! Am I a bulldozer that I should want to come up against walls? To be either inside or outside them is to be a prisoner.'

'Let us not quarrel until we have found some point of agreement,' he said. 'Here are the stars. Can't we agree about them?'

'If we are both indifferent to them,' she said, looking out and impudently winding his arm about her. The staircase had attained the zenith of its travels and moved slowly sideways along the upper edge of Eyebright. They stood on the top step with night flashing their images back at them from the glass.

Eva Coll-Kennerley was a human, but not of any common stock. She was a velure, born of the dense y-cluster worlds in Vermilion Outer, and her skin was richly covered with the brown fur of her kind. Her mercurial talents were employed in the same research department that enjoyed Belix Sappose's more sober ones; Derek had met her there on an earlier visit to Pyrylyn. Their love had been an affair of swords until her scabbard disarmed him.

He looked at her now and touched her and could say not one word. When she flashed a liquid eye at him, he essayed an awkward smile.

'Because I am oriented like a compass towards strong men, my lavish offer to you still holds good. Is it not bait enough?' she asked him.

312

'I don't think of you as a trap, Eva.'

'Then for how many more centuries are you going to refrigerate your nature on Abrogun? You still remain faithful, if I recall your euphemism for slavery, to your Mistress, to her cold lips and locked heart?'

'I have no choice!'

'Ah yes, my debate on that motion was defeated – and more than once. Is she still pursuing her researches into the transmutability of species?'

'Oh yes, indeed. The medieval idea that one species can turn into another was foolish at that time; now, with the gradual accumulation of cosmic radiation in planetary bodies and its effect on genetic stability, it is correct to a certain definable extent. She is endeavouring to show that cellular bondage can be –'

'Yes, yes, and this serious talk is an eyesore in Eyebright! Do you think I can hear of her when I want to talk of you? You are locked away, Derek, doing your sterile deeds of heroism and never entering the real world. If you imagine you can live with her much longer and then come to me, you are mistaken. Your walls grow higher about your ears every century, till I cannot – oh, it's the wrong metaphor! – cannot scale you!'

Even in his pain, the texture of her fur was joy to his warmsight. Helplessly he shook his head in an effort to brush her clattering words away.

'Look at you being big and brave and silent – even now! You're so arrogant,' she said – and then, without perceptible change of tone, 'Because I still love the bit of you inside the castle, I'll make once more my monstrous and petty offer to you.'

'No, please, Eva!'

'But yes! Forget this tedious bondage of Abrogun and Endehabven, forget this ghastly matriarchy, live here with me. I don't want you for ever. You know I am a eudemonist and judge by standards of pleasure – our liaison need be only for a century or two. In that time, I will deny you nothing your senses may require.'

'Eva!'

'After that, our demands will be satisfied. You may then go back to the Lady Mother of Endehabven for all I care.'

'Eva, you know I spurn this belief, this eudemonism.'

'Forget your creed! I'm asking you nothing difficult. Who are you to haggle? Am I fish, to be bought by weight, this bit selected, that rejected?'

He was silent.

'*You* don't really need me,' he said at last. 'You have everything already: beauty, wit, sense, warmth, feeling, balance, comfort. *She* has nothing. She is shallow, haunted, cold – oh, she needs me, Eva.'

'You are apologising for yourself, not her.'

She had already turned with the supple movement of a velure and was running down the staircase. Lighted chambers drifted up about them like bubbles.

His laboured attempt to explain his heart turned to exasperation. He ran down after her, grasping her arm.

'Listen to me!'

'No one in Pyrylyn would listen to such masochistic nonsense! You are an arrogant fool, Derek, and I am a weak-willed one. Now release me!'

As the next room came up, she jumped through its entrance and disappeared into the crowd.

V

Not all the drifting chambers of Eyebright were lighted. Some pleasures come more delightfully with the dark, and these were coaxed and cosseted into fruition in halls where illumination cast only the gentlest ripple on the ceiling and the gloom was sensuous with perfumes. Here Derek found a place to weep.

Sections of his life slid before him as if impelled by the same mechanisms that moved Eyebright. Always, one presence was there.

Angrily he related to himself how he always laboured to satisfy her – yes, in every sphere laboured to satisfy her! And how when that satisfaction was accorded him it came as though riven from her, as a spring sometimes trickles down the split face of a rock. Undeniably there was satisfaction for him in drinking from that cool source – but no, where was the satisfaction when pleasure depended on such extreme disciplining and subduing of self?

'Mistress, I love and hate your needs!'

And the discipline had been such ... so long ... that now when he might enjoy himself far from her, he could scarcely strike a trickle from his own rock. He had walked here before, in this city where the hedonists and eudemonists reigned, walked among the scents of pleasure, walked among the ioblepharous women, the beautiful guests and celebrated beauties, with My Lady always in him, feeling that she showed even on his countenance. People spoke to him; somehow he replied. They manifested gaiety; he tried to do so. They opened to him; he attempted a response. All the time he hoped they would understand that his arrogance masked only shyness – or did he hope that it was his shyness that masked arrogance? He did not know.

Who could presume to know? The one quality holds much of the other. Both refuse to come forward and share.

He roused from his meditation knowing that Eva Coll-Kennerley was again somewhere near. She had not left the building!

Derek half-rose from his position in a shrouded alcove. He was baffled to think how she could have traced him here. On entering Eyebright, visitors were given sonant-stones, by which they could be traced from room to room; but judging that no one would wish to trace him, Derek had switched his stone off even before leaving Belix Sappose's party.

He heard Eva's voice, its unmistakable overtones not near, not far ...

'You find the most impenetrable bushels to hide your light under –'

He caught no more. She had sunk down among tapestries with someone else. She was not after him at all! Waves of relief and regret rolled over him ... and when he paid attention again, she was speaking his name.

With shame on him, he crouched forward to listen. At once his warmsight told him to whom Eva spoke. He recognised the pattern of the antlers; Belix was there, with Jupkey sprawled beside him on some elaborate kind of bed.

'... useless to try again. Derek is too far entombed within himself,' Eva said.

'Entombed rather within his conditioning,' Belix said. 'We found the same. It's conditioning, my dear – all conditioning with these Abrogunnans. Look at it scientifically: Abrogun is the last bastion of a bankrupt culture. The Abrogunnans number mere thousands now. They disdain social graces and occasions. They are served by parthenogenically bred slaves. They themselves are inbred. In consequence, they have become practically a species apart. You can see it all in friend Ende. A tragedy, Eva, but you must face up to it.'

'You're probably right,' Jupkey inserted lazily. 'Who but an Abrogunnan would do what Derek did on Festi?'

'No, no!' Eva said. 'Derek's ruled by a woman, not by conditioning. He's –'

'In Ende's case they are one and the same thing, my dear, believe me. Consider their social organisation. The partheno slaves have replaced all but a handful of true men. They live on their great estates, ruled by a matriarch.'

'Yes, I know, but Derek –'

'Derek is caught in the system. They have fallen into a mating pattern without precedent in Starswarm. The sons of a family marry their mothers, not only to perpetuate their line but because a productive female has become rare by now. Derek Ende's "mistress" is both mother and wife to him. Add the factor of longevity and you ensure an excessive emotional rigidity that almost nothing can break – not even you, my sweet Eva!'

'He was on the point of breaking tonight!'

'I doubt it,' Belix said. 'Ende may want to get away from his claustrophobic home, but the same forces that drive him off will eventually lure him back.'

'I tell you he was on the point of breaking – but I broke first.'

'Well as Teer Ruche said to me many centuries ago, only a pleasure-hater knows how to shape a pleasure-hater. I would say you were lucky he did not break – you would only have had a baby on your hands.'

Her answering laugh did not ring true.

'My Lady of Endehabven, then, must be the one to do it. I will never try again – though he seems under too much stress to stand for long. Oh, it's really immoral! He deserves better!'

'A moral judgement from you, Eva!' Jupkey exclaimed amusedly.

'My advice to you, Eva, is to forget all about the fellow. Apart from everything else, he is scarcely articulate – which would not suit you for a season.'

The unseen listener could bear no more. A sudden rage – as much against himself for hearing as against them for speaking – burst over him. Straightening up, he seized the arm of the couch on which Belix and Jupkey nestled, wildly supposing he could tip them onto the floor.

Too late, his warmsight warned him of the real nature of the couch. Instead of tipping, it swivelled, sending a wave of liquid over him. The two unglaats were lying in a warm bath scented with essences.

Eva shouted for lights. Other occupants of the hall cried back that darkness must prevail at all costs.

Leaving only his dignity behind, Derek ran for the exit, abandoning the confusion to sort itself out as it would. Burningly, disgustedly, he made his way dripping from Eyebright. The hastening footsteps of Jon followed him like an echo all the way to the space field.

Soon he would be back at Endehabven. Though he would always be a failure in his dealings with other humans, there at least he knew every inch of his bleak allotted territory.

ENVOI

Had there been a spell over all Endehabven, it could have been no quieter when My Lord Derek Ende arrived home.

I informed My Lady the moment his lightpusher arrived and rode at orbit. In the receptor bowl I watched him and Jon come home, alighting by the very edge of the island, by the fjord with its silent waters.

All the while the wind lay low as if under some stunning malediction, and none of our tall arborials stirred.

'Where is my Mistress, Hols?' Derek asked me, as I went to greet him and assist him out of his suit.

'She asked me to tell you that she is confined to her chambers and cannot see you, My Lord.'

He looked me in the eyes as he did so rarely. 'Is she ill?'

'No. She simply said she could not see you.'

Without waiting to remove his suit, he hurried on into the building.

Over the next two days, he was about but little, preferring to remain in his room while My Lady insisted on remaining in hers. Once he wandered among the experimental tanks and cages. I saw him net a fish and toss it into the air, watching it while it struggled into new form and flew away until it was lost in a jumbled background of cumulus; but it was plain he was less interested in the riddles of stress and transmutation than in the symbolism of the carp's flight.

Mostly he sat compiling the spools on which he imposed the tale of his life. All one wall was covered with files full of these spools – the arrested drumbeats of past centuries. From the later spools I have secretly compiled this record; for all his unspoken self-pity, he never knew the sickness of merely observing.

We parthenos will never understand the luxuries of a divided mind. Surely suffering as much as happiness is a kind of artistry?

On the day that he received a summons from Star One to go upon another quest, Derek met My Lady in the Blue Corridor.

'It is good to see you about again, Mistress,' he said, kissing her cheek. 'To remain confined to your room is bad for you.'

She stroked his hair. On her nervous hand she wore one ring with an amber stone; her gown was of olive and umber.

'Don't reproach me! I was upset to have you go away from me. This world is dying, Derek, and I fear its loneliness. You have left me alone too often. However, I have recovered and am glad to see you back.'

'You know I am glad to see you. Smile for me and come outside for some fresh air. The sun is shining.'

'It's so long since it shone. Do you remember how once it always shone? I can't bear to quarrel any more. Take my arm and be kind to me.'

'Mistress, I always wish to be kind to you. And I have all sorts of things to discuss with you. You'll want to hear what I have been doing, and –'

'You won't leave me alone any more?'

He felt her hand tighten on his arm. She spoke very loudly.

'That was one of the things I wished to discuss – later,' he said. 'First let me tell you about the wonderful life form with which I made contact on Festi.'

As they left the corridor and descended the paragravity shaft, My Lady said wearily, 'I suppose that's a polite way of telling me that you are bored here.'

He clutched her hands as they floated down. Then he released them and clutched her face instead, cupping it between his palms.

'Understand this, Mistress mine, I love you and want to serve you. You are in my blood; wherever I go I never can forget you. My dearest wish is to make you happy – this you must know. But equally you must know that I have needs of my own.'

'I know those needs will always come first with you, whatever you say or pretend.'

She moved ahead of him, shaking off the hand he put on her arm. He had a vision of himself running down a golden staircase and stretching out that same detaining hand to another girl. The indignity of having to repeat oneself, century after century.

'You're being cruel!' he said.

Gleaming, she turned. 'Am I? Then answer me this – aren't you already planning to leave Endehabven again?'

He said haltingly, 'Yes, yes, it's true I am thinking … But I have to – I reproach myself. I could be kinder. But you shut yourself away when I come back, you don't welcome me –'

'Trust you to find excuses rather than face up to your own nature,' she said contemptuously, walking briskly into the garden. Amber and olive and umber, and sable of hair, she walked down the path, her outlines sharp in the winter air. In the perspectives of his mind she did not dwindle.

For some minutes he stood in the threshold, immobilised by antagonistic emotions.

Finally he pushed himself out into the sunlight.

She was in her favourite spot by the fjord, feeding an old badiger from her hand. Only her increased attention to the badiger suggested that she heard him approach.

His boscises twitched as he said, 'I'm sorry.'

'I don't mind what you do.'

Walking backward and forward behind her, he said, 'When I was away, I heard some people talking. On Pyrylyn this was. They were discussing the mores of our matrimonial system.'

'It's no business of theirs.'

'Perhaps not. But what they said suggested a new line of thought to me.'

She put the badiger back in his cage without comment.

'Are you listening, Mistress?'

'Do go on.'

'Try to listen sympathetically. Consider all the history of galactic exploration – or even before that, consider the explorers of worlds without space flight. They were brave men, of course, but wouldn't it be strange if most of them only ventured into the unknown because the struggle at home was too much for them?'

He stopped. She had turned to him; the half-smile was whipped off his face by her look of fury.

'And you're trying to tell me that that's how you see yourself – a martyr? Derek, how you must hate me! Not only do you go away, but you secretly blame me because you go away. It doesn't matter that I tell you a thousand times I want you here – no, it's all my fault! I drive you away! That's what you tell your charming friends on Pyrylyn, isn't it? Oh, how you must hate me!'

Savagely he grasped her wrists. She screamed to me for aid and struggled. I came near but halted, playing my usual impotent part. He swore at her, bellowed for her to be silent, whereupon she cried the louder, shaking furiously in his arms, both of them tumultuous in their emotions.

He struck her across the face.

At once she was quiet. Her eyes closed almost, it would seem, in ecstasy. Standing there, she had the pose of a woman offering herself.

'Go on, hit me! You want to hit me!' she whispered.

With the words, with the look of her, he too was altered. As if realising for the first time her true nature, he lowered his fists and stepped back, staring at her sick-mouthed. His heel met no resistance. He twisted suddenly, spread out his arms as if to fly, and fell over the cliff edge.

Her scream pursued him down.

Even as his body hit the waters of the fjord, it began to change. A flurry of foam marked some sort of painful struggle beneath the surface. Then a seal plunged into view, dived below the next wave, and swam towards the open sea, over which an already freshening breeze blew.

Tyrants' Territory

From the heavy and turbulent cloud layers of Askanza VI, rain fell solemnly. It pattered on the roof of the overlander making its way down into a coastal valley. Craig Hodges, sitting at the wheel, nodded reflectively to himself. If he and his Planetary Ecological Survey Team (PEST for short) passed this world as safe for habitation, future colonists would still have plenty to worry about from the weather alone. Askanza, the sun, never broke through VI's clouds.

Craig smiled. He had little sympathy for colonists at the best of times. All his affections went to these unexplored planets on the fringe of Earth's ever-expanding spatial frontiers. Each of them, however luxuriant, however barren, presented its own special problems and guarded its own special secrets.

Bumping its way down a mile-long slope, the overlander came onto a plateau. From here, but for the rain which now gave signs of abating, there should have been a good view ahead. Craig stopped on the edge of the plateau, peering forward. He was reluctant to leave the advantage of high ground without knowing what he was going into, particularly in a coastal region. Coasts were focal areas for life on almost any planet, and a lifetime of PEST service had taught Craig caution.

Craig was not exactly anticipating anything momentous in the way of life on this moonless, tideless, grassless ball; still, any form of anticipation could be misleading on a new world.

The dwindling curtains of rain parted, dimpling away across an expanse of grey water. So Craig got his first glimpse of the sea, and his first surprise.

From the quiet face of the waters rose tall and thin pillar-like struc-tures. Irregularly spaced, they varied in height, and rose from a few yards off shore to about a mile out to sea.

Adjusting his binoculars, Craig studied them with interest. In the glasses, the pillars glinted with a diversity of subdued colour. Some were opaque, some semitranslucent. Their surfaces, as far as he could make out, were by no means regular. Some looked sharp-edged and geometrical, some haphazardly ragged, some rounded. Some were as much as fifty feet high.

Pleased speculation filled Craig. Here was something he had not met with before – a man could ask for no more than that. On first sight Askanza VI had threatened to be dull; now he knew it would not be.

The PEST ship had landed several hours ago on a high tableland beyond the mountains through which Craig Hodges had driven. Craig and his two colleagues, Barney Brangwyn and young Tim Anderson, made their usual preliminary ride-around before splitting up. They had seen little but barren land, curious rock formations, some stunted trees and a large number of surprisingly symmetrical boulders; Askanza VI was no beauty spot. Then they had separated to take up their customary positions eighty miles apart at the three corners of an equilateral triangle, Tim staying by the ship, Barney and Craig moving off in their overlanders.

Thus did the PEST work. Briefly, their job was a two-fold one: to discover if a new planet harboured any species which would unduly menace the farmers and other colonists; and – if such a species existed – to suggest how it might best be dealt with without destroying the ecological balance of the planet. Time had shown that the most economical way of making the necessary observations was to have three trained men sitting eighty miles apart from each other, interpreting what they saw. Old exploratory methods of hacking one's way round a planet until one eventually blundered into trouble had been superseded long ago.

When he had made a careful survey of the pillars, Craig put down his binoculars. He estimated one to every seventy-five square yards of shallow sea, but their irregular placing made it difficult to be accurate.

Now most of the rain had cleared, and for the first time Craig saw into the valley below him. It was full of moving creatures!

Climbing out of the cab, Craig jumped down and went forward for a closer look. He was now almost the required eighty miles from base, so that this busy valley might well be regarded as his Plot for investigation. Fantastic rocks outcropped from the ground as he descended. As before, there was no plant nor flower anywhere, nor even a blade of grass; although a few mosses grew by the rocks. The heavy clayey ground ran right down to the water's edge.

When Craig found a suitable vantage point down the slope, he stopped to observe, raising the glasses again to his eyes.

From the complex nature of their activity, the creatures might be reckoned to possess intelligence, although it was difficult to decide what they were doing. At the far end of the beach they had raised a high earthwork which looked unmistakeably like a defence. The creatures themselves varied in size but not in shape. Craig mentally labelled them turtles, for it was to that reptile they bore most resemblance with their huge carapaces and flipper-like extremities. From the chunky shell, six limbs and a head protruded. One pair of limbs were legs and feet, another arms and hands, while the intermediate pair served the intermediate purpose, being used sometimes to handle objects, sometimes to be walked on. Their heads were large and clumsy, with one eye and a beaky mouth. The mouths, as Craig could see, contained big teeth. Since these creatures when erect stood about five feet high in their armour plating, their total appearance was formidable.

Many of these turtle-like beings worked about a structure which was a baffling mixture of rock and metal. Others were parading about the strip of beach. Some dug in the ground, some stood as if in contemplation.

At a sound behind him, Craig turned.

He saw now that the outcropping rocks he had passed had been hollowed out on their seaward side for some depth. Turtles were coming out at him, moving fast, some on two legs, some on four.

Seen this close, they were daunting. For all their speed, they looked enormously heavy. Their flippers, thick and closely scaled, would have been capable of felling a man. They charged at Craig with snapping jaws, a small bony antenna flicking on their foreheads. Craig did not stop for a second look.

A few of the creatures who came charging out bore cup-like objects in their flippers. As Craig turned, the first cup was thrown at him.

It came hard, flung with force and accuracy.

Craig dodged and it shattered on the ground nearby. He slipped on the clayey slope, and began to run back to the overlander as fast as he could. The turtles were after him. They made no cries, but already other turtles were hurrying up from the valley. They moved fast, jaws snapping.

The overlander was only a few yards away. As Craig reached the door, one of the cups struck him on the shoulder. It broke, splashing liquid over his uniform. He whirled; the turtle who had thrown it was almost on him. Reluctantly, even in the heat of the moment, Craig pulled out his gun and fired. The shot caught the creature full in the breastplate and bowled it over backwards as Craig swung himself up to safety. Gunning the engine, he backed away. Another fiercely-flung cup struck the door as he did so.

Swinging in a wide arc, Craig began to head his vehicle for the slopes. His shoulder was burning painfully; he ignored it, so angry was he with himself for his carelessness. He had fallen into the elementary error of anticipating Earth-like behaviour from an Earth-like creature. These things which looked like turtles had a ferocity and certainly a turn of speed unknown to the beings they most nearly resembled on Earth.

The overlander reached the foot of the mile long slope and stopped, its wheels slithering in mud brought down by the recent rain. Cursing quietly, Craig switched to caterpillar, shutting down the drive as the retractable tracks came into position. As he opened up again, there was a grinding noise outside while the vehicle lurched forward and then fell back again. Something had jammed the tracks. He was stuck.

Another attempt to move on dual drive failed.

Leaning half out of the cab window, Craig saw that one of the turtles was wedged with its shell broken between the track plates. Its feeble movements awoke compassion in him, even as he cursed it, for he would have to dislodge it before the overlander would move again.

He jumped out hurriedly. This turtle must have hung on and taken an uninvited ride, or it would have been left behind with the others. It was too bad for all concerned that it had attempted to meddle with the tracks.

Grabbing a crowbar from an external kit locker, Craig levered at the creature's shell. His shoulder was paining him badly. The main body of turtles was now only a hundred yards away, coming up fast. To add to Craig's troubles, night was coming on, Askanza's dull light thickening into dusk. The planet had an eleven and three quarters hour long day, which meant only about six hours of daylight in these latitudes. Not, Craig thought, the happiest of places, even for colonists.

The injured turtle gave a creaking groan as Craig applied pressure. Its shell was formidably tough and would not budge, locked as it was between plates and against a drive wheel. Craig could see he would need a sledge hammer to break it up. He climbed back into the overlander: there was no time now to do more – the other turtles had caught up with him again. A minute later, some fifty of them were grouping round the vehicle. They hammered and slapped against it until the interior echoed with sound. The light was exceedingly bad now; Crain switched on an upper searchlight to see what was happening outside. Certainly the light rattled the turtles. They hurried out of the beam but did not retreat far. In the reflected light, their eyes glittered emerald green. Their antennae flicked about alertly.

The overlander was, among other things, a mobile fortress. Craig could have wiped out every creature present by half a dozen means, but killing was not to his taste or his policy. He sat for a moment high up in the cab, watching to see what would happen next.

Obviously the turtles were curious about the vehicle. They were hostile, yes, but something more than mere blind hostility directed their actions. On the edge of the gloom, they waited now with the impatient patience of reasoning beings.

Grunting with the pain of his shoulder, Craig retreated into the small room at the back of the cab. If they disliked light, light they should have. Pressing a wall stud, he sent an arc light rising ten feet above the overlander's roof on a telescopic leg. When he switched on, brilliance poured in through the windows at him.

With a pounding of flippers, the turtles retreated again, some still flinging cups against the vehicle.

'Splendid!' Craig said, and retired to the lab to treat his shoulder.

It was red and blistered, from his collar bone down to his elbow. A simple test satisfied Craig that he had been bombarded with a fairly strong solution of sulphuric acid. He anointed himself, bandaged himself, and went to view his visitors through the overhead blister.

The turtles kept their distance in a ring some forty yards off, milling about impatiently.

'I'm still within acid-cup throwing range,' Craig said to himself.

He loaded the flare rifle, setting its timer to fire every fifty seconds and its altitude at two hundred feet. As soon as the first flare burst overhead, he climbed outside with a sledgehammer.

Green light bathed the land as the temporary star burned viridian-fierce overhead. While the turtles fled from the brightest light Askanza VI had ever seen, Craig got to work, hammering at the wedged carapace. He was dragging the last chunk of shell from the track as the third flare went up. By now the unfortunate turtle was dead. Taking up its great head and a chunk of shell and body, Craig climbed back into his vehicle once more, switched off the flare rifle and arc light and started moving.

The overlander responded without trouble now, dragging itself easily out of the mud and heading up the slope. As it did so, the turtles closed in again and began to follow. Their persistence was impressive.

Ignoring them, Craig climbed the slope. Glancing at his watch, he saw it was time for his group call with Tim and Barney. He had, of course, no intention of returning to the ship. His Plot had its little problems; but it was problems he was here to investigate.

After driving half a mile, he halted and switched on his overhead arc again. In three minutes, the first of the pursuing turtles thudded up, to stand at a respectful distance outside the circle of light.

By now it was almost completely dark, the stuffy unpunctured darkness that had covered the face of Askanza every night since it was created.

Craig went below to the wireless, turned onto Frequency Modulation and called Tim. In a short while, both Tim's and Barney's voices came through, Tim quiet and deferential as usual, Barney full of bounce.

'Nothing very exciting to report here,' Tim said. 'No life at all visible, except through a microscope. Well, that's not strictly true; I have found a worm fifty millimetres long! How fortunate that a day so dull should be so brief. I've occupied myself taking soil samples and borings. The crust of the planet is loaded with ore. Its mineral wealth will make Askanza VI an industrial bonanza in a decade, heaven help it. Seems funny to think of the millions of years of peace it's had, and in ten years' time it'll be lusty and brawling with materialism. ... It's been pouring here ever since you two left, a steady acidic shower – I've kept figures, since they vary slightly from hour to hour.'

'Just as well the ship and vehicles are fully proofed,' Barney grunted.

'Despite that, the soil's okay,' Tim went on. 'Nature seems to have preferred the inorganic to the organic here, but with implantations of suitable microorganisms I see no reason why Earth-type crops shouldn't be grown here in a year or two. Rice probably, in this climate!'

'It's dry in this region,' Barney said. 'I'm sheltered by the mountains, tucked in a valley, and fourteen miles from what the radar shows to be ragged coast. It's been so mild I ate my meal in the open.'

'What have you been doing besides eating, Barney?' Craig inquired.

'Since you ask, I've been fiddling with the search radio, among other chores. As you can hear, our reception at 85 Mc/s is brilliant, but some of the other frequencies are surprisingly congested. There's some curious mush on the short waves – sounds almost like *musique concrete* at times. If nothing better offers itself tomorrow, rather than waste my time here I'll return to you, Tim, and use the ship's radio equipment to chart the various sky layers. If the colonists come here poor guys, they'll need wireless, so a few preliminary findings won't hurt – that is, if it's okay with you, Craig?'

Craig hesitated.

'The sky's not our job, Barney, nor is wireless reception,' he said. 'If there are no reflecting layers at all topside, the colonists can still use direct wave, as we are doing. Have you found nothing of interest on the ground?'

Back in his own vehicle, Barney twiddled a curl of his beard round a finger and studiously kept any irritation out of his voice as he replied.

'There are some six-legged things crawling about – look like turtles with large heads,' he said. 'They seem to move very intermittently, and are sluggish when they do move. Ugly devils, but harmless for all their array of teeth. I'm afraid I just can't see them in the role of Plimsol Species, Craig. Fodder for Colonists I'd call them, until they all get killed off and eaten.'

Craig stared incredulously at his amplifier.

'They ... drag themselves round on all six legs?' he asked.

'Yes. When I went over to them and kicked them, they retracted into their shells. The heads don't retract, being a bit too big for that. When in that position they look like boulders. What have you been doing, Craig? Seen any boulders walking about?'

'My boulders walk on their hind legs,' Craig replied. With typical caution, he kept his report very brief, saying only that he had seen large numbers of the turtles. He made no mention of the fact that he was still surrounded by them, although he warned Barney and Tim about the acid throwing.

'This little habit would be a considerable menace to colonists without overlanders to retreat into,' he said.

'You must have hold of a different species there, Craig,' Barney said after a pause. 'My babies haven't learned to walk upright yet, never mind throw acid. Sulphuric acid, you say? Where would they get that from? You don't suppose they build their own Glover towers?'

Tim answered his question.

'I've found samples of normal salts that would be useful in preparing the acid – barytes for one – but you're not suggesting these creatures have enough intelligence to –'

'I'm trying to avoid suggesting anything at the moment,' Craig said dryly.

Recognising the note in his voice, Barney dropped that line of approach and tackled Tim.

'What do your turtles do, Tim? Are yours vertical or horizontal?'

There was a second's silence, and then Tim said in a strained voice, 'I haven't seen any round here at all. ... Hang on, will you? Something's moving outside. ...'

He went off the air. Craig sat where he was, eighty miles away over the mountains, drumming his fingers and trying to visualise what was happening. He knew, with a half-mystical certainty, that any planet was a different place by night from its daytime self; ask any child on Earth and they would say the same thing. The atmosphere changed. ...

By now the darkness was total. Thunder grunted disconsolately round the horizon like distant gunfire.

Tim's voice came back in a minute, a note of relief in it.

'Hello, Craig and Barney. I've got the turtles too! Most curious. There must have been a crowd of them hereabouts, but during the daylight they were absolutely doggo. I took them for big stones – your boulders, Barney. Now they're getting up and walking about.'

'See they don't pinch the space ship,' Barney said. 'Are yours travelling on all-sixes?'

'No. They're walking on their hind legs – or on their two hind pairs, like Craig's. They're pretty busy, too. Some of them are trying to investigate the overlander. What do I do?'

'Shine a bright light and they'll keep their distance,' Craig advised.

'I've already discovered that.'

'Good boy.' Craig had to suppress an urge to be fatherly to Tim; his voice sounded very young over the FM. He could not resist adding, 'And don't let them throw acid at you. It's painful.'

'Are you keeping something back from us, Craig?' Barney growled. 'You're not having some sort of trouble with these critters, are you?'

'You sleep tight, Barney, and don't worry. I'm fine. We'll buzz each other at eight tomorrow morning. Adios and out.'

So they closed down. Barney scratched his head, feeling sure Craig was holding something back. He knew Craig of old. Both Craig and Tim sounded like they were having a more interesting time than he was himself. Promising himself that tomorrow he would go hunting turtle eggs and try a little private research, Barney settled down to read a book.

It was a collection of Conrad's tales. To Barney Brangwyn's mind, only Conrad of all the old authors conveyed the sense of a planet as a planet. He read: '... Nothing moved. The fronds of palms stood still against the sky. Not a branch stirred along the shore, and the brown roofs of hidden houses peeped through the green foliage, through the big leaves that hung shining and still like leaves forged of heavy metal. This was the East of the ancient navigators, so old, so mysterious, resplendent and sombre, living and unchanged, full of danger and promise. ...'

As another sort of 'ancient navigator', Barney knew that what Conrad had written almost exactly six and a half centuries ago contained a true vision of the universe: that behind all the sunlight, however vivid, lay an impenetrable darkness which could be expressed in scientific terms as energy or in religious terms as God. Whatever he or the turtles might do, that darkness remained – yet he could hold that concept in his mind and at the same moment hope to outdo Craig.

Before Craig retired to his bunk, he took a look at the creatures surrounding his overlander. They were still outside the circle of light, still active, though perhaps less so than they had been when down by the shore.

He stood for a long while, stolid and unmoving, looking out. The thunder was dying now as night fully established itself.

Craig considered. These creatures seemed to have three different patterns of behaviour over a remarkably small stretch of territory. Where he was, by the coast, they behaved like a true Plimsol species; they were active, aggressive, curious. Where Tim Anderson was, their activity was nocturnal only and they seemed slightly less formidable. Where Barney Brangwyn was, they behaved merely like lower animals – like clumsy tortoises. There had to be a reason for this curious deviation, but as yet Craig had insufficient data to uncover it.

Abruptly he turned from the window, and climbed into the cab. Getting into the driver's seat, he started the engine and drove the overlander further up the long slope onto level and higher ground, until he estimated he must be about three miles from the coast. Then he went to see what the turtles were doing.

Most of them followed the overlander; they covered the ground steadily, if not as vigorously as they had moved hitherto. Many seemed to be suffering from very human bouts of indecision about coming on or going back. Eventually some forty of them grouped themselves beyond the range of Craig's light and sat themselves down to wait.

Shaking his head, he went to his bunk.

The puzzle was still with him. Unable to sleep, Craig rose again after twenty minutes and went to the little laboratory. There he pulled from the deep-freeze the remainder of the turtle who had been caught in the caterpillar tracks and began to dissect it.

He concentrated on the head first. The face was closely scaled with chitinous scales. The antenna was cartilage, and scaleless. The mouth was tongueless, with amazingly strong teeth which scooped sharply forward in the lower jaw. Pulverising one of them and analysing the powder, Craig found it to consist principally of iron tungstate and magnesium phosphate. Mineral substances lodged between the other teeth made it clear that these tough little weapons could be used for digging into softer rocks. A quick examination of the digestive tract indicated that much of the turtle's nourishment also consisted of minerals, broken down by microorganisms so that they could pass into the bloodstream and nourish the body tissues.

The turtle's single eye was a wonderful organ. As he worked under an optical microscope, Craig recorded his findings on tape.

'... The turtles have both night and day vision,' he said. 'Their visibility spectrum must be much wider than ours, enabling them to see into both the infra-red and the ultra-violet. This is of course consistent with what one would expect from a cloud-obscured world like Askanza VI, but it also indicates a species coping with its environment with considerable success. "Turtle" is a misleading name for these creatures, and I shall hereafter refer to them as pseudo-chelonia. We shall then be less likely to underestimate their intelligence.

'Now I am going to open the brain case and examine the brain ...'

The skull was extremely dense, almost defying Craig's best saw. As he increased revs on the motor, the saw moved faster, biting down into the curving bone. Suddenly there was a loud explosion and the skull cracked.

Craig stopped the motor. Picking up the skull, he examined it. With a needle torch he peered into the hole the saw had made. The report had been caused by an implosion, not an explosion. The pseudo-chelonia had a vacuum where their brains should have been! Dividing the vacuum space, in place of grey matter, were only one or two bony and bare shelves.

Craig stared down in amazement, and the solitary eye stared back at him.

He thought incongruously of what Tim had said over the wireless: '... the millions of years of peace it's had ...' but what sort of peace had reigned in these bony cavities over those long years?

*

The dun-coloured morning dawned to the tune of more thunder, which died away in half an hour. Craig woke late. He looked outside as he dressed.

Certainly the view was impressive, if bleak. With the rain holding off, he could see some distance in all directions. Behind lay the mountains, rounded and bland. Ahead, the great planes of land sloped down towards the sea, hiding it from sight. All around were only simple shapes, rarely broken by a stunted tree.

The pseudo-chelonia lay silent, like boulders left by a mighty outgoing tide. Only one or two of them stirred feebly.

Grabbing a bar of condensed ration, Craig jumped down onto the ground. He chewed his breakfast as he walked. The creatures spread raggedly. Yesterday's tyrants were today's sluggards; nearer the overlander they were still as stones. Further away, down the slope, one or two moved on all-sixes as if in pain towards the distant sea.

Craig sat on the nearest specimen.

'You certainly have something to contend with,' he remarked, tapping it reflectively, 'And I think I have an inkling as to what it is.'

When he had finished his breakfast, he rose, grave and solid and methodical, to make the group call.

'I could have had turtle eggs for breakfast, only I didn't fancy their metallic content,' Barney announced. 'I don't mind living off the land, but not when it's so indigestible.'

'I could have had some too,' Tim said. 'I've been up most of the night watching, and I've seen these – what do you call 'em, Craig? – these pseudo-chelonia laying eggs in approved turtle style. And then along came three creatures like alligators and made a spirited attack on the egg burial spots.'

'Interesting,' Craig commented. 'What happened?'

'The pseudo-chelonia made a spirited defence. They warded off the alligators with acid contained in clay cups. Despite that, two of them were killed and a lot of eggs taken. These alligators are fast and tough. I was able to film the whole incident for the record.'

'Can you see anything of them now?'

'The alligators? No. They made off before dawn. And then with the light and the thunder, the pseudo-chelonia just seemed to be overcome by sleep. I can see a few of them now, all absolutely motionless, looking like boulders again.

'Ah well, I'm going to bed for four hours.'
'We'll be calling you,' Craig said. 'Adios and out.'
He had his day's programme all planned.

Avoiding his yesterday's route, he drove down to and then along the coast. The beautiful pillars still protruded from the sea. Overhead, cloud still merged with cloud everlastingly. The pseudo-chelonia were still active, and thickly distributed along the sea's margins.

Today their activities were more comprehensible to Craig, in the light of what he knew about their habits and their metabolism.

Mainly they appeared to be building – or rather, turning rocks into buildings. This they could do in two ways, dependent on the nature of the rock with which they dealt: either by scraping away the rock with their teeth, or by pouring acid into the metallic veins in the rock and then pulling the uneaten rock away. These proceedings accounted for many of the curious rock formations the PEST had seen.

Craig also knew that much of the creatures' actual food came from the rock. Like plants, they had the ability to convert inganic matter into the living substance necessary to all forms of animal existence. And through his binoculars he soon observed the skill with which the pseudo-chelonia, beings without fire, prepared their acids, collecting and dissolving salts in little hollowed bowls of rock.

Several times armed parties came up to investigate the man who was investigating them. Craig avoided a crisis by moving on.

At last he came to the raised earthwork he had seen on the previous day. Unmistakeably, it was artificial, built by hundreds of determined flippers working in organised fashion.

From its look, it might have stood for centuries. Craig did not inspect too closely, since several pseudo-chelonia were inside it. Instead, circling them, he brought the overlander to the other side of the fortification – and here he found the remains of the enemy against whom the fortification had been built. A litter of bones and skulls told Craig he was looking at the end of some of the alligator species Tim had described.

Selecting a fresh skull, Craig stowed it away before driving on another hundred yards to get further from the earthwork. Doubtless this was no man's land between alligator and turtle territory, but it was the first unpopulated stretch of shore he had found. A fast and cold river flowed down into the muggy sea. The pillars that grew here were few and stunted. Craig drove right down to the waterline, hurriedly launched a collapsible boat, and chugged out to a pillar that rose only three feet above the waterline. On his way he picked up a sample of sea water for analysis.

The pillar was brown with patches of blue, the colours glinting even in the dull light, and just too thick for Craig to get his hands round.

When he hacked at it with a knife, it splintered easily. In little time, he had the stump of it in the boat and was back ashore.

He had cut things fine. Several pseudo-chelonia were coming rapidly along the beach, flinging themselves over the earthwork and running towards him. Putting the pillar stump and his water sample into a deposal locker, Craig collapsed the boat and snapped it into a side rack. He swung himself up into the cab just as the first creature burst round the corner, flippers swinging.

It took a snap at him. Missing, it took a bite at the overlander instead. For many a long day, the heavy metal of one wing bore the imprint of tooth marks, the most awesome teeth Craig had ever come across. Given half an hour on their own, these chaps could have wrecked the big vehicle utterly.

But now the overlander was speeding off, out of harm's way. Accelerating, Craig shook off any pursuit before stopping in a shallow inland dell to examine the specimens.

As he had long suspected it would be, the pillar was natural, an alien accretion similar to the coral reefs of Earth. It consisted of crystals of metallic salts, iron chloride and copper and nickel sulphate among others, many of the crystals being abnormally large. It reminded Craig of a 'magic' chemical garden he had grown in water glass as a boy.

His sample of sea water proved to contain traces of many metals considered rare on Earth now, including tungsten and germanium.

When he had made the analysis, Craig sat looking out over the land to the placid sea. The sea on Askanza VI covered five sixths of the planetary surface. Here as on Earth, it had cradled life. Yet here, Craig was now fairly positive, it still held absolute power even over those creatures which had long since left it for dry land.

A man had in him much of the sea from whence he came. Wombed within water, he passed through a fish stage as a foetus; born, he carried all his life a tide in his veins and the taste of salt in his blood. But for all that, he had turned his back to the beaches in a way the pseudo-chelonia could never manage to do.

It was so, at least, if his theory was correct. To prove that conclusively, he needed equipment that only the PEST ship contained. Climbing down to the cab once more, he headed the overlander for home.

Rain came cascading down again as he touched the hills. It slowed him to little more than twenty miles an hour over the rough, so that another of Askanza's brief days was almost over before he sighted the PEST ship. Nevertheless, the journey was not entirely wasted, since it supplied confirmation that his theory was at least near the mark.

Four miles inland, all traces of the pseudo-chelonia died away. They began again after another fifteen miles; but all the creatures he saw lay face down against the bare ground as if dead, their carapaces shining dully in the yellow downpour.

Donning oilskins, squelching through the downpour, Craig hurried into the ground lock. Tim Anderson was there to greet him; the young man had seen his vehicle drive up. Something in his attitude told Craig he was uneasy.

'Coming back empty-handed!' he exclaimed as he greeted Craig. 'You've not much chance of indulging your favourite hobby of parasitology here, Craig.'

'No,' Craig agreed. 'There's little diversity in the life forms, but the wonder seems to be that anything organic has established itself at all.'

As they went up in the lift, Tim said, 'Then no doubt you've noticed the life forms seem to be either large size or microscopic.'

'I had noticed – and I notice Barney's vehicle outside. He's back already then?'

Tim shot him a veiled look.

'Barney's back,' was all he answered.

Barney himself greeted them in the lounge. He was consuming a plateful of canned pork, gooseberry sauce and potatoes, and demolishing a bottle of Aldebaran wine. He waved genially to Craig.

'Beat you to it. Have a drink?'

'Love to,' Craig admitted, peeling off his oilskins and stuffing them into a dryer. As he got a glass, the evening's thunder began.

'Everything tied up?' Barney inquired mildly, pausing with uplifted fork.

'What makes Askanza VI tick?' Tim asked.

'By the way you both ask me, I can see you all ready know all the answers,' Craig said. 'Well, yes, I think I know some of them myself. I'll tell you my ideas, and you can stop me when I go wrong.'

'The man's modest,' Barney said.

'I admire the resourcefulness of this world,' Craig said. 'Its conditions are not unlike those on Earth's neighbor planet Venus which – you may remember from your elementary textbooks – supports no life at all. Here we have at least two tough forms of life, the pseudo-chelonia and the alligator-things, which have managed to evolve despite an almost complete lack of anything but minerals. Minerals there are in abundance, which as Tim says should make this a very prosperous world *if* the colonists move in.'

'The earliest forms of growth here – pre-living forms – are crystal accretions, which rise out of the shallow seas like masts. I've seen them along the coast. When I first saw them, I had the impression of wireless masts – and oddly enough I was not far wrong. However, perhaps that is not the right end to begin the story at.'

Barney and Tim exchanged glances as Craig went on.

'Let's take the turtles first. They have no brain in any sense that we know of. Instead, they have nature's equivalent of a wireless receiver in their heads. There is even a vacuum in the middle of their skulls, where bony shelves impregnated with metal form a natural triode valve. The alligators function on the same principle.'

'They do,' Tim affirmed. 'I shot one and its brain case imploded.'

'Yes. No smaller reptiles exist because a big heavy head is required to house such an arrangement.

'Their motive power is of course their own. But their – shall we say their thoughts, primitive though they are? – their thoughts are radio waves.

'Life, as we know, develops as it can. We must expect that eventually research will show why these creatures have receivers instead of brains. Nature, however, works with what it has, and here it had a perpetual source of radio emission.

'For me this is the most interesting fact of all. The silent seas of Askanza are gigantic low-powered transmitters. How it works in detail I don't know, although I suggest we find out tomorrow. Roughly, though, the main items would seem to be these. Cold levels of water from rivers etcetera send up temperature differences in the sea which are transformed into small electric charges. These are influenced by the heavy metallic suspension in the seas. At the same time, the water containing germanium, various depths act in effect as gigantic transistors, amplifying the potential signal.

'The crystal pillars serve as aerials. Day and night they radiate the message of the sea, and the pseudo-chelonia and their enemies pick them up. Do you follow this, Tim?'

Tim shook his head, moving from the window where, as he listened, he had been watching the first motionless turtles come to life with the night.

'I'm with you, Craig, although the way you've deduced all this fills me with wonder and anguish.'

'I've only fitted together the facts we discovered – and kept an open mind, remembering the old PEST rule, "Necessity forms the only basis for comparison between systems." What we find on Askanza VI is the best possible operable system in the circumstances.'

'That's all very well, Craig, but what first started you adding the facts towards the right answer?' Barney inquired. Lighting a cigar, he added, 'And don't be afraid to boast. You don't know how oppressive your modesty can be.'

Craig smiled.

'Then I must boast on your behalf. You gave me the lead with your remark during our first group call. You talked about the curious mush you picked up on the short wave. That was the call of the sea – calling all life on Askanza!'

'Ha!' Tim exclaimed. He snapped his fingers and started walking round the room.

'Craig, the next bit I pieced together for myself,' he said. 'What Barney said started me wondering too, particularly when he mentioned sky layers. Obviously the atmosphere is disturbed; thunder night and morning must mean something. What it means here is that the Appleton or F-layer which normally reflects short waves back to the ground is dissolved during the day. During the night-hours it re-establishes itself. Barney and I have proved this is so with the ship's transmitter.

'Working on the idea that our turtle friends were controlled by short wave radio, I saw this would explain why they were doggo by day and active by night. The signal would not reach them by day, but would radiate into space and be lost.

'Then I asked myself why your turtles and Barney's didn't fit with this neat theory. Directly I thought of locating the transmitter by the coast I had my answer.'

'Yes, when you get that far, the rest's a matter of elementary radio theory,' Barney said. 'The coastal creatures get their transmission direct, so the presence or absence of an F-layer doesn't worry them. Up to maybe three miles inland, the beasts are active day and night, as Craig found. I was on the fringe of a skip area, where the ground wave's given out and the sky wave only reaches under freak conditions – but on planetary scale, such freak conditions must be pretty prevalent. Perhaps my beasts were explorers, shuffling along in a land where for them thought would hardly reach. Put like that, it makes them sound oddly impressive.'

'They are impressive,' Craig agreed. 'And right now I can hear some of them clumping round the ship. Tim, better switch on external lights before they eat their way in.'

Obediently, Tim climbed up into the cabin and punched the external switchboard. Barney and Craig were watching the pseudo-chelonia scamper heavily for the darkness as he returned.

'It's all clear enough,' Tim said, 'except for one thing. God, I know it's impressive, this tideless sea broadcasting its message for millennia, and every creature on the planet picking it up. But – *what does it say*?'

Craig spread his hands wide.

'What does the sea still say in your blood, Tim? Something simple in its origin, infinitely complex in its working out; in a word: Survive!

The turtles are our brothers in that they are doubtless getting the same message.'

For a minute they were silent, each occupied with his own reflections. Craig was the first to speak again.

'There's one further point, Tim,' he said. 'Just now you mentioned that the pseudo-chelonia were *controlled* by radio. I don't think that is any more accurate than saying that humans are controlled by thought. They seem more to be *guided*, as we are guided; it may sound a subtle difference, but it's a big one. Their movements show primitive signs of individuality: hesitation, for instance.

'Finding out exactly how they behave within their own groups will be valuable work for the scientific bodies who'll follow us. It should shed a lot of light on human impulses.'

He stood up, his face clouded.

'And so we've got everything taped. Or have we? We know in outline how the Plimsol species ticks. We know it's plenty tough. It can live on dirt and bite through anything, while I'd say one of those fore-flippers could break a man's leg. But there's only half of our task. Little as I love colonists, I hate to think of them facing up to these armoured monsters with buckshot. My prediction is that they won't take long to lose their fear of bright lights. They may be generally doggo in the daytime, but who wants to die at sunset? In short, what recommendations can we possibly make to PEST HQ about dealing with the brutes?'

Grinning, making a rude sign he had picked up in a dive on Droxy, Barney stood up.

'That sounds like a cry to your man of action,' he said. 'This is where I come in.'

Craig emitted a hollow groan.

'Tell me the worst,' he invited.

'No, I've something to show you in the control room,' Barney said. 'While you and Tim were cogitating so powerfully yesterday, I was after turtles' eggs, if you remember. I found I couldn't eat the things, so I hatched 'em in an improvised incubator. Come have a look-see.'

He led the way up into the control room, smiling as he went. He hated what he had discovered, and he knew Craig would hate it even more; that did not prevent his seeing the diabolically funny side to the whole business.

On the control room floor was a heavy box with a visiplex top. Inside it, on a layer of sand, lay three baby pseudo-chelonia, each measuring about a foot long.

'Good heavens!' Craig exclaimed. 'How old are they?'

'About a day old. You've not seen the eggs. They're as big as cannon balls and almost as heavy. The female only lays about half a dozen at a time – and that must be a pretty painful process. Better her than me.'

Barney showed Craig how he had screened off the box, so that even though it was night and the F-layer established overhead, no radiations were getting through to the three creatures.

'Otherwise they'd be biting tunnels through the hull,' he said. 'Believe me, these babies have milk teeth like buzz saws.'

He went over to the transmitter on one side of the room, unhooked an aerial, placed it in with the pseudo-chelonia and returned to the set. He switched on, starting up a music tape.

'Just in the interests of science,' he said grimly. 'I am going to give these babies a snatch of Debussy's *La Mer* on their frequency. Here it comes.'

Craig and Tim heard the music, damped right down, from the tape player. Barney's babies heard it in their heads. At once they began to move.

They moved uncertainly, like puppets twitched by the hand of a drunkard. First they went forwards, then they went backwards, then they shuffled sideways. Their heads rolled in ungainly fashion. Their six limbs retracted then shot out again. It was horrible to watch them.

'That's enough, Barney,' Craig said.

'I'll give 'em a bit more volume,' Barney said, twiddling a knob.

At once the pseudo-chelonia were seized by convulsions. They leapt and bucked like unbroken steers, clattering against the side of the box, waving their limbs frantically, wagging their antennae. They threw themselves about like creatures gone crazy, even twisting onto their backs and running into each other.

'All right, Barney, turn it off,' Craig said, in a shaken voice. Tim Anderson too looked slightly rattled.

'Those beings are blessed – or cursed! – with intelligence,' he said. 'Think how they must feel with an alien madman bawling inside their heads.'

'Horrid, I agree,' Barney said flatly. His three specimens slumped back into immobility as he switched the radio off. Leaving the tape recorder still playing its quiet melody, he got up, returning Craig's straight stare.

'And that's how the colonists are going to cope with our Plimsol species,' he said. 'Just a little demonstration for you, Craig. The miners and farmers who touch down here in a year or two aren't going to need shotguns or blasters. They only have to switch on the short wave to burn these critters' brain boxes out. ... It's not pretty, but it's simple – and nice and safe. Why are you looking so grim?'

Tim, recovering, slapped Craig on the back and said, 'At our moments of triumph, our leader always turns philosophical and sad.'

'Maybe you're right,' Barney said, leading the way back to the lounge and the bottle of wine. 'He will now tell us that we've done our stuff in record time, but that nevertheless we are degenerate. The ancients, he will remind us, had a saying "to understand all is to forgive all". And now the PEST motto means something less than that. "Capite Superare": "Comprehend To Conquer" ... Shows how the race is going downhill ... Have a drink, Craig.'

'I will,' Craig said mildly, holding out his glass, 'when you've finished bullying me.'

As the three of them drank, he said, 'If I looked grim, it was because I realised something you may have overlooked.'

He sat down in a chair and surveyed the two of them.

'After your demonstration, Barney, we can do nothing but send off a report that will soon bring the colonists flocking in. Askanza is going to be a tough planet for a long while. It's going to demand a lot of work from everyone.'

'We should worry,' Tim said.

'Yes, we *should* worry! You think the colonists will kill off the pseudo-chelonia by Barney's method?'

'Of course. What else?'

'In no time, one colonist brighter than the rest is going to find a way of broadcasting – not death, but something more deadly – orders. It won't take them long to find out a way either; you know as well as I do what the main sort of colonist is like: he's society's misfit, a reject. How many millions of these tough beasts do you think there are on Askanza? In no time they'll be transformed into a radio-controlled army, working, dying, killing, for a few tinpot tyrants crouching behind transmitters.'

Barney spilt half his drink down his beard.

He jumped up.

'My God, Craig, you have the nastiest ideas!' he said.

'You think I like them? It makes me shudder just to think of the future of Askanza – but as Pontius said, once I've filed my report it's out of my hands.'

Tim gazed fearfully out of the window. Beyond the ring of lighting, the turtles waited for they knew not what. Beyond them was only the blackness, warm and unlit. And beyond that blackness: a deeper blackness.

'*Our* job's finished,' he said. 'Let's get to hell out of here – and make sure we never come back.'